PRAISE FOR THE SPINE-TINGLING SUSPENSE AND GRIPPING ROMANCE OF
ANDREA KANE

"Andrea Kane expertly juggles suspense and romance."

—Iris Johansen

NO WAY OUT

"A tightly woven romantic thriller . . . this fast-paced tale will appeal to fans of Lisa Gardner."

—*Publishers Weekly*

"Another of Kane's absorbing tales of romantic suspense."

—*Booklist*

"Exciting suspense and terrific emotional drama. . . ."

—*Romantic Times*

THE GOLD COIN

Also by Andrea Kane

Published by POCKET BOOKS

ANDREA KANE

SCENT OF DANGER

POCKET STAR BOOKS

New York   London   Toronto   Sydney   Singapore

An *Original* Publication of POCKET BOOKS

A Pocket Star Book published by
POCKET BOOKS, a division of Simon & Schuster, Inc.
1230 Avenue of the Americas, New York, NY 10020

ISBN: 0-7434-4613-5

First Pocket Books printing February 2003

10 9 8 7 6 5 4 3 2 1

POCKET STAR BOOKS and colophon are registered trademarks of Simon & Schuster, Inc.

For information regarding special discounts for bulk purchases, please contact Simon & Schuster Special Sales at 1-800-456-6798 or business@simonandschuster.com

Front cover illustration by Shasti O'Leary Soudant

Printed in the U.S.A.

DEDICATION

To organ donors everywhere, who offer a future to those who need it. And to the dedicated medical professionals whose skill and commitment make that future a reality.

ACKNOWLEDGMENTS

With deep gratitude, I acknowledge those who were an integral part of my writing *Scent of Danger*.

I was fortunate to have outstanding consultants who helped me create the authenticity I strove for. Any divergence from that authenticity is my responsibility—a literary license I sparingly availed myself of only when necessary to tell the story.

In that vein, I specifically want to thank:

Hillel Ben-Asher, M.D., whose medical knowledge and diversity of expertise never fail to impress me. Almost as impressive are his patience in sharing that knowledge, and his prompt and thorough responses to my countless detailed questions.

Desiree Laz, RN, Clinical Transplant Coordinator, Department of Surgery, Albany Medical Center Hospital, who educated me in the kidney transplant process, taking me through the procedure from evaluation to completion, addressing all my questions. Her personal commitment to her career, her patients, and the future of transplant surgery is humbling.

Randy Slaughter, who generously shared his experience as a kidney donor with me, providing me with technical information, literature, and his own perspectives so that I could gain the necessary insights to integrate the medical aspects of this procedure with the personal and emotional ones.

Alex Senchak, EMT, who brought the world of an emergency medical technician to life, explaining his training and experience, and helping me convey a realistic portrayal of a gunshot victim. Emergency medical teams save lives every day. The maturity, wisdom, and levelheadedness of its members, some of whom are so young, is inspiring.

I want to thank the following people for their contributions, every one of which made *Scent of Danger* a stronger book:

Scott Mayer, for his meteorological insights, which helped me explain the atmospheric conditions that aggravated Sabrina's heightened olfactory sense.

The Cornell "hotelies" who shared curriculum details and the vast range of career opportunities available to Sabrina, and to them, after graduation.

Peggy Gordijn, for her bird's-eye view of Mt. Sinai Hospital, particularly 11 West. My only request is that, next time, she's just a visitor.

Andrea Cirillo, for championing me through a year filled with emotional and professional challenges, for knowing when to step in and when to give me space, and for providing a potpourri of story-enhancing tidbits— from the security bars on brownstone windows to designer toilets.

Caroline Tolley, for a twelve-year partnership, an enduring friendship, and more memories than I can fit on a page. Thanks for believing in me from day one, and never wavering in that belief. The Smith and Wo's scene is my tribute to you, from appetizer to dessert.

Brad Kane, management consultant extraordinaire, incomparable brainstorming partner, and one-of-a-kind support system that defies words. No matter how many years go by, you're still the greatest guy in the world.

Wendi Kane, for going but still staying, for cheering and critiquing, and for having the heart, the wisdom, and the maturity to understand that reshaping is inevitable, but retaining is the ultimate prize.

I want to close by highlighting the fact that there is a serious shortage of organ donors at this time. Some eighty thousand people are on waiting lists, and that list grows longer every day. March is Kidney Month. I urge you to visit the National Kidney Foundation's website at: http://www.kidney.org and learn more about kidney disease, what's being done to educate the public, what the Kidney Foundation does to assist those in need, and what you can do to help.

SCENT
OF
DANGER

1

Monday, September 5th, Labor Day, 5:45 P.M.
New York City

He'd been shot.

He never saw his assailant. Never heard him. Only the pop from behind. An instant later came the burning heat in his back. He pitched forward at the panorama of windows he'd been facing when the attack occurred. He broke his fall by planting a palm on the wall, bracing his weight long enough to twist around and scan his office doorway.

Empty. Whoever had done this was gone.

Pain lanced through him and weakness invaded, spreading through him in widening bands. His legs gave out. He crumpled to the carpet, trying to grab onto his desk for support. His fist clutched nothing but air.

He landed on his belly, his arms doing little to cushion the fall. Automatically, he turned his head to one side to protect his face and make breathing possible. It didn't do much good. He couldn't seem to bring in enough air. And when he did—Christ, the smell of the oriental rug made his stomach lurch. Sickeningly sweet, like a suffocating air freshener. It was that cleaning stuff the maintenance staff used. One more whiff and he'd puke.

He shifted a bit, resorted to breathing entirely through his mouth. The rug was wet, he noted, and getting wetter, saturating through with something sticky. *My blood,* he thought vaguely, feeling oddly detached as the fluid continued to seep from his body.

Cobwebs of dizziness blanketed his brain. He was losing consciousness, and he knew it. But there was no way to help himself. He couldn't move. Couldn't crawl to the door. His phone . . . the cord was dangling from his desk . . . no, he couldn't reach it. He'd try to yell . . . what good would that do? It was Labor Day. No one was in except him and Dylan. And Dylan's office was at the opposite end of the building. Making a racket would be futile. All he could do was hope that Dylan hauled his butt back here before it was too late.

Footsteps sounded, slowing as they reached the office.

"Okay, Carson, I've got those files you wanted. We can go over them later. Right now, it's time we got into that personal matter I . . . *Jesus Christ!*" Dylan's words ended on a strangled shout. He flung aside his papers and was next to Carson Brooks in a flash, squatting down beside him. "Can you hear me?" he demanded, groping for a pulse.

"Yeah." Carson's voice sounded hoarse, faint. "Shot," he pronounced, licking his lips so he could speak. "But not . . . dead. Not . . . yet . . . anyway . . ."

"And you're not going to be." Dylan bolted to his feet. "Don't try to talk. I'll get an ambulance." He snatched the telephone, punching in 911. "This is Dylan Newport," he reported tersely. "I'm calling from Ruisseau Fragrance Corporation, 11 West 57th Street. A man's been shot." A pause. "No names, no press. Just send an ambulance, and fast. Yes, he's breathing. But it's labored. He's conscious, yeah, but barely. And he's lost a lot of blood. Looks like his lower back." Another pause. "Right. Fine. Just get that ambulance here *now*. Twelfth floor, back southeast corner office." He slammed down the receiver. "Lie still," he ordered Carson, squatting down again. "Don't try to move or talk. The paramedics are on their way."

"Pushy bastard . . ." Carson taunted lightly, his speech slurred. "I'm not . . . even dead . . . and you're . . . already giving . . . orders. . . ."

Dylan said something in reply, but Carson couldn't make out his words. He felt as if he were floating outside himself. Was this how it felt to die? If so, it wasn't so bad. What sucked was all he was leaving undone, not to mention the big question mark in his life that would now die a mystery.

Twenty-eight years. Funny, it hadn't mattered until recently. And ironic that when he was finally about to act, the chance to do so was being snatched away.

"Dammit, Carson, stay with me!"

He would have answered Dylan. But his mind was drifting back to another time, twenty-eight years and a lifetime ago. That pivotal twist of fate had changed everything. A seed that had grown into an empire.

A seed. What an ironic metaphor.

One sperm specimen . . . twenty grand. No risk, no strings, nothing to lose. What a deal.

Stan had been right. It *had* been a deal, one that had changed his life.

And maybe created another.

Carson, you've got it all. The IQ. The looks. The youth. The charm. Go for it. If she bites, you'll make a bundle.

She had. And he had.

He'd plowed forward from that day on. Never looked back. Not till a few weeks ago. Funny, how a fiftieth birthday made a man take stock . . .

"Where's the victim?"

Strange voices. Pounding footsteps. The Clorox smell of institutional clothes.

Paramedics.

"In here." Dylan's urgent reply as he led them in. "It's Carson Brooks."

His eyelids fluttered. Through a blurred haze, he made out two pair of uniformed legs hovering over him.

The paramedics squatted and began working on him.

"Heart rate a hundred fifty."

"Blood pressure a hundred over sixty."

"That's very low for Carson." Dylan's lawyer-voice. Hard-hitting. Authoritative. Daunting even to his most formidable opponents. "His pressure's usually somewhere around one-fifty over a hundred. He suffers from hypertension. He takes Dyaxide to control it."

"Any other preexisting medical conditions you know of?"

"No."

"Okay." Pressure on his back. His lids were lifted and pinpoints of light pierced his eyes. "Pupils dilated. Can you hear me, Mr. Brooks?"

"Y-yes."

"Good. Hang in there. We're just trying to slow down the bleeding."

"Respiration shallow. No obstructions."

"Start the oxygen. Set it at fifteen lpm. Let's get him on the backboard."

"Right." Two more paramedics had materialized in the room and were now rustling around with some equipment.

Idly, Carson noted the intricate pattern of the oriental carpet. The floral configurations had more red in them than before. And the color was spreading.

An oxygen mask was fitted over his nose and mouth, its elastic strap secured behind his head. "Breathe normally, Mr. Brooks. This will help."

It did—a little. He rasped in the oxygen. The air freshener smell grew faint.

"His pulse rate's dropping. And his heart rate's up. We've got to move him—now." Another flurry of activity, and a long board was propped against his side. "Okay, on the count of three. One, two . . . three."

He heard his own groan as they maneuvered him onto the board and secured his head and body. The sound reminded him he was still alive. He had to stay that way. He had to find out who'd shot him. He had to protect his legacy.

And he had to know if Ruisseau was his only legacy, or if he had another one out there—one that was a living, breathing human being.

Determination was suffocated by the fog enveloping his brain.

"Stay with us, Mr. Brooks." The paramedics were talking again. They'd lifted him onto a stretcher and were moving. They were racing him through the lobby toward the front door. Strange, he didn't remember the elevator ride down.

"Is he conscious?" Dylan grilled.

"In and out." The glass doors blew open. Thick summer air enveloped them. Manhattan pollution. A hint of it seeped around the oxygen mask and invaded his nostrils. There were flashing lights—police cars flanking the ambulance. One cop rushed up to the paramedics. More ran into the building.

He was transported to the ambulance. "Mount Sinai?" Dylan was asking the paramedic who'd climbed in beside him.

"Yup. We'll get over to Madison and fly straight uptown. With the siren on, we'll be there in minutes."

"I'm riding with you." Dylan was getting in even as he spoke.

"Uh, Mr. Newport . . ." The ambulance driver turned

and cleared his throat uneasily. "The police want to talk to you about—"

"Fine." Dylan cut him off at the knees. "Then they can meet us at Mount Sinai. I'm riding there with Mr. Brooks. That's not up for debate. And like I said, you're bringing in a 'John Doe.' No names, no press. Let's go."

There were no further arguments. Doors slammed. A siren screamed. The ambulance zoomed off.

"Heart rate's up to a hundred seventy. BP's down to ninety over fifty." The paramedic leaned closer. "Mr. Brooks, can you tell me how old you are?"

"To-o old. F-f-ifty."

His voice mingled with the scream of the siren. The traffic on Madison Avenue seemed to part like the waters of the Red Sea.

"Carson." Dylan's voice was low, very close to his ear.

"Still . . . alive . . ." he managed.

"I never doubted it. You're indestructible."

"Yeah . . . tell that to whoever . . . did this."

"Talking isn't what I have in mind for that bastard." A pause. "Did you see who it was?"

"Saw nothing . . . too fast . . . and from behind." Carson drew a slow, raspy breath. "Dylan . . ."

"We'll get him, Carson. Don't worry."

"Not that." A weak shake of his head. He was fading. For now or for good, he wasn't sure. But, just in case he'd be around to hear the answer, he had to try. "That situation . . . I was wrestling with . . . the confidential one . . ."

"I remember."

He swallowed, fighting the waves of darkness. "If I've got a kid . . . I want to know. Find out."

2

Tuesday, September 6th, 9:30 A.M.
Center for Creative Thinking and Leadership
Auburn, New Hampshire

"Good morning, everyone. Welcome to CCTL."

Sabrina stepped into the conference room, strolling over to the head of the elegant teak table and simultaneously assessing the new management team of Office Perks, a Boston-based accessories-for-the-workplace company.

The composite of the group was pretty standard. Eight executives, five men, three women. Most in their mid-thirties, a few in the forty to forty-five range. That included Robert Stowbe, the company's newly appointed chief executive officer, who was forty-four and at the helm following a large, heavily publicized merger. He'd handpicked his new department heads. And, as Sabrina's research had confirmed, he'd done a pretty good job. Edward Rowen, the chief financial officer, had done a decent job of increasing profits at his previous position; Harold Case, the VP of sales, was a shrewd cookie who knew his clientele; Lauren Hollis, the VP of information technology, was a workhorse, if a bit lacking in creativity; Paul Jacobs, the VP of strategic planning, had vision and initiative; Lois Ames, the VP of marketing, was well connected and open to new ideas; Jerry Baines, the VP of research and development, had a good track record but was a bit of an autocrat when it came to running his department; and Meg Lakes, who promised to be a perky, energetic VP of human resources.

Now came the hard part. Taking a talented, aggressive bunch of people and transforming them from a collection of ambitious individuals into an integrated management team.

Making that happen was Sabrina's job.

Whether or not she was successful, only time would tell.

After spending four years as a management consultant—three in the big leagues and one right here at CCTL—Sabrina had learned that no team was standard, few transitions took place without a snag, and nothing should be taken for granted.

Still, her track record was pretty damned good. Which was why so many corporations that were either expanding or needed a jolt of adrenaline to get them back on track sought her out.

"I'm Sabrina Radcliffe," she began, intentionally staying on her feet even though everyone else was seated—a routine ploy aimed at retaining control of a meeting. "As you know, I'm the president of CCTL. I won't waste time spouting my background and credentials, since I'm sure you've done your homework and know all about my reputation, and CCTL's. So I'll just invite you to take full advantage of our facilities—for recreational and mental health, as well as for professional growth.

"Plan on being busy over the next four days. We'll be holding frequent team meetings. Workshop times are listed on the agendas you received with your registration packs. That having been said, you'll also notice we left chunks of unscheduled time. That's where your mental recharging comes in. We cover both ends of the spectrum: unwinding and pumping up. For starters, our staff offers stress management and yoga classes. We also have a state-of-the-art health center—you'll have full use of that. And, last but not least, Lake Massabesic is right at our doorstep; it's great for sailing, canoeing, or hiking. Do whatever moves you."

Sabrina gauged the attention span of her audience. Time to talk food.

"On to meals."

Everyone sat up a little straighter. Not a surprise. Food did it every time.

"Our chefs are unbelievable," she continued. "They've been recruited from top restaurants worldwide. So don't expect to lose weight. You won't. Unless, of course, that's your goal. If you do have specific requests or dietary restrictions, be sure to let them know. They'll be happy to work with you."

Sabrina's fingers swept over her cranberry silk blazer and slacks. "Dress at team meetings is business casual. The last thing we need is constrictive ties and waistlines. I'm convinced that anything that inhibits breathing, also inhibits creativity."

A few smiles.

Time to allow for assimilation of information.

"I'll get into the specifics of our team meetings later, after you've had a chance to settle in," she concluded. "For now, let me assure you of this: My staff is exceptional. Put yourselves in our hands, give us your all, and we'll send you home ready to take on the world and win."

11:15 A.M.
Mt. Sinai Hospital

Dylan gulped down the last of his coffee, crumpled the Styrofoam cup, and tossed it in the garbage.

The past sixteen hours had been a surrealistic blur.

The ER. Then the OR. Carson had been in there for ages, undergoing extensive surgery to repair organs and suture blood vessels. Now he was in the ICU, stuck with tubes and IV drips, hooked up to all kinds of monitors, and with no definitive assurances of recovery.

Christ, what a nightmare. Dylan shut his eyes, massaging the throbbing sockets to ease a headache that wasn't about to go away. Not without food, sleep, and results. He'd made the necessary phone calls, set in motion what needed to be done. But there were so many damned loose ends to connect. . . .

"I can't take this uncertainty much longer. Not knowing, not hearing a word—I'm losing my mind." Susan Lane jumped up from the waiting room chair, her entire body taut with worry. She raked her fingers through her sleek frosted-blond hair, rumpling it even more than it already was. It occurred to Dylan that he'd never seen Susan so disheveled. At forty, Carson's significant other looked thirty, and was always impeccably made-up and dressed. Not this morning. After a night of pacing, she was definitely the worse for wear. Then again, so was he.

"Why don't they tell us something?" she demanded.

"Probably because there's nothing new to tell," he replied. "Carson came through the surgery. He's a fighter. He'll make it."

"He has to." Susan sounded as if she were trying to convince herself rather than Dylan. She started pacing again, her voice choked as she remembered aloud. "I had a feeling something was wrong. He was very late, even for Carson. This wasn't a boring dinner party, it was a night at the U.S. Open. I should have listened to my instincts. I should have called."

"It wouldn't have mattered, so don't beat yourself up. The match started after seven. Carson was shot before six."

"Right. And you didn't call me till almost ten," Susan reminded him, pain and accusation lacing her tone. "When I was sitting in Carson's courtside box with my cell phone turned off."

"I called you as soon as I could think straight." Dylan felt as if he were talking about something that had happened a year rather than a night ago. "I'm sorry you had to hear about Carson through voice mail. I'm sure my message shocked the hell out of you." He blew out a weary breath. "Frankly, I don't remember much about those first few hours."

"I'm sure you were a wreck," Susan acknowledged, her demeanor softening. "I didn't mean to jump all over you like that. I just keep thinking that if I'd gotten here sooner, it might have made a difference. Maybe if he heard my voice, or knew I was there . . ." She swallowed hard. "Anyway, what's done is done. All that matters is for Carson to pull through this."

She walked over to the ICU, circling it as she tried to see in. But the curtains were drawn, as they had been since Carson's surgeon went inside. "Dr. Radison's been in there a long time."

Dylan crossed over to stand beside her. "Radison's being thorough. You know his reputation as well as I do; he's the best there is. He's more than aware we're still out here. He'll give us an update as soon as he can."

"Mr. Newport?"

The voice came from the corridor behind them. Dylan turned, not particularly surprised to see Detectives Barton and Whitman standing there. They'd questioned him last night before Susan arrived—about his relationship to Carson, Carson's lifestyle, his friends and enemies—the usual criminal investigation rundown. He'd responded on autopilot, although he doubted those responses had been too coherent. Not that it mattered. Even if he'd been in top form, he'd still be high up on their suspect list. He'd been the only other person at Ruisseau when the shooting took place. His tight relationship with Carson and the edge it gave him in the company was no secret. And by now they'd done their homework. They knew what kind of background he had, and they knew how much he stood to gain if Carson didn't make it. So here they were, back to probe further. Unless of course they'd found out something . . .

"Detectives." He shoved his hands in his pockets, trying to assess their demeanor. They sure as hell didn't look like satisfied law officers who'd just made an arrest. "Do you have anything for us?"

"Nothing you don't already know." Frank Barton's reply had a definite edge to it—an edge and an implication. "We spoke to the two guards who were on duty at the building last night—the one at the front door and the one monitoring the video surveillance. They saw nothing and no one, except you and Mr. Brooks. We reviewed the surveillance tapes and confirmed that. So if anyone else got into the building, they used the freight entrance." Barton didn't meet Dylan's gaze, but instead shot an inquisitive look at Susan.

"This is Susan Lane," Dylan supplied in a stiff tone. "Her name's on that list of Carson's friends I gave you. Susan, Detectives Barton and Whitman."

"Ms. Lane." Eugenia Whitman acknowledged the introduction. "I'm glad you're here. We were going to contact you later today to ask you a few questions. Now we can do it here."

Susan nodded. "Of course. Whatever I can do to help."

"Good. Also, just so you know, we're posting twenty-four-hour security outside Mr. Brooks's hospital room, just in case whoever did this decides to try again. Officer Laupen should be showing up any minute now. He'll be taking the first shift." Whitman's attention switched back to Dylan. "You seem to be in better shape than you were last night. Does that mean there's positive news on Mr. Brooks's condition?"

Like they hadn't already called the hospital and checked, Dylan reflected dryly.

"It means last night I was in shock," he said aloud. "That shock is wearing off, so today I'm a little more collected. As for Carson, he's hanging on. He had a lacerated artery, a pierced lung, and a perforation of his intestines. He's also lost huge amounts of blood. So with regard to the prognosis, the jury's still out. For the time being, he's doped up and in ICU. His surgeon's in with him now. If you stick around, I'm sure you can hear the latest firsthand."

"That's what we had in mind," Barton assured him. "I understand from the surgeon's report that the bullet wasn't removed."

"You understand correctly. The bullet's in Carson's chest, lodged somewhere close to his lung. Taking it out would have been more dangerous than leaving it."

Barton folded his arms across his thickening middle. "So we have no bullet, no weapon, and a victim who can't talk to us yet."

Dylan noticed he didn't say anything about having no motive or suspect.

"Talking to Carson won't help. He didn't see his assailant." Rather than provoking the detectives, Dylan repeated what he'd told them last night. "He was shot from behind. He said the whole thing happened too fast for him to turn around."

"According to your story, he said that in the ambulance. Unfortunately, no one but you heard him." Detective Whitman fiddled with the ends of her short puff of curly platinum-blond hair—a deceptively casual gesture, since she was studying Dylan intently.

"The paramedics were a little busy, Detective." Dylan was starting to get pissed. "They were working to save Carson's life. He only managed a few words. And the only one he spoke to was me." He met Whitman's cool stare. She was tall—almost as tall as his own six foot one—with pale coloring, a straight, stick-thin build, and cottonball hair. She looked just like a Q-tip.

"Um-hum." She scanned her notes. "That's what you told us."

"And that's what happened. Look, let's not waste time debating the facts. You can confirm them with Carson the minute the doctor gives his okay."

"That's why we're here, Mr. Newport. To see if the victim's story matches yours."

That did it.

"Look, Detective," Dylan said icily, "I hear your message—loud and clear. For the record, you're barking up the wrong tree. But you'll find that out for yourselves. Just don't waste too much time in the process. I want you to get whoever did this. Dig around. Carson's shooting wasn't random."

"That's one point we agree on. It wasn't random. But it wasn't robbery either. When the ambulance brought Mr. Brooks in, he had five hundred dollars and a solid gold money clip in his pocket. Neither was touched. And since, allegedly, the assailant had vanished without a trace by the time you walked onto the scene, he would have had more than enough time to snatch those items before taking off."

"Robbery? That never occurred to me. Yeah, Carson's rich, and he's high-profile. But if someone wanted to rob him, they'd have mugged him on the street corner, not gone up twelve floors to shoot him in his office."

"Makes sense." Barton eyed Dylan thoughtfully. "So tell me, Mr. Newport, do you have a particular motive in mind?"

Mine, you mean, Dylan mused silently. Aloud he replied, "It could be any one of several. Revenge. Greed. A desperate need for financial survival. As I told you last night, Carson's not your average CEO, or even your average self-made man. He grew up in the streets. He started with nothing, and made a fortune by busting his ass, and relying on nothing but his brains and his instincts. He's a brilliant chemist and businessman—a true genius, if you ask me. People like that bring out the worst in their enemies."

"And why would those enemies choose to act now?" Whitman probed.

"C'est Moi." Susan realized aloud where Dylan was headed. "It hit the market in June. Carson's shooting has to be related to that." She gave Whitman a quizzical look. "Have you heard of it?"

"The fragrance that rocked the nation?" Whitman's sarcasm was so thick you could cut it. "You'd have to be dead not to. The sensationalism surrounding that ad campaign caused riots at every cosmetic counter in the country."

"It's not the campaign," Dylan said tightly. "It's the product. The ads just captured the world's attention. But it's the scent itself that's caused the rest of the fragrance industry to go into a tailspin."

"Because it turns every woman into a goddess," Whitman said.

"It's a perfume, Detective, not a magic potion. It doesn't create what isn't there. It just enhances what is. Truly the ultimate fragrance. Ask around. Or, better yet, try some yourself."

"I'll do that. As soon as we solve this case." Whitman wasn't about to be sidetracked. "So let's say this perfume is all it's cracked up to be. How does its success tie in to Brooks's shooting? The product's already out there. Why would killing Brooks change that? Ruisseau's a solid company. I'm sure it wouldn't fold without its CEO."

"No, it wouldn't. But in the case of C'est Moi, there's an Achilles' heel," Dylan explained. "Its formula is unique. It took almost two years to develop. The process was done in absolute secrecy."

"By Brooks's R&D team."

"No. By Carson himself."

An intrigued lift of Whitman's brows. "Brooks invented the formula?"

"Yup. And he's the only one who knows it."

For the first time, the detective looked startled. "The only one? No one else is privy to that information?"

"Not a soul. Including me, by the way. But there are lots of folks who'd like to be. It's raking in millions."

"So you think someone tried to kill Brooks to get the formula."

"Or to stop production in its tracks. Not only has C'est Moi made millions in a few short months, it's also cutting into the sales of every other perfume manufacturer in the business. Their stocks are plummeting. That doesn't exactly endear Carson to his competitors."

"You didn't mention these details before."

"Frankly, I assumed you'd done your homework. Or were you too busy doing a background check on me?"

Before Whitman could respond, the door to the intensive care unit swung open, and Carson's lead surgeon strode out, brows drawn as he studied a chart.

"Dr. Radison." Dylan went straight over, blocking the surgeon's path. "How is he?"

The surgeon halted, glancing up from his clipboard with a guarded expression. "He's holding his own."

"Is he conscious?" Barton demanded.

Dr. Radison gave the detectives a measured look. "He drifts in and out. A lot of that's due to the pain medication."

"Was he awake just now?" Whitman pressed.

"Yes." The surgeon held up a palm, setting immediate limits to the oncoming request. "He's on an endotracheal tube and a respirator. So he can write, but he can't speak. Plus, he's not up for a long interrogation. A few questions, but that's it." His gaze flickered back to Dylan. "He scribbled down that I should send you home. His note said you'd better be rested enough to work round the clock till he's back."

A corner of Dylan's mouth lifted. "That sounds like Carson."

"Does he know I'm here?" Susan interrupted.

Radison nodded. "I told him. He was pleased to hear it, until I added that you'd been here all night. At that point, he scrawled down that he wants you to go home and rest, too."

"Is there anything else we should know about Mr. Brooks's condition before we go in?" Whitman was already inching toward the ICU.

"Actually, yes." Dr. Radison's tone stopped her in her tracks. "We have an additional complication. If you remember, I said the bullet nicked Mr. Brooks's abdominal aorta."

"You also said you sewed that up," Dylan countered.

"We did."

"So?"

Dr. Radison rubbed a hand over his square jaw. "It's not as simple as that, Mr. Newport. The aorta is the body's main artery. It's crucial in supplying blood to the organs. In this case, the spot the bullet nicked resulted in a reduced blood flow to the kidneys. That, combined with the large amount of blood he lost overall, and the septic shock resulting from the infection caused by the damage done to his intestines, all add up to a major source of concern. I just ran a CT scan. I'm not happy with what I saw. Kidney function is down eighty percent. Unless that improves, I'm inserting a temporary fistula and starting dialysis."

"Dialysis." Dylan repeated the word slowly. "Are you saying you expect his kidneys to shut down completely?"

"That's a worst-case scenario. It's possible they'll just need some help before they take over on their own."

"So this problem is temporary."

A brief hesitation. "That's my hope."

Dylan tensed. "But it could be permanent."

"Possibly, yes. And, taking into account Mr. Brooks's vital lifestyle, his resistance to physical restrictions of any kind, I want to be prepared."

"Oh, God." Susan pressed her palms to her cheeks. "You're talking about a transplant."

"I'm only talking about laying the groundwork," Dr. Radison clarified. "Just in case." He glanced back at his file and frowned. "Unfortunately, Mr. Brooks has no family. He's also got type O positive blood, which reduces the potential pool of compatible donors. We'd better start alerting anyone close to him who'd be willing to be screened for a match—again, just in case." He inclined his head. "I assume we should start with the two of you?"

"Absolutely," Susan returned immediately.

"Hmm?" Dylan's mind was racing. Thank God he'd made those calls already. He'd set things in motion, a fact that had just taken on a whole new dimension. Ironic that Carson had picked now to search for his child. That request had just escalated from sentimental curiosity to urgent necessity.

"Mr. Newport?" Radison's tone suggested he'd been trying to get Dylan's attention. "I asked if you know your blood type."

"Sorry. I was just digesting everything you said. I'm O positive."

"The same as Mr. Brooks. Good. Ms. Lane just told me she's A negative. That won't work."

"Does that mean I'm compatible?" Dylan asked.

"I'm afraid it's not that simple. It's just step one. We need to draw your blood so we can do tissue-typing, as well as . . ."

"I'll get down to the lab and have that done right away." Dylan could feel the detectives watching him, gauging his reaction. He couldn't ask to speak to Dr. Radison alone, not without arousing further suspicion. Besides, now wasn't the time to spill his guts to the surgeon about the chance that Carson had a biological child. Not until he knew whether this person actually existed.

"Something wrong, Mr. Newport?" Whitman inquired.

"I'm just making a mental switch from focusing on Carson's enemies to focusing on his friends." Dylan pulled himself together quickly enough to cover his tracks. "I'll call everyone I can think of. The more people willing to get screened, the better chance we'll have of finding a compatible donor." His jaw set. "I assume the rest of our conversation can wait until I've made those calls and had some blood drawn?"

"I'll start on the calls, Dylan," Susan offered, her voice shaky, as if she were battling shock. "It will make me feel useful. You, at least, can give blood. I can't even offer him that." She swallowed hard. "Whoever I leave out—business associates, old girlfriends, whoever you think might help—you can make those calls afterward."

Dylan nodded. "Is that all right with you?" he asked the detectives.

"Certainly," Whitman assured him, her poker face back in place. "We want to talk to Mr. Brooks anyway— and Dr. Radison, if he can spare a minute. After that, we'll chat with Ms. Lane. We're not going anywhere, and I assume neither are you. We'll catch up later, here. Unless you're going home to rest, as Mr. Brooks suggested?"

"No. Rest isn't an option." Dylan's jaw tightened a fraction more. "I'll be right here at the hospital—unless I'm in a taxi, or home showering and changing. In any case, I'm reachable."

"Fine." Barton turned to Susan. "You'll wait?"

"Of course. I'll be outside the building, making calls from my cell phone. Get me when you're ready." Her eyes glistened with unshed tears. "I want whoever did this caught and punished."

"So do we," Barton assured her. "And don't worry. He will be. Soon."

With a speculative glance at Dylan, Barton followed his partner into the ICU.

3

2:30 P.M.
341 West 76th Street

Dylan stepped out of the shower to a ringing telephone. He swore softly, knotting a towel around his waist and making a mad dash for the bedroom.

It was probably one of those pain-in-the-ass detectives at the other end, ready for another round of grilling. He was in no mood for it, either. He'd been in perpetual motion for the last three hours.

First, he'd given blood. Then, he'd checked on Carson, who'd drifted off to sleep, after what was evidently a short session with the detectives. Whitman and Barton had moved on to interviewing Susan, an interview Dylan interrupted long enough to get the list of people Susan had reached.

She was in the process of describing to the detectives how she and Carson had met, and their mutual interest in YouthOp, the charitable organization that she headed and Carson supported. Dylan hadn't stuck around to hear the rest. No doubt the cops would get around to asking her questions about him. Well, that would be a dead end. He and Susan got along fine. All she really knew about him was how tight he was with Carson. And since Carson was a very private man— one who wasn't in the habit of discussing his relationships, business or personal, not even with Susan—and who never divulged the details of what went on at

Ruisseau, there was no fuel Susan could add to the detectives' fire.

When Dylan got home he'd spent over an hour on the phone, managing to round up four or five people who were willing to be screened. Not that he blamed the ones who said no. Having respect, even affection, for someone was one thing. Giving them an organ from your body was another.

That's where blood relations came in.

And, with luck, came through.

He'd gone into the shower, letting the hot water spray over his head and down his back, hoping it would ease his tension and frustration. Fat chance of that. He was so tight he was practically vibrating. And now the damned phone was ringing.

He snatched up the receiver just before the call went to voice mail. "Yeah, hello."

"Dylan?" the voice on the other end asked. "I was just about to hang up and try your cell phone again."

"Stan." Equal amounts of relief and apprehension flooded Dylan, and he sank down in a chair. "Tell me you have something for me."

"I do. It took a while because the doctor's retired. My guy had to find out where the records were stored. Then, he had to get his hands on them. But he managed."

"Are you sure they're legitimate?"

"Positive. I worked there, too, remember? I know the doctor. I know where he retired to. I also know what his forms and his letterhead look like. And the fax I got is authentic. It gave me the woman's name, her personal data, the works. The rest was easy. Our PI traced her, and her family. Gloria Radcliffe. She's a fashion designer, lives in Rockport, Massachusetts. Her family's loaded; from Beacon Hill, just like I remembered. It's all here. Now that I know where you are, I'll fax all the information directly to your apartment."

"Now."

"Of course now." An uneasy pause. "How's Carson?"

"His kidneys aren't functioning right. He might need a transplant."

Stan swore under his breath. "Do they have him on dialysis?"

"They didn't when I left. By now, they might. Let's cut to the chase. Does Carson have a living child or not?"

"Yeah. A daughter. Her name's Sabrina. Born June third, nineteen seventy-five, Newton-Wellesley Hospital—almost ten months to the day from when Carson made his donation. Born perfectly healthy, according to her birth records."

"You've got those?"

"Right here in my hand. I'm reading from them now."

"Is her blood type listed?"

"Um . . ." A pause, as Stan skimmed the page. "Here it is. O positive."

Dylan blew out a breath of sheer, utter relief. "I assume you've got current information on this Sabrina Radcliffe. Where is she now?"

"She runs some high-level corporate training center near Manchester, New Hampshire. It's a combo business center and resort. She lives there."

That clinched it.

"I can fly to Manchester in an hour. I'll talk to Carson's surgeon. Then, I'll jump on a plane. In the meantime, you keep Carson's name out of the press, just like we discussed. Cash in some favors. Do whatever you have to. It'll just be for a day, until I can get to Sabrina Radcliffe. And Stan—thanks. This could be Carson's best chance, maybe his only chance."

"Wait a minute, Dylan." Stan cut him off before he could hang up. "Are you nuts? You can't just burst into that training center tonight—no phone call, no warning, and lay this on that girl."

"Watch me."

"But . . ."

"Look, Stan. This isn't just a sentimental request anymore. We're talking about Carson's life. You know the kind of man he is; he won't accept a damned thing from anyone. Long-term dialysis? Depending on hospitals, tubes, and machines? That would destroy him."

"I'm not arguing with you. But someone has to be the voice of reason here. What you're about to do will turn Sabrina Radcliffe's life upside down. To begin with, you don't even know if she's a compatible donor. More important, you don't know if she's willing. Yeah, Carson's her biological father. But they've never even met. It's possible she's not even aware he exists. Who knows what her mother's told her? The path Gloria Radcliffe took was pretty radical for the seventies; I doubt she shared the details with her kid."

"That kid is twenty-seven now. She'll handle it."

"Maybe. Maybe not. You have no clue how she's going to react, or if she'll cooperate."

"I'll cross that bridge when I come to it."

"She might throw you out on your ass."

"And her mother might sue me," Dylan added dryly. "She'd win, too. She's got enough grounds to have me disbarred and a bunch of us tossed in jail. Obtaining confidential medical records and divulging their contents without permission—that's criminal *and* unethical. But it's a chance I'll have to take."

"Dylan . . ."

"Don't worry. Your name won't ever be mentioned.

I'm in this alone. But come hell or high water, I'm flying up to Manchester. I've got to."

"Yeah . . . I know you do." As Stan spoke, Dylan's fax machine started to ring. "That's everything you'll need—all seven pages' worth. Good luck."

3:15 P.M.
Mt. Sinai Hospital

Dylan blew by the ICU waiting room and went straight to the desk. "I need to see Dr. Radison," he told the nurse. "It's urgent."

She glanced up from the chart she was reading. "Mr. Brooks is resting comfortably, sir. There's no cause for alarm."

"I'm not alarmed. I'm time-stressed. I've got to talk to Dr. Radison—now." He glanced back over his shoulder, noting the cop posted outside Carson's door, and eyeing the ICU with a somber expression. "That's a dialysis machine Carson's hooked up to, isn't it?"

"Yes. Dr. Radison started the procedure about an hour ago. But there haven't been any complications. Mr. Brooks is responding well; his blood pressure's steady and he's showing no major side effects or discomfort."

"That's because he's too drugged up to understand what that machine means to his life." Dylan leaned forward. He wasn't about to be placated or put off—not on this one. "Is Radison in surgery?"

"No, but . . ."

"Then page him."

The nurse eyed Dylan for a minute. Something in his expression must have convinced her, because she picked up the phone and complied.

*   *   *

Across the waiting room, Detective Barton slid forward in his chair and started to get up.

"Wait." His partner stopped munching on her potato chip long enough to stretch out an arm and deter him.

"Why? Newport's a wreck. His defenses are way down. It's the best time to put the screws in."

"I agree. But let's get the whole picture first. Let's find out why Dylan Newport's so freaked out. Whatever it is, it must be pretty serious if he's insisting on paging the surgeon. Let him do his thing. Then we'll do ours."

Dylan felt the detectives scrutinizing him. He didn't give a damn. If Radison responded as expected, he'd have to tell the cops about his plans anyway.

"Mr. Newport?" Radison strode into the corridor, brows knit. "I understand you need to see me. The nurse said it was urgent."

A tight nod. "Is there somewhere we can speak in private?"

"Of course." The surgeon led him down the hall into an unoccupied room. "What is it?" he asked, shutting the door.

"Carson's on dialysis. Does that mean his kidneys are worse?"

"It means they need help. Whether they'll rally and function normally on their own, it's too early to tell." The surgeon frowned. "This isn't an unexpected crisis. We discussed the possibility of dialysis."

"Yes. But there's something I didn't know; something I just found out. It might make a huge difference if Carson's kidneys don't kick in as we hope." Dylan met Radison's gaze. "Carson has a biological child he isn't aware of—a daughter. She's twenty-seven and lives in New England. I don't have a detailed medical history on her, but I do have one crucial fact—her blood type. She's O positive."

Radison stared. "How did you come by this information?"

"That's not important. What's important is, it's accurate. Now you need to give me some facts. First of all, how likely is it that Carson's daughter's a match?"

A pause, as the surgeon weighed his response. "There are no guarantees. But, excluding an identical twin or sibling, a parent or child is the most likely individual to be a donor match. You've already overcome one hurdle by telling me that father and daughter have the same blood type. That's step one. There's still tissue-typing to check for common genes, and a crossmatch test to perform. Until both of those are done, I can't tell you if this would be a go. After that, she'd see a nephrologist, who'd do a full evaluation, including a battery of lab tests. Last, she'd undergo a renal angiogram. The good news is that, if Mr. Brooks and his daughter are compatible, there are added benefits, should a transplant become necessary. Common genetic backgrounds will lower the risk of kidney rejection. And the odds of success are improved when the donor is young—which, in this case, she is. So if you're asking me if this is an encouraging discovery, the answer is yes."

"That's good enough for me." Dylan shot a quick look at his watch. "How soon do I need to get her here?"

Radison's frown returned. "You want a timetable. Frankly, before I even broach that subject, I feel compelled to remind you that Mr. Brooks is this young woman's father. He's been shot, and is in critical condition. For that reason alone, she should be advised immediately. She has every right, and every reason, to see her father."

"Point taken." Dylan wanted an answer, not a lecture. "But with regard to the medical urgency . . ."

"You're not under the gun. Even if Mr. Brooks's kidneys fail completely and don't recover, we wouldn't perform a transplant until his wounds have healed, and until he's been infection-free for six to eight weeks. On the other hand, that time frame is deceptive, because it also takes six to eight weeks to complete a full donor evaluation. Bottom line? If Carson Brooks's daughter is willing, the screening process should begin right away." He gave Dylan a quizzical look. "Would you like me to make the telephone call?"

"No." Dylan shook his head. "This is a delicate situation. Very few people know the truth—including, very possibly, the young woman herself. News of her paternity could come as quite a shock to her. That's why I asked if we were racing the clock. I want a chance to do this in person. You just gave it to me. I'll fly up to her home tonight and break the news. Hopefully, I can convince her to come back with me." Dylan's lips tightened. "But first I need to clear my plans with the detectives lying in wait outside."

"There's our guy." Whitman crumpled up her empty potato chip bag and tossed it into the trash as Dylan plowed his way over to them.

"Yup," Barton agreed dryly. "Certainly no need to track him down. He's heading straight for us. And, boy, does he have something on his mind."

"We're about to find out what."

"Detectives." Dylan stopped directly in front of them. "You said you had more questions for me. Ask them now. Because in ten minutes I'm leaving for the airport. I've got a plane to catch."

"Do you?" Detective Whitman shot him an interested look. "To where?"

"Manchester, New Hampshire. The flight leaves La-Guardia at six ten. It arrives at seven thirty-two. I'm staying in Auburn, just eleven miles from the Manchester airport. I'll give you the address and phone number. That way you can keep tabs on me—you know, make sure I don't flee the country."

"Sudden, isn't it?" Barton ignored Dylan's sarcasm. "Not to mention that this trip must be pretty important for you to leave Mr. Brooks during his medical crisis."

"It's *for* him that I'm leaving."

Whitman responded by jerking her head in the direction of the empty lounge across the way. "Let's talk in there."

With a tight nod, Dylan complied, and the three of them filed into the room.

"What's in Auburn?" Whitman demanded the instant the door was shut behind them.

"Not *what—who,*" Dylan corrected. "And the answer is Carson's biological daughter."

Whitman's Q-tip brows shot up. "I thought he had no living relatives."

"We all thought that. We were wrong. I just found out about this woman's existence. I informed Dr. Radison. He wants her to be screened right away."

"Makes sense. So call her. Telephones are a lot quicker and more convenient than planes."

With great irritation, Dylan rubbed the back of his neck. "I've already told you more than I should have—none of which is to be made public," he added meaningfully. "I only disclosed this much because you'd demand a credible reason for my leaving town, and so you'll understand why the media needs to be kept out of this, at least until tomorrow. But this is a personal, not a police, matter. I can't get into the details without breaking Carson's confidence."

"We're not interested in leaking a scandal," Barton said tightly. "We're interested in solving a crime. We said we'd put off the press, and we will. As for relevance, it's up to us to decide what does and doesn't pertain to our investigation. So you'll have to give us a little more information than you have. Why the trip?"

"Let's just say that my news might catch Carson's daughter off-guard."

"News of the shooting?"

"News of who her father is."

"I see." Whitman pursed her lips. "She doesn't know. And you're going to be the one to break it to her."

"I'm the only one Carson entrusted with this information, and with the job of finding her, so, yes. It's my responsibility."

"Entrusted?" Whitman pounced on him like a hunter on its prey. "So Carson Brooks does know he has a biological child. You just said . . ."

"He suspects. He's not sure," Dylan said, cutting off her interrogation. "Let's not play cat and mouse. Not now. Later, you can get into this with Carson. Use the next seven minutes to grill me on whatever you've been saving up. Then I'm out of here. Unless you plan on stopping me."

"Now why would we do that?"

"Because you think I shot Carson."

"Did you?"

Dylan stared Whitman down. "No."

Barton tore open a pack of gum and popped a stick in his mouth. "Do you own a gun, Mr. Newport?"

"Ah, now we're getting down to it. I'm sure you already know I don't. I didn't borrow or steal one, either. Besides, if I was the one who shot Carson, what did I do with my weapon? Toss it out the twelfth-floor window or down an elevator shaft?"

"That's one of our question marks. No weapon. No bullet."

"But lots of motive and opportunity," Whitman chimed in. "You were the only other person at Ruisseau at the time of the shooting."

"The only other *known* person," Dylan amended.

"Right. That gave you both the time and the access. As for motive, the amount of money, company interest, and corporate power that would go to you if Carson Brooks was out of the way is staggering."

Dylan's eyes glinted. "True. I'd get a bundle. I'd also lose the closest thing to a father I've ever had. The trade-off sucks."

"You've known Mr. Brooks for nineteen years." Whitman skimmed some pages that Dylan recognized as Child Welfare records. "You came to him with a colorful background. In and out of five foster families . . ." A pointed pause. "Three juvenile arrests."

"I fought with fists, not guns."

"Yes, and frequently, too. Street brawls, discipline problems in school."

"That's right. I had a lousy childhood." Dylan's jaw tightened. "Now skip ahead. Read the part about *after* I met Carson Brooks. Straight A's, work-study program, corporate internship. Graduated from Columbia University and Columbia Law School with honors. Did any of that register? Because if it did, you know the difference Carson's made in my life."

"He's certainly been a generous benefactor. Any idea why? I mean, why you?"

A muscle in Dylan's cheek flexed. "You'll have to ask Carson that one, too. Now, are you going to let me go to Auburn, or not?"

Whitman studied him for a long moment. Then, she nodded, tearing off a scrap of blank paper and handing it to Dylan. "Write down Mr. Brooks's daughter's name and address," she instructed. "And keep your cell phone on. If we need you, we'll find you."

4

Sabrina was just finishing up an evening workshop when her assistant, Melissa Andrews, poked her head in.

"Excuse me, Sabrina," she murmured, looking distinctly uncomfortable—a rarity for the thirty-five-year-old dynamo, who could cope with just about anything. "May I see you for a moment?"

"Sure." Sabrina took the cue, gathering up her notes and gesturing for the group to disband. "We were just about to call it a night anyway. These folks need a little R&R." She smiled politely around the room. "The evening's yours. Enjoy it."

She walked into the hall, edging toward the quiet alcove where Melissa had already positioned herself so they could talk in private. "What is it?"

"There's a man here to see you," Melissa reported, folding her arms across her breasts and tapping one manicured nail against her sleeve. "His name's Dylan Newport. Evidently, he's corporate counsel for Ruisseau Fragrances."

"Ruisseau?" Sabrina's brows rose with interest—an interest that was rapidly eclipsed by puzzlement. "Their corporate counsel? That's odd."

"Almost as odd as showing up at my desk at eight o'clock at night, insisting on speaking to you and *only* you, now if not sooner. He practically forced me to interrupt your workshop. I swear, I think the guy would have broken down the door if I'd said no."

"That sounds pretty extreme." Sabrina frowned. "We've never done business with Ruisseau, so this can't be a legal suit."

"It isn't. I specifically asked him if he had documents for you. He said no. I pressed him as hard as I could. He finally acknowledged that he wasn't here on legal business. That's as much as I could get out of him. He refused to say another word, except that it was you he needed to see. Tonight." Melissa shot her a questioning look. "You're not having an affair with him, are you?"

"Yeah, right," Sabrina retorted, her mind racing to find a logical explanation. "I barely have time for a nap, much less an affair."

"I didn't think so. It's too bad, though. He's hot. *Really* hot. But he's not your type. This guy's too earthy."

"Thanks for the assessment." Sabrina wasn't bothered by Melissa's bluntness. Her assistant was as plunge-in-and-get-it-done about relationships as she was about work. "But whatever this Dylan Newport wants to see me about, it's not sex."

"Like I said, too bad. Anyway, he's definitely a man with a mission. He won't take no for an answer. Rather than test his limits, I decided to interrupt you."

"A wise move. Where is he now?"

"In the office behind the reception area. I showed him in there to keep the disruption to a minimum. He's waiting for you, pacing around like a caged lion."

"Then let's not waste time—his or ours. Let's find out what he wants."

"Have fun." Melissa patted her shoulder. "I'll be at my desk. Just hit the intercom and bellow if you need me."

"I think I can handle this." Sabrina was already on her way, heading down the hall, her thoughts moving faster than her feet. Why would an attorney for Ruisseau Fragrances be here, demanding to see her?

Only one way to find out.

She cut across the marble and glass reception area and made a beeline for the rear office.

Stepping inside, she nearly collided with the tall, dark-haired man who was pacing near the doorway. "Mr. Newport?"

When he turned toward her, Sabrina knew instantly why Melissa had described him the way she had. He *was* earthy. And hot—if you went for the dark, rough-around-the-edges type. He was certainly both those things, more dangerous-looking than classically handsome, right down to his penetrating gaze and strong, slightly crooked nose that suggested it had been broken at least once. His stance and build were equally tough and Sabrina could sooner picture him in a black T-shirt and jeans than in the herringbone blazer and conservative wool slacks he had on.

No, definitely not her type.

"I'm Sabrina Radcliffe," she informed him, extending her hand. "I understand you're here to see me."

He returned her handshake as if on autopilot, something akin to startled realization flashing in his eyes. Then, he stepped back, scrutinizing her with fierce, unnerving intensity, his stare raking her from head to toe—not in the usual suggestive manner Sabrina had been subject to all too often, but in a clinical way, like a scientist might examine a specimen under a microscope.

"Do I get the part?" she asked pointedly.

Her meaning sank in, and he broke off his physical inspection, his gaze rising to meet hers. He looked a little shell-shocked, although why, she had no idea. "Yeah, you get the part. I hope you'll want it."

Okay, so he *was* here to hire her. But why the timing? And why an attorney?

This was getting more fascinating by the minute.

"I'm intrigued." Sabrina tucked a wisp of hair behind her ear. "Ruisseau's last quarter was incredible. You blew away all your competition. Your company's clearly on a roll. So why seek out CCTL now? Don't get me wrong—we can always find ways to make a company better. But it's a rare CEO who thinks that way when profits are sky-rocketing. And it's rarer still to have him or her send corporate counsel to do human resources' job. So what's the scoop?"

To her surprise, a crack of laughter escaped Dylan Newport. He gave a hard, disbelieving shake of his head, rubbing the back of his neck as if to assimilate some major discovery.

"Care to share the joke with me?"

"Sorry. It's been a pretty intense day. And there's no joke. Just some unexpected enlightenment."

"You lost me."

Her guest's amusement faded, and he leaned past Sabrina to shut the door. Then, he gestured toward a chair. "Sit down, Ms. Radcliffe. The conversation we're about to have is not going to be easy."

Normally, she'd remain standing. But something in his voice made her comply.

He pulled around another chair so he could face her, lowering himself into it. "I didn't come here to hire you."

"Then why did you come?"

He interlaced his fingers, staring at them for a moment before answering. "You know a lot about Ruisseau's success. Why is that?"

Sabrina blinked. "I'm a management consultant. My clients are companies, big and small, public and private. It's my job to know what's going on in the business world. And I'd hardly say I know a lot about Ruisseau; only what's been in every financial newspaper and on every television network in the country."

"Yeah, well, check out the early morning business news tomorrow."

She jumped on that one. "Why? Will Ruisseau be a news item? Is that why you're here? Has something major happened?"

A humorless smile. "That's the understatement of the century. It's only because we called in a few favors and because we're a private company that I managed to keep things quiet until after you and I talked."

This was getting more outrageous by the minute. "Why would you need to talk to me first, especially if you don't plan to hire CCTL? Where does my company fit into all this?"

"It doesn't. *You* do."

Sabrina's gaze narrowed. "How? And I want an answer, not another question."

"Fine. I'll cut to the chase. The reason I'm here is because of your father."

"My . . ." Sabrina broke off. After all this buildup, Dylan Newport's visit was obviously a mistake. Whoever he was looking for, it wasn't her. "You've been misinformed. My father's not alive, much less affiliated with Ruisseau."

"You're wrong, Ms. Radcliffe. He's both." A resigned frown. "I was hoping this wouldn't come completely out of left field. No such luck, I see. Were you told your father is dead, or just a nonentity?"

An odd, uneasy sensation formed in the pit of Sabrina's stomach. She'd heard this song and dance before, but never from a reputable attorney, and never with such an intricate scenario to back it up. Why would Ruisseau's corporate counsel represent a two-bit hustler when there was so much at stake?

He wouldn't.

The cerebral part of her was dying of curiosity. The instinctive part wanted to turn around and run.

She started to get up, eyeing the file Dylan Newport pulled out of his leather case. "I repeat, you're talking to the wrong person. Now if you'll excuse me . . ."

"Your mother's Gloria Radcliffe," he announced, stopping Sabrina in her tracks. "She's a fashion designer from a prominent Beacon Hill family. You're her only child. You were born on June third, nineteen seventy-five, at Newton-Wellesley Hospital. You blasted your way through school and, at the ungodly age of nineteen-going-on-twenty, got your degree from the Cornell School of Hotel Management. You worked in the Ritz-Carlton's management trainee program for a year, then went back and got your MBA from Harvard. For three years, you were employed at Haig, Lowell, and Fontaine—one of Boston's most renowned management consulting firms— and you were well on your way toward becoming their youngest junior partner when, a year ago, you did a one-eighty, leaving to start the Center for Creative Thinking and Leadership. At that time, you recruited top talent from all over the country to form your staff. You're quite a success story. Still think I have the wrong person?"

Slowly, Sabrina sank back down. "Okay, what's this about? Why did you dig up my entire history? Or maybe I should ask for whom? In fact, maybe I should see some identification. You claim you're a lawyer. I'm starting to think you're a PI."

"I'm not. If I were, I'd be handling this conversation better." He pulled out his license and company ID, handing both to her. "Proof enough?"

Sabrina skimmed them, then handed them back. "Fine. You are who you say you are. That still doesn't explain . . ."

"How much do you know about your father?" he interrupted. "Or, more to the point, the details surrounding his becoming your father?"

The way he said that—she had a gut feeling he had facts to back up his allegations. So, obviously, did whoever had sent him. They knew exactly how she'd been conceived. Which explained the way Dylan Newport was staring at her, as if he were checking for some resemblance, something concrete to lend credibility to his client's claim.

Still, she could be wrong. This could be nothing more than another run-of-the-mill case of a con artist who assumed she was the product of a one-night-stand, and was looking for a windfall. An incredibly good con artist, if he'd convinced Dylan Newport to represent him.

"You're representing a man with an alleged claim," she stated, testing the waters. "Is your client going after my mother? Because if he is, it won't work. My mother's got an amazing memory for the men she's been involved with. This hoax has been tried before—my long-lost father showing up, trying to extort money from my family—and he and his lawyer have been slapped with lawsuits so big they'd make your head spin. Although, I must say, I'm surprised that an attorney of your standing could be so easily duped. Or that you'd stoop so low and risk so much."

"Hold it." Dylan Newport shook his head. "There's no alleged claim. And I'm certainly not going after your mother, or anyone else in your family. I'm just trying to get a handle on how much of the truth you've been told."

"You tell me."

"Fine. You were conceived through donor insemination. You never met your biological father. Is that consistent with the information you've been given?"

So she'd been right. He did have the facts.

Sabrina's eyes glittered. "It is. It's also a private aspect of my life—not one I'm ashamed of, by the way, but one I don't discuss with strangers. I must say you've gone to great lengths, Mr. Newport. Prying into confidential medical records, divulging that information—you've already given me grounds to have you disbarred. Keep talking and we'll add charges of extortion and fraud to invasion of privacy. Try leaking this bogus claim to the news—and you'll be spending time in jail."

"Thanks for the warning." Dylan Newport's unflinching stare said that none of her threats were news to him. And, in spite of it, he was still pushing ahead with this.

Why?

The obvious answer was that whatever he was about to tell her was true. And damned important to the higher-ups at Ruisseau.

The pit in Sabrina's stomach became a full-fledged knot.

"Your assessment is right," he was continuing. "At least partly right. You'd get me on the invasion of privacy charge. Add emotional distress, for that matter. But you'd lose on extortion and fraud. Because I don't want money, and the claim I'm making isn't bogus. It's real. The fact that I'm willing to go to these extremes despite the risk should tell you that."

"Fine." Sabrina acknowledged his claim with a tight nod. "So you know whose sperm was half-responsible for my conception. Congratulations. Now comes the bad news. You've conducted this whole extensive, shady investigation for nothing. I'm not interested in learning the donor's name or anything about him. Not now. Not ever."

"Yeah, I picked up on that."

"Then why are you pursuing this?"

"Because I have no choice."

"There's always a choice."

"Not in this case. A man's life depends on it. He could die. He means as much to me as if he were my father. As luck would have it, he's yours."

"Die?" Another jolt out of left field. Sabrina's mind had been going down the corporate path, assuming that Dylan Newport was bailing out some company exec who was being blackmailed with this juicy scandal. But life and death? That steered things in a whole different direction.

Sabrina's shoulders lifted in a baffled shrug. "Are you suggesting this man is terminally ill and thinks meeting me will help?"

"No. He doesn't even know you exist. Nor is he in a position to find out. He's lying in ICU fighting for his life. By the way, *he* has a name. It's Carson Brooks. Who, as a side issue, doesn't need your money. He has millions of his own."

Whatever Sabrina had been about to say vanished with that bombshell. Beyond pretense, beyond trying to assimilate facts, she simply stared.

Dylan looked away, swearing quietly under his breath. "Look, Ms. Radcliffe—Sabrina—I'm not trying to tear a hole in your life. But I don't have the luxury of time, and . . ."

"Carson Brooks," she interrupted, seeking some sort of clarification. "The CEO of Ruisseau. He's my father."

"Yes."

"You said he could die. What happened? Did he have a stroke? A heart attack?"

"Neither. He was shot."

This was turning into a bad detective movie. "Who shot him?"

"We don't know. It happened last night in his office. The police are investigating. Maybe after news of the shooting is released tomorrow, we'll get some tips that will give us a clue."

More pieces fell into place. "So that's the media-fest you were referring to that you managed to hold off until tomorrow. The networks and newspapers will be getting word of the assault."

"Right. And that's all they're getting word of. You, your relationship to Carson—that information was given only to the police and Carson's surgeon. So you can cross slander off your list, too. Although, to be frank, having Carson Brooks for a father is something to be proud of, not to renounce. Still, your relationship won't be made public. We'll try to keep it quiet as long as we can."

"Thank you—I think." Sabrina's head was swimming. "I'm not sure what to say." A guarded look. "Will he be all right?"

"He's in pretty bad shape."

"I'm sorry to hear that. But I'm also confused. Where do I fit into all this? You worked round-the-clock to find me, not to mention going out on a limb that could have cost you your law license. Why? I doubt it was to prepare me for an eventual news leak. So what is it you want?"

From the expression on Dylan Newport's face, Sabrina knew they'd reached the moment of truth.

"Besides his internal injuries, Carson's kidneys have shut down," he informed her. "He's on dialysis. A transplant is a real possibility. It's crucial that we find a donor match. The odds of that happening are best when the donor and the recipient are blood relations. Which you two are. In fact, you're Carson's only blood relative. So you see, Sabrina, I'm here for more than your sympathy. I'm here for your cooperation. You have to be tissue-typed. My records show that you and Carson have the same O-positive blood, but you'll need to take a confirming blood test. The next step would be—"

"Stop." Sabrina was on her feet, reality punching her in the gut. "You came up here to get me to volunteer one of my organs to . . . to . . ."

"To your biological father, yes." Dylan rose, too. He looked concerned, but not contrite. "I realize this is a lot to absorb, not to mention being a huge sacrifice."

"A sacrifice?" Sabrina repeated. "I don't know this man. I never met him. He was faceless, nameless . . ." She broke off, reason telling her she had to be sure. "You obviously brought proof that he's my father. Show it to me."

Dylan held up the file, then placed it carefully on the glass table behind him. "Everything is in here. Read it. I'll go grab some dinner and give you a few hours alone. We'll talk later—say, eleven o'clock?"

Sabrina's head was spinning. "You're staying in the area?"

"Until tomorrow. Then I'm flying back. I'm hoping you'll decide to come, too—not only to get tissue-typed, but to meet your father. Think about it, Sabrina. I know this is a shock. But you'll get past it. Carson Brooks is a brilliant, vital man. You could save him from a life that, to him, would be no life at all."

With a final penetrating stare, Dylan headed toward the door.

"Wait." Sabrina stopped him in his tracks. "Eleven is too soon. I need more time."

He turned back. "You want to speak with your mother." It was a statement, not a question.

"Yes. And not on the phone. In person."

"In person?" He frowned, giving her another of those hard, assessing looks. "You're driving to Rockport?"

"That's where she lives," Sabrina returned tersely. She didn't bother questioning how he knew where her mother's home was. His background check had been thorough. He'd known her mother was from Beacon Hill and what she did professionally. Why wouldn't he know the rest? "I've got to see her right away. The reasons should be obvious."

"They are. But Rockport's an hour and a half away. Are you sure you're up to driving? It's late. And you're upset."

"I'm fine."

He didn't press the point. "You'll spend the night there."

"Probably. Maybe. I'm not sure." Sabrina wished he'd go away and let her think. "My mother's been in Manhattan on business all week. Her plane landed at Logan around seven. I doubt she got home before eight, and that's if the plane landed on time. She's bound to be exhausted. And this news . . ." Sabrina drew a shaky breath. "It's bound to throw her. So I can't give you an exact time as to when I'll be back. You'll just have to be patient."

"Fair enough. I'll get a hotel room. I'll call your assistant with the telephone number when I have it."

"You can stay here at the Center," Sabrina offered tonelessly. "We have more than enough room." She walked over to the glass table, tore off a Post-it, and scribbled something down. "Give this to the receptionist. She'll take care of the arrangements." She handed him the Post-it. "Whatever my decision, I'll get it to you tomorrow."

"Fine." He cleared his throat. "If it makes any difference, for weeks now Carson's been wrestling with the idea of conducting an investigation to learn whether or not he has a child. He didn't intend to intrude on your life. He just wanted to know. It was on his mind the night he was shot. I rode with him in the ambulance. He was fully aware he might not make it. He asked one thing of me: to find you—if you existed. I planned on doing that, even if this kidney crisis hadn't come up. The difference is, you would never have had to know about it. I'm truly sorry for dumping all this on you. But I'm sorrier for Carson." He pulled open the door. "I'll be waiting for your call."

Sabrina sat alone in the office for a long time, reading through the file and thinking.

Then, she reached for the phone.

5

Gloria Radcliffe loved her home. The two-hundred-year-old Cape was small and charming and, even with its view of the ocean, far more modest than her current income reflected. But it was the first thing she'd bought with her own money—almost three decades ago—and it was the place she'd brought her infant daughter home to raise right after she was born.

Her parents had been incensed. Then again, they often were when it came to her decisions. Rockport had been a poky town back then, a far cry from Beacon Hill. A beach community of clam chowder joints, bed-and-breakfasts, and would-be artists, it was exactly where she wanted to live.

It still was. She'd done some of her best sketches here, and that was the case to this very day. Even a week in the Big Apple, with all its glamour and excitement, couldn't detract from the simple joys of being home.

That was especially true this time. Her excursion to New York had been more draining than she'd expected.

She shut the door behind her, gazing around appreciatively, savoring the soft cream and taupe furnishings, and the gleaming hardwood floors. She carried her two pieces of Louis Vuitton luggage into the master bedroom, then headed for the kitchen, opting for a quick bite to eat and a hot bath before she unpacked.

Forty minutes later, she padded out of the bathroom, tying the belt of her silk dressing robe. She sat down at the dressing table, ready to begin her ritualistic beauty regimen.

Her make-up-free reflection looked back at her. She was fortunate, and she knew it. Mother Nature had been kind to her. She'd aged well. The general consensus was that she looked forty-five rather than sixty-one, thanks to a naturally slim figure, skin that hadn't wrinkled, and hair that—with a little help from Jean-Paul, her genius of a hairstylist—was still a lustrous honey-brown. Her good looks were something she'd once taken for granted and now appreciated fully. Not out of vanity, but out of pragmatism. In the fashion business, aging was a no-no. Being old meant being out of touch with the times *and* the trends. And that meant being a fashion designer who was passé.

She'd just finished applying her moisturizer when the telephone rang.

Frowning, she glanced at the clock. Nine twenty-five. It was unusual for anyone to be calling this late.

She walked over and picked up the receiver. "Hello?"

"Hi, Mother, it's me."

"Sabrina." Was it her imagination or did her daughter sound strained? "Is everything okay?"

"I know it's late," Sabrina replied, evading the question. "You probably just got in from the airport. But I have to talk to you."

No, it definitely was *not* her imagination.

Gloria's grip on the receiver tightened. "Of course. What is it?"

A long sigh. "Would it be all right if I drove out there?"

"Tonight?"

"Yes. I realize you're probably on your way to bed, but it's important."

This was totally unlike Sabrina. She wasn't the dramatic type. Yet her voice sounded unnaturally high and out of sorts. "Sabrina, are you ill?"

"No, nothing like that. I just got hit with some news that threw me. It affects both of us. I really need to discuss it with you, right away. Apparently, time is of the essence."

There was no point in playing guessing games. The sooner Sabrina got here, the better. "Fine. Are you leaving now?"

"Yes. I'll be there before eleven."

10:48 P.M.

Sabrina turned onto the cobblestone driveway, the headlights of her Lexus RX300 illuminating her mother's front lawn. She threw the gear shift into park and turned off the ignition, resting her forehead against the steering wheel for one weary moment.

The long drive hadn't helped. She was still just as unsettled as she'd been when Dylan Newport left her, maybe more so, since analyzing the situation had forced her to confront the numerous painful consequences that might arise.

Consequences that would vastly impact her mother, send ripples through every facet of her life, both personal and professional.

She could just see the headlines now: *High-profile CEO Carson Brooks revealed to be biological father of Sabrina Radcliffe, youngest member of the rich, socialite Radcliffe family.*

And once the tabloids got hold of it, they'd exploit the juicy tidbit to death. The result would be a media extravaganza with the Radcliffes smack in the middle of it. So much for Gloria's privacy, her carefully sculpted way of life. As for Sabrina's grandparents—what a nightmare that would be. The whole topic of how she'd been conceived was considered taboo in their book. Not only wasn't it discussed, it was deemed as having never happened. After their unsuccessful attempts to dissuade Gloria from going through with the donor insemination, they'd dealt with it through denial, never touching on the subject of Sabrina's father, wordlessly designating the subject as taboo among their friends and colleagues. And given how much influence Abigail and Charles Radcliffe wielded in the Boston country club set, they had no trouble getting anyone who was anyone to take the hint.

So, Sabrina came into the world, a welcome, beloved daughter and granddaughter. Gloria had taken the wise course, privately telling Sabrina that a father didn't factor into her life and then, as soon as Sabrina was old enough to understand the birds and the bees, explaining the donor insemination process—and her grandparents' unwillingness to acknowledge it. Sabrina heard her mother's message loud and clear. And the truth remained buried in the silent woodwork.

Until now.

Sabrina loved her grandparents dearly. But she also understood what they were about. They'd been elitist and rigid in their youth. Now, vital as ever but well into their eighties, they were positively implacable. Their reaction to this bombshell would be predictably severe. Not to mention the fallout Gloria would experience from them as a result.

And that was just from being told that this forbidden secret had been dug up, and that Sabrina knew her father's identity. If things progressed beyond that point and

Sabrina went ahead with the tissue-typing, then all hell would break loose. There'd be *no* chance of keeping her relationship to Carson Brooks under wraps, the tabloids would burst onto the scene, and her grandparents would totally freak out. And, no matter how you sliced it, she'd be responsible for their angst—angst that would only escalate if it turned out she was a compatible donor and decided to go through with the transplant. She meant everything to her grandparents—*and* to her mother. Putting her health at risk might just push them over the edge.

With a huge sigh, Sabrina climbed out of her car, wishing she knew how to bypass the land mines and arrive at a decision that was right for everyone. Any way she viewed this, it was a lose-lose situation.

Except maybe for Carson Brooks. He might stand to win. If that were the case . . . well, when one weighed physical survival against emotional well-being, the scales tipped heavily in favor of survival.

Sabrina was halfway up the front walk when Gloria pulled opened the door and stepped outside, rubbing the sleeves of her robe against some internal chill that defied Indian summer.

"I tried your cell phone three times," she said in greeting, eyeing Sabrina anxiously as she crossed the threshold. "I wanted to make sure you were calm enough to drive. You didn't answer. After the way you sounded on the phone, I was really starting to get frightened."

"I'm sorry. I guess I forgot to turn on my phone," Sabrina replied, slipping off her lightweight jacket and hanging it up.

"That's a first. You're never unreachable, especially since you started CCTL." Gloria's features were tight with concern. "You're really upset. What's this about?"

Sabrina studied her mother, noting that she looked tired—not a surprise given a week-long business trip. She also looked out-of-sorts, thanks to Sabrina's cryptic phone call and mystery visit. Well, things were about to get a lot worse. Her announcement was about to blow the lid off Pandora's box.

"Sabrina, whatever's bothering you is serious." Gloria was watching the play of emotions on Sabrina's face, her concern tangibly mounting. "I've never seen you like this. You're sheet-white." She drew her daughter over to the living room sofa. "Sit. I'll pour you a glass of merlot."

"Pour one for yourself, too," Sabrina advised.

A wary look. "All right."

Once she'd dispensed with that task, Gloria settled herself on the sofa next to Sabrina and handed her daughter one of the two wine goblets. "Now tell me what's happened."

With a fortifying sip of merlot, Sabrina turned toward her mother. From her peripheral vision, she spied the matching pieces of Louis Vuitton luggage clustered just inside the master bedroom and was reminded again how late it was, how intrusive her barging in this late must be. "I'm sorry, Mother. You haven't even had a chance to unpack."

"I'll do that later." Gloria waved away the notion. "You're stalling. That's not like you either."

"You're right. It's not. But the subject I'm about to get into was a closed chapter in our lives. Unfortunately, it's been pried open with a crowbar."

"*What* subject?"

"My conception."

That was obviously the last thing Gloria had expected. "Your conception? Why on earth would that come up?

And why would it cause you a problem?" An angry spark lit her eyes. "Don't tell me we have another con artist on our hands."

Sabrina shook her head. "Unfortunately not. That would be old hat, certainly not enough to freak me out like this. No, Mother, no con artist. This time we have the real thing. And he comes with a built-in crisis we have to deal with."

Gloria had gone very still. "You'd better explain."

"That's why I'm here." Sabrina steeled herself. "Mother, I know who the sperm donor was. I have more than enough proof. We'll get to that part later. First things first. You'll recognize his name. He's an extremely visible man. Visible enough so I doubt my biological ties to him can be kept under wraps for long. It's Carson Brooks, head of Ruisseau Fragrance Corporation."

Slowly, Gloria blew out her breath. For a long moment she said nothing. When she spoke, her voice was filled with quiet resignation. "Yes, I know. I don't need proof." She cleared her throat. "Now, how do *you* know, and what's this crisis you're referring to?"

Sabrina's jaw had nearly struck the coffee table. *"You know?"*

Another pause, as Gloria forced herself to address an issue she'd clearly wanted to avoid. "Not through any concrete proof. But, yes. I figured it out a long time ago."

"How long ago?"

"Maybe ten years."

Okay, Sabrina was about to lose it. This night was turning into The Twilight Zone. "How could you figure it out? Based on what? I thought the donor was anonymous."

"He was—at least by definition."

"What does *that* mean?"

Gloria swirled the remaining merlot around in her goblet. "It means I was never told his name. But I had lots of other information at my disposal. I had an entire personal profile. Most particularly, I had his photo—a very clear photo of a man who, even at twenty-two, had a face that was too striking, too charismatic to forget. Of course, at the time, he was a nobody. He couldn't have had any idea how high-profile he'd become. So he had no way of predicting that I'd wind up with an unexpected means of identification. His physical appearance hasn't changed much over the years. Same compelling features, piercing blue eyes, and an interesting scar on his right cheek. That was the giveaway. It's on the arch of his cheekbone, a curved, jagged slash, like he was cut by a bottle cap. It's very distinctive. So when I saw it again on the business news, on the face of a man who's an older version of a photo I once memorized feature for feature, I recognized it. That's how I knew."

"I don't believe this." Sabrina was still reeling. "You put all this together ten years ago—and you never said anything to me?"

This time her mother's chin came up. "What would you have liked me to say? 'Guess what, Sabrina, I figured out who helped make you'? He was a sperm donor, not a father. He had no obligation to me, and I had no more right to invade his privacy than he had to invade mine. More important, I didn't want to throw your life into chaos. I know you. If I'd told you, you'd have become personally vested, even if you somehow restrained yourself from going to him, which I'm not sure you'd manage to do. You'd have pored over articles on Carson Brooks, read everything about Ruisseau that you could get your hands on. It would have done more harm than good. I'm your mother. My job is to protect you. That's why I said nothing." Gloria finished with an air of finality. "We can debate my decision later. For now, I'd like some answers. How did you find out about Carson Brooks? What crisis forced him into your life? And why is time of the essence?"

Sabrina had given up trying to digest anything. As for the explanation her mother was demanding, there was no way to ease into it. Nor did she have the wherewithal to try. So she just went for it.

By the time she finished, Gloria had turned pale. "Are you suggesting that they want *you* to donate a kidney?"

"If I'm a compatible donor, yes. That's pretty much the size of it." Sabrina's lips gave a wry twist. "Ironic, isn't it? He was my donor, now I can be his."

"Sabrina." Gloria was visibly struggling for control. "Am I to assume you're actually considering this?"

Wearily, Sabrina massaged her temples. "A man's life is at stake. A man I'm biologically tied to and whose recovery might depend on me. How can I *not* consider it?"

"Because there are risks involved. . . . Because you don't even know this man. . . . Because after all I've done to make sure—" Gloria broke off. "How bad are his injuries?"

"It sounds like it's touch and go."

"Then he might not make it. So why are the doctors focusing on a kidney? They should be focusing on saving his life."

"They are. But it takes time to find a compatible kidney donor, even in instances where the victim does have living relatives. In this case, there's only me. And if I don't fill the bill . . ." Sabrina fell silent for a moment, then placed her wineglass on the coffee table and turned to face her mother. "But you know what, Mother? You were right. Now that I know the truth I can't ignore it. He might not be my father, but he did father me. Now he might die. I've got to at least meet him. I might not have another chance. As for the rest, we'll play it by ear. I don't know if I'll agree to be tissue-typed. Maybe I won't have to make that decision. Maybe the doctors will already have found another donor. Or maybe I won't be a compatible match."

"Maybe." Gloria sounded dubious, her lips thinning into a tight, apprehensive line. "I take it news of the shooting hasn't hit the media yet."

"Not until tomorrow. Dylan Newport was keeping things quiet until he could reach me. The financial networks will get hold of it first thing tomorrow. As for my existence, my relationship to Carson Brooks, that he'll try to keep a lid on as long as he can."

"Right. Which will be about twelve minutes, knowing the media." Gloria polished off her wine and rose, nervously tightening the belt of her robe. "This is going to snowball like crazy."

"Not if I do nothing but meet the man."

Her mother shot her a who-do-you-think-you're-kidding look. "True. But that's not the way it'll play out. If you can help him, you will."

Sabrina didn't deny her mother's words. She wasn't sure she could—not in good conscience. The truth was, Gloria was probably right.

Walking over, she touched her mother's arm. "I realize what I'll be exposing you to. It's not fair to you, or to Grandmother and Grandfather. I don't know what to say except I'm sorry. Do you think they're up for this?"

A short, humorless laugh. "Your grandparents? They're tough as nails, and twice as strong as we are. They'll be fine." Her wry humor vanished, and she swallowed, her voice trembling a bit as she added, "Unless something should happen to you. That would kill them—and me."

"Mother . . ."

Gloria waved away Sabrina's assurances. "Don't. Not yet. We'll cross that bridge when we come to it." She paused to collect herself. "In any case, your grandparents will prevail. What they'll do to us, now that's another story." An overwhelmed shake of her head. "This is all so unbelievable. Carson Brooks—shot. Do the police know who did it?"

"No. They're investigating."

"I assume that that attorney—Dylan Newport—told the police about you?"

"He had to, yes. The police know. Carson Brooks's doctors know. But that's it."

"For now." Gloria angled her head, her eyes widening as a different thought occurred to her. "How did this Dylan Newport find out about you—from Carson Brooks? Does Carson Brooks know he's your . . . your . . ."

"Not yet." Sabrina spared her mother the discomfort of using the word "father" to describe Carson Brooks. "Evidently, he was toying with the idea of finding out if his sperm donation had resulted in a child. But he didn't have time to follow through. He asked Dylan Newport to do that for him. I've seen the investigation results. They're real."

"Getting them was also illegal, no matter how Mr. Newport managed it."

"I know. But does it really matter at this point?"

Sighing, Gloria replied, "No. If we initiated legal action, it would only magnify the scandal that's already going to swallow us whole." She stared off into space for a moment before looking back at Sabrina, her eyes filled with tears. "Dylan Newport is waiting for your answer?"

Sabrina nodded. "I told him he couldn't have it till tomorrow. He's staying at the Center."

"And you're staying here." Gloria crossed over to the hall, opening the linen closet and tugging down a blanket and pillow. "I'll make up your old bedroom. It's after midnight. You're exhausted, physically and emotionally. I was worried enough when you drove here an hour ago. Now you're in even worse shape. Get some sleep. You'll drive home after breakfast. That'll give you plenty of time to give Dylan Newport his answer . . ." She turned back to her daughter. ". . . and to catch a late afternoon flight to LaGuardia. Which I presume you'll be doing."

It was a statement, not a question. Sabrina answered it anyway. "I think so, yes."

"Fine. I'll go with you."

Sabrina was touched but not surprised by her mother's selfless generosity. And she was all prepared with her answer.

"No you won't," she refused gently. "You just got back yourself. You're worn out and probably a week behind on your sketches. You need to get past this and get back to work."

"That's not likely to happen."

"You'll make it happen. You love your work. In the meantime, you're going to have your hands full. Breaking this news to Grandmother and Grandfather will be an ordeal unto itself. If I know you, you'll want to drive down to Boston and tell them right away, so they're not caught off guard."

Gloria couldn't deny that one. She gave a frustrated sigh, torn between familial obligation and maternal support.

Sabrina helped ease the impasse. "Mother, let's be practical. We have a better chance of keeping my hospital visit hush-hush if I go alone. You're well known on the Manhattan fashion scene. I'm not." Sabrina cut off Gloria's protest, giving her arm a warm squeeze. "I appreciate your offer. But it's better this way. I'll make the initial appearance on my own. You, in the meantime, deal with Grandmother and Grandfather. Then—assuming I take this any further—we'll talk about emotional support, all ways around."

Reluctantly, Gloria nodded. "I suppose that makes sense. Let's not get ahead of ourselves. After all, who knows how this will play out?"

"Exactly," Sabrina agreed, too tired to analyze the past or contemplate the future. "Who knows?"

6

Detectives Eugenia Whitman and Frank Barton had been partners for ten years. Around the Midtown North Precinct, they were known as "Stick" and "Stone"; Eugenia for her beanstalk figure and stinging interrogation style, and Frank for his solid build and blunt delivery. Eugenia was subtle in approach and patient in timing— until she closed in for the kill—at which point, look out. Frank was the ultimate Type A, a cut-to-the-chase kind of guy to whom temperance was an ordeal. He readily admitted that he lacked Eugenia's patience and people skills, but was the first to add that what he lacked in finesse, he more than made up for in good, old-fashioned gut instinct.

Outside work, their lives were as different as their personalities. Frank was a homebody. Happily married to the same woman for fifteen years, he liked tinkering in his workroom, cheering at his kids' soccer games, and investing in the stock market to ensure his family's future. He was battling middle age—and its accompanying spare tire around his middle—with a vengeance, dieting and going to the gym, and hating every minute of it.

Eugenia—or Jeannie as she preferred to be called— was divorced, and relieved to be so, after a five-year try at marriage. During that time, she discovered that permanently entwining her life with someone else's was definitely not for her. Since then, she'd been very much her own person, indulging her need for spontaneity and diversity of interests through avenues ranging from solitary excursions to the Museum of Natural History to nights out clubbing with her friends. A self-proclaimed junk-food addict, she snacked nonstop, yet never gained an ounce. Thanks to a super-fast metabolism, she still tipped the scales at exactly the same hundred and thirty pounds as she had the day she'd reached her current height of five foot eleven, back in the eighth grade.

Frank and Jeannie never socialized together when they were off duty. But when they were on duty, well, everyone at the precinct agreed that they were a formidable team that lived up to the adage "sticks and stones may break your bones"—although their way of breaking guilty suspects was a lot more civil, but no less effective.

This morning what they wanted to break was this case.

They arrived at the precinct early, gulping down their first cup of coffee while watching the early business news that included the breaking story of Carson Brooks's shooting. As soon as the news clip ended, they put in a call to Dr. Radison, and inquired about Carson Brooks's condition. Hearing he was conscious but undergoing tests, they left the station, picked up some breakfast, and headed over to Mt. Sinai.

The place was hopping when their Ford Crown Victoria pulled into the hospital parking lot, TV news vans lined up as close to the entrance as they could get, business correspondents and their camera crews getting set up for whatever medical updates they could obtain.

"They're circling like hawks," Frank noted from behind the steering wheel. He pulled off to the side and parked where they could keep an eye on things, opening up the brown bag that contained his breakfast.

"Security's tight," Jeannie assured him, popping her third Dunkin' Munchkin into her mouth. "The press won't be getting in anytime soon. In fact, they won't be getting anything at all, except the prepared statements Dr. Radison issues."

"Yeah, you're right." Frank scowled at the dry bagel, taking an unenthusiastic bite and washing it down with a gulp of black coffee.

"That bad, huh?" his partner inquired, licking the final crumbs of chocolate glaze off her fingers, and reaching into the box for a powdered Munchkin.

"Worse." He shot her an irked look. "Do you have to look like you're enjoying those things so much? It's bad enough having to smell donuts when I'm eating this piece of cardboard and counting these goddamned points. But, I sure as hell don't need to watch you suck down every drop of glaze and every speck of sugar. Cut it out, Jeannie."

Her pale brows rose, and she reached for a napkin, wiping her fingers in a more conventional way. "My, aren't we in a foul mood today. Ah, last night was your weekly weigh-in. What happened—were you up a pound?"

"I maintained," he grumbled. Giving up on the rock-hard bagel, he tossed it back into the bag. "That's worse than gaining. At least when I gain, I've had fun doing it. When I maintain, I've eaten zip, but my body doesn't co-operate. So I get on that goddamned scale, and my Weight Watchers leader looks at me with those cow eyes, like I'm a kid who needs a hug. Then she gives me a pep talk that makes me want to puke. And I'm right back where I started."

Jeannie's lips twitched. "Sounds like a blast."

"It's not." Frank took another gulp of coffee. "Neither is this case. And keeping things quiet until this morning was a major pain in the ass."

All humor vanished. "Yeah, it delayed grilling Brooks's competitors, that's for sure." Jeannie rubbed her temples, pensively. "On the other hand, we had enough conversations to know that Brooks has lots of money, lots of visibility, and, as a result, lots of enemies. Okay, maybe enemies is too strong a word. Let's say people with a motive to get rid of him."

"True. But how many of them had access to his office? Or to the building, for that matter?"

"All the assailant would need is a key and access to the freight entrance," Jeannie pointed out. "It was Labor Day. Security was light. Two guys and a camera, both stationary. Remember, we're not talking about a high security building here. Eleven West 57th's got a bunch of corporate offices in it. Ruisseau's top-secret stuff is done at the research facilities in Jersey."

"But the man who invented C'est Moi wasn't in Jersey. He was in his office, right here in Manhattan. So was his attorney. Yeah, there's the freight entrance. But there's also the obvious. No one but Brooks and Newport was seen entering the building that day."

Jeannie propped her elbow against the window and turned to face her partner. "You really think Dylan Newport did it?"

A shrug. "He's got a sketchy background. He'd get big bucks and controlling interest in the company if Brooks died."

"Yeah, and he was the only one who knew Brooks had a daughter—one who might very well inherit if Brooks found her and changed his will before leaving this world.

That's more than enough motive. But it doesn't answer my question. Do you think Newport did it?"

Frank polished off his coffee and crushed the Styrofoam cup. "I can't decide. Part of me thinks he did. Part of me thinks he's too smart to be that dumb. We know he wasn't lying about Brooks not seeing his assailant. Not only did Brooks confirm the story, but the path the bullet took tells us that the shot was fired from an angle that was behind and below the victim. The shooter was either hunched down or crouched in the doorway when he discharged that bullet. There was minimal chance of being spotted."

"The other thing is I can't help feeling that Newport's concern for Brooks is real. Either that, or he's one hell of an actor." Jeannie rotated her shoulders in a counterclockwise direction to ease her tension. "As for entry keys, every employee at Ruisseau had them. Plus, during those few minutes we had with Brooks, he said that the doors to Ruisseau and to his office, were unlocked. Which means that the rest of the building employees, including security and maintenance—anyone with keys to the building—are suspect. So are their family and friends outside work who have access to those keys. Add to that the fact that the assailant could have bypassed the surveillance camera by avoiding the lobby and taking the stairs, and we're back to square one."

"I realize Brooks was half out of it when we talked to him. Even so, he was pissed as hell when we implied Newport was a suspect. His glare could've lanced through us, and he underlined the words 'no way' about six times. He's devoted to the guy."

"That's going to complicate the investigation," Jeannie murmured. "And it's not just Newport he's defensive about. That glare didn't go away. He's protective of all his employees, whether or not they're personal favorites of his. It's kind of like family loyalty. I'm sure it'll go both ways. We'll soon find out. I doubt we'll get much cooperation from his staff. But now that the news about Brooks is out, we can get the investigation into full swing. We'll head over to Ruisseau right after Radison gives us an update and lets us in to see Brooks."

"If he lets us in to see Brooks."

"He will. Brooks is conscious. We know that much. We also know that Radison's taking him off the respirator and endotracheal tube to see how he does on his own. All we need are a few minutes with him so we can get a better handle on the personal rapport he has with his employees, and which of them might have it in for him. Brooks isn't going to bad-mouth anyone, so we'll have to read between the lines and watch his body language."

"In the meantime, do we tell him about his daughter?"

Jeannie contemplated her partner's question, then gave a thoughtful shake of her head. "No. Not yet. Let's see if Dylan Newport shows up with her like he said. Give him a day to play this out before we stick our noses into it."

"For Brooks's sake or the Radcliffes'?" Frank asked. He and Jeannie had done their homework, checking into the name that appeared on the slip of paper Dylan Newport had given them. They knew just what kind of a hornet's nest this was going to stir up.

"For *everyone's* sake," Jeannie replied. "Including ours. This is a personal situation. Considering the players, it could get very sticky."

"Yeah." Frank made a disgusted sound. "Talk about complications we didn't need. It would be a lot easier if Brooks's daughter had turned out to be an average woman. Instead, she's part of a big-time country club family. This whole thing is like a soap opera—one with lots of potential lawsuits."

"You got that right. It's a pretty safe bet that if Gloria Radcliffe never told Brooks she was pregnant, much less that he had a daughter, the Radcliffes aren't going to be thrilled about being dragged into this."

"I can't figure out Gloria Radcliffe being involved with Carson Brooks back then—not in a long-term affair or a one-night stand. He was a college-age nobody when their daughter was conceived. Gloria Radcliffe was an established designer and a socialite in her mid-thirties. What's the deal with that?"

Jeannie shrugged. "He's a charismatic guy. Maybe he was sexy even as a twenty-two-year-old kid. Lots of women are attracted to guys that age. Why—don't you know rich men of sixty who are shacking up with girls young enough to be their granddaughters?"

"Yeah, and it makes me sick. But you're just proving my point. There's usually an agenda in situations like that. Where's the agenda here? Gloria Radcliffe is a class act. Back then, she was a knockout. You saw the newspaper clippings we dug up. Between her money and her looks, believe me, she'd have men breaking down her door."

"Fine, then I guess Carson Brooks just turned her on. He's far from an average guy. Maybe he knew exactly what women are about, even then. Remember, this is the guy who invented C'est Moi."

"Yeah, right. How could I forget."

Jeannie gulped down the last of her coffee. "Speaking of C'est Moi, what do you think about the idea that someone was trying to silence Brooks because he was the only one who knew the formula?"

Frank grimaced. "I want to toss that theory in the garbage. But the truth is, the stuff is raking in a fortune.

And if Brooks is eccentric enough to keep the formula to himself, yeah, I guess it's possible."

A corner of Jeannie's mouth lifted. "Don't sound so skeptical. That whole pheromone thing is a big deal now. And Brooks incorporated it in a product that does handsprings around his competitors. He capitalized on a hot trend, and raked in a huge chunk of the perfume market. The man's a genius."

"No arguments. I'm well acquainted with the C'est Moi rage. My wife was first on line to buy a bottle. Said it was supposed to make the wearer irresistible."

Jeannie grinned. "And did it work? Was she irresistible?"

"I wouldn't know. She didn't buy it. She thought there was a man's brand, too. Turned out they've only marketed a woman's so far."

The grin widened. "Linda wanted to buy it for *you* to wear?"

"Yup. Like I'm not irresistible enough."

Jeannie patted his sleeve sympathetically. "Don't sweat it. From the ads I've seen, they're coming out with the male version for Christmas. I'll give Linda a heads-up call. That way, we'll make sure you find a bottle in your stocking."

"Gee, thanks."

"Look at the bright side. Linda might be so turned on, you won't see the light of day for a week. Think how much weight you'll lose."

"Cute. Really cute." Frank shot her a look. "I'm not in the mood for jokes. In fact, I'm feeling pretty testy today."

"No kidding."

"Starving to death will do that to you. So will lack of sleep. Especially when it comes from working on a case like this."

Sobering, Jeannie nodded. "I'm with you there. This investigation gets more involved by the minute. Rather than narrowing things down, we've got a growing list of suspects, a ton of alibis to confirm—and very little to go on."

"I'd say I wish we already found the weapon, but I doubt it'll help us, even when we do," Frank added in disgust. "We know from the shell casings on Brooks's rug that the gun was a twenty-two caliber. Not exactly an uncommon choice. And I doubt it'll have a name tag on it. More likely, when we trace it, we'll find out it was hot. That'll be another dead end."

"Let's hope we have some luck at Ruisseau today." Jeannie glanced at her watch. "It's eight-forty. Brooks must be out of radiology by now. Let's see if we can get a word with him."

8:45 A.M.
Center for Creative Thinking and Leadership

Dylan swallowed the last of his muffin and coffee, then left the lounge on his floor that served light breakfast, and headed down to the reception desk for the third time that morning.

"Any word from Ms. Radcliffe?" he asked.

The young woman looked up from her paperwork. "No, Mr. Newport. She's still not back." She cleared her throat, evidently deciding he was losing patience with that response. "Why don't I buzz her assistant, Melissa Andrews? She might have heard from Sabrina."

"There's no need, Kim." Sabrina's voice came from behind him. "I'm here. I'll talk to Mr. Newport."

He turned, struck again by Sabrina Radcliffe's startling resemblance to Carson. It wasn't so much her features, which were softer, more delicate and refined. But her coloring—the contrast of jet black hair and intense

blue eyes—plus that high forehead, and her manner-
isms—the way she held her head, the stubborn line of her
chin and jaw when she was speaking, the astute, no-
nonsense delivery . . . damn, it was like seeing a smaller,
slighter, feminine version of Carson. The rest of it—the
fluidity of her movements, her innate poise, and her pa-
trician bearing, not to mention the incredible body that
only a dead man wouldn't notice—those attributes she
obviously owed to her mother.

She looked exhausted, with lines of fatigue around her
eyes and dark circles beneath them. At the same time, she
was composed, her corporate training kicking in to help
her hide whatever emotional turmoil she was experiencing. He wished she were more readable; he was good at
seeing through people, and he would have given a king's
ransom to be able to read her mind.

What had she decided to do—or not to do—about
Carson?

"Let's go up to my office," she said quietly.

He nodded, following her down the hall and up a short
flight of stairs. Her office was in a private alcove at the
end of a plant-lined corridor, with only her assistant's cubicle sharing that section of the building.

"Hi." Melissa Andrews greeted Sabrina, then started
as she saw who was with her. Glancing from Sabrina to
Dylan and back again, she sat up straighter, her brows
arching with interest. "Did you just get back?"

"Um-hum." Sabrina paused beside Melissa's desk,
rummaging through the early morning memos and telephone messages already waiting for her. "*I* did. Mr. Newport didn't. He spent the night at CCTL. I spent the night
at my mother's. I'm assuming Mr. Newport slept alone.
But you can check with him after our meeting." Sabrina
looked up. "Anything urgent I should know about?"

"Nope. Business as usual." Her assistant didn't seem thrown by the curt, no-bullshit reply. For his part, Dylan had to bite back a grin. If that response wasn't Carson, nothing was.

"Good." Sabrina plucked out two memos and one phone message, handing them to Melissa before placing the rest of the pile back where she'd found it. "Deal with these. Also, ask Deborah and Mark to divvy up my workshops for the next day or two. Everything else can wait till I come back."

"Back? You're going away?"

"Briefly, yes. I'll fill you in on where and when after I meet with Mr. Newport." Sabrina gestured for Dylan to accompany her into her office. "Hold all my calls," she instructed Melissa. "I'm out to everyone except my mother."

Dylan followed her into the office and shut the door behind him. "You decided to come to New York," he stated flatly, seeking the confirmation he needed.

Sabrina poured herself a glass of water, taking a few bolstering swallows before she turned to face Dylan. "Yes, I did." She set down the glass, tracing the rim with her fingertip. "I caught the business news this morning. His condition sounds iffy. I want to meet him. That's all I'm committing to for now."

"Fine," Dylan replied. It wasn't really, but it was a start. Meeting Carson was the first step toward helping him.

"I've got a few loose ends to tie up," Sabrina continued, feathering her fingers through her hair in a weary gesture. "Then, I'll throw some things in a bag. Give me fifteen minutes. There's a ten forty-five flight that gets into LaGuardia at noon. Will that work?"

"Yeah, it'll work." Dylan cleared his throat. Despite his relief over her decision, he couldn't help feeling responsible for the emotional chaos he'd thrust into her life. Getting into this with her mother couldn't have been pleasant. And now—facade or not, she looked pale and faraway. "Are you okay?"

"As okay as you'd expect." Her chin came up—a clear indication that she wasn't about to lower her guard. "Don't worry about me, Mr. Newport. I hold up well under pressure. Besides, it's not me I'm concerned with. It's my family. I'm trying to think of ways to keep the press from jumping all over this."

"You could start by calling me Dylan."

As intended, his abrupt change in subject and tone came at her out of left field, rattling her facade, if not lowering it. She blinked, eyeing him warily. "And how exactly would that help?"

He shrugged, folding his arms across his chest. "You just said that your trip to New York, at least for the time being, is purely to meet Carson. That won't necessitate a disclosure of your biological ties to him. So, whatever media's hanging around Mount Sinai won't have the slightest idea who you are or why you're there. They'll just see you with me and assume we're friends—unless you raise a red flag by referring to me as Mr. Newport, that is."

Sabrina's brows rose. "Why do I get the feeling that the business correspondents of the world are used to seeing you with women—and not the kind the tabloids would label as friends?"

"Colleagues then," Dylan suggested, sidestepping that loaded question. "If anyone asks about you, I'll say you're a management consultant assisting Ruisseau during this crisis period."

"Very smooth. Quick, too. You must be a real asset—Dylan. It's no wonder Carson Brooks hired you."

He found himself grinning. "I'll take that as a compliment."

"Do that." There was a challenging light in her eyes, one Dylan suspected was an integral part of her. Verbal sparring, winning—he recognized the traits.

"I'll leave you to get your professional life in order," he said, reaching for the door. "I'll take care of the travel arrangements. I'll meet you in the lobby in fifteen minutes."

"Melissa will take care of our travel plans. She knows what hotel to book for me. And I guarantee you, she's more efficient at organizing itineraries than you are."

Another attempt at retaining the upper hand.

Dylan couldn't help himself. When it came to a challenge, he was too used to rising to the bait. "I don't doubt that she is," he acknowledged smoothly. "Shall I stop at her desk on my way out? I can relay our plans *and* confirm that I slept alone last night." One dark brow rose. "As opposed to with you, I assume?"

A slight flush stained Sabrina's cheeks—her only overt reaction to his provocative remark. "Something like that. If I remember correctly, she said you were hot. She also said you weren't my type. She was right."

"About which?"

"The latter. Which makes me unqualified to answer the former."

Dylan's lips twitched. She was good. Very good. Carson would be proud. "Touché." He opened the door. "We'll continue this battle of wits on the plane. For now, let's call it a draw." He paused, speaking bluntly and without forethought. "You're going to like him, you know. I realize you don't want to. But you will."

7

Jeannie and Frank were frustrated.

After waiting forever for the go-ahead from Dr. Radison, they'd finally gotten in to see Carson Brooks—for a five-minute session max, given how touch-and-go his condition still was. He was wiped out from the extensive testing he'd undergone, as well as from the possible infection indicated by the increased fluids present in his chest. His voice was raspy and irritated from the endotracheal tube, and his breathing wasn't great on its own. He was weak as a kitten—hardly up for a pointed interrogation session. And whenever they asked about specific Ruisseau employees, he became agitated. Especially if the question happened to involve Dylan Newport.

In short, three of their five minutes were gone and they'd learned absolutely nothing of value.

"Mr. Brooks." Jeannie pulled up a chair at the foot of his bed, trying a softer tactic. "You're exhausted. We don't want to push you. We also understand you view us as the enemy. We're not. We're not out to attack your company, or harass your employees. But someone tried to kill you. Our job is to find that someone. We want to keep you safe. I think you'll agree that, if your assailant happens to work at Ruisseau, he or she doesn't deserve your protection."

Carson turned his head slightly, staring past the tubes in his nose and fixing his probing blue gaze on her. "Nice try, Detective," he wheezed out. "But the bonding technique . . . won't work with me. I don't need . . . to feel loved. I need to survive. I'm not protecting anyone. . . . If I knew who put this bullet in me . . . I'd hand . . . the son of a bitch . . . over to you on a silver platter." He stopped, dragging in a few labored breaths. "But I'm not listening to you . . . spout crap about Dylan. Or the rest of my team . . . without good reason. If you want to know . . . if any of them shot me . . . ask them."

"We will. We're going over to Ruisseau this morning." Jeannie glanced quickly at her watch. "Let's talk about C'est Moi. Ms. Lane suggested that your attack might be tied to its success."

"Smart girl . . ." Carson rasped, his expression indicating he'd been thinking along the same lines. "That wouldn't surprise me."

"Is it true you're the only one who knows the formula?"

A nod. "In my head . . . Not written down anywhere . . ."

"I don't get it," Frank said. "That formula is a gold mine. Didn't you patent it?"

"Nope." Carson wet his lips with the tip of his tongue. "Took the risk not to. . . . Bigger risk if I had . . . Would have had to put the formula in writing. More chance of the secret leaking." A pained smile. "Besides, didn't you ever hear that mystery . . . in consumer products . . . is a great marketing ploy? Worked with the secret Coca-Cola formula . . . Did the same with C'est Moi."

"True. But getting nothing in writing—those are high stakes you're gambling with," Frank said in amazement.

"I'm . . . used to it. High-stakes gambling . . . is the only way to come out on top. . . . That's how I built . . . my company."

"So let's say someone was desperate to shut down the production of C'est Moi, so desperate they'd shoot you. Any particular rivals spring to mind who fill that bill?"

"Cut-throat bastards, yeah. Cold-blooded murderers, not off-hand . . . Primary competition's Etienne Pruet . . . Based in Paris and New York. Strong, at least on paper . . . Call Jason Koppel at Merrill Lynch . . . Great industry analyst . . . trustworthy, too . . . I've known him twelve years . . . Pick his brain. Maybe someone's company's . . . worse off than I know."

The door opened and Dr. Radison walked in. "That's it for now," he stated flatly, checking Carson's IV fluids and cardiac monitor as he spoke. "Mr. Brooks needs his rest."

"Of course." Jeannie stood, following Frank's lead as he inched away from the bed. "We'll get started with what we have."

"Do . . . that. . . ."

She halted. "Unless you can think of anything we overlooked?" she added quickly, hoping to jog his memory before Dr. Radison intervened. "Anything you were too fuzzy to remember yesterday? Did you notice anyone in the building? Was there someone in particular you might have clued in to the fact that you planned to work on Labor Day?"

"Didn't need to make an announcement . . . I'm at Ruisseau every day . . . holidays included. I ran late. . . . Supposed to leave around five . . . U.S. Open . . . Was really looking forward to it . . ." Carson coughed. "Didn't see anyone . . . Don't remember much . . . Dylan went to get files. . . . I went to windows. . . . Heard pop . . . Felt pain . . . Smelled burning . . . Smelled . . ." He dissolved into a spasm of coughing.

"That's it, Detectives," Radison broke in. "I mean it. No more for this session."

Jeannie made an apologetic gesture. "We're on our way. You take care, Mr. Brooks. We'll be back another time."

"Wait." In a slow, pained motion, Carson turned his head in their direction. "Go easy . . . on my team. Even if one of them's guilty . . . which I don't believe . . . the rest are innocent . . . Remember that. . . ."

"Will do."

Officer Laupen glanced up as Jeannie and Frank walked out of the hospital room. "Hey, Stick, Stone. Any breakthrough?"

"Nothing to write home about," Jeannie replied tersely.

"Sorry."

"So are we," Frank said.

The two of them headed briskly down the hall.

"We're on our own now," Jeannie muttered. "We can't push Brooks any more, not till he's stronger. If we want a rundown on his staff, we'll have to get it elsewhere."

"Yeah, but from whom? Dylan Newport?"

Jeannie shrugged, reaching the elevator and pressing the down button. "We'll pick his brain, yeah. He's certainly on the inside track. But in the meantime, he's in New Hampshire. We're here. Let's go meet the Ruisseau gang and see what we can dig up on our own."

Frank nodded. "We'll duck out the back way. The last thing we need is a swarm of reporters to deal with."

They left the building and headed for the parking lot. Once outside, they automatically punched their cell phones back on, having followed ICU regulations to turn them off.

Jeannie had one message waiting for her. She listened to it carefully, then turned to her partner.

"Dylan Newport called a few minutes ago. He's on his

way home. He'll be landing at LaGuardia around noon. Sabrina Radcliffe's with him."

11:15 A.M.
Manchester Airport

The jet accelerated down the runway and took off, slicing the skies as it climbed to its cruising altitude of thirty thousand feet.

Sabrina stared out the window, watching the wisps of clouds rush by, wondering what was waiting for her at the other end of this flight.

"You haven't said ten words since we left CCTL," Dylan commented beside her.

"I didn't have anything to say." She angled around to face him.

"I dropped a bomb on you last night. You must have a million questions. Ask."

Right. Ask. Sabrina sighed, thinking that she'd never felt so displaced in her life. Oh, she was used to being a fish out of water. She'd learned early on to become thick-skinned, and to draw on her own inner resources to cope. But this one was a doozy to contend with, even for her.

"I'm not sure where to begin," she answered frankly. "This whole thing is still too surreal. It's also too personal. I'm not really comfortable getting into it with you. I realize Carson Brooks knows you. But I don't. I don't know you, and I don't know him." She shot Dylan a pointed look. "You, on the other hand, know my entire life history. I understand why you felt compelled to dig it up. I'm not blaming you for doing it. That doesn't mean I'm happy it was done. I'm a private person. My life is my own."

"Yeah, I figured that out. I respect it, too. Believe it or not, we're a lot alike in that way." He drummed his fingers on the armrest between them, searching for the right way to get through to her. "Look, if you think about it, I don't know the first thing about you. All I've got are biographical specs."

"Nice try. But PI's dig up a lot more than stats."

"Not in this case. I wasn't investigating you; I was just locating Carson's child. No in-depth personality traits, no activity log. The one intimate detail I know about you is that you were conceived through donor insemination. And that's pretty cut and dry. Hell, it's damned scientific and boring compared to the way most people were conceived, and by whom. Have you watched *Entertainment Tonight* lately?"

Sabrina had to bite back laughter. The image of Dylan Newport glued to his TV set for nightly updates on what Hollywood's stars were up to was priceless. "No, I can't say that I have. Why? Do you watch it regularly?"

A corner of Dylan's mouth lifted in a crooked smile that made Sabrina understand why Melissa had described him as hot. "Nope. Most nights, I'm at my desk around that hour, with stacks of files and a quart of roast pork fried rice in front of me. But my secretary Nina watches the show religiously. And you should hear the stories she brings in. The stuff they reveal about people is as intimate as you get. And millions of viewers tune in to see those clips. Now *that's* personal."

He paused as the flight attendant stopped beside their seats and inquired if they'd like a beverage. Dylan ordered a cup of black coffee for himself, then turned questioningly to Sabrina.

"Cranberry juice," she responded. The flight attendant handed her a can of juice and a plastic cup, which she took with a businesslike smile. "Thanks."

"See what I mean?" Dylan asked with a hint of teasing

in his voice. "Talk about lack of personal details. I didn't even know your beverage of choice."

"Point taken." Sabrina was beginning to enjoy the lighthearted banter. It felt good to smile. Plus, a nice, superficial conversation was all she could handle right now.

The tight knot inside her loosened a bit.

"I'll fill in the missing blank for you, then," she supplied. "I usually drink either juice or water. As for coffee, I'm not crazy about decaf. So I reserve my coffee-drinking for the morning. Too much caffeine makes me nuts."

"Then I must be certifiable. I drink the leaded kind—strong, black, and all day long." Dylan punctuated his words with an appreciative swallow. "Okay, so it's juice and water. What about wine or mixed drinks? Do you do those?"

"Merlot. But only in moderation or I get a killer migraine."

"I rest my case. That's two personal preferences I didn't see anywhere on my fact sheets."

She couldn't help but chuckle. "You must be a very effective attorney. You're shrewd and disarming. I recognize the traits from my own corporate training."

"That training is something I *do* know about you. You've got quite a résumé. So I'm flattered." Dylan set down his cup. "While I'm learning nuances about you, let me ask something about your career. You were well on your way to a partnership. What made you leave the fast track and start your own company?"

"Are you really interested? Or just choosing nice, safe topics that will help lower my guard and make me less ambivalent about meeting Carson Brooks?"

"Both."

She hadn't expected him to be so frank. Nevertheless,

she appreciated it. The less he tried disguising his agenda, the less additional work he'd create for her. She had no energy to cut through pretense to get at truth. As for his question, she was fine with it. The reasons for her career path weren't a secret.

"I left for a number of reasons," she replied. "I wanted to run my own organization. I was arrogant enough to believe I could do things better, and without a lot of corporate politics. I'm not very good at games, especially when playing them means compromising on what's best for my client. I also believed I could combine work and play into an ideal learning experience. So I guess you could say my striking out on my own was a combination of ideals, ethics, and ego. Plus, I had to get out of Boston. The city air was having an adverse effect on me."

Dylan's brows rose. "Allergies?"

"No. I just have a hypersensitive nose. Cities are always a bit much for me to handle. I'm a mess in L.A., with all the car emissions. Same with Denver. New York's not a picnic, but it's not as hard on me as Boston is. Maybe it's because there are so many bodies of water around Boston. One of the guys in my CCTL team took some meteorology courses. He subscribes to the theory that conflicting land breezes keep the stagnant air hanging around the city longer. Or maybe it's because Boston's older than New York, with lots of historic buildings. They're beautiful, but the mustiness drives me crazy." She shrugged. "There's no particular rhyme or reason to what affects me. Some smells do. Others don't."

"Not a surprise," Dylan startled her by saying. "You have a heightened olfactory sense. That makes every smell more acute." He went on, speaking as if he were reciting information he'd stored in his memory. "The fact is, even the average person can distinguish thousands of odors. Our noses contain sensory neurons. Different neurons respond to different odors and—in some way that's beyond my nonscientific mind's ability to comprehend—they end up stimulating specific patterns of behavior. With you, the effects are even more extreme. A heightened olfactory sense is a gift and a curse. As for why certain things trigger it adversely, who knows? It's just one of life's mysteries."

Sabrina put down her cup in amazement. "You sound like a textbook. How do you know so much about this?"

"Carson taught me. Of course, he explains it with all the right chemical phrases and molecular drawings. I just nod a lot. As for why he's so well versed on the subject, it's because he has the same trait. I guess it's hereditary."

Whatever Sabrina had been expecting, it hadn't been that. She'd always thought of her acute sense of smell as an idiosyncrasy. But an inherited trait . . . "Wow," she murmured aloud. "That possibility never occurred to me."

"Me, either. But listening to what you just said, it's obviously true. In Carson's case, it's one of the reasons why he's so amazing at creating the fragrances he creates. C'est Moi, for instance, was his baby all the way—from test tube to stores."

"Right." Sabrina responded on autopilot. "I skimmed some articles that mentioned it was Carson Brooks, and not his R&D team, that came up with the formula."

Actually, she'd done a lot more than skim those articles. She'd been fascinated by Carson Brooks's hands-on involvement in his company's success, the way he'd combined business savvy with chemical genius and come up with a unique fragrance formula that had knocked the industry on its butt. He was the most versatile, brilliant CEO she'd ever come across. As for C'est Moi, under normal circumstances, she'd be asking a million questions about Carson Brooks's unique integration of human pheromones in the fragrance production, probing his market research, his assimilation of facts. But right now, it didn't seem to matter. In fact, for the life of her, she couldn't think of a thing to say.

So, she'd inherited her heightened olfactory sense from him. How weird, learning she had such strong commonalities and hereditary ties to a father who'd been a nonentity in her life until yesterday. And learning about them from a third party who saw this man every day, worked by his side, well that made the whole scenario seem even more bizarre. She felt both involved and detached, and she wasn't sure which she preferred.

"How did you meet Carson Brooks?" she heard herself ask.

Dylan had been watching her intently. He didn't seem surprised by her question. "Through a work program he initiated," he replied in a matter-of-fact tone. "Over nineteen years ago. Carson was barely past thirty, and Ruisseau was less than a decade old. But the company was growing like gangbusters. Carson needed help—kind of a guy Friday and errand boy rolled into one. Rather than advertise in the newspaper, he went to a high school in a crappy section of New York City. He was hoping to give some underprivileged kid a break."

"And you were that kid." Sabrina eyed him thoughtfully. "You must have jumped at the chance."

A hollow laugh. "Hardly. I fought it tooth and nail. I already had more than enough structure in my life. School. Community service. Chores. I barely had enough time for a life."

Puzzled, Sabrina studied the hard line of his jaw. "What kind of life did you want?"

"One that was a crash course in self-destruction. One that made me feel powerful—and sent me home drunk and bleeding more nights than not. The rest of the time I spent cutting classes I didn't want to attend and breaking rules I didn't want to follow. That's where the community service came in. Social Services thought it would re-orient my thinking. It didn't. I felt patronized and pissed off."

"I see."

"No you don't. And don't bother trying. Suffice it to say, my life was a far cry from Beacon Hill."

"I get the message loud and clear." Sabrina looked away. "I'm prying. Fine. Consider the subject dropped."

"That's not what I meant." Dylan drained the rest of his coffee. "Sorry—I didn't mean to come off as abrupt. The truth is, I was stating a fact, not cutting you off. Ask whatever you want to about my past. It doesn't bother me to talk about it. It's like another life."

"It's really none of my business."

"Actually, it is. You should know the kind of man Carson is. If this doesn't tell you, nothing will."

"All right. Go on."

"Like I said, Carson needed some part-time help. He showed up at my school during one of my countless detention periods. He'd reviewed my records, both academic and personal, then set up a meeting with my principal and, ultimately, with me. He pulled up a chair, told me I reminded him of himself at my age—except that he was already in the gutter by age sixteen, while I had two more years to go before I got tossed there. He advised me to lose the anger, because no matter how pissed off I got, life would still be unfair, and it would still be up to me to even the odds. He said I was smart and tough, and that I could choose to rot in the streets or

make something of myself. He added that unless he'd
sized me up wrong, I was too shrewd not to take his job
offer. Said he'd pay me a decent hourly wage, and increase it monthly as I proved myself. Along with the
added pay would come added responsibilities, including
a chance to work on some projects with him, once we
had a better idea where my talents and interests lay.

"In return, I had to clean up my act, show some respect to my foster parents, go to school, cut out the
drinking and brawling, and work my ass off." Dylan
gave a reminiscent chuckle. "Talk about shrewd. He
never patronized me, never showed me a shred of disre-
spect or censure. It was hard to abuse myself with someone like that believing in me. From that point on,
everything changed. My grades skyrocketed. I finished
high school with straight A's and a corporate internship
at Ruisseau. I got into Columbia on scholarship. They
gave me a huge financial aid package. The remainder of
my expenses were subsidized by Ruisseau. I graduated
with honors, and went on to Columbia Law, where I did
the same. The day I got my LLD, Carson had a brass
plate engraved, 'Dylan Newport, Corporate Counsel.' I
helped him hang it on my office door. It's been there
ever since. As have I. So you see, I owe Carson Brooks
everything."

Sabrina had been totally absorbed in Dylan's story.
Now, she blinked, an odd lump forming in her throat.
Surprisingly, the lump wasn't pity. It wasn't even admiration, although she felt tremendous respect for what Dylan
had accomplished. It was envy. There was an incredible
bond that existed between him and Carson Brooks—a
bond that had formed over nineteen years. They were
tight. Really tight. And here she was, a total stranger,
about to meet her "father" for the first time.

The whole situation was becoming more and more unsettling.

"So now you know my life story," Dylan was saying. "That makes us even."

"I suppose."

He was watching her intently again. "If I can help make this easier for you, let me know."

"I'm not sure that's possible." She wet her lips with the tip of her tongue. "When you called the hospital before, was he conscious?"

"Yeah. The police were with him."

"Will they tell him about me?"

"I asked them to stay out of it. I think they'll go along with that. They know we're on our way back to New York. I'm sure they'd rather leave emotional disclosures to friends and family, and stick to solving the crime."

"Do they have any leads?" Sabrina asked. "Anyone who might have a grudge against him? Anyone who stands to gain huge amounts of money or power if he dies? Or are they concentrating on digging up information on Ruisseau's rival companies—checking out people who'd benefit by killing off the competition?"

"They have their suspicions." A muscle flexed in Dylan's jaw. "I don't know how far they've gotten with the investigation. We'll find out soon enough."

Sabrina was taken aback by the hostility in his tone. He was certainly bugged by something pertaining to the investigation. Was he unhappy with the detectives' speed and thoroughness, or was it the direction they were taking that was ticking him off?

She opened her mouth to ask.

He cut her off before she could.

"Do you want to talk to Carson by yourself, or should I be there with you?"

That was enough to startle her back to the face-to-face meeting that was about to occur. "By myself?" She blinked. "Don't you think that's a little extreme? The man is fighting for his life. He has no idea I exist. If I march in there and announce who I am without any preparation from you—God, I can't imagine a shock like that being good for him."

Dylan was shaking his head, his earlier hostility having vanished as quickly as it came. "That's not what I meant. For his sake—and yours—I planned to go in first and lay the groundwork. What I wanted to know is, once I've given him the facts and introduced you, do you want me to stay or leave?"

"Oh." Sabrina hadn't actually thought that one through. Still, it was a no-brainer compared to the other decisions she'd made since yesterday. "Under the circumstances, I think that choice should be his. I'll go along with whatever he decides."

"Good enough. One more thing. As I said, Carson's heavily medicated. I'm not sure he's cognizant of the fact that he's been on dialysis, or that he might need a kidney transplant. It's going to hit him hard when he finds out. So let's not get into it just yet."

"Don't worry, I won't say a word. It's better that way anyway, since I haven't made any decision about what my next step will be—until after I've met him."

The words sounded hollow and insincere, even to Sabrina.

What's more, she realized with an abrupt flash of insight, they sounded equally insincere to Dylan. He'd led her right where he wanted her, acquainting her with Carson Brooks by presenting him in the most likeable, emotionally-compelling light possible. And he'd managed it either totally by chance, through his own opportune, yet genuine affection for the man, or through one of the most cleverly manipulated conversations she'd ever fallen victim to.

Sabrina didn't know why that bothered her so much. Maybe it was because she hated being bested, and she rarely was. More likely, it was because it drove home how emotionally involved in this whole situation she was. She hadn't expected it. It made her feel much too vulnerable. And she had no intention of letting Dylan Newport play on that vulnerability, no matter how worthy his motives were.

She edged a quick, sideways glance at him. He was putting up his tray, then repositioning his seat as the plane began its rapid descent into LaGuardia.

He was either giving her the space she needed to get herself together, or giving her a chance to steep in her newfound personal connection to Carson Brooks—a connection he'd made sure to foster.

Putting her at ease. Sharing his own personal story. A little flirtation. A hint of humor. A touch of compassion.

Nice work.

Sabrina snapped her own seat upright, feeling Dylan's gaze slide over her. He was assessing her, trying to figure out how won-over she was.

Good question.

A meeting was one thing; donating her kidney was another. Especially when donating her kidney meant affecting not only her life but the lives of her family.

Deliberately, Sabrina kept her face averted, busying herself with her seat belt, not giving Dylan anything definitive to go on. She wasn't ready to commit herself. Not yet.

But the next phase of the decision-making process loomed just a cab ride away.

8

Roland Ferguson was fifty-six, and had been Ruisseau's VP of human resources for eleven years. He'd left corporate America at forty-one to start his own recruiting firm. He liked being his own boss, and had fully intended on keeping and running his small but successful company until retirement.

That was before Carson Brooks got ahold of him.

He'd called Roland out of the blue. But he'd sure as hell done his homework. He knew Roland's résumé inside out, including every promotion he'd ever received from the three different human resource departments he'd worked in, as well as the promising reputation he'd established since going out on his own. And, yes, he was impressed. Impressed *and* impressive. Carson Brooks was a dynamo. Saying no to him was almost as hard as saying yes. "No" meant walking away from the opportunity of a lifetime; "yes" meant committing yourself body and soul to your work.

It was a tough choice.

Not that Carson gave you one. When he wanted something, he was like a dog with a bone. And he wanted Roland to head up HR. It wasn't just what he'd seen on paper. He liked Roland's style, his inherent people skills. And he wanted those skills applied at Ruisseau.

After two weeks of intense negotiations and equally intense soul-searching, Roland had hired a manager for his recruiting firm, and had gone to work for Carson Brooks.

Two months later he'd sold his company outright and made his stay at Ruisseau permanent.

His job wasn't easy. Working for a hard-assed genius with the energy level of an eighteen-year-old and a 24/7 work ethic produced an environment that was fast-paced, high-pressure, and crackling with ambition. Which meant equal amounts of success and tension, commitment and rivalry.

As a result, Roland had faced his fair share of hostile employees and explosive situations.

But the current crisis blew the rest of them out of the water.

Nothing had prepared him for the past two days. First, walking into Ruisseau and finding a roped-off CEO's office that was now a crime scene. Second, hearing that Carson was hovering somewhere between life and death. And third, enduring the somber aura enveloping the office, not to mention the taut apprehension emanating from an office full of coworkers who were now attempted murder suspects.

Including him.

He'd seen the two detectives briefly, first yesterday when they'd dropped in on the team of cops scouring Carson's office for clues, then again this morning when they'd arrived around ten-thirty, only to vanish into the executive wing for almost an hour, presumably to interview people.

Now it was his turn.

There they were in his office, pressing him for whatever leads they could find.

God, this was a political nightmare. And it might end up being a personal one, as well.

He had to be careful.

"Mr. Ferguson, we appreciate your time." Detective Whitman was seated adjacent to her partner in one of the two chairs directly across from Roland's desk. "We'll try not to keep you long."

"I'll help in any way I can." Roland pulled off his glasses, rubbing his eyes in a few unsteady motions before shoving the glasses back onto his nose. "I still can't believe this happened."

"We understand your shock. Hopefully, Mr. Brooks will pull through. In the meantime, it's up to us to find out who's responsible." Whitman glanced over her notes. "Let's start with some basics. In total, how many employees work at Ruisseau?"

"Just over a hundred. That includes the part-timers, and the R&D staff at our New Jersey research facility in Englewood Cliffs. We also have about a dozen interns in the various departments. In addition, there's our European Operations, headquartered in Paris. It's got a managing director and a half-dozen employees."

She nodded. "And how many of the people you just described would have access to Mr. Brooks?"

That question was safe enough. Answering it candidly required no finger-pointing. "If you're asking about the chain of command here, it's very informal. Carson's not into protocol. If the custodian came up with a great idea, Carson would meet with him. So I don't think you can zero in on anyone using that method." Roland cleared his throat, giving the detectives a cautious look. "I realize you're just doing your job, but do you really believe someone at Ruisseau shot Carson?"

"We don't know, Mr. Ferguson," Detective Barton retorted. "Why? Do you think someone here's guilty?"

"Definitely not."

"How can you be so sure? Are you saying that no one here was unhappy or disgruntled? That no one ever felt pissed about the way he or she was treated, or bitter about being passed over for someone else when it came time for a promotion?"

"Of course I'm not saying that," Roland replied defensively. "But feeling angry or overlooked is a far cry from taking a shot at someone."

"I agree. Someone else doesn't." Barton leaned forward. "We've spoken to all the company VPs, other than Claude Phelps, the VP of research and development. His name's come up several times in our discussions. What's your take on him?"

They were starting to head into choppy waters.

Roland kept his features schooled, opting for a basic rundown rather than a personal critique. "Claude's office isn't located here. It's at our New Jersey research facility, for obvious reasons. He makes weekly trips into the city to attend management committee meetings. The rest of the time he stays in touch by phone or e-mail. Oh, and Carson rides out to Englewood Cliffs a lot, maybe three or four times a week when he's working on something. So he sees Claude pretty frequently."

"Yes. That much we already knew." Whitman was staring at him. He hoped that didn't mean she'd interpreted his reply as being intentionally ambiguous. "We also know that Phelps has been with Mr. Brooks since the company's inception."

"Pretty much. Claude started about six months after Ruisseau got off the ground. Stan Hager's the only employee who's been here longer. He and Carson knew each other as kids."

"Stan Hager. Right. The chief operating officer." Whitman's clipped tone said she wasn't about to be diverted. "We already spoke briefly with him. When we saw him today, he was on his way to the hospital. We arranged to have an in-depth talk with him there." Her eyes narrowed slightly. "Let's get back to Claude Phelps, shall we? I asked for your opinion, not a job description."

Roland made one last-ditch effort, just in case whatever they'd heard about Claude was vaguer than he thought. "I don't know him very well. We rarely see each other, except at meetings, and we never socialize outside the office. He takes his work seriously, that much I can tell you. He only uses a fraction of his vacation time each year." Seeing the expectant look on Whitman's face, Roland realized she was waiting for more. "What in particular do you want to know?"

"For one thing, why you're uncomfortable talking about the guy. Is it because he's been a problem lately, like we've been told? Or do you just dislike him?"

There was no way out of this one. Not when it was clear they'd been told about Claude's disruptive conduct. He had to open up. If he didn't, someone else would fill in the missing pieces and the cops would be right back in his office for details—and answers as to why he hadn't leveled with them right away.

Still, he had to handle this delicately.

Lowering his gaze, Roland steepled his fingers in front of him. "My personal feelings aren't the issue here. I just don't want to bad-mouth someone who's been a loyal employee for twenty-seven years. But, fine. Since you've already heard bits and pieces, yeah, Claude's had some problems recently."

"What kind of problems?"

"The last few times he showed up at the New York office, he'd been drinking. He wasn't out-and-out drunk," Roland hastened to clarify. "But there was definitely alcohol on his breath. And his behavior was out of character."

"In what way?"

"Claude's kind of a quiet guy, keeps to himself. On these occasions, he was loud and belligerent. He made a couple of unpleasant scenes during each visit. In his defense, he's taken quite a verbal beating since the release of C'est Moi—everything from friendly ribbing to nasty comments. A few business analysts have gone so far as to speculate bluntly on why Carson needs Claude at all. That's a low blow, especially for Claude. His professional ego's always been a little shaky. He's taking this very hard."

"So it seems." Whitman didn't look surprised by anything he'd said, although she did jot down an additional note or two. "Okay, so the bottom line is that Phelps is freaked out because Carson Brooks came up with the bank-breaking formula for C'est Moi, and that, as a result, Phelps is being labeled a lame duck."

"That pretty much sums it up, yes."

"You said he's taking this hard. Explain."

Roland gave an uncomfortable cough. "Like I said, the last few times he showed up here, he'd been drinking. He dropped in on a few executives, ranting about how he was being cut out of C'est Moi's success and squeezed out of his job. In one case he went so far as to claim he'd come up with the preliminary formula. He ruffled a lot of feathers. Four written complaints were filed with my office. Eventually, I was asked to have a talk with him, and to issue a gentle warning about his behavior. I did. He didn't take it well."

"Meaning?"

"He blew up at me. He called me a few unpleasant names, then paced around my office, waving his arms and yelling that Ruisseau would be nothing without him. He threatened to sue the company if he was fired, said he'd show Carson just how essential he was."

"Those were his exact words?"

"Yes."

"Did anyone else hear him say that?"

Roland shrugged. "It's possible. His voice was raised at the time. Either my secretary or someone passing by my office might have overheard. If so, I haven't gotten wind of it. That wouldn't surprise me. Ruisseau's a tight organization. We don't gossip about each other."

"Yeah," Barton muttered. "We noticed. We've got to pry information out of you people with a crowbar."

"That's loyalty, Detective. It's one of the traits Carson Brooks insists on from his staff."

"Right. Well, whoever shot him wasn't loyal."

"That's why I don't think someone here is guilty."

"Let's get back to Phelps's threat," Whitman interceded. "You were the only person actually in the office with him when he issued it."

Damn, this woman just wouldn't be sidetracked.

"Yes." Roland shifted uncomfortably beneath Whitman's scrutiny, feeling compelled to defend himself by stating the obvious. "All meetings between employees and Human Resources are conducted in private. That's company policy. It's especially important in cases like this, where there's a reprimand involved."

"It sounds like he was pretty agitated."

"He was." Roland couldn't leave it at that. If he was the one who hung Claude out to dry, it would get out, and his name would be mud. "Detective, I realize how this sounds. But please put it in context. Claude was furious. He felt professionally vulnerable and personally attacked. So, yeah, he threw a few threats around. But they were all business-related. He never once hinted at violence."

"Professionally vulnerable," Whitman repeated. "In other words, his job was on the line." Her gaze hardened. "You said you were asked to have a talk with Phelps and issue a warning. Who asked you to do that?"

Roland swallowed. "Carson Brooks."

A swift exchange of glances between detectives. "We'd like to have a look at those written complaints," Barton informed him.

"I anticipated you might." Slowly, Roland opened his drawer and removed the sheets of paper he'd placed there earlier, sliding them across the desk. "Here. I made copies for you. But I think you're barking up the wrong tree. Claude's all bluster. He wouldn't shoot anyone."

"Everyone's capable of violence, given the right circumstances," Barton refuted, picking up the pages. "And we're barking up *every* tree, not just this one. We plan to find out who did this."

"I understand."

Whitman was still watching him. "I'd like access to *all* the personnel files. And there's no need for you to make photocopies. We'll copy what we need."

Roland's gut knotted. He didn't like Detective Whitman's tone, or the vibes he was picking up from her. Whatever she was thinking, it wasn't good. "All right," he agreed, trying to seem as cooperative as possible. He reached for his phone. "I'll arrange for you to have immediate access."

"Fine. We're heading back to the hospital now. We'll check back with you later today." Whitman paused. "By the way, where were you on Monday evening, between the hours of five and six?"

His forefinger paused on the keypad. "At my home on

Long Island. Throwing some franks on the grill for our annual barbecue. I was there all evening."

"I assume someone can verify that?"

"My wife." He licked his suddenly dry lips. "Why? Am I a suspect?"

"This is an attempted murder, Mr. Ferguson. Everyone's a suspect."

"Until our alibis are confirmed," Roland amended.

"Until we find the assailant." Whitman wasn't giving, not an inch. "Which we will, Mr. Ferguson. You can bet the bank on it."

1:35 P.M.
Mt. Sinai Hospital

Pop.

The sound echoed inside his head. White-hot pain. It lanced through him, a bolt of lightning in his back. Colors. A kaleidoscope rushing up at him. And that sticky-sweet smell. Blood. His blood. Oozing from his body . . . Trickling down his back . . . draining away his life.

Dying. He was dying. And it was too soon . . . too soon . . .

He heard his own groan at the same time that a firm hand shook his shoulder.

"Carson? Carson, it's me."

He jerked awake, fighting the cobwebs that clung to his mind as a result of the drugged sleep. A nightmare. He'd been having a nightmare—or rather reliving one that had actually occurred. But it was over. He was alive. The wetness trickling down his spine was sweat, not blood. And the concerned face swimming into view over the sea of tubes and monitoring equipment was Dylan's.

"Are you all right?" he demanded.

Carson forced a half-grin. "I've been better. . . . But

I'll live . . . I think." A raspy breath. "You ordered me to . . . if I remember right."

Dylan's features relaxed. "You remember right."

"Where the hell have you been? . . . It's been . . . a day . . . maybe more. . . ."

"*You* gave *me* some orders, too." Dylan pulled up a chair, sank down beside the bed. "I've been busting my tail to carry them out. No easy feat, I might add."

Carson's brows drew together. "What're you talking about?"

"I'm talking about the person you asked me to locate." Seeing Carson glance around, Dylan added, "Don't worry. We're alone."

Physical discomfort became secondary, as Carson studied Dylan's expression. "Well?" he demanded.

"I'd pass you a cigar, but there's no smoking in ICU."

That was the answer he'd been looking for. "I have a kid," he realized in awe. "Damn . . . A kid."

A corner of Dylan's mouth lifted. "She's far from a kid. Actually, she's a knockout. She looks a lot like you, only better. More feminine and minus the scars. She's smart, too, and successful. Even you'll be impressed."

"*She,*" Carson repeated. "I have . . . a daughter." It was the strangest feeling, one he couldn't quite describe. "Tell me . . . about her."

"I'll do one better. I'll introduce the two of you."

Carson stared. "Now?"

"Can you think of a better time?"

The way Dylan phrased that . . . Suspicion clouded the picture, and Carson's gaze flickered to the various contraptions he was hooked up to. "You tell me. . . . Am I out of time? . . . Is that it? . . . Am I losing this fight? . . ."

"Not a chance."

"Then why did she agree to come? . . . How did you

find her? . . . Who . . . ?" Winded, he broke off, suddenly and painfully aware how much he was taxing himself.

"Try to be quiet and listen for a minute. I know it's against your nature, but try," Dylan advised wryly. "That way you can save your strength for your daughter. Stan helped me dig up the information I needed. Once I got the basic specs—her name, her address—the rest was easy. She lives in Auburn, just outside Manchester, New Hampshire. I flew up there last night and told her about you. She wants to meet you. She's waiting outside. I'm sure she can answer the rest of your questions better than I can. Okay?"

"Did she already know . . . about me?"

"Not who you were, no. But that her father was a sperm donor, yes."

"She took . . . the news okay?"

As always, Dylan was straight with him—no sugar-coating, no bullshit. "She was shocked. She came around. It's a sticky situation. She's strong and gutsy, but she's also very tight with her family. Her mother's in a high-profile industry, and her grandparents epitomize Boston high society. A scandal wouldn't be welcome."

Carson frowned. "I remember . . . the woman was from Beacon Hill . . . that's all I ever knew. . . . Who is she? . . ."

"Her name's Gloria Radcliffe. She's an upscale fashion designer. Fairly well known, too. She must be— Susan's already bought half her fall line. She's in the lounge right now chewing your daughter's ear off about how much she loves Gloria's designs."

That didn't sit well with Carson. "You told Susan about . . . ?"

"Nope," Dylan assured him quickly. "I gave her the same story I gave the press—that Ms. Radcliffe is a management consultant assisting Ruisseau during this crisis period."

"Nice story." Carson eyed his friend. "Management consultant? . . . Can she pull it off?"

"No problem there. She can pull it off fine, since that's just what she is. A pretty sought-after one, too. You should see her list of clients."

It was ludicrous and unjustified, this surge of pride that rushed through him. He'd contributed nothing to this young woman, except his genes. He hadn't raised her, had never even met her. But still . . . hell, she was his daughter.

"So, are you ready for your introduction?" Dylan asked.

A slow nod. "Yeah."

Dylan rose. "I'll be right back."

Carson shut his eyes, deliberately conserving his strength for what lay ahead. It was bound to be a difficult meeting. He didn't delude himself. He never had, never would. No matter what Dylan said, this young woman must be completely thrown by what she'd learned. As for meeting him, she'd be curious, yeah, but she'd also be uncomfortable as hell. Why not? She didn't know him from Adam, yet he was being introduced as her father.

Christ, this was bizarre.

He opened his eyes as two sets of footsteps entered the room.

"Carson," Dylan said, stepping aside so the woman accompanying him could approach the bed. "This is Sabrina Radcliffe." He kept the introduction simple, avoiding any use of the word father. "Sabrina, Carson Brooks."

Sabrina. So that was his daughter's name. It suited her, too, he thought, studying her intently. Beautiful and classy.

Dylan was right. There was a resemblance. Her coloring was the same as his, and there was a certain look about her—her chin, maybe, or the way she held her head—that she'd gotten from him. Dylan was also right that she was a knockout. She had a fineness and poise about her that screamed breeding, traits she'd obviously inherited from her mother.

He couldn't believe how choked up he was.

"Hello, Mr. Brooks." Her voice was steady, but her hand trembled as she extended it to him. "I'm glad you're up to seeing me."

He met her handshake solemnly, proud as hell that she had the guts to put up such a brave front. "I've wanted . . . to find out about you . . . to meet you . . . for a long time. . . . Thanks for coming."

She extricated her grip. "The doctor says you're holding your own."

"I'm too . . . tough to die . . . without a fight. . . ." He gestured toward the chair. "Sit." He waited until she'd complied. "Dylan says . . . you're a management consultant. . . ."

She nodded. "I own and run a company called the Center for Creative Thinking and Leadership. Companies send their management teams there for training."

Carson's brows lifted. "CCTL is you? . . . I just read up on it. . . . Top-notch reputation . . . Considered sending my team there . . . for brush-up. I'm . . . impressed."

Sabrina's lips curved slightly. It was a tight smile, but a smile nonetheless. "Given the source, I'm flattered. I've read about you, too. I'm familiar with Ruisseau's successes. Not only are you a corporate genius but you're personally involved in every facet of your company, a policy I think more CEOs should adopt. It's fitting that Ruisseau is named after you—albeit in French."

"Yeah, well, 'Ruisseau' has . . . an exotic, romantic . . .

ring to it. . . . No one wants to buy . . . a perfume called 'brook.' Sounds like a drinking hole for trout . . ."

A flicker of amusement lurked behind the guarded veneer in her sharp blue eyes—*his* eyes. She had a definite sense of humor. But she wasn't ready to let down her defenses. Instead, she opted for another tight smile. "I see your point."

Enough about him. He didn't want to talk about his accomplishments. He wanted to hear about her. "Tell me . . . about your life . . . your mother. . . . She wanted to make . . . an exceptional child. . . . Obviously, she succeeded." He began to cough.

"Are you all right?" Sabrina half rose.

He waved away her concern. "Fine . . . But listening hurts less . . . than talking."

"Okay." She got the message and sat back down, considering what she wanted to say. "I don't know how much Dylan's told you."

"Not much," Dylan supplied. "Just your name and profession."

"He also said you . . . were a knockout. . . ." Carson added. "He's right."

Sabrina shot Dylan a look that Carson couldn't quite make out. Wariness or discomfort, maybe, mixed with something else.

Whatever it was, Dylan picked up on it. "Do you want me to leave?" he asked.

"Not on my account," she replied. "Unless Mr. Brooks feels otherwise?" A quizzical glance at Carson.

He shook his head, waving Dylan toward a chair. "I have no secrets . . . from Dylan. . . ." He wet his lips. "Sabrina . . . I know this situation's awkward . . . But call me Carson. . . . Mr. Brooks seems pretty ridiculous . . . under the circumstances. . . ."

"I suppose so," she agreed. "All right, I'll try." She cleared her throat. "You asked about my mother. Her name's Gloria Radcliffe. She's a fashion designer with her own label. She has clients everywhere—including New York. In fact, she just got back from showing her latest designs here."

"Back? She . . . lives in New Hampshire?"

"No, in Rockport, Massachusetts."

"A . . . good place . . . for an artist . . . to call home." Carson couldn't miss the warmth with which Sabrina spoke of her mother. "You're very . . . proud of her."

"Yes, I am."

"Did you . . . tell her . . . you were coming . . . to see me?"

"She knows." A troubled expression flickered across Sabrina's face. "She wishes you well."

"But she'd . . . preferred if you'd . . . stayed away."

A sharp intake of breath. "It's not as black and white as that, Mr. Broo— Carson. It's complicated."

"Most things are. . . ." He paused. "Twenty-eight years ago . . . she was determined to . . . go it alone. . . ." He saw the glint of surprise flash in Sabrina's eyes. "No, I never . . . spoke to her . . . firsthand," he clarified. "But I was given . . . some background . . . by the medical personnel. Your mother's . . . criteria were pretty stringent. . . . She was blunt about the fact . . . that no man . . . would fill the bill . . . as a mate. . . . So she wanted one who could fill the bill as an ideal sperm donor . . . to make an extraordinary child. . . ."

"I see." Clearly, she'd known only pieces of the puzzle. It gave Carson some pleasure to know he was able to fill in more.

"She stuck to her guns . . . and never married?" he asked.

Sabrina nodded.

"Not . . . surprised . . ." He angled his head, glanced at Sabrina's left hand. "You're not wearing a ring. . . . Are you a die-hard soloist . . . too?"

"A die-hard soloist?" This time her smile came naturally. "That sounds like I'm in flight school."

He chuckled, wincing a little at the resulting pain in his chest—a pain he stubbornly ignored. "Okay, then . . . what's the female equivalent . . . of a bachelor—a bachelorette?"

"I get the picture." She feathered her fingers through her long, dark hair. "And, no, I'm not militant about staying single. But I strongly suspect that's the way things will play out."

"Because you work . . . all the time." It was a statement, not a question.

"Something like that, yes."

"And you're different . . . out of sync with others . . . A loner and a maverick. . . ."

The practiced look was back in place. "Are we describing me or you?"

It was a good business ploy, one Carson recognized well. She was reclaiming a position of power, turning a defense into an offense. Good for her. She was sharp and self-protective. Regardless, he was right.

"Both of us," he answered frankly. "But for now, you . . . I assume there's no one special . . . in your life. . . . ?"

She looked like she wanted to slug him for butting in where he didn't belong.

"Cut me . . . some slack," he urged. "I just . . . found out . . . I'm a father. . . ."

Her brows rose. "Fine. I'll placate you—this time. No, there's no one special."

"Change that."

"What?"

"I said . . . change that."

"I don't believe this." Sabrina was at the edge of her seat again, looking like she was about to bolt. "I never met you before today, never even knew who you were. And here you are, analyzing me and handing out romantic advice?"

"You got it," he confirmed. "Because I'm . . . an expert on the subject. . . . I know . . . what you're cheating . . . yourself of. . . . I just found out the full extent of it . . . when you walked in. I was a damned fool. . . . Don't be the same. . . ."

She said nothing for a minute, just stared at him, and the myriad of emotions crossing her face told him he'd struck home.

"I didn't mean . . . to upset you. . . ."

"You didn't," she assured him, her tone deceptively light. "I hear this on a daily basis from my assistant. She lectures me about being a workaholic, insisting that it's the unhealthiest of lifestyles."

"She's right. . . . You grow old . . . alone."

"Is that why you wanted to meet me?" Sabrina asked. "You think you're growing old alone? Because that's certainly not what the media reports."

"There's alone . . . and there's alone." He was beginning to fade, but dammit, he had to finish. "I have a full life. . . . Ruisseau . . . Susan . . . And Dylan's like a son. But no continuity . . . I didn't realize . . . until recently. Then I started thinking . . . that you might be out there. . . . Had to know . . ."

Moisture dampened Sabrina's lashes, and she quickly blinked it away. "I think you should rest. Contrary to what you believe, a lot of people care about you. Dylan, for one. And Ms. Lane, who from what I hear hasn't left the hospital since yesterday."

"Susan's great." Carson was stunned to taste the salt of his own tears. He couldn't remember the last time he'd cried, if ever. "But a relationship . . . at my stage . . . is something different. . . . It's not a family . . . kids. . . . I wish I'd realized . . . sooner. Don't . . . make that mistake." He didn't wait for her to answer. "I want to . . . get to know you. I realize . . . I have no right . . . but think about it. Discuss it with your mother . . . if you need to." His jaw set. "And don't do it . . . because I might die. Do it because you want to . . . and so do I."

"I will. I'll think about it. I—I've got to go." Sabrina rose, her motions jerky and her eyes damp.

"Don't cry."

"I'm not." She needed to lie to protect herself. Carson understood. She wasn't ready to bare or share emotions yet. It was too soon. Hell, he hadn't known he possessed these kind of feelings himself until now.

"I'm not crying," she repeated, seeing the knowing look on his face. "My eyes are just watering. It's the antiseptic smells. Hospitals do that to me."

"Yeah . . . to me, too."

"Sabrina has a heightened olfactory sense," Dylan contributed, joining the conversation for the first time. "I told her it must be hereditary."

Carson marvelled at the wonder of genetics. "I guess it must be." He reached out a hand, touched Sabrina's sleeve as she turned to go. "Will you . . . be back?"

She swallowed, gazing at him for a moment before she nodded. "Yes. I'll come by later. I can't promise more than that."

"I understand." He was relieved he'd gotten this much.

And he was so tired he could hardly keep his eyes open.
"Then . . . later . . ."

"Fine. Now get some sleep." She headed for the door.

Dylan leaned over the bed. "I'll be back in a while,"
he said quietly. "I just want to get Sabrina to her hotel."

Carson nodded. "Good. Make sure she's okay." His
lids drooped. "We'll talk . . . when you get back."

9

Dr. Radison was waiting outside ICU when Dylan and Sabrina emerged.

"How did it go?" he asked.

"Fine. It went fine," Sabrina replied dazedly. She felt exhausted and too off-balance to speak, much less go into detail.

"He's still so damned weak," Dylan reported. "And his breathing's labored."

"We need to talk about that. Mr. Brooks's chest is filling up with fluid. He's fighting an infection, and he's losing. The chest tube's going back in this afternoon. The respirator and ET tube will probably follow suit tonight. Tomorrow morning I'm going in and removing the bullet."

Dylan tensed. "You said that would be risky because of where it's located."

"Not as risky as leaving it. Not at this point."

A muscle flexed in Dylan's jaw. "What time are you operating?"

"Nine-thirty. The good news is, the bullet shifted after piercing the lung. It's now lodged closer to the skin. I'll make a small incision and extract it. I don't expect complications. Hopefully, the antibiotics will take over. In the meantime, I want him to rest. Minimal visitation. One person at a time. Five minutes max."

"Understood. What about his kidneys?"

"They're still not responding on their own. But the dialysis did its job. And his blood pressure's stable. So, first things first. Let's get rid of the infection. Then we'll discuss the kidney options."

Sabrina felt the doctor's gaze slide to her. It was a reflexive gesture. Nonetheless, it served as a blatant reminder of the pivotal role she might be called on to play.

Her insides clenched.

Dylan was looking elsewhere. He'd twisted around, and was scanning the lounge to determine who was there. Sabrina followed suit, unsurprised to see Susan Lane hovering near the window, her face lined with worry, and Stan Hager—whom she'd met briefly before going in to see Carson—seated on the couch, slumped forward, his head in his hands. From the opposite direction, two official-looking suits were approaching—one man, one woman—bearing down on them like two lions about to pounce. It didn't take a genius to figure out they were detectives.

"Oh, joy, rapture," Dylan muttered under his breath. "Here come Whitman and Barton." He turned back to Dr. Radison. "Have you brought them—or anyone else for that matter—up to speed on where things stand with Carson, or about your plans to remove the bullet?"

"No. I wanted you and Ms. Radcliffe to know first." Dr. Radison cleared his throat. "I assumed there'd be questions. And I wasn't certain who'd been told about the biological ties between the patient and Ms. Radcliffe."

"I appreciate your discretion. But the detectives know. I told them before I flew up to Auburn. I'm sure that's why they're here—to meet and greet Carson's daughter." Dylan turned to Sabrina, presumably to give her some insight into what to expect. He took one look at her sheet-white face, and changed his mind. "Are you okay?" he demanded, frowning. "You look like you're about to collapse."

"I'm fine." She was beginning to sound like a broken record. And the truth was, she was anything but fine. She was on major overload. And the doctor's update had only made things worse. Dammit. More surgery. More risk. No improvement in kidney function. Less time to make an increasingly critical decision.

"Sabrina." Dylan's tone was more gentle than she'd heard him use until now. "I told Carson I'd take care of you, starting with getting you over to your hotel. If you're not up to speaking with those detectives, say the word. I'll tell them you're drained and their questions will have to wait. I've gotten good at putting them off. Besides, they already think I'm scum. This will just feed into that opinion."

"What?" Sabrina didn't understand what he was talking about.

"Never mind. Just say the word and I'll delay this interrogation."

"That's not necessary," she said tonelessly. "There won't be any interrogation. Since I never met Carson Brooks before today, I don't have much to tell them. So let's go ahead and get this over with."

"You're sure?"

A nod. "Yes. As long as we can go into an empty office or lounge. I won't have this conversation in the open."

"You can use my office," Dr. Radison offered quietly. "You'll have all the privacy you want there."

"Thank you." Sabrina assessed the detectives as they closed the gap between them. The woman looked like a cornstalk with hair and an ice-blue gaze so razor-sharp it reminded Sabrina of Superman's X-ray vision. As for the man—well, excluding his suit and the slight paunch around his gut, he could have passed for a bouncer, complete with bulldog expression and kick-ass demeanor.

They stopped in front of her, and the bouncer spoke first. "Mr. Newport, Doctor Radison." A questioning glance at Sabrina. "I assume you're Sabrina Radcliffe."

"I am."

"I'm Detective Barton. This is my partner, Detective Whitman." He gestured toward the cornstalk, who acknowledged the introduction with a nod. "We're investigating the shooting."

"So I've been told," Sabrina replied.

"I'm sure you have." Barton slanted a look at Dylan— one Sabrina could swear was accusing.

If so, she'd have to set them straight. Dylan had actually been very close-mouthed on the subject of the investigation. Whatever Sabrina had picked up on had been based on attitude, not words.

"In any case, Ms. Radcliffe," Barton was continuing, "we'd like to talk with you. *Alone.*" Another sharp glance at Dylan. "You don't have a problem with that, do you, Mr. Newport?"

Anger glinted in Dylan's eyes. "Nope. Like me, Ms. Radcliffe is perfectly capable of taking care of herself."

The tension here was so thick you could cut it with a knife.

"Good." Barton turned to Sabrina. "Is now all right?"

Sabrina nodded, wondering at the dynamics here. Whatever was going on, it clearly went beyond a difference in philosophy. The detectives didn't like Dylan, and the feeling was mutual. Why?

"Dr. Radison said we could use his office," she informed them. "I'd prefer that this conversation remain private. I'm sure you understand."

"No problem." There was a hint of compassion in Detective Whitman's tone—whether it was because she was naturally less abrasive or because she and Barton played good cop, bad cop, remained to be seen. "Let's go."

"I'll wait for you in the lounge," Dylan told Sabrina. "As soon as you're done—which, as I see it, should be ten minutes max given how little you can do to help the detectives build their case—I'll get you over to your hotel so you can rest."

Talk about pointed. And obvious. Coming from a man who knew all the rules of subtlety, as well as how to turn on the charm to achieve his goals, it seemed as if Dylan *wanted* to antagonize the cops.

Whatever was bugging him, he was ripping mad.

She shot him a curious look. "Thanks."

Closeted in Dr. Radison's office, the detectives didn't waste any time.

"Mr. Newport seems very protective of you," Whitman said. "Yet you've only known him since yesterday." She perched at the edge of the desk, her long legs crossed in front of her, while her partner stood, arms folded, near the windows. They were clearly establishing a dominant stance, but Sabrina didn't care. She was worn out and stressed to the max.

"It's Carson Brooks he's protective of," Sabrina corrected, easing back in a thick leather chair and eyeing the detective to determine if her earlier personable manner was indeed a facade. "For obvious reasons, Dylan views me as an extension of his mentor—and a possible lifeline, as well."

"So it's true that you're Carson Brooks's biological child," Detective Barton clarified.

"Yes."

"Did that news come as a surprise to you? Or were you aware of your paternity?"

"I had no idea Carson Brooks was my father." Sabrina didn't appreciate the dubious glint in his eyes and, reflexively, her chin came up as she prepared for a less amiable talk than she'd expected. "Frankly, I was shocked."

"Shocked." Barton repeated the word with more than a trace of cynicism. "You're a very bright woman, Ms. Radcliffe. You've got an IQ that's through the sky, and a career that's based on identifying problems and figuring out solutions. Are you saying you never questioned your mother about something as fundamental as who your father was? That you never demanded answers?"

Okay, now Sabrina was getting pissed. "That's definitely *not* what I'm saying."

"In that case, are you suggesting your mother refused to answer, that she never told you she and Carson Brooks were once involved?"

"I'm not saying that either. And, with all due respect, Detective, I'd appreciate your losing the attitude. You don't win allies by biting their heads off. Nor do you get answers by firing questions so rapidly there's no time for answers."

Was it Sabrina's imagination, or did Detective Whitman shoot her partner a cool-it look?

Barton's tense response was to yank out a pack of gum, unwrap a piece, and pop it in his mouth. "Fine. I'll chew. You talk."

"Sounds fair." Sabrina gave him a tight-lipped smile. "To begin with, my mother and I discussed my conception as soon as I was old enough to understand the facts of life. She answered all my questions. As for mentioning Carson Brooks or the fact that they were involved, she didn't. Because they weren't. You're apparently unaware that I was conceived through donor insemination. My mother was unmarried and unattached. My father was an independent sperm donor. I learned yesterday that that donor was Carson Brooks."

Both detectives looked startled by the revelation.

"That explains a lot." Detective Whitman spoke first, having chewed over the various ramifications. "An independent sperm donor. So Mr. Brooks was anonymous."

"Right."

"Which means that neither he nor your mother knew the other's identity."

Well, that wasn't entirely true. And Sabrina knew enough about law enforcement to know that if she shaded the truth, it would come back to haunt her.

"That's too broad a generalization," she clarified.

"Fine. Narrow it down for us."

"They didn't know each other's names, no. Nor did they ever meet. But my mother had specific, strict criteria in mind for the man who fathered her child, which was why she chose this route to begin with. So it wasn't just a case of the donor leaving a sperm deposit and going home. Carson was given enough facts to make that clear. As for my mother . . ." A brief hesitation. Odd, how calculated her mother's motives sounded, when she'd really just been a clever, levelheaded woman doing the best she could to ensure her child was all he or she could be. "It was more complicated for her."

"How so?"

"To begin with, the entire donor insemination process was relatively uncommon in those days. And my grandparents were against it."

"Because of their social status."

"Among other reasons, yes. Anyway, my mother handled the whole procedure very discreetly, through a private fertility specialist. I don't know all the details, but I do know she insisted on seeing medical, intellectual, and social backgrounds on all the prospective donors."

"That's understandable. But she still never knew any of their identities, including that of the actual donor."

"Not at the time, she didn't."

Whitman's brows rose. "Are you saying that changed?"

God, Sabrina didn't want to go there. But she had no choice. "Yes, that changed. But before you jump to conclusions, it was strictly coincidental. Besides all the background information my mother received when she was choosing a sperm donor, she got photos of each candidate."

"Photos." A lightbulb seemed to go off in Detective Whitman's head. "In other words, she saw a photo of Carson Brooks—and studied it closely. Over the past dozen years, his face has been plastered on the cover of *Business Week* and shown regularly on CNN and CNBC. He's a striking guy. My hunch is that no woman could forget his face. Am I right? Did your mother recognize him at some later date?"

"Yes, she did."

"When?" Barton was back in the picture. He'd stopped chewing gum and was staring her down.

Warning bells screamed inside Sabrina's head. "I'm not sure. Several years ago, I think. She told me this last night, after I learned Carson was my father."

"Several years ago," Whitman repeated, scratching her head in puzzlement. "Why didn't she say anything to you before now?"

"She was protecting me, Detective Whitman. She was afraid I'd try making contact with a man who, as far as she knew, had no interest in having me in his life. And she was right. I would have."

"She might have been right about you, but she was wrong about Mr. Brooks. As we understand it, he was in the process of trying to locate you—or at least to determine if he had a living son or daughter."

"I realize that now."

"But your mother didn't?"

"Of course not. How could she?"

Rather than answering, Whitman asked another question of her own. "You said you spoke with your mother last night. Did you tell her about Mr. Newport's visit and about your plans to go to New York and see Mr. Brooks?"

"Absolutely. It was a big step on my part, one that could lead to an even bigger step. I wanted to prepare her."

"So you phoned her?"

"No, I drove over to her house."

"To Rockport?" Whitman gave a low whistle. "Wow. It must have been close to midnight by the time you got there. Between Mr. Newport breaking his news to you, and the hour plus drive from Auburn to Rockport—I can't imagine you getting there sooner. You must have scared her to death, waking her up like that."

"I didn't wake her." Sabrina had a bad feeling about this. She was being led somewhere. She just wasn't sure where or why. "She'd just gotten home from the airport."

"She'd been away?"

"On a business trip, yes."

"For how long?"

"A week."

"Where did she go?"

"To New York. She's a clothing designer. And Manhattan is the center of the fashion industry."

"True." Whitman pursed her lips. "So she was here since last . . . ?"

". . . Wednesday," Sabrina supplied.

"Hmm. That's five days before Labor Day."

"Which is when Carson Brooks was shot." Barton fired away like a canon. "Now *that's* an interesting coincidence. And what were your words—that your mother was protecting you? I'm sure she was, not to mention protecting her elderly, vulnerable, and socially connected parents, too. The question is, to what extreme would she go to do that?"

Sabrina felt as if she'd been punched in the gut as the detectives' deplorable, utterly insane intimation struck home. They had to be kidding. They couldn't possibly believe . . .

"Ms. Radcliffe?" It was Detective Whitman addressing her, but this time that calm, even tone did nothing to cool Sabrina's rage. "Are you all right?"

Ice chips glittered in Sabrina's eyes. "No, I'm damned well not all right. If your partner is trying to imply that my mother is a suspect in the shooting of Carson Brooks, then he's lost his mind, I'm sickened, and this meeting is over." She started to get up.

"We're not implying anything," Whitman quickly refuted, stretching out a detaining arm. "Believe me, Ms. Radcliffe, there's a long, long list of potential suspects. Your mother's just another name on the list. We'll have to talk to her, of course, to establish her whereabouts at the time of the attack. If she was on a business trip like you said, I'm assuming she was probably with clients who can confirm her story. Also, if we determine that she had no foreknowledge of Carson Brooks's decision to find you, her motive would become more obscure. So please—don't overreact."

"I'm not the one who's overreacting," Sabrina shot back, with a pointed glare at Detective Barton. "Your partner is. I realize he wants to find the assailant. So do I. But not this way. He needs to take a few training classes at CCTL. They would improve his people skills."

Whitman's lips twitched. "We'll keep that in mind. Won't we, Frank?"

Barton scowled. "Yeah. Right."

"Let me ask *you* a question now." Sabrina was sticking her nose where it didn't belong, and she knew it. But with the detectives backpedaling to try to appease her, she had the upper hand—for a brief time. "What's the situation between you and Dylan Newport? Why is there so much animosity?"

"Why? Has he said something?" Whitman's comeback was whip-quick, although her expression remained nondescript.

Sabrina had definitely struck a nerve. "He doesn't need to. It's obvious. What I can't figure out is the basis for it. Did you grill him the way you grilled me? Is that what pissed him off so much? Or are you hassling people he thinks are innocent?"

"We grill everyone, Ms. Radcliffe," Barton said tightly. "This is an attempted murder, not a petty theft. As to whether someone's innocent or guilty, time will tell. Time and a thorough investigation. Who knows what Newport's problem is? Some people get riled up when we get close to the truth. Especially if uncovering that truth means wrecking their efforts, their freedom, their future—or all three."

Sabrina blinked in stupefied amazement. "You can't possibly mean you think Dylan shot Carson?"

"I didn't say that."

"You didn't have to." This guy was *really* starting to

get on her nerves. "Let's stop playing games, Detective. You're implying that Dylan's a suspect—not a random name on a very long list, but a *prime* suspect," Sabrina amended. "Why?"

She was greeted with silence.

"Need I remind you that I'm Carson Brooks's daughter," Sabrina heard herself say. "I'm entitled to know the status of the investigation."

Whitman's brows rose. "You certainly took on your new role in a hurry."

"I improvise quickly."

"That's an understatement. Okay, look, we have nothing concrete to tell you. Let's just say that Mr. Newport was the only other person we can place in the building at the time of the shooting, and that he would benefit big-time if Mr. Brooks weren't around."

"Financially, you mean." Sabrina shook her head in disbelief. "Do you have any idea how much Carson means to him? How far back they go? The life Carson yanked him out of?"

"We do." Whitman leaned forward with interest. "Evidently, so do you. You know a great deal about Mr. Newport considering you two just met."

"We had an hour's plane ride to talk. I'm nosy. I ask a lot of questions. And I'm a *very* good judge of character. Dylan Newport is tough, arrogant, street-smart and book-smart. You might even be able to add manipulative to that list. The jury's still out on that one. But his feelings for Carson are as real as they come. He'd never harm the man, much less for money. And he'd certainly never be stupid enough to do it in a situation where every drop of circumstantial evidence would point at him."

"I doubt you realize what Carson Brooks is worth. The thought of inheriting that kind of wealth entices even the most noble of people to commit criminal acts. As for the poor choice of timing, I agree. But time wasn't on Mr. Newport's side, not when Carson Brooks had already clued him in to the fact that he was launching a search for you. To be more precise, he didn't just clue him in. He confided in him—and *only* him—then asked for his help. Talk about waving a red flag. If you turned up, a genuine heir, that could change everything, especially the allocation of assets to an outsider, no matter how dear. The prospect is enough to push a smart, cautious man into taking dumb, reckless risks."

"Nice theory." Sabrina looked from one detective to the other. "Where's the proof?"

"If we had proof, he'd be in custody," Barton replied.

"Right." This time when Sabrina got to her feet, she wasn't going to be stopped. "No wonder he's bent out of shape. Not only do you think he tried to kill a man he loves like a father, he's probably afraid that since you have him all but in handcuffs, you're not exactly busting your tails to find the real shooter."

"Wait a minute." Whitman blocked her path. "I resent the hell out of that. Yeah, we have our qualms about Dylan Newport, but that's all they are—qualms. We have qualms about a bunch of people. And we're investigating every one of them—every person who might have a grudge against him, every individual who might gain something from his death. Until we find a theory that's fact, this case will stay wide open—and so will our minds. We're *very* good at our job. We *will* find the person who did this. So tell Mr. Newport not to be so damned paranoid, and not to bitch about how we're conducting our investigation."

Sabrina stared Whitman down. "He hasn't bitched, at least not to me. If he does, I'll pass along your message.

In the meantime, I've had enough for one day. I'm exhausted. I'm going to get some rest. I'll be back at the hospital later this evening. If you need to reach me before then, I'm staying at the Plaza Athenée."

"Until when?"

"I haven't set a departure date."

"Does that mean you're planning to be tissue-typed? Have you decided to volunteer one of your kidneys to your father?"

"I haven't thought that far ahead. When I do, I'll let you know. Now, if you'll excuse me . . ."

Sabrina sidestepped Detective Whitman and walked out.

10

Gloria put down her sketch, which was less inspiring
than anything she'd done since she was a first-year design student. It was no use. She couldn't concentrate. Not
with all that was going on.

She went into the kitchen, made herself a cup of tea,
then curled up on the sofa to drink it and think. The
phone call from Sabrina hadn't held any major surprises.
She'd met Carson Brooks. She'd been moved by the experience, whether or not she chose to admit it. She'd
been sucked up into a vortex of activity and emotion, and
they both knew how it was all going to play out, at least
as far as Sabrina's decision was concerned.

No, none of that was a surprise.

It was the speed with which everything was unraveling that was alarming. The police interrogation, the
media clustered outside the hospital, the sacrifice that
Sabrina was going to have to make without being given
nearly enough time to prepare herself.

Gloria's hand trembled on her cup. She'd restrained
herself from getting involved as long as she could.

She had to fly back to New York.

It was inevitable, really. Those detectives would be
contacting her soon enough anyway, and it would make
things easier if she talked to them in Manhattan rather
than here. It would, at least, keep her parents removed

from the heart of the scandal. As it was, she had to stop off and see them on her way to the airport, break the news to them about what was going on.

She could hardly wait.

Sighing, she put down the cup and massaged her temples. Twenty-eight years was a long time, but a person didn't forget a pivotal milestone like the one that had started all this and, ultimately, created Sabrina. Gloria hadn't come to her decision lightly. Donor insemination was still somewhat of an eyebrow-raiser in the mid-seventies, even when the parties involved were a married couple. But for an unmarried woman such as herself, one who wanted to bear and raise a child alone, it was a major tongue-wagger. Which to her parents, who were so enmeshed in their Beacon Hill world, translated into scandalous behavior.

Then again, they'd come to expect that kind of behavior from Gloria. She'd always been a maverick. Growing up in the fifties, coming into her own in the sixties, she was too intelligent for a woman, too outspoken to keep her opinions to herself, too creative to fit in, too beautiful and well bred to abandon the country club life and—sin of all sins—become an artistic bohemian rather than an affluent housewife.

Of course she would have preferred finding the right man—one who loved her for who she was, rather than who he wanted to make her. But that wasn't in the cards. She knew that early on. She was too much the free spirit, too individualistic. Finding her soul mate would be like finding a needle in a haystack.

Time didn't prove her wrong. Every man she got involved with was a colossal disappointment. They either wanted to possess her or to change her. She could abide neither.

So marriage was out. But, oh, how she wanted a child—one she could bond with through pregnancy and childhood; one she could love, give every emotional and intellectual advantage to, and encourage to be his or her own person. She had so much to offer. And if she could only integrate her own attributes with those of someone who was equally dynamic but different from her, with entirely distinctive traits of his own—what an extraordinary child she could share with the world.

With that thought, the idea was born.

And so, at the age of thirty-three, with her bio-clock ticking loudly in her ear, Gloria had taken the plunge.

Finding the right doctor had been imperative. He had to be an accomplished fertility specialist, as well as open-minded, and discreet. Because the path she was taking was far more unorthodox than the customary one in which you paid the donor a nominal fee, got him to relinquish all paternal rights and—with a topical knowledge of the donor's background, interests, and profession, along with his clean bill of health and basic specs—you went for it.

Even now, she smiled, remembering how intrigued Dr. Oldsman had been by the intricacy of her plan. He'd chuckled, saying it was stretching the boundaries but not breaking the rules. Sure, offering twenty thousand dollars to a sperm donor was outrageous. But given how specific she was about what she wanted for the father of her child, how high she'd set the bar, and how extensive was the testing and paperwork she required, it was understandable. And since she had the luxury of money on her side, why not use it to her advantage?

Her criteria had been lofty, but clear. The donor had to be exceptional, both physically and mentally. He had to have strengths that would augment hers; a scientific mind to offset her creative one, and an ambition level as fiery as her own. She wanted to maximize her child's chances of being successful, no matter what direction he or she took.

Each donor was, of course, required to submit to an extensive medical examination. But that was just the beginning. He was also required to take various exams testing his knowledge and intellectual abilities, plus he had to participate in a personal interview with Dr. Oldsman, the transcript of which—with the full knowledge and consent of the donor—was given to Gloria for review. Last but not least, each donor was required to fill out a questionnaire, supplied by Gloria, one that explored his talents and aspirations.

Gloria pored over each candidate's questionnaire and interview transcript. She also scrutinized his test results—medical and intellectual—looking for just the right combination of qualities.

She'd quite nearly given up finding them.

Then, Candidate #67 had crossed her desk.

She remembered every detail of his application. He had an IQ of 176, and a propensity for chemistry and business. He was determined to use those talents to start his own company, build it from the ground up, and make it thrive. He planned to do that with the twenty thousand dollars he received, should he be selected as the donor. His passion was infectious. His charisma and self-assurance practically leaped off the pages. His age was ideal—a youthful twenty-two—and his health was perfect. His sperm count was also exceptionally high—a major plus since, given Gloria's age, she wanted to minimize the risk of failed attempts. All in all, his specs were outstanding. The only negative was his sketchy ancestry. He was a street kid, an orphan whose parents had been high-school lovers. They'd gotten through the pregnancy, then taken off in separate directions, dumping their kid in the process. On the positive side, from the information Gloria managed to dig up, there'd been no drugs or alcohol involved, and the baby was born in perfect health. So, okay, she couldn't trace his lineage back three generations. Given her own experiences, she wondered if that mattered. The truth was, she was far more impressed by ambition and potential than she was by pedigree.

The clincher was his photo. He was drop-dead gorgeous. And, yes, that damned well mattered. The world was such that, just or unjust, people judged others by their appearance. Cold, hard facts showed that being attractive opened doors both personally and professionally. If Gloria could give that advantage to her son or daughter, she'd be a fool not to.

So Candidate #67 got the nod of approval—and the twenty thousand dollars.

The procedure went flawlessly. Sabrina was the result.

And, Gloria suspected, so was Ruisseau.

Odd, how she and Carson Brooks had each gotten what they wanted. She got her precious daughter; he got the company he was burning to start.

Their lives should never again have touched.

But they had.

And now she had to see through what she'd started.

7:25 P.M.
Mt. Sinai Hospital

"Dylan?"

Hearing Carson's gravelly voice, Dylan snapped out of the doze he'd fallen into moments before.

"Hey. You're awake." He pulled the chair over to the bed, studying his friend. His breathing wasn't great, even though they'd put the chest tube back in. His color wasn't all that terrific, either. But his eyes were relatively clear, considering everything he was enduring, and the pain medication that was being pumped into his body.

"Is that a surprise?" Carson's voice was still hoarse and weak, and his speech was slow. "I've slept more these past few days . . . than I slept in fifty years combined."

Dylan's lips twisted into a grin. "I can't argue that. But you look more like yourself."

"You look like shit."

"You sound more like yourself, too." Dylan felt a surge of relief he couldn't begin to define. "I see signs of the old Carson. Hell, you can insult me all you want."

A hint of a smile. "Sounds tempting . . . maybe later." The smile faded. "We have things to talk about."

"Yeah." Dylan had a pretty good idea what was coming. Carson wanted details, something he wasn't looking forward to supplying. But he'd never lied to Carson before, and he wasn't about to start now. "Sabrina first?"

A knowing look, as that sharp blue gaze bore through him. "Coward. That's the easy part of our talk."

"Cut me some slack. You've been out of commission since Monday. I'm off my game."

"I'll let you off the hook this time. . . . But only because I want to talk about my daughter." Carson said the word awkwardly, but with an awed expression Dylan had never seen before. "So, okay, yeah, Sabrina first." Raw pride took over. "She's incredible, isn't she?" He didn't wait for an answer. "Man, do I have amazing sperm."

"*One* amazing sperm," Dylan corrected wryly. "We can't vouch for the rest. Maybe it was just the luck of the draw."

"Maybe," Carson agreed, not bothered in the least by

Dylan's ribbing. He held his friend's gaze. "Is she freaked out?"

"She's beat. Those detectives did a number on her before she left for the hotel. I guess they implied her mother might have been the one who shot you."

"Her mother?" Carson repeated in astonishment.

"To keep you from contacting her. It sounds pretty lame to me."

"To me, too . . . How the hell would she know my plans?" A pause. "Besides which, I thought the cops had decided *you* shot me."

Dylan started. "They actually laid that one on you?"

"Not in so many words . . . But I'm a pretty smart guy . . . even with all these damned drugs in me." Carson rested a few seconds. "They're being assholes. I told them so. They think I'm just protecting you. They'll figure out the truth . . . soon enough."

"Thanks," Dylan said simply.

"For what? Trusting you not to put a bullet in my back?" Carson snorted in disgust. "Give me a break . . . and some credit for knowing you." An off-handed shrug—and a wince. "Besides, I ruled you out. If you wanted me dead, I'd be in a box . . . not a hospital."

"Cute." Dylan knew Carson was trying to make light of the accusations, but he couldn't laugh off something of this magnitude. Still, it took the edge off his rage knowing Carson had dismissed the detectives' speculations without a second thought.

"Lighten up, Dylan. . . . They don't know you, or how tight we are. . . . They're just doing their job. They've got a great rep. . . . I had Stan check them out. They'll get it right. . . . Look at the bright side. I'm not gonna die . . . so I'll be around when they find whoever shot me. . . . Then I can make them apologize to you . . . in public, if it helps."

"What'll help is seeing you on your feet, and seeing whoever did this in jail."

"Sounds good." Another short rest. "When's Sabrina coming back to the hospital?"

Dylan glanced at his watch. "I checked in with her about an hour ago. She sounded pensive. I guess she's dealing with her family, and the shock of finding out who her father is. But she's holding her own. She said she'll be here around eight."

"She's got a lot more to be pensive about than putting a name to a sperm specimen. . . . And her family's got a lot more to worry about than a scandal. . . . But then, you already know that. Which brings us to our next topic . . ." Carson was forced to stop and rest his lungs. He began coughing, and gestured for some water.

Dylan poured him a cup, helped him drink it. "Maybe we should cut this talk short."

Carson waved away the notion. "Not a chance . . . We're finishing this before Dr. Kildaire comes in . . . and tosses you out."

As usual, Carson wasn't going to take no for an answer. "Okay," Dylan agreed. "What topic's next—Ruisseau?"

"Nice try. But you know better. I'm not worried about Ruisseau. . . . Not with you and Stan there . . . I have some thoughts . . . but we'll talk about those later." A concerned pucker formed between his brows. "Just tell me one thing . . . are the detectives bugging anyone?"

"*Everyone.* We'll survive. We're tough." Dylan braced himself for Carson's typically intensive probing. "So what's the next topic?"

"Sabrina's real reason for coming—what is it?"

"I already said, she wanted to meet you. Is that so odd?"

"No. But it's only part of the reason . . . and it doesn't explain the urgency of the visit. . . . She's a workaholic. She's got a pretty intricate business to run . . . yet she just dropped everything and flew here. . . ."

"She thought you might not make it. Now she knows you will."

"Which takes the focus off me . . . and gives her time to decide whether or not she wants a relationship with me."

"Right."

"So you think she'd jump on a plane . . . and run home to work it through . . . with her family." Carson was starting to fade. But he was fighting it tooth and nail. "But she didn't do that, did she? She's still here."

Dylan blew out a breath. "Maybe she wants to get to know you better. Maybe she's curious. Maybe—"

"Dylan—stop. I saw the dialysis machine." Carson raised his wrist. "And I know what this shunt-thing is for."

Silence.

"Stop looking like a dog who got caught peeing on the rug. . . . I called Radison in . . . made him tell me about it. I know my kidneys aren't kicking in." Carson shut his eyes for a minute to regather his strength. Then, he opened them. "Tell me the truth. Did you bust your ass . . . to find Sabrina . . . in case I needed a transplant?"

Dylan didn't avert his gaze. "That, and because you asked me to."

A shaky nod. "Did you talk to her about the idea?"

"Yeah. She hasn't given me an answer."

"I don't . . . blame her. Christ . . . it's a huge sacrifice. I'm a stranger. . . ."

"You're her father."

The barest hint of a smile. "Not really . . . Not in the ways that matter . . . You know that, too. You're just too stubborn to admit it . . . and too close to me to be objective. . . . Those are lousy traits for a lawyer. . . ."

"So sue me."

"Give her room, Dylan. . . . Her family won't make this easy on her. . . . They're old money—lots of it. . . . Grandparents are very proper. . . . They're also in their eighties, and not about to mellow. . . . It was hard enough on their daughter. . . . She's made quite a name for herself in the fashion industry. . . ."

Dylan's brows rose. "For someone fighting for his life, you've managed to do lots of homework."

"Stan ran the check for me. It wasn't hard to get a profile on the Radcliffes. . . . They're very visible. . . . I had to know something about my daughter's family . . . her *real* family. . . ."

"And did they meet your expectations?" Sabrina inquired from the doorway.

"Actually . . . yeah." Carson angled his head in her direction, not missing a beat. "Come in . . . and pull up a chair."

Curiously, Dylan watched Sabrina, gauging her reaction. She was leaning against the doorjamb, arms folded across her breasts. Her expression was unreadable. If she was expecting contrition, she was talking to the wrong guy. Carson never apologized for being thorough.

"You're only allowed one visitor at a time," she reminded him. "I'll wait."

"The hell you will," Carson refuted, gesturing for Dylan to stay put as well. "Forget the rules. . . . Radison's gone for the day . . . and I won't tell."

Sabrina's lips twitched. "All right." She walked over, nodding her thanks to Dylan as he dragged over an armchair for her. "So, Dylan, are you the one who played Magnum, PI again?"

"Not this time," Carson supplied. "This time it was Stan. You met him?" He waited for her affirmation. "He and I go way back. . . . He's the only other person who knows about you."

A troubled frown. "You told him?"

"I didn't have to. . . . He worked for the fertility specialist your mother went to. . . . He's the one who clued me in to the donor search . . . she was doing . . . twenty-eight years ago. . . ."

"Oh. Wow. I didn't know that."

Carson regarded her steadily. "I won't tell anyone about your relationship to me. . . . That choice is yours."

"I doubt it'll work out that way," she murmured. "But that's life. It'll be up to me to do damage control."

"You're worried that news of who you are will leak out."

"Not leak . . . pour. And it's my family I'm worried about, not me."

"Speaking of that . . . are you ticked off that I . . . checked them out?"

"No. I would have done the same thing. The difference is, I didn't have to. I already knew a fair amount about you professionally. And Dylan filled me in personally." She broke off, drawing an unsteady breath, then sweeping her hair up and off her neck and sitting quietly, as if she felt light-headed. Studying her more closely, Dylan wondered if maybe she did. He was struck by how pale and strained she looked, even more so than earlier today. The hotel break hadn't done her much good, other than giving her a chance to shower and have it out with her family. She'd changed her clothes, too, and in her khaki slacks and light blue short-sleeved sweater, she looked younger and more vulnerable than the sophisticated corporate woman he'd dealt with until now.

She also looked on the verge of collapse.

"Sabrina, you're still white as a ghost," he heard himself say. He got up, poured her a glass of water and pressed it into her hand. "Have you eaten?"

"Um-hum." She managed a weak smile between sips. "Not fifteen minutes ago. Cranberry juice and crackers."

"What kind of a meal is that?"

"The kind the hospital lab gives you when you start to black out. It's embarrassing to admit, but I'm a baby when it comes to needles. Also, my blood pressure tends to be on the low side of normal. So when it comes to anything more than a couple of vials, I tend to get woozy."

The implication struck home, and Dylan's gaze fell to the inside of her forearm, where a cotton ball was pressed against the crease, held in place by a Band-Aid. "You donated blood."

She nodded. "I thought it was a good idea. As you know, Carson and I are the same blood type. The hospital's banking my blood specifically for him, just in case he needs it." She looked like she wanted to say more, then thought better of it.

Dylan caught on right away. And he prayed his assumption was fact and not a pipe dream. "Carson knows about the dialysis and the possibility of needing a kidney transplant," he said pointedly. "So there's no need to avoid talking about it."

"I see. Well, I'm glad I don't have to dance around the subject. I'll just tell you both that the lab took a separate blood sample to use for tissue-typing. We'll have the results in about a week."

"Wait a minute," Carson barked.

Sabrina's head came up, and she eyed Carson warily.

Dylan turned toward him, too, although he wasn't the least bit surprised by his friend's response. In fact, he'd been expecting this. And if Sabrina was expecting otherwise, if she'd anticipated some big, emotional scene, she was about to be surprised for the second time.

Addressing the fundamentals first, exploring the benefits of personal gain second, that was Carson's way. And given his newfound sense of responsibility when it came to Sabrina, and the direct part he'd played in triggering her current crisis, he wasn't going to make this easy for her.

"Yes?" Sabrina inquired.

"Let's start with your family. . . . Do they know about this?" Carson's hard stare pinned her to the chair.

Sabrina wasn't rattled. Nor did she dodge the question. "I spoke to my mother a little while ago. She'd already guessed. Now comes the harder part. She has to tell my grandparents. After that, we'll deal with the fallout. Anything else?"

"Yeah. Health risks—yours. Privacy invasion—also yours. Screwing up a lot of lives, and a lot of relationships—yours again . . . Listen, Sabrina, I don't like this. . . . You're not just opting to—"

"I already have," she interrupted. "It's my choice to make, not yours. Now, stop getting yourself all worked up, or I'll call Dr. Radison and get him back here."

"He left the hospital, remember?"

"I have his beeper number."

"You can't use it. There's no emergency."

"I'll lie."

Carson scowled. "You're a real ball-breaker, aren't you?"

"I wonder who I take after," was her wry response. She waved away his continuing protests. "We're getting ahead of ourselves. This tissue-typing is more complicated than it sounds. Besides checking for common genes, they have to do a crossmatch test, see if your immune system has produced any antibodies that might kill off my kidney. Until that's determined, we won't know if I'm a compatible donor. Let's save the arguing for afterward."

"Does that mean that if all systems are go you'll agree to be the transplant donor?" Dylan demanded. "Have you thought that far ahead?"

"No, she hasn't," Carson snapped out.

"Yes, I have." Sabrina ignored Carson's pointed objection. "*If* the test results indicate that I'm the best match, and *if* Carson's own kidneys don't resume on their own, then he'll get one of mine." She eased to the edge of her chair and started to get up. "Now, if it's okay with you gentlemen, I'll head back to the Plaza Athenée. You're right about my being a little weak. I'd rather be at my best for this battle of wills. Let's put it on hold until tomorrow. For tonight, all I had in mind was checking in on Carson to make sure he was holding his own. Which I have, and he is. So I'll . . ." She stopped, groping at nothing as she started to black out.

Dylan grabbed her before she fell, anchoring his arm around her waist. "You'll head back, all right. But not before you eat a decent meal."

"Dylan." It was Carson's command-and-control voice. "Get her out of this damned hospital. Take her to a steak house . . . to Smith & Wollensky's; it's not far from the Plaza Athenée. . . . Order the biggest piece of meat on the menu. . . . Get one for yourself, too. You've eaten nothing but hospital crap all day. . . . After dinner, take Sabrina back to the hotel. . . . Walk her up to her room. . . . Then, go home and get some sleep. You look like a zombie." He paused to regain his strength. "Don't worry about me. . . . I'm talked out. . . . Need to rest."

"Yeah, you do," Dylan agreed.

"And don't show up here at dawn. . . . Susan's already doing that. . . . So are the cops, to snatch up that bullet the minute Radison gets it out . . . Besides, I want you here afterward. . . . When they're gone . . . we need to talk. . . ."

"About Ruisseau?"

"Yeah."

"I'll be here."

"Not just you." Carson gestured from Dylan to Sabrina. "Both of you. The three of us have things to work out . . . alone."

11

Sabrina surveyed the bustling Third Avenue steak house and its tightly packed tables. Seventy percent of those tables were filled with groups of men, ten percent with groups of women, and twenty percent with a mixture of both. The restaurant was filled to bursting—mostly with professionals who worked in midtown and had stopped for business or social dinners before heading home—yet no one seemed to mind the crowd. To the contrary, everyone was having a rip-roaring time, laughing and stuffing their faces.

She and Dylan were lucky to have gotten a table. Partially because the place was hopping, and partially because neither of them was dressed appropriately. While most of the patrons were wearing jackets or suits, Sabrina was wearing khakis and Dylan was wearing a sport shirt and jeans. Fortunately, Dylan knew the maître d', who greeted him warmly, and whisked them right off to an upstairs table.

Before she'd slid in her chair, Dylan had already confirmed that she liked seafood, and ordered the two of them a mixed seafood appetizer. When it came, he instructed Sabrina to wolf down at least half of it, along with two small rolls, before taking her first sip of merlot. As a rule, she didn't take kindly to being strong-armed. In this case, she didn't put up a fight. Dylan was right.

She already felt light-headed; drinking wine on an empty stomach would knock her right out.

The steaks arrived, sizzling and huge, along with three side dishes: hash browns, creamed spinach, and asparagus. It was enough to feed an army, and Sabrina felt well up to the task.

She dived in with relish.

"This is fabulous," she pronounced a few minutes later, swallowing another bite of filet mignon, and washing it down with merlot. "Either the New York restaurants are even better than I remember, or I didn't realize how hungry I was."

A corner of Dylan's mouth lifted. "Maybe both."

"I take it you eat here often."

"Every Wednesday night at eight o'clock sharp. Carson, Stan, and I catch up on business matters over dinner. This is our regular table. It's a great arrangement—no ringing cell phones, no meetings, no distractions. We get twice as much accomplished. We also get our weekly red meat fix."

"Sounds like a winning combo to me." Sabrina paused, toying with her food. "By the way—thanks."

"For what?"

"For dinner. And for catching me before I cracked my skull on the hospital floor."

"You're welcome on both counts." Dylan resumed eating his sirloin with gusto. "I must admit, I've sprung for lots of dinners, but the knight-in-shining-armor bit was new. I'm glad my reflexes were quick enough."

"They were. As for being a first-timer, never fear. There are two tables over there who'd love to help you practice—and perfect—your reflexes." Sabrina couldn't believe she'd said that. It must be the wine talking.

Dylan's forehead wrinkled in puzzlement. "You lost me."

"The women behind us," she explained, gesturing with her glass. "There's a table of four to my right, and a table of six to my left. They've been salivating over you since we sat down, and openly gaping since our appetizers arrived."

One dark brow rose. "I'm flattered you noticed."

"Don't be. They're not exactly subtle. I think the waiter's about to trip on their tongues." Sabrina's lips curved. "I guess this proves Melissa's right. You must be hot."

Dylan's expression remained impassive. "If that's the criteria, then you're bordering on scalding."

Sabrina blinked. "Huh?"

"A third of the men in this room are in the process of undressing you with their eyes. Another third are trying to decide if your bra unhooks in the front or the back. And the last third are already fantasizing about what positions you like best in bed, and planning how fast they can get you there." Dylan calmly helped himself to another roll.

Laughter bubbled up in Sabrina's throat. She couldn't help it. The images Dylan had conjured up were too priceless. As for what he'd said—well, it had to be the most outrageous thing anyone had ever said to her. "You're quite the cynic, aren't you?"

"Nope. Quite the realist."

"You've condemned every man in the room? Surely there must be a few exceptions."

"Not unless they're gay or dead."

Sabrina gave an astounded shake of her head. "How do I respond to that? Do I say thank you?"

Dylan's hand paused on his wine goblet. "I don't know. How do you usually respond when men say you're beautiful and sexy?"

"I'm not sure you want to know."

"Try me."

Debating whether or not to do just that and to blurt out the truth, she took another sip of merlot. She was drinking too much, too fast, and she knew it. But it was only her second—and final—glass. She had no intentions of getting sloshed. But the thin wire of tension inside her was about to snap. The day had simply been too much. And if she didn't have some relief, find some way to unwind, she'd shatter.

"Slow down," Dylan murmured, as if reading her mind. "Drink more water and less wine."

Her brows rose. "Why? Are you afraid I'll take you back to my hotel and have my way with you?"

There was that lopsided grin again. And damn if Melissa wasn't right. He was hot. *Very* hot. And very earthy. As for being her type, what was her type anyway?

She really had drunk too much wine. Time for water. She reached for her glass.

"An interesting thought," Dylan commented. "Intriguing as hell, too. But not terribly realistic."

"Really." Sabrina's chin came up, and she found she was irrationally annoyed by his assessment. "Why is that?"

He propped his elbows on the table and leaned forward, until she could see the tiny orange flecks in his eyes. "One, because knights-in-shining-armor don't take advantage of women who are tipsy and at the end of their ropes. Two, because Carson would rip my head off if I touched you. And three, because my guess is you have a lot more experience with corporations than you have with men. Am I right?"

Sabrina could actually feel the hot color flood her cheeks. "It depends on what you mean by experience. I've been hit on by the best of them."

"All of whom you shot down."

No reply.

"I guess it's time to change the subject."

"No." Sabrina shook her head. "Not until I set you straight."

"About?"

"Whatever conclusion you've come to. It's one of two. Either you've decided I'm an ice queen, or that I'm a raging feminist who likes castrating men. For the record, I'm neither."

"And, for the record, I didn't think you were."

Sabrina pushed away her glass, folding her hands firmly in front of her. "I'm not in the habit of explaining myself. I'm not even sure why I'm doing so now, except that I just met my father for the first time, and you're the closest person in the world to him. So maybe I care what you think of me. Or maybe it's because you opened up to me on the plane, and I don't think you're in the habit of doing that either. Or maybe it's just because I'm strung out and a little drunk. It doesn't matter. I'll give it to you in a nutshell."

She leaned closer. "When you're a kid, being supersmart means being alone. Going to college at sixteen when you're as unprepared as a middle-schooler means being alone, too. Jumping into the workforce at twenty and spending half your day saying no and the other half fighting to get ahead because you're bright and qualified, not because you're pretty, means being alone. And meeting an occasional man who shows a glimmer of promise at being different, only to find out he's threatened by your brains and your ambition means being alone. So, no, I don't have lots of experience with men. Frankly, it's just not worth it."

To her astonishment, Dylan gave a thoughtful nod. "Yeah, I guess it wouldn't be."

"You don't seem surprised."

"I'm not. Men are simple beings. Most are driven by either sex or power. Sometimes both. They're threatened by women they can't conquer or outshine. With you, that's next to impossible. So they walk."

Sabrina wasn't thrilled by the way that made her come off. But she knew it was meant as an observation, maybe even a compliment. Besides, she was more impressed by Dylan's insight into the male psyche, and his candor about the same. It was rare to meet a man who recognized the truth about his own species, much less one who was willing to admit it.

Lastly, she was amused by the conclusion he'd drawn. "Nice analysis," she commended. "One correction. When I said it wasn't worth it, I didn't mean for *them.* I meant for *me.*"

"I know. But it works both ways."

"I guess it does." She propped her chin on her hand. "I notice you didn't include yourself in the 'them.' So tell me, which category do you fall into? Are you driven by sex or power?"

He shrugged. "It varies. Sometimes sex, sometimes power. But I'm luckier than most. I've got a healthy ego. So I don't waste time trying to prove myself."

Sabrina started to laugh again. "Do you have any idea how arrogant you sound?"

"Why? You just described yourself as pretty and intelligent. I didn't accuse you of being arrogant. You were just stating facts. They were also gross understatements, by the way. But facts nonetheless. I'm merely doing the same about myself. Fact: I'm driven, and driven hard. By many things, sex and power included. I'm a normal male—just an unusually secure one who happens to be more complex than most."

"Anything else?"

"Attributes, you mean? Sure. I'm smart, tough, and persistent. I can also be charming, attentive, and funny. That depends on the person I'm with."

"Or on whether you're with her in or out of bed."

One dark brow rose again. "Did I say that?"

"You didn't have to."

"So now it's *you* judging *me*. Or doesn't the reciprocal apply?"

Sabrina couldn't refute that one. "You're right. I apologize."

"You're forgiven." He glanced at her now-empty goblet. "No after-dinner drink for you. But they do make an unbelievable dessert. A chocolate basket filled with white chocolate mousse and drizzled with raspberry sauce. *If* you like chocolate, that is."

"Who in their right mind doesn't?" Sabrina leaned back with a sigh. "But I'm about to burst."

"This dessert's worth bursting for. We'll split one." He signaled for the waiter. "Do you want coffee?" he asked Sabrina as the waiter hurried over. "And, yes, I remember—decaf."

"I'd love some."

Dylan ordered the chocolate basket and two coffees—decaf for her, regular for himself.

When dessert came, they stopped talking long enough to enjoy it. Dylan was dead-on. This sinful, incredible chocolate nest was worth bursting for.

"M-m-m, fabulous," Sabrina murmured, swallowing another chocolaty mouthful.

"Better than that." Dylan had been studying her over the rim of his coffee cup, an enigmatic expression on his face.

"Something on your mind?" Sabrina inquired.

"As a matter of fact, yes—since we left the hospital." He set down his cup. "I was wondering what made you change your mind."

She didn't even pretend to misunderstand. "About the tissue-typing or the transplant?"

"Both."

"I think you know the answer to that."

"Meeting Carson."

"Not just meeting him. Talking to him. Seeing how much I resemble him. Liking and respecting him, much as I tried to stay removed." She gave an acquiescent wave of her hand. "Go ahead and say I told you so, if that's what this is about. You were right. I underestimated how much this experience would affect me. I couldn't—I can't—turn my back on him." She was a little startled by the fervor of her own response. Then again, she was startled by a lot of what she'd said tonight.

"This isn't about being right," Dylan replied, interlacing his fingers on the table. "It's about my saying thank you. I'm very grateful." He met candor with candor. "Look, Sabrina, I'm not the manipulative SOB you suspected I was on the plane." Another lopsided grin when he saw the glimmer of surprise in her eyes. "You're not the only one who's perceptive. I'm a pretty good mind reader myself. Sure I knew what you thought. You were wrong. Yeah, I want you to go through with the transplant—*if* it becomes necessary. I don't think I made any secret of that. But as for the rest—every word I said about Carson was true. He's one of a kind. I think you saw that today for yourself."

"I did." Sabrina frowned. "He's fighting so hard to come back. He must know what an uphill battle it is."

"He knows. But Carson's been a fighter all his life."

A brief hesitation. "Maybe I can offer him an incentive. And I don't mean my kidney. That's a separate thing entirely."

"You want to open the door to some kind of relationship."

She shot him a quizzical look. "Do you think it would make a difference?"

"A difference?" Dylan gave an ironic laugh. "I think it would give Carson the motivation to jump out of that hospital bed and host a party."

"That's a little on the optimistic side. I'd settle for him taking a sharp turn for the better."

"I second that."

"So you don't think the idea's crazy?"

"The only thing that would be crazy would be your walking away from a chance to get to know him." Dylan's jaw tightened, as did his tone. "Then again, my perspective is different from yours. You see how much this is going to screw up your life and your family. I see how lucky you are. And frankly, no matter how much you're sacrificing, it's hard for me to feel sorry for you."

Sabrina should have been put off by the harshness of the comment. Instead, she found herself contemplating its basis. There was too much emotion behind it, too much personalization.

Mentally, she reviewed what Dylan had told her on the flight to New York. He'd said he owed Carson everything.

Just how bad was the life Carson had rescued him from?

"Now you're angry," Dylan surmised, as the silence between them stretched out. "Don't be. I'm not callous to what you're going through. This whole situation came at you out of left field. But compassion only goes so far."

"I'm not angry. And I didn't expect you to feel sorry for me. Actually, I was thinking."

"About . . . ?"

"You. Your commitment to Carson. How strong it is. How far back it goes. On the plane, you mentioned having foster parents."

"When I wasn't living on the streets, yeah."

"These foster parents—was it a bad situation?"

"Which time?"

She blinked. "How many families did you live with?"

"Five. Four of which I'd like to forget. The fifth was the couple I was living with when I met Carson. They were decent people. They were older and childless. They really wanted to make a difference; they just weren't sure how. They tried. It wasn't their fault that I was too desensitized to be reached."

He sounded dispassionate enough. But Sabrina had the feeling she was poised in the eye of the storm. "Am I overstepping?"

"Nope." Dylan took another gulp of coffee. "I told you, my past is part of another life. It doesn't bother me to talk about it. Ask whatever you want."

"The other four families—were they cruel to you?"

"They varied from screwed up to emotionally abusive. Oh, and number four was physically abusive, too. Unfortunately, that's the family I was with the longest, and during my so-called formative years. I left there with lots of scars—some physical, some mental—and lots of anger. I became the classic street kid. I racked up three juvenile arrests and more drunken brawls than I can recall. The only thing I wasn't stupid enough to get into was drugs."

Sabrina was suddenly and completely sober. "What about your biological parents?"

"What about them?"

"Did they die?"

"My mother did—eventually. At least that's what I've been told. We never got to know each other. And my father? Your guess is as good as mine. I never even met the guy."

"He took off when he heard your mother was pregnant," Sabrina deduced quietly.

"Oh, long before that. I was the product of a weekend fling in Newport, Rhode Island. My parents were college kids having some fun. My father—Jamison something-or-other; he didn't give my mother his real last name—was a spoiled rich kid looking for some action. He found it. My mother went through with the pregnancy. She even managed to get word to Jamison— one of those friend-of-a-friend-of-a-friend deals, where the last in line actually knew Jamison, and his real last name. That plan fell flat. Jamison blew her off in a hurry. So she had me, dumped me on the steps of a New York City church, then spent the next bunch of years in and out of rehab as she drugged and boozed herself to death. End of story."

Sabrina wasn't fooled by the unemotional recounting. No one emerged from a life like that without baggage. "So you never found out who your father is."

"Nor am I interested."

"I can understand why." She didn't bother pointing out that she'd said those exact same words to Dylan yesterday, when he'd confronted her with Carson's identity. Because she couldn't. The circumstances of her conception were entirely different from Dylan's. In her case, Carson had donated his sperm in an honest, impersonal business transaction. In Dylan's case, this Jamison kid had "donated" his sperm by having reckless, irresponsible sex, then walking away from the consequences without even supplying a last name. Talk about scum.

"And the name Newport—" Sabrina murmured, "I take it that's not a coincidence?"

"None at all. I needed a last name, since I didn't know my father's and had no desire to keep my mother's. So I picked one, courtesy of where I was conceived. Pretty clever, huh?"

"Clever, yes. But a pretty lousy thing to have to choose for yourself." Sabrina couldn't muster up any banter, not on this one. "No wonder you think I'm an ungrateful bitch for being ambivalent over my situation."

"I don't think you're an ungrateful bitch. You're protecting your family. I understand that. But I'm protecting mine—Carson. Maybe now you can fully understand why."

"I can." Abruptly, Sabrina found herself wondering if Dylan resented her. How could he not? Here she was, just waltzing into Carson's life when Dylan had been a constant in it for almost twenty years.

It was a sobering thought.

"Stop looking so grim," Dylan said with a tight smile. "I turned out fine. Arrogant, I think you called me."

She relaxed a bit. "I did, didn't I?"

"Um-hum. You also called me hot."

"No," she corrected, rising to the challenge. "I said you *must* be hot. That was supposition, not fact or personal opinion."

A chuckle. "Are you sure you're not an attorney?"

"Positive." Sabrina's eyes twinkled. "Attorneys are sharks."

"Ah, as opposed to management consultants who are newborn kittens."

"We are. We just insist on keeping our claws—just in case."

"I'll remember that." Dylan flashed her that sexy, crooked smile. "I wouldn't want to get scratched."

The waiter appeared at their table, clasping his hands behind his back and gazing expectantly at Dylan. "Will there be anything else tonight, Mr. Newport?"

Dylan shot a quick glance at his watch, and blinked in surprise. "It's almost eleven-thirty. When did that happen? Thanks, no, just the check."

"Very good, sir." He hurried off to prepare it.

"I didn't mean to keep you up this late," Dylan told Sabrina apologetically. "You've had a hell of a day. You need to get some sleep."

"So do you," she reminded him.

"I'll get it. First, I'm taking you back to your hotel. Don't waste your breath," he added quickly, cutting Sabrina off as she began protesting, saying she was perfectly capable of hailing a cab and seeing herself back. "I gave my word to Carson. Besides, I want to." He paused, clearing his throat. "Anyway, after that I'll swing by Ruisseau. Then I'll head home."

Sabrina's brows rose. "And I thought *I* was the workaholic."

"I just want to pick up some papers to run by Carson tomorrow. He likes to pretend he's happy leaving Stan and me in charge, but don't believe him. He's never happy unless he's in control."

That sparked a thought.

"Dylan, that reminds me, why did Carson make that request before we left? Why would he want me there when you two catch up on Ruisseau?"

"Not a clue." Dylan shrugged. "But Carson's mind works round-the-clock. He must want your input on something. Remember, he knows your professional reputation. Maybe he wants to tap your brain on how to make the transition easier for the staff while he's incapacitated. Maybe he wants to ship the whole management team up to Auburn so you can give them a refresher course. I don't know. But we'll find out tomorrow."

12

It was a local anesthetic Radison administered. But Carson had had a restless night—first, fighting the ET tube they'd reinserted to help him breathe, then thrashing around from the discomfort of the abdominal and chest tubes. So they'd given him something to relax. As a result, he found himself fading in and out during the twenty or thirty minutes that the minor surgery was taking place.

The problem was that every time he slept, he relived the shooting.

Same scenario. He, standing at the window, wondering whether or not he had a kid, waiting for Dylan to come back so they could finish work and talk about whatever was bugging his friend. Something was definitely bugging him. He'd been on edge the whole afternoon.

He never heard a sound, not even a footstep. Nothing before the pop. Then, the pain, the colors, and that sweet smell. Oh, and the carpet cleaner. He'd smelled that, too. Almost as sickening and powerful an odor as the blood. The voices of the paramedics. Losing sensation in his limbs. The cobwebs in his brain. And the pop . . . over and over. The smell . . . it wouldn't leave his nostrils. Damn, he wished he could wipe it away. But it wasn't going anywhere. And the more he slept, the more it plagued him.

Vaguely, he heard a *ping,* and he frowned, wondering if that was a sound he'd forgotten. Like something solid hitting tin. It rattled around. He turned his head, trying to clear away the haze.

"That was the bullet, Mr. Brooks." Dr. Radison's voice was calm. "Just relax. I'm stitching you up."

"Smell . . . blood . . ." He was rasping again, his throat irritated by the ET tube they'd, thankfully, removed this morning.

"Sorry, not this time. Not enough to bother even your nose. The incision's too narrow to cause much bleeding. This time we got lucky. The bullet cooperated by being close to the skin. Whatever you smell, it's not blood."

"Heard the pop . . . felt the sting . . . smelled . . . smelled . . ."

"You're just reliving the shooting. It's over now. You're on the mend." Radison paused, addressing someone else in the room. "Detective Whitman's outside the door. Call her in. I initialed the base of the bullet for ID purposes. She can bag it and take it with her." With that, he turned back to Carson. "Okay now," he said, continuing in his original soothing voice. "Another few minutes and I'll be finished here."

"What . . . time?"

"It's ten-thirty. I know you want to speak with Mr. Newport and Ms. Radcliffe. I called them both, told them you were off the respirator and would be up for visitors around noon. Until then, I want you to rest."

". . . Too much rest already." Carson blinked, cracking open his eyes in time to see a nurse leaning into the hall and gesturing to someone outside ICU. An instant later, Detective Whitman stepped into the room.

"Hey, Detective . . ." he called out, his voice slurred and gravelly. "Get your asses in gear . . . on my case, will you?" He swallowed, a corner of his mouth lifting ever so slightly. ". . . I'd hate to spread the word . . . that some amateur . . . outsmarted New York's finest. . . ."

Whitman shot him a look. "I appreciate the kick in the pants, Mr. Brooks. So will my partner. My precinct, too, for that matter. Shame alone will get us moving."

"Yeah, well, it should. . . . And move in the right direction . . . and to the right people."

Her expression didn't change. But Carson knew she'd gotten the message. "How about leaving the crime-solving to us, Mr. Brooks. You just worry about getting well. Cooperate with poor Dr. Radison. Let him do his job. And let us do ours. That's what professionals are for."

"Sometimes." Carson wasn't nodding off without getting the last word. "Other times they need help. . . ."

"This isn't one of those times."

"Glad to hear it . . . Now, let's see some proof. . . ." A challenging spark lit his eyes before they slid shut. "Find the bastard."

11:15 A.M.

Sabrina stepped out of the elevator and headed for ICU.

She knew she was early. Dr. Radison had said noon. But she'd been awake since six, her emotional overdrive having won out over her exhaustion. And, after two hours of paperwork, a long hot shower, and two essential phone calls—one business, one personal—she'd virtually run out of things to do to keep her mind occupied.

The first call had been to Melissa to tell her that she'd be in New York a few days longer than expected, and that she'd check in later today.

The second call had been to her mother. Gloria sounded as tired as Sabrina did, and almost as strung out.

She told Sabrina that she was flying to New York later today, both to be there for her daughter and for the more practical purpose of meeting with the detectives to answer their questions. *That* was the easy part. The hard part was that, on her way to the airport, she was stopping by to see her parents. They had to be told, and now, before the media got hold of the story.

Sabrina had felt like Cruella De Vil. She couldn't help it. No matter how valid her feelings were or how righteous her intentions, and no matter how much her mother swore otherwise, Sabrina felt so damned responsible for the pain and anguish she was about to cause. She loved her grandparents. She didn't want them upset or strained. And she sure as hell didn't want her mother to take the brunt of it when these old wounds were opened up—especially since the old wounds now came with new, uncertain consequences.

Her head about to explode, Sabrina had left the hotel, hopped into a cab, and made her way to the hospital.

She went straight for the coffee machine—buying a cup of the fully leaded variety this time—then veered toward the nurses' station. She'd check on Carson's condition, after which she'd wait in the lounge for Dr. Radison to call her in.

"Ms. Radcliffe?"

Sabrina turned to see Susan Lane seated alone in the lounge. She was perched at the edge of a sofa, two empty Styrofoam cups on the end table beside her, one full cup in her hand. She looked wrung out, so peaked and tired that Sabrina's heart went out to her.

"Hi." Sabrina walked over, and sat down. "You look exhausted. Have you been here long?"

"Hmm? . . ." A vague glance at her watch. "About four hours, I think. After a while, I lose track of time. One minute blends into the next."

The slight quaver in her voice made Sabrina tense. "Is everything all right? There hasn't been a turn for the worse, has there?"

"No, nothing like that." Susan put down her cup. "I guess the aftermath's just hitting me hard. It feels like months, not days, since Carson was shot. And I still can't seem to absorb it. He's such a vital man. I can't stand the thought of him lying there, fighting, not even knowing if he'll make a full recovery." She waved away her own words. "Anyway, the bullet's out. Whether or not it was the cause of the infection, we'll have to wait and see."

"From what I hear, Dr. Radison is the best. He'll figure out the source of the infection. Then he'll eliminate it."

"And then what?" Susan ran a shaky hand through her frosted blond hair. "God knows how much damage was done, how many more complications will crop up. There's also this crisis with his kidneys. I still can't believe . . ." She broke off, shot Sabrina a rueful look. "I'm sorry. You didn't come by today to hear me go on and on like that." A puzzled knit of her brows. "Actually, why did you come?"

Sabrina was half-tempted to just blurt out the truth. After all, the press would soon be all over this, so what was the point of keeping it a secret, especially from someone as close to Carson as Susan was?

On the other hand, Susan looked too out-of-it to process a story of this magnitude. And Sabrina wasn't really up for launching into a blow-by-blow recounting of her conception.

So she settled for providing a fragment of the truth. "Carson's having some kind of meeting with Dylan. He didn't supply the details, but he did ask me to participate."

"Makes sense." Susan's half-smile was tender. "I should have guessed. From what Dylan told me, you're no average management consultant. You're exceptional. And Carson? He's the heart and soul of Ruisseau. He worries about it like a father worries about his child. Not just the company, the employees, too. They're like his family. He's probably trying to think up ways to keep morale high and productivity at a peak while he's recuperating. You must have tons of experience in that area. I'm sure he's counting on that."

A father worrying about his child. That reference carved a hollow ache in Sabrina's gut, one she steeled herself against. She didn't want to go there—not now. "You're probably right," she replied instead. "And, yes, I do have experience working with teams who need guidance to stay focused and unified. Losing a team leader—even temporarily—can be disruptive to group morale and, as a result, to group performance. I'm sure Carson's well aware of that, which is why he's concerned."

"Only Carson would worry about his company when his life's on the line." Pride laced Susan's tone. "He's one of a kind."

One of a kind. Funny, those were the exact same words Dylan had used to describe Carson. What an amazing man to have such a profound effect on those he was closest to.

Sabrina inclined her head, studying Susan thoughtfully. Her devotion to Carson was obvious. As was her respect, which bordered on awe. She'd scarcely left the hospital, or Carson's side, for days. Just how serious were they?

Even as she cautioned herself that she had no right to pry, that Carson's love life was none of her business,

Sabrina heard herself ask, "Have you and Carson been together long?"

"About a year and a half." Susan didn't seem the least bit put off by the question. "We met at a charity function I was hosting. I've hosted dozens. Never have I been so impressed by a contributor before in my life."

Sabrina took a sip of coffee. "Impressed how? It doesn't sound like you're referring to the sum he donated."

"I'm not. Although the check he wrote was exceptionally generous. But contributing money is easy when you're rich. Caring enough to contribute your time, to offer your personal involvement, that's something else."

"I agree." Sabrina's interest was piqued, once again, by learning more about Carson Brooks. Each story let her glimpse another facet of him. This time, it was Carson Brooks the philanthropist. "What charity are you affiliated with, and what kind of personal commitment did Carson make?"

"YouthOp." Susan settled back as she warmed to her subject. "It's a combination mentoring and educational program for troubled, low-income kids. We're still in our embryonic stage. But we're growing. So far, we've initiated a work-study program, a big brother program, even some cultural and recreational activities. Our teenage volunteers are referred to us by schools and social services. They donate time and emotional guidance—not professional guidance, but a been-there-done-that kind of approach—to elementary school kids. In return for helping the younger ones get their heads on straight, they get opportunities to intern at our participating companies, and educational assistance—either in working toward a high school equivalency diploma or going for a college degree. The latter includes scholarship money."

"What a wonderful organization. Do you have any government funding?"

"On a local level, yes. We're still lobbying for state and federal funding. Until then, we have to rely heavily on personal and corporate contributions."

"And Carson is one of those contributors." Sabrina understood the scenario better than Susan realized. She knew what Carson had done for Dylan; this kind of thing was right up his alley.

"Not just a contributor," Susan amended, confirming Sabrina's speculation. "Carson opens the doors of Ruisseau to the teenage mentors. He offers them internships, scholarships, even chances to make pocket money. As for the little ones, he's a major supporter of the big brother program. He sponsors trips to amusement parks, movies, ball games." A grin. "He's even been known to attend a few of those ball games, when he can tear himself away from Ruisseau. Oh, and then there's the annual camping weekend."

"Carson goes camping?"

Susan chuckled at the disbelief in Sabrina's voice. "You mean the tough city boy? Yup, he sure does. The last weekend of June every year. I can vouch for it, since I'm there, too."

Okay, now that vision was even more incomprehensible than the last. The thought of Susan Lane, the ultimate cosmopolitan woman who wore every one of Gloria Radcliffe's most expensive, high-end designs, marching through muck and mire and sleeping on a cot or, better yet, in a sleeping bag? No way.

"Are we talking about camping-camping?" Sabrina tried. "You know, hiking, sleeping in layers so you don't freeze, roughing it in the great outdoors—that kind of camping? Or is there another, less rustic kind I'm unfamiliar with?"

"No, that's the one." Susan's eyes twinkled. "Gotcha, didn't I? Well, not only do I go, I help run the event. I also hike four miles, pitch a perfect tent, and build a mean campfire. *And* I cook dinner over that campfire, all weekend long. That's three whole days with no designer clothes, no soft mattress, and no makeup. Impressed?"

"Actually, stunned. You're a better woman than I. And here I was, all proud of myself because I can finish the two-hour hike at Lake Massabesic in an hour and a half, and then go on to beat any of my coworkers in a canoe race. But when I'm done, I drag myself home to a yoga class, a hot bath, and a soft bed."

Susan laughed, reaching over to give Sabrina's arm a sympathetic pat. "Before you write off those accomplishments, I should tell you that my camping weekend isn't really as big a stretch as you'd think. Despite the way I come off, and the fact that I've lived in—and loved—Manhattan for fifteen years, I was raised in a rural town in upstate New York. I can milk a cow and plant tomatoes with the best of them. Back then, it was home cooking, not restaurants, and fresh air, not air-conditioning. So a few days of roughing it doesn't phase me. Although, I must admit, I prefer AC to humidity and a toasty bed to the freezing ground any time. And bugs . . . yuck. But the kids don't know that. And I don't plan to tell them."

"Your secret's safe with me," Sabrina assured her. With another fascinated shake of her head, she reminded herself of one of the iron-clad rules of her profession: Never judge a book by its cover. If this wasn't a perfect example of that, nothing was.

Studying the fashionable woman beside her, seeing the genuine pleasure on her face as she discussed the kids she helped, another, more important thought occurred to Sabrina. "I'm really impressed," she told Susan. "Not just with Carson, with you. Clearly, you love what you do, and you do it with your heart and soul. Helping those kids gives you great joy."

"Yes, it does." Susan's lightheartedness faded, her expression turning earnest. "I feel for them. And you're right, I have a tendency to throw myself into whatever I do. That was certainly the way it was when I first started YouthOp." She paused, and it was apparent she was trying to keep herself emotionally in check. "But, the truth is, my dedication to YouthOp is no longer rooted solely in altruism. Not since I met Carson." A hard swallow. "I'm sure you're aware of Carson's background. He's been written up in every business publication in the country—the street-kid-turned-business-mogul success story. Well, everyone sees him as he is now, a secure, dynamic, successful CEO. I keep picturing him as he must have been then—a frightened kid, a troubled teen—always alone, usually on the streets. If a program like this had existed back then . . . Well, let's just say I wish someone had extended a hand to him."

"I agree." Sabrina was deeply moved by Susan's words. "But in looking at Carson now, I see more than a successful CEO. I see a very lucky man—one who has loyal friends like Dylan and Stan, and a sensitive woman like you in his life. To my way of thinking, he's got a lot to be thankful for—and to live for."

Susan's eyes misted. "That's very kind of you."

At that moment, Stan Hager strode into the lounge. He was a stocky man of medium height with steel-gray hair and tight, solemn features. He glanced around the room until he spotted them. And when he did, and recognized the emotional scene taking place before him, he went sheet-white.

He was beside them in an instant. "What is it? Is Carson worse?"

"No, no, nothing like that." Susan dabbed at her eyes. "I didn't mean to frighten you. I was just talking about Carson and getting all sentimental. His condition's status quo. Dr. Radison removed the bullet. Detective Whitman took it to ballistics. Carson's resting now."

"But you saw him this morning?"

"Yes, before the surgery."

"And he was all right?"

"He was tired, but holding his own."

"What about his spirits—were they good?"

Susan blinked, startled by the barrage of questions. But a slight smile curved her lips as she answered. "Let's see. When I walked in, he immediately started complaining to Dr. Radison about not being allowed a conjugal rights visit. If prisoners are entitled to them, why not hospital patients, was his argument."

Stan relaxed a bit. "Sounds normal for Carson."

"I thought so." Susan made a puzzled gesture. "Is there a particular reason why you're more concerned than usual?"

A brief hesitation. "He just sounded a little distracted when I called earlier. But he hadn't slept well. That was probably it."

"He did have a rough night," Sabrina confirmed, watching Carson's friend and wondering why he seemed so on edge. "I'm sure Dr. Radison left orders for him to be given something to help him relax before surgery."

"Yeah, true." Stan rubbed the nape of his neck as if it pained him. Abruptly, he seemed to realize how extreme he must be coming off, and how closely Sabrina was scrutinizing him. "Forgive my manners, Ms. Radcliffe," he said, addressing her for the first time. "I didn't even say hello."

"That's quite all right. You're worried. Everyone is.

And by the way, please call me Sabrina, both of you. I'm not big on formalities." *Another thing Carson and I have in common,* she reflected silently.

She saw her own thought mirrored on Stan's face. But aloud all he said was, "We're all on a first-name basis. So you do the same."

"Absolutely," Susan concurred. "Oh, Stan. I'm sure you're here for that meeting Sabrina was just telling me about. Dylan hasn't arrived yet, but he must be on his way. I know Dr. Radison said noon, but if Carson's still groggy, the meeting could get a late start. Is that a problem?"

"Hmm? No, it's fine."

Sabrina had the distinct feeling that Stan didn't have a clue what meeting Susan was talking about. How odd was that? The guy was COO of Ruisseau, an aggressive go-getter, and a key officer of the corporation. Why would Carson leave him out of the loop? It made no sense, especially since Stan was in the loop about everything else. Besides, the official word was that Carson was bringing Sabrina on as a management consultant, a process his COO would be actively involved in. For Stan not to be right in the thick of things would seem strange and, most likely, out of character.

"Stan?" Obviously, that was the case, because Susan looked astonished. "You are here for that meeting, aren't you?"

Realization struck, and his entire demeanor changed. "Of course. Just for the first few minutes though. Doctors orders. When I broached the subject, Radison put his foot down about three of us being in Carson's room at once. So I'll get a recap from Carson later today." He frowned. "I'm not sure what time. Whenever I wrap up with Whitman and Barton."

Sabrina leaned forward. "The detectives?"

"Yup. They're coming by my office at two-thirty." He tried to sound nonchalant. Instead, he sounded like a rubber band about to snap. "They're grilling everyone at Ruisseau. They've been trying to pin me down to do the same. We set up an official meeting. From what I've heard about these interrogation sessions from the rest of the staff, I'm not looking forward to it."

"I don't blame you," Sabrina muttered, grimacing in remembered irritation. "Everything you heard is true."

"Are you saying they interrogated *you?*" Susan looked stunned, and Sabrina wanted to kick herself for opening up Pandora's box. "Why?"

"Sabrina was with Dylan when she met Detectives Whitman and Barton." It was Stan who intervened, running welcome interference for her. "They must have heard she was a management consultant and assumed she had an established business relationship with Ruisseau. Besides, they're covering all their bases by talking to everyone Carson knows—which is what they should be doing."

"In any case, they now know Carson and I just met." Sabrina took over, shooting Stan a quick, grateful smile. "So they'll be doing their interrogating elsewhere."

Dylan walked into the lounge, followed by Dr. Radison.

"Sabrina," Dylan greeted her. "Carson's awake, alert, and asking for us."

"Ordering me to get you is more accurate." The doctor gave an exasperated shake of his head, gesturing for Sabrina to head down to ICU. "Go ahead. But don't be fooled by his bravado. He's still very weak, and he's fighting that infection. I'll give you fifteen minutes. No more than that. And if he starts to tire sooner, you'll have to leave, whether he likes it or not."

"Of course." Sabrina turned to Susan. "Did you want to see him first?"

"That's not necessary, although I appreciate your asking. Knowing Carson, he's got Ruisseau on his mind. Business now, personal time later." Susan glanced at Stan. "Didn't you say you were popping in?"

"Sure did." Stan rubbed his palms together, gazing intently at Dr. Radison. "I know you set a limit of two visitors max, but I'll just stay for two minutes."

The doctor frowned. "All right, two minutes," he conceded. "But that's it. I don't want him overwhelmed. He thinks he's Superman. He's not."

Stan's smile was tight. "Tell that to Carson."

12:20 P.M.
Midtown North Precinct

Jeannie strode over and sat down next to Frank's desk. "Mission accomplished," she announced. "Ballistics has the bullet." A frown. "Not that it'll do us much good. They already warned me that the bullet's in so-so shape. The grooves are distorted. Plus, we've got no weapon to match it with. The damn twenty-two's probably at the bottom of the East River." She groped in her pocket for the Milky Way bar she'd stashed there. Man, did she need a sugar-fix. "In any case, ballistics will do what they can, then get back to us." She tore open the candy bar wrapper, then, seeing the dark scowl on her partner's face, reconsidered and tucked the whole Milky Way, wrapper and all, back in her pocket. "Sorry. Too early for candy anyway."

"Yeah. Right." Frank yanked open his desk drawer and pulled out a Ziploc filled with neatly sliced carrot sticks. "In that case, try these instead. They're my mid-morning snack. Linda gave them to me, partly out of desperation and partly out of pity. And for a special treat, she packed a matching bag of cucumber slices for my mid-afternoon snack. I don't know how I'll contain myself until then."

Jeannie stifled a smile. "Poor Linda. You must be a bear to live with these days."

"You can say that again. The good news is, I take out most of my lousy mood on you, so I'm not as bad when I get home."

"Gee, thanks. How are the kids handling this get-in-shape program of yours?"

A proud grin spread across Frank's face. "They're the best. Matt's been working out with me at the gym twice a week. He's developing quite a set of biceps for a thirteen-year-old. And Katie—the number one chocoholic in her fourth grade class—has developed a sudden preference for fruits and vegetables. Coincidentally, she wanted—and got—the same snacks in her lunch bag today as I did. Linda offered her a devil dog, some Oreos, you name it, but she chose the carrots and cucumbers. She said she's studying food groups in school, and she wants to eat healthy."

"You've got great kids."

"Yeah, I do." He nodded, looking significantly less grumpy than he had a moment ago. "Damn if the two of them and Linda don't keep me going. And Bruno, who takes me on a half-mile tear every morning. I'm telling you, that shelter was wrong about him being part weimaraner, part Saint Bernard. The way those long legs of his shoot out from under him—he's got to be three-quarters greyhound."

Jeannie chuckled. "Maybe. Or else Matt's slipping him a little food bribe on the side—one of Linda's awe-some tacos, maybe—to make sure you get another daily workout." Satisfied that she'd taken the edge off Frank's lousy mood, Jeannie propped an elbow on his desk and met his gaze. "We've got to talk."

"How did I guess?"

"Because you know me. And you know what I'm about to say is true. Look, Frank, I know this whole Weight Watchers and gym thing is tough. I might not have firsthand experience with dieting, but I've got enough experience with eating to know that not being able to do it sucks. That doesn't excuse your hard-assed attitude yesterday."

She didn't cut him any slack, knowing he'd do the same for her if things were in reverse. What Frank needed right now was a good slap in the face, not tea and sympathy. "You went over the edge yesterday with Sabrina Radcliffe. You nearly ripped her head off, and with no justification. She's not a suspect. She's barely even a player, given the fact that she just found out Carson Brooks is her father and therefore has zero firsthand exposure to the guy."

"Well, she's certainly in the picture now. She made that crystal clear."

"True. She's a smart woman, with good eyes, good ears, and a personal stake in finding Brooks's assailant."

Frank got the picture. "You're suggesting she could be an ally. That she might help us filter through the suspects. And that I blew our chances by getting in her face at the hospital yesterday."

Jeannie didn't deny it. But she didn't rub his face in it either. "Let's just say that going that rough on her is only going to put her on the defensive. And if she dislikes or distrusts us, you can forget her lifting a finger to help our investigation."

"She won't lift a finger to help if our investigation implicates her mother, either," Frank pointed out.

There was no arguing that one. *"If,"* Jeannie stressed. "In the meantime . . ."

"Yeah, yeah, I know." Frank tossed the bag of carrots aside. "You're right. I drilled her too hard. Especially when I slammed home the idea that her mother's a possible suspect. She was royally pissed off. I'm not even sure I blame her. But, my short fuse aside, I don't think we can dismiss the possibility of Gloria Radcliffe's involvement, not after what came to light in that chat."

"I agree. She was in New York at the time of the shooting, and she sure as hell wants to keep her family's connection to Carson Brooks quiet. Of course, all that's circumstantial, and contingent on whether she knew Brooks was about to contact their daughter, and whether she can establish an alibi. If the answers to those questions are yes and no respectively, then we'd have motive and opportunity. So your reasoning was dead-on. It was your delivery that needed some toning down."

Deciding enough was enough, Jeannie waved away Frank's self-reproach, reaching for the bag of carrot sticks and taking out two—one for each of them. "Lecture over. Besides, there's a bright side to this. Your heated interrogation broadened the spectrum so it doesn't seem like we're on a witch hunt for Dylan Newport. That's the last thing I want Carson Brooks thinking. He's already not too happy with our progress, or the direction we're taking. He made that very clear to me this morning, even with a local anesthetic dulling his faculties."

Frank studied his partner intently. "You're not worried about what Brooks thinks. The truth is, you really don't believe Newport did it."

Jeannie released a harsh breath. "I told you, it doesn't

sit right with me. His commitment to Brooks is just too real, and his mind's too sharp to plan a crime in which the key circumstantial evidence points to him." Her jaw tightened. "In the meantime, we're at no loss for suspects. The list seems to grow, rather than shrink. Roland Ferguson gave off some strange vibes when we talked to him yesterday. He's also got no witness to corroborate his whereabouts Monday evening but his wife. And she's so jittery, it's like trying to make eye contact with Road Runner. I actually had palpitations when we left her house."

"Stan Hager's a nervous wreck, too," Frank murmured, lacing his fingers behind his head. "I know we've only talked to him sporadically while he's pacing around outside ICU, but he's so hyper he's about to pop. I called him this morning to set up a meeting, and he fell all over himself setting up a time. I swear he was practically vibrating. He explained it away by saying he feels the weight of the company on his shoulders, but I'm not sure I buy it. He and Brooks go back thirty years—and he's lived every one of them in Brooks's shadow. I feel like he's holding something back; I just don't know what."

"What time's our meeting with him?"

"Two-thirty."

"Okay." Jeannie glanced quickly at her watch, and gave an exasperated sigh. "In the meantime, we've got three major competitors of Ruisseau we still need to do rundowns on. And now we've got Gloria Radcliffe to check into."

"Don't forget Claude Phelps," Frank reminded her. "We've got our heart-to-heart with him in an hour. He's making a special trip in to the corporate office just to meet with us."

"I can hardly wait. Sounds like a loose cannon, too, if you ask me."

"Agreed." Frank rubbed his eyes. "As you said, the list just keeps on growing."

"Let's slash a few names." Jeannie picked up the phone. "It's time to start setting up a few more appointments and verifying a few more alibis."

13

12:35 P.M.
Mt. Sinai Hospital

The upper half of Carson's bed was at a slight incline when the three of them walked in. He looked pale, but his eyes were sharp and alert.

"Don't even think about doping me up," he warned the nurse, who was in the process of adjusting his IV. His speech was still a little slow, but it was much clearer than yesterday. And, although he spoke in staccato phrases, he wasn't nearly as winded as before. "I mean it," he reiterated, glaring at the uniformed woman as she jotted down a few notes. "No drugs. I'll live with the pain. I'm conducting business. I need to be lucid."

She lowered her clipboard and rolled her eyes, looking more frustrated than intimidated. "Fine. But after your visitors leave . . ."

"We'll discuss it then. So long." A meaningful look until, muttering under her breath, the nurse left.

"You're obviously the most popular patient in ICU," Dylan observed dryly. "They'll probably throw a huge party when you leave."

"That's the point. If I'm a pain in the ass, maybe they'll kick me out sooner." Carson's gaze shifted immediately to Sabrina. "You look better. Did Dylan feed you?"

"Fed me and delivered me to my door," Sabrina confirmed. "He obeyed your orders to a tee. And I do feel better. I'm fine."

"Liar. You're a wreck." With that, his gaze shifted to Stan. "Morning, Hager. Or is it afternoon? Either way, I didn't expect you. Have you been hovering around, too, making sure I don't crap out on you? Because I'm not planning to die. So relax."

"Thanks for the reassurance." Stan didn't miss a beat. "Now I can sleep tonight. And here I thought I had to wait for the doctor to give me a prognosis. Stupid me. As for hovering around, don't flatter yourself. I dropped by because the coffee's good here, and I'm too lazy to brew my own."

"Well, buy yourself a cup and get over to Ruisseau. They need you. I don't. Christ, between you, Dylan, and Susan, I have three damned mothers."

Listening to this exchange, Sabrina's lips twitched in spite of herself. "Are you always this obnoxious?" she asked Carson.

"Only when I'm not running the show."

"Which happens about as frequently as a solar eclipse," Stan clarified. He patted Sabrina's shoulder in a paternal gesture. "You'll get used to him. We all do. Just take him with a grain of salt. His bark's a whole lot worse than his bite. Especially with you, I have a strong feeling."

"Thanks for the pep talk." Sabrina was fascinated by the change in Stan. Gone was the man who was so taut he was practically vibrating. This man was relaxed, witty, comfortable as he bantered with his oldest friend.

Interesting.

" 'Bye, Hager," Carson told him purposefully. "No need to stay. You know what this meeting's about. You know what I'm proposing. You can guess why. But Sabrina needs to hear the details first. I obviously want my attorney present, too. Problem is, Radison's being a stickler about the two-visitors-max rule. He says I'm weak and can't handle too much stimuli." A wry grin as Carson stopped to catch his breath. "I told Radison you were too boring to count as stimuli. But he wasn't buying. So, beat it. I've got limited time to get this show on the road. Check in with me later."

"That's what I planned," Stan agreed, totally unruffled by Carson's ribbing and, more significant, clearly aware of the agenda for this meeting. Okay, so Sabrina had been wrong. Whatever Carson was about to get into, Stan was privy to it. So why had he acted so out of touch when Susan brought up the subject of the meeting earlier? And why the complete mood swing?

Evidently, she had yet to figure out what made Stan Hager tick.

"I wasn't even going to stay this long," he was continuing. "But Susan was asking questions about today's powwow, wondering why I wasn't in the thick of things. I didn't know how to play it, since I had no idea if you'd told her the truth about Sabrina yet."

"No. Not yet."

"I figured as much. So I appeased whatever doubts she had by making myself part of the meeting. Which is why I'm poking my head in for the opening remarks."

Carson nodded. "Good move. Thanks."

"Sure." Stan paused, scrutinizing Carson for a moment, and Sabrina saw a muscle working in his jaw, as if he were fighting some internal emotional battle. "You're still wiped out," he pronounced. "Don't overdo. That's not just the doctor's orders; they're mine." He cleared his throat, his composure restored. "I have a vested interest in your getting well. Running the company without you is a pain. It's cutting into my social life."

Carson's brows rose. "Two ex-wives and work. You call that a social life?"

"No. That's why I need time to get one. So start healing, fast."

"I'm working on it. Now get going. I just lost three of my fifteen minutes."

"Only two. And I'm on my way." He slanted a look of mock sympathy at Sabrina. "Try to hang in there."

"I'll do my best," she assured him.

The instant Stan was gone, Sabrina turned to Carson. "What's this about? What details do I need to hear? What is it you're proposing? And why am I the reason Dylan's here in his official capacity?"

"Sit," Carson replied, pointing to a chair. "You, too," he ordered Dylan.

"Did you know more about this meeting than you let on?" Sabrina muttered to Dylan as they got themselves settled.

"Nope." Dylan seemed as unruffled as Stan had been. "But getting blindsided by a punch and jumping up to come out swinging is business as usual with Carson." He yanked out a pad. "All set."

Carson adjusted his pillow, waving away Sabrina's offer to help. "That's not what I need you for." Impatiently shifting his weight so the tubes and drains caused him the least amount of discomfort, he grimaced in annoyance, then settled back, his hard stare fixed on Sabrina. "What I need you for, is Ruisseau. I've got to make provisions. Because I don't know when—or *if*—I'm getting out of here."

He cut off Dylan's immediate and vehement objection. "Don't interrupt me. I've got to talk before I run out of steam. And, Dylan, let's cut the bullshit. I'm fighting like hell. But that bullet did a good job on my insides.

My intestines, my lung, my kidneys—that's a lot of organ damage. There's plenty of room for complications. I've got to get things in order, just in case. That's where Sabrina comes in."

Sabrina was as thrown by Carson's grim assessment as Dylan was. It was the first time she'd heard him allude to the possibility that he might not make it. Somehow, she'd assumed he'd never considered losing this battle. He was a fighter, a survivor.

He'd pull through. He *had* to pull through.

She swallowed, hard. "You're a strong man, Carson. You're not going to die."

"Glad to hear it. But you're not God. And, even if I do live, I'm not getting out of here anytime soon. I won't be at my desk. I won't be running my company." He took a few more breaths. "No matter what happens, Ruisseau needs to be protected."

"You have Dylan and Stan for that."

"You're my daughter."

It was the first time he'd actually said those words. And Sabrina felt them like a blow to her gut. "Carson . . ."

"Hear me out," he commanded. "Then you can blow me off if you want to. This has nothing to do with Dylan or Stan. Not personally or professionally. Stan's my COO. He's also my oldest friend. He'll continue to be both. Dylan's my corporate counsel. He's also my surrogate kid. Our bond's unique. That won't change. Neither will Dylan's place in my life or my company. Satisfied?"

Sabrina sucked in her breath. "I don't know what I am, or what you want of me," she replied, totally stymied as to where Carson was going with this. "I assumed you wanted to utilize my consulting expertise. Actually, I didn't even assume that. I thought that whole story was a smoke screen, one Dylan had invented to explain my being here. Then you asked me to sit in on this meeting. Now you're implying you want me to take on some major role in helping to protect Ruisseau. I'm not qualified. . . ."

"You sure as hell are." Carson pushed himself up a bit more, trying to find a position that would help him get out his words faster and with more fervor. "You've fixed companies that are in the Dumpster. Mine's flying high. You understand the corporate sector. You're skilled at strategic planning. You're creative and proactive, and you've got the guts to use those qualities. You're a born leader. And you know what makes people tick. That's essential in understanding consumer products marketing, as well as corporate politics. You're smart. You're experienced. And you've got my blood flowing through your veins—right down to my heightened olfactory sense. Who better than you to see Ruisseau through this crisis?"

Sabrina's adrenaline had begun to pump. It wasn't the flattering portrayal, although it was certainly nice to hear that Carson thought so much of her. It was the reason for his blow-by-blow delineation of her assets. It had been done very deliberately, not to praise, but to lead up to something. And whatever that something was, every instinct told her it was big. Very big.

"What did you have in mind?" she questioned.

A hint of a smile. "Intrigued, huh?"

"Curious," she corrected. "Wary, but curious."

"You sense a challenge. And your adrenaline's picking up, no matter how much you wish it wouldn't. You can't help it. Like I said, it's in your blood."

"Carson, stop baiting me. What is it you want me to do?"

"On a simple, superficial level? Exactly what you said. Come on as a management consultant. Work with Stan. Assess the major issues facing Ruisseau. Set up an action plan for each key initiative. Drive the company forward. I'll pay you double your normal rates, to cover the inconvenience of keeping you away from CCTL for so long. Speaking of CCTL, I'd suggest you turn things over to that consultant you hired away from the snooty firm in L.A.—Deborah Ogden. Between her and that other winner you hired—Mark Weiss—they can run things for a few months. Whatever help they need, your assistant Melissa Andrews can provide. As for you, you can fly home weekends, be there Friday through Sunday—if you take Ruisseau projects to work on while you're in Auburn, and on the plane. You'll have to burn the candle at both ends. Because you're going to be busting your ass for me. I don't tolerate less."

The lengthy speech obviously taxed Carson's strength, because he finished by leaning back against his pillow to rest.

Sabrina was speechless—something that was getting to be a habit when she was around this man. He'd done major research on CCTL, that was for damned sure. "Exactly how much do you know about my company?"

"Just as much as I expect you to know about mine." He shut his eyes for a moment, trying to hold on to his rapidly ebbing strength. "Dammit," he muttered. "Goddammit."

"Carson, maybe that's enough." Dylan spoke up for the first time. "You said your piece. We've only got a few minutes left before Dr. Radison comes in and tosses us out anyway."

"Screw Radison." Carson forced his head upright. "Sabrina, you asked what I want you to do. The consulting part just skims the surface. The rest is more substantial, and more complicated. I want to make you an officer of the company. Specifically, president. Dylan can draw up the paperwork. He and Stan can also be the only ones who know about the appointment, if that's the way you want it. I told you yesterday, I'm not pushing you to announce who you are. Wait as long as you want." Weakly, he angled his head toward Dylan. "There'll be legal loopholes, like how does she vote at board meetings if no one knows she's president. Maybe by proxy. I don't know. That's your job. Come up with something. But I want her in there . . . if she'll do it." A heavy-lidded stare at Sabrina. "Will you?"

You could have heard a pin drop in the room.

Sabrina couldn't begin to process Carson's request. Talk about a bombshell. She'd expected something major—but this?

Abruptly, she stood up and turned away, staring at the bare wall across the room. She was shaking, too overwhelmed to speak. She'd had it. This just might be the straw that broke the camel's back.

"Like I said, you're a wreck." There was no trace of sarcasm or banter in Carson's voice when he spoke, only comprehension and regret. "I'm sorry. You're on overload. You don't need more pressure. Certainly not from me. I wish I had more time . . . that I could let you think this through. Whoever shot me didn't give me that luxury. I need to take care of Ruisseau—for now, maybe for good. So I'm asking—will you do it?"

"I . . ." Sabrina edged a sideways glance at Dylan, who was scrutinizing her closely, his expression nondescript. "I don't know. I can't just give you an answer at the drop of a hat. It's too huge a—"

"Which part's the problem?" Carson's voice was

raspy now, and he was starting to sound winded. "I assume it's not the consulting."

"No. No, of course not."

"Okay, then, is it the lifestyle—having two residences and a weekly commute? Is it being away from CCTL? Having a vested interest in two companies?" A sharp intake of breath. "Or is it being tied to me? If it is, say so. You've got the right."

"That's not it." She turned around to face him, this time making no move to hide the tears in her eyes. "I *want* to know you. I was going to bring that up myself. Ask Dylan. We talked about it last night. You just happened to beat me to it. As for making me an officer of Ruisseau, I . . . I'm touched and I'm flattered. And the challenge—you're right. I'd be lying if I didn't admit it excites me. But the enormity of what you expect—I'm not sure I can deliver. A long-term consulting project I could manage no problem. But the presidency of a company, *your* company, that's not just a temporary thing. Even if I agreed to stay at Ruisseau until you were well and back at the helm—which you *will* be—I couldn't make the arrangement permanent. It would involve my being in New York five days a week, reducing CCTL to less than my number one priority. I can't do that. CCTL is my baby, the same way Ruisseau is yours."

"We could work something out. . . ." Carson was forcing out the words. "Half week here . . . half week there . . . any arrangement we could . . . Don't say no."

"Carson, please—stop," Sabrina burst out. "Not for me, for you. You're exhausted. Don't talk. Just rest. Let me think."

She raked both hands through her hair, her mind racing wildly. Arbitrary thoughts ran through her head. President of Ruisseau—my God. It was the opportunity of a lifetime. She'd be working for a genius—a genius who was her father. She'd have a chance to get to know him, to share in his vision, to be part of a company he'd created and raised from infancy. And she wouldn't have to give up her own growing company. CCTL would still be hers; Carson had as much as said so. He understood the way she felt about her "baby." He'd been in that position himself.

Her presence at CCTL over the next few months was already in question, thanks to Carson's immediate health crisis. She was hell-bent on seeing through her kidney-compatibility process. And that meant time. To begin with, the tissue-typing results wouldn't be back for a week. Even if she flew home in the interim, she'd return to New York once the results were in. Then, if they showed she was the best donor match, she'd need to be examined by a nephrologist, go through a battery of tests. Finally, if the transplant became a reality, she'd be out of commission for at least a month. In which case, CCTL would have to do without her.

She'd made contingency plans for these circumstances as she'd tossed and turned in her bed last night. The funny thing was that her line of thinking had been identical to Carson's, only shorter-term. She'd take a leave of absence until she recovered from the surgery. During that time, she'd leave Deborah in charge, with Mark as backup and Melissa in the wings. When it became feasible, she'd go in part-time, handling as much as she could by phone and e-mail.

Why couldn't the same plan work on a long-term basis? She'd physically be at CCTL every week for three-to-four day stretches—two days of which would be weekends, when Ruisseau was closed anyway. During that time, she'd run the show at CCTL and conduct her

workshops. The rest of each week she'd spend at Ruisseau, learning the ropes, sharing her expertise, and working her butt off. Deborah would be her point person at
CCTL. If any problem arose, she could just pick up the
phone and call. By the same token, there were always
telephones and e-mail for client contact, so Sabrina
would never truly be out of touch.

It was a feasible solution.

Maybe. Maybe not. Oh, it was doable for a while,
even a long while. But for good? What if she couldn't
swing it? What if there was an overlap in crises, and both
companies needed her at the same time? What if she
couldn't handle a steady diet of Manhattan pollution, or
tolerate the corporate politics she'd gladly left behind?

Then there was her family. Her mother was due here
this afternoon. How would she take this? She knew how
ambitious Sabrina was. She'd understand her daughter's
excitement over the opportunity she was being offered.
But what if the scandal leaked out that much sooner because of Sabrina's very visible presence at Carson's side?
And if she knew for a fact that it would—should that influence her decision? What if her grandparents took this
as some kind of betrayal?

"Forget the what-if's. . . . Name your terms. . . ." It
was as if the man could read her mind. "I won't . . . lock
you in . . . to anything irrevocable. . . . You can get out . . .
if you want to. But it's my legacy . . . and so are you." He
licked his lips. "There's one more thing I have to dump
on you . . . before you decide."

"I don't think I can deal with any more."

"You have to. It's C'est Moi. The scent's a breakthrough. . . . Momentum strong . . . Someone has to keep
it going, build on it . . . and expand the line. That someone is you. You'll have to know the formula. Can't let it

die with me . . . I'll tell it to you now . . . explain it step by step. But verbally. No paper. You'll have to memorize it. And no one can know about this. I want you safe from whoever went after me."

Sabrina was past reeling and into numb. The formula for C'est Moi? She'd done enough reading to know the unique cloak of secrecy that surrounded Ruisseau's newest fragrance. Carson had invented it. And only he knew what went into it. If he was going to share that information, it should be with someone who could translate formula into fact, use it to Ruisseau's advantage. Blood relation or not, she was completely unqualified to fill that role. "Carson, that's definitely a mistake. I'm not a chemist. I wouldn't be able . . ."

"Doesn't matter . . . We have chemists. Stan and Dylan will choose the right one to replace me . . . if it comes down to that . . . and he or she will work with you. But your sense of smell . . . and your gut instincts . . . you'll know where we need to go from here. You'll have to queue up timetables for other C'est Moi spin-offs after the men's version takes off. . . . And marketing . . . you're trained . . . and smart. You'll know what to do. . . . You'll see."

He eased his head over to give Dylan a pained look. "After they find the shooter . . . I'll share the formula with you, too. If I'm not around anymore, Sabrina will do the honors. I want both my kids to have that formula. . . . But, right now, it would be a mistake . . . for you to have it. Those damned detectives . . . I'd be giving them more ammo to use against you. . . . If you knew something they saw as motive for you to get rid of me . . . they'd jump on it. Better if you don't know, for now." He started coughing, and he moaned with pain, his hand going reflexively to his chest.

"Carson . . ." Sabrina took two steps toward him.

He waved her away. "I'm . . . fine . . . just . . ." Another hard wince.

"That's it." Dylan bolted to his feet. "This meeting is over." He turned to Sabrina, his expression grim, his entire body taut. "I'm going to see what the hell's keeping Dr. Radison. That gives you and Carson a few minutes alone. Decide what you want to do, about the appointment and the formula. If you've got memorizing to do, do it fast. When I get back, we're leaving. Carson's getting some sleep, if I have to call that nurse back in here to add knock out drops to that morphine drip."

Dylan was visibly freaked out. It didn't take a shrink to see that. Whether it was over Carson's decisions—which had to have shocked him as much as they had her—or over the bleak possibilities conjured up by Carson's assessment of his medical condition, Sabrina wasn't sure.

She merely nodded, staring dazedly after Dylan as he left.

"Sabrina . . ." She turned to see Carson studying her expectantly, gritting his teeth against the pain. "He'll be okay. . . . Give him space. And give *me* your answer."

She should need time. Leaping before she looked wasn't her thing. When it came to decisions of magnitude, she acted only after a thorough analysis of the facts. And this was the heaviest decision she'd ever had to make.

"Yes," she heard herself say. "My answer's yes. I'll do it."

Relief flashed across his face, easing the tight lines of pain. "I'm glad," he returned, a deliberate understatement. "Thank you. Although, if you're made of . . . what

I think you are, I think that one day . . . you'll be thanking me."

Sabrina sidestepped that one, at least for now. Besides, she had another matter on her mind—one that needed to be addressed before this meeting ended. "What about Stan? Where does he fit into all this?"

"Same as always . . . Runs the company's day-to-day operations . . . In on almost everything . . . But not the formula . . . He's got a crappy memory. . . . Can't retain a damned thing . . . Forgot his first wife's birthday four years in a row . . . probably why they're divorced."

"Got it." Sabrina wasn't up for humor. Not when beads of perspiration were dotting Carson's forehead, showing her how much he was suffering. Further, she sensed there was more to this issue with Stan than he'd let on. "So you're not giving him the formula. And my guess is, you don't want me, or eventually Dylan, to clue him in to the fact that you gave it to us."

A raspy chuckle. "You're good. Damned good. And you're right. I don't."

"Which is the real reason why you didn't want him staying till the end of this meeting."

"Um-hum. Not lack of trust . . . Meant it about his memory . . . But he wouldn't believe that. . . . He'd take it the wrong way. . . . Stan's insecure enough. . . . Don't want to add to it. Easier to say it was personal . . . about you coming on as president. He knows . . . you're my daughter. . . . Understands what I want for you . . . what you can bring to Ruisseau . . . No resentment there . . . Don't worry."

"I wasn't. Not about me."

"Not about anything . . . It's all under control."

So *that* was the missing link. Stan Hager was insecure. And insecurity made people act in strange ways, do strange things. Carson was far from naive. Regardless of what he said, how lightly he touched on—and seemed to dismiss—the subject of Stan's low self-esteem, he was aware of its significance. He didn't want to bad-mouth Stan. That much was clear. But what was also clear, at least to Sabrina, was that Carson recognized that Stan ran the risk of being a loose cannon. Bottom line? He was protecting his friend *and* his company.

"The basis for Stan's insecurity—is it anything I should know about?" she asked carefully.

"Nothing sinister . . . or specific . . . We'll discuss it next time. . . . Right now, all we've got time for is the formula."

Sabrina placed her hand on Carson's arm. "Are you sure you're up for this?"

"Yes."

"Just as important, are you sure this is what you want?"

"That depends—are you sure it's what *you* want?"

She met his gaze, pain-filled but intense. Was she sure? Very. She didn't know why, but somehow she was.

Slowly, she nodded. "Yes. I'm sure." An attempt at a smile. "As sure as I'll ever be. My entire world's been turned upside down these past few days. I don't expect it to right itself anytime soon."

"With me for a father? . . . And a boss? . . . Don't count on it." With great effort, Carson raised his arm, sticking out his hand to seal things in a handshake. "So you're on board. Welcome to the team."

"Yes, I'm on board," she echoed. "And thanks." She met his grip, feeling a sense of comfort at the physical contact. Was that some unfathomable instinct because he was her father? Or was it just relief that he had enough strength left to master a handshake?

"Go to Ruisseau tomorrow morning. . . ." Carson instructed. "Dylan will have the paperwork done by then. . . . Stan will introduce you around. . . . Nothing formal . . . Just a top-notch consultant who's there to help Ruisseau stay on track . . . Won't make an official announcement till you're ready . . . Anyway, come see me afterward. . . . I want your take on my people . . . my company. . . ."

"Only if you promise to be at the top of your game when I report in," Sabrina returned lightly. "Meaning you rest, follow doctor's orders, and stop causing trouble. Too much to ask? Tough." She forced a teasing smile to her lips as she echoed what he'd said to her earlier. "You're going to be busting your ass for me. I don't tolerate less."

A tight grin permeated his physical distress. "I'll keep that in mind. . . . Now let's get to the formula. . . ."

"Right." Sabrina wet her lips, focusing all her energies on her powers of concentration. "All I know is that it's based on human pheromones, right?"

"Pheromones and a compound that enhances male receptivity to those pheromones . . ." he clarified. ". . . Variations in men's brand, obviously . . . But both are blends of natural essences and synthetic chemicals. . . . Musk. Cinnamon and ginger . . . Orange. Three floral scents . . . Other stuff. I'll give it to you exactly. And I'll have Dylan and Stan run you over to the lab later today. . . . You can check out R&D firsthand. . . . Now listen . . . and lock what I tell you into your brain."

14

Ruisseau Fragrance Corporation

Stan stood at his office window, staring out at the line of buildings across West 57th Street, wondering if anyone in any of those jaillike grids called offices could possibly be as strung out as he was.

He felt like a goddamned hamster in a maze. Well, he was tired of running. Tired of scrambling to stay ahead. Tired of looking over his shoulder. Tired of keeping secrets and doing damage control. Tired of trying to be more than he was.

And most of all, tired of answering these detectives' questions.

"Mr. Hager?" It was Detective Whitman again, shoving another question down his throat. She and her partner had been at it for almost an hour, right on the heels of raking poor Claude over the coals. Claude had emerged from the interrogation looking like a broken sparrow, making Stan's guts twist with a sense of foreboding as he tried to imagine what they had in store for him.

Well, now he knew. They'd poked, prodded, and probed into every last facet of his life. They knew about his two divorces, his personal habits, and his professional rise at Ruisseau. They'd delved into his take on every corporate officer, every company executive—from upper management down to middle management—then moved on, dissecting every one of Ruisseau's divisions, trying to determine who might have even the slightest beef with Carson Brooks. From there, they'd explored the in-house clashes Carson had been involved in—even on the most peripheral level—over the past month or so, including such trivial incidents as when he'd demanded that the custodial staff switch rug cleaners.

Then came reviewing Ruisseau's chief competitors, a topic that always made Stan's guts twist. He could tell Whitman and Barton had done their homework. They'd gotten Jason Koppel's name from Carson, and they'd gone over to Merrill Lynch to meet with him. They knew exactly which companies' profits had taken a downslide since C'est Moi hit the market. They ran through each of them with Stan, questioning him about which high-level execs he knew at each company and whether any of those people were, in his opinion, unbalanced or over the edge.

He was a fine one to ask.

Oh, they'd tackled every subject imaginable, concentrating particularly on him—his state of mind, his feelings about Carson, his status at Ruisseau. Over and over, they came back to the fact that he had no alibi for Monday evening, that he'd *allegedly* been alone in his apartment, sleeping off a seventy-hour workweek, when Carson was shot. They kept harping on how difficult it must be to stand in your best friend's shadow, day after day, year after year, in all facets of your life.

The one thing they *hadn't* done was issue any accusations. Not yet. But after fifty-five minutes, they were working their way there. In fact, judging from the more intense tone and personal direction of the interrogation these past few minutes, they were about to go for the jugular.

Sure enough, Whitman confirmed his suspicions by starting the process. "You and Mr. Brooks go back thirty years. That's longer than any other employee—actually any other person in Carson Brooks's life."

Give the woman a cigar, he thought. "That's true." He turned around to face her, folding his arms across his chest and resupplying his history with Carson—the safest course of action he could take. "Like I told you before, we met at City College. I was taking classes there when I wasn't doing odd jobs to pay the rent. Carson was cleaning offices, but making extra cash tutoring college freshmen."

"I didn't need a refresher, Mr. Hager. I know how you two met." Whitman's gaze bore straight through him.

"Yeah. It's unbelievable," Barton muttered. "I still can't get over it. A high school dropout tutoring kids who had more education than he did."

Stan's jaw tightened. "Carson's a genius. He could have taught college-level chemistry when he was in eighth grade. And he didn't drop out of high school; he was kicked out for being a smart-ass. He got his diploma the year we met, not that he needed it. He knew more, and taught others more, than any professor ever could. He made his first million, actually several million, by age thirty. Oh, and for the record, he never lied to the kids he tutored. They knew he didn't have any formal education. But guess what? When they saw those A's on their exams, they didn't care."

Barton crossed one leg over the other, his gaze narrowing a bit. "That was admiration you heard, not censure, Mr. Hager. Why are you so defensive? More important, why are you so jumpy? You've been a wreck since we walked in. Actually, longer. Since this investigation began."

"You're right. I have. Look, Detective, my oldest friend's been shot. His life's hanging in the balance.

That's thrown me for a loop. On top of that, I'm operating on zero sleep. When I'm not at the hospital, I'm here, pushing to run this company the way Carson would want it run. I think that's grounds to be on edge, don't you?" He didn't wait for an answer. "So tell me, what else do you want to know?"

"What I want, is to get back to my original question," Whitman responded, like a damned dog with a bone. "Since you know Mr. Brooks for so long, can you think of anyone from your past who might have it in for him?"

With a half-laugh, Stan shook his head. "You're joking. We weren't exactly high-visibility types. We were dirt poor, Detective. Punks who were lucky to afford a room. We shared a hole-in-the-wall in those days—a cockroach-ridden dump in a downtown tenement that was barely big enough to hold two mattresses and a lamp. Carson didn't have a pot to piss in. Believe me, no one viewed him as a future candidate for making it big. So if you're picturing him being stalked by someone from our youth, someone who bided his time in the hopes of making a windfall, you can forget it."

"That's not what I was picturing. But, fine. Let's play this your way. What about later? Thirty years is a long time, providing lots of opportunity to meet people and form relationships."

"Most of that time was filled by the blood, sweat, and tears of building Ruisseau. That doesn't leave much time for forming close personal attachments. There were women, if that's what you're asking. Plenty of them. But never anyone serious. Never anyone who'd stand to gain anything if Carson were out of the way."

"Interesting the way you keep getting back to money," Whitman noted. "There are other reasons to kill someone, you know."

"A woman scorned, you mean." Stan tried that route, shrugging away the idea. "First of all, Carson's not the sentimental type. He doesn't do the head-over-heels-in-love thing. Never has, never will. I think that's why he never married. He's already married—to Ruisseau. He also doesn't mislead women. They know where they stand. It's Ruisseau first, sex and recreation second. So none of his ex-lovers would be home nursing a broken heart. It doesn't fit. Besides, they've all been out of the picture for a long time now. Carson and Susan have been exclusive for well over a year. She's nuts about him, and he seems very happy with her. So, no, I don't think this is a spurned-lover deal."

"I don't remember suggesting it was." Whitman leaned forward, staring him down in a way that said she'd grown tired of his evasion tactics. "Actually, my thoughts were going in an entirely different direction. I was wondering if there's anyone you can think of who might carry a grudge against Mr. Brooks? Anyone who's known him for years and has watched his success explode like wildfire—with women, with business, with pretty much everything he's touched? Anyone who might have felt cheated by that success?"

"Anyone, Detective? Or me?" Stan went for the direct confrontation approach, slapping his palms on his desk. "Why don't you ask me straight out? Better yet, I'll save you the trouble. Do I hold a grudge? No. For what? Carson's worked for everything he has. No one handed it to him. Sure, he's got a lot going for him, but he never took the easy way out, and he never forgot his friends. Which brings me to your next question: Do I feel cheated? Nope. Carson was always incredibly generous with me. When he started Ruisseau, he took me right along with him. When the company's profits skyrocketed, so did mine.

"Now, I'll answer the questions you're about to ask. Am I grateful? Yup. More than you can imagine. Have I ever wished I could trade places with Carson? You bet. He's got it all, and only a fool wouldn't wish for the same. Would I kill him to get it? Not for all the money, power, or position in the world. Oh, and one more thing. I have no desire to be CEO of Ruisseau, even if Carson asked me to be. I'm collapsing under the weight of that position right now, and it's just a temporary arrangement. I've got more than enough on my plate being the company's COO. My job's exciting, challenging, and rewarding. I like coming to work each day. I've got a seven-figure income, a retirement plan that'll keep me living in style for the rest of my life, the respect of my colleagues, and the pleasure of working with people who are also my friends. Does that about cover it?"

"If you say so." Whitman put away her pen. "Except for one thing—you don't happen to own a gun, do you?"

"No," he bit out.

"Okay, Mr. Hager. I think that's enough." Barton rose, exchanging a quick glance with his partner. "We'll be on our way now. If you think of anything else, you know where to find us. And if we need you, we know where to find you."

Stan waited until the detectives had gone. Then, he shut the door behind them, crossing over to drop into his plush leather chair. He propped his elbows on his desk, put his head in his hands. He should feel relieved. He didn't. He was far from out of the woods. Any one of several people could tip the scales against him. Starting with his ex-wives. If Whitman and Barton talked to either Lily or Diane, it was highly possible something would be said to raise their antennae.

And then there was Ferguson. He was the biggest potential liability of all. If he caved under pressure, or got scared enough, he might slip. One wrong word and Dick and Jane Tracy would come rushing back over here. Then what would he say? How could he explain the situation without making it look as seedy as it was? And how could he keep the detectives from making the assumption that, if he'd gone this far, he'd have the motive and the incentive to go the rest of the way?

Yanking open his drawer, Stan shoved aside a copy of the memo from Pruet calling an emergency meeting in Paris, and pulled out the bottle that contained his ulcer medication. His insides were on fire. They hadn't stopped burning since Monday. He popped a pill in his mouth, then went over to his office's fully stocked bar, pouring himself a glass of mineral water. He threw back his head, swallowed his medication in two hard gulps.

Talk about paying for his mistakes in spades. He was doing that. Every day of his life.

Being second best sucked.

7:40 P.M.
Plaza Athenée

Gloria Radcliffe arrived at the hotel in time to check into her room, freshen up, and go downstairs for a cocktail. She needed one.

The visit with her parents had gone pretty much as expected. They were angry, shocked, worried, and a few other choice adjectives they'd tossed her way.

She was weary. She was also worried. She'd reached Sabrina by cell phone when her plane landed. Her daughter had visited Carson Brooks twice that day. She'd then been whisked away by limo to a business meeting in Englewood Cliffs, and was now on her way back to Manhattan. Riding with her was Ruisseau's COO and its corporate counsel—Dylan Newport, the man who'd brought Sabrina to New York in the first place. Sabrina had asked Gloria to meet her at the hotel around nine o'clock for a late dinner, at which time she'd fill her in.

Well, that left an hour and twenty minutes. Gloria could spend it agonizing over things she couldn't change and wasn't privy to, or she could take a proactive step that had to be taken sooner or later.

Sooner was better for the psyche than later.

She turned on her cell phone, punched in the number the operator provided.

Two rings, and an answer. "Midtown North."

"Yes." Gloria glanced down at the piece of paper where she'd written the names Sabrina had given her a short while ago. "I'm trying to reach either Detective Whitman or Detective Barton. This is Gloria Radcliffe."

7:45 P.M.
Midtown North Precinct

Jeannie leaned across Frank's desk and drew a line through Claude Phelps's name. "That's another one down," she pronounced. "He might be a twitching nut job, but he's got ninety witnesses who were with him and his wife at his thirty-fifth wedding anniversary celebration at the Marriott Marquis on Monday evening." She tossed down her pen. "So that leaves us with one less suspect."

Frank munched on a cucumber slice. "Maybe I'm getting soft because I'm such a nut job myself these days, but I felt sorry for the guy when we questioned him. He obviously knew we'd heard horror stories about him twenty times over. That made him even more neurotic. I think he was half-expecting us to read him his rights on the spot."

"Yeah, I felt the same way. Funny thing is, nut job or not, I'm not surprised he has an alibi. Or a family who loves him, for that matter. There's something endearing about Claude Phelps, hyper though he is."

"As opposed to Stan Hager." Frank polished off another cucumber slice. "He's a wreck, too, but he's a hell of a lot smoother about it than Phelps is."

Jeannie nodded. "Hager gave us quite a runaround. He desperately wanted to keep the spotlight off himself. Now the question is, why? Is it because he's afraid of looking bad—to Brooks, to the company, maybe even to the industry as a whole if some nosy business reporters start speculating—or is it because he really has something to hide?"

"I'm on the fence on that one," Frank replied with a shrug. "The whole staff of Ruisseau speaks highly of him. That includes the handful of employees in their European operations. Hager commands a great deal of respect everywhere. And his loyalty to Brooks, and to the company, is undisputed by anyone—across the board. Still, just in case we decide to dig deeper, I made a couple of calls, got us the scoop on Hager's exes. Wife number one—Lily—remarried a dozen years ago. She lives on Long Island, with her husband and their ten-year-old son. Wife number two—Diane—decided her huge alimony checks were the only permanent fixtures she needed in her life. She's cruising the Greek Isles now, with her latest lover. She's due back in New York next week."

"A woman after my own heart," Jeannie noted wryly.

"I kind of guessed that would be your reaction." Frank resealed the remaining cucumber slices in their Ziploc.

"Which is why we both know the way this should play out, if we go the route of talking to the ex-wives."

"Sure do." A corner of Jeannie's mouth lifted. "You'll take the lead with Lily and I'll do the same with Diane. That gives you the family man angle, and me the woman-to-woman thing—two liberated divorceés living high on the hog." Jeannie grimaced. "Except in my case, it's minus the high on the hog. I knew I should have married for money. Then, when the marriage ended, I'd be set for life." She dug in her pocket, plucked out the Milky Way bar she'd shoved away earlier, and frowned as she saw it looked rather the worse for wear. "Great. Instead, I get squashed candy and a cranky partner."

"You want sympathy? Go somewhere else." Frank was studying the list of suspects. *"Any* candy— squashed, stale, even moldy—beats cucumber slices. As for your partner, I've been a puppy dog since you ripped into me this morning. So eat your Milky Way and count your blessings."

Frank's forehead creased in concentration. "We've eliminated most of the employees at Ruisseau's competition. As for Susan Lane, she's clean. Not only was she on her way to the U.S. Open when the shooting took place, she's got no motive. I've checked and double-checked. Brooks wasn't cheating on her. Hager was right about that. As for monetary gain and social status, the only way she'd continue enjoying those is with Brooks alive. She gets to attend all high-profile events on his arm. He's the single largest contributor to her YouthOp charity. And she's not named in his will."

"Right. So if inheriting was her goal, she'd be better off keeping him around long enough to make her Mrs. Carson Brooks, *then* bumping him off." Jeannie chewed her candy thoughtfully. "The other big question mark is Gloria Radcliffe. I tried reaching her. No answer. I left a message on her voice mail. I'm sure my call won't come as a surprise. Her daughter must have given her a heads-up about the direction our questions took. I can't wait to hear her answers."

The phone on Jeannie's desk rang, and she plucked it from the receiver. "Whitman."

"Stick?"

"Yeah, Parsons, it's me. What's up?"

"I've got a call for you. I think you'll want me to patch it through."

"Who is it?"

Getting her answer, Jeannie sat up straighter, covering the mouthpiece with her hand. "Speak of the devil," she hissed at Frank.

"Gloria Radcliffe?" he mouthed.

A hard nod. "Absolutely, put her through," she instructed. A pause. "Ms. Radcliffe, hello. I assume you got my message." She frowned. "That's odd. I left it this afternoon. Have you checked your voice mail?" A pause, and Jeannie's brows shot up a notch. "In Manhattan? Your daughter didn't mention you were here. Oh, I see. So where are you now? Yes, that's close by. The precinct is on West 54th. If you go south on Fifth Avenue . . ." Jeannie broke off, abandoning the idea of direction-giving. A quick glance at her watch, and an equally quick decision. "My partner and I were just heading out. Stay put. We'll meet you in the hotel lounge. We can talk there. Right. We're on our way."

Jeannie was scrambling to her feet even as she put the phone back in its cradle. "She's at the Plaza Athenée. Apparently, she flew in a couple of hours ago to be with her daughter. She's waiting to have dinner with her. Sabrina's

still at the hospital. She's meeting her mother in the hotel
lounge at nine. That gives us over an hour. Let's get moving. If we want a shot at the truth, or at catching Gloria
Radcliffe in a lie, we'll do better if her daughter's not
there. No moral support. No chance to embellish on a
story to downplay guilt. I want to talk to Gloria Radcliffe
alone."

15

Russ Clark took his two slices of pepperoni pizza and his medium-size Coke and slumped into a booth. He'd been walking for over an hour trying to clear his head.

It hadn't helped.

He'd been an intern at Ruisseau for almost two years now.

If anyone had asked, he'd say the sun rose and set on Carson Brooks. Thanks to him, Russ was off the streets. Not only that, he was a high school grad—one who'd gone on to Queens College, and was working his way toward the journalism degree he'd always dreamed of.

Mr. Brooks had met with him personally a month or two after he'd started working in Ruisseau's mail room. He'd told Russ what a fine job he was doing, then said he'd been reviewing Russ's application and noticed that he'd written a gripe column for his school newspaper—at least until his gripes became too raunchy to print.

Russ had steeled himself for a lecture, or worse. Instead, Mr. Brooks had asked him if he liked writing, or just griping. When Russ finished hemming and hawing, and finally spit out what he wanted his future to be, Mr. Brooks had moved him to the publicity department.

At first, Russ had been a gofer, but now he was actually helping write copy. It wasn't the same as investigative reporting, but it did teach him how to gather information and present it clearly and concisely. It was cool, it was something to put on his résumé when he graduated, *and* he got paid for it.

Finally, things for him were looking up.

Last month everything had changed.

It started on the day he overheard that conversation, and gotten wind of what was going on. It made him furious. So, to appease himself, to hone his skills as a reporter and, most of all, to look out for Mr. Brooks, he'd started poking around.

Tonight he'd hit pay dirt. Only he wished to hell he hadn't.

Because now he had to do something with it.

Polishing off his pizza and downing his remaining Coke, Russ chucked out the paper plate and cup. Then, he headed toward the subway.

Diagonally across the street, a pair of eyes watched him with interest.

8:15 P.M.
West 73rd Street

Sabrina was bone-weary and mind-numb.

Talk about being bombarded with stimuli. After the emotional meeting with Carson, an afternoon of follow-up calls to CCTL, and an early-evening check-in at the hospital to see how Carson was doing, she'd been herded into the limo with Dylan and Stan, driven out to tour the R&D facility, then driven back to Manhattan. During the return trip, she'd been sucked into an impromptu meeting. No surprise who'd orchestrated the tour and the meeting, straight from his hospital bed, no less. Carson was intent on immersing Sabrina in Ruisseau and in defining her roles there—both her official and her unofficial ones—as soon as possible, so that Dylan could finalize the paperwork, Stan could orchestrate a nine A.M. meeting to introduce her, and both men could give her a rundown on the "who's who" and the "what's what" in advance.

Using Carson's limo for the meeting made sense. It was large, cushy, and, most of all, private. Stan began by giving her a procedural summary of what she could expect the next morning, while Dylan scribbled snippets of amendments on whatever legal documents he'd already banged out. Next, Stan piled a ton of documents in her lap—from Ruisseau's latest financial statements, to its fourth quarter projections, to the current marketing campaign for C'est Moi—advising her to familiarize herself with them as quickly as possible. He'd also given her a company directory, complete with titles, departments, and telephone extensions, suggesting she get a feel for the staff. Finally, he'd tossed her the keys to an apartment Carson had talked her into accepting, flourished a business card with his home phone number written on it, and waited while their driver pulled over and stopped on Riverside Drive. Then, he jumped out of the limo.

When she'd stared at him dazedly, trying to figure out why she was still sitting there with Dylan, while Stan was obviously leaving—sans the limo—he'd informed her that the car and driver were at her disposal, that she should feel free to go anywhere she wanted, and that she should get a good night's sleep. He'd then promptly climbed into another car—one that was waiting to take him back to work—and zoomed off.

Anywhere she wanted? What Sabrina had wanted was to crawl into bed, pull the covers over her head, and collapse.

The problem was, she couldn't collapse. Certainly not at the hotel, where her mother was waiting for her. Besides, it wasn't that she wanted to avoid Gloria. She wanted to touch base with her, to hear how things had gone with her grandparents, and to fill her in on the pivotal decisions she'd made that day. Just not at that moment. Not right away.

If only she could go somewhere for a reprieve, she'd thought wistfully. Just for a little while. Not a noisy bar or a crowded restaurant. But somewhere quiet, where her thoughts and emotions—both of which were on overdrive—could come down a peg or two. Then, she'd be ready for her nine o'clock dinner, and the issues she and her mother had to discuss.

Dylan must have read her mind, because he'd leaned forward, given the driver an address, and settled back in his seat.

The driver had brought them to what Sabrina realized was her new Manhattan residence. And, she had to admit, the cozy brownstone was the perfect medicine.

She'd explored the place from the ground floor up, climbing the three flights of stairs with newfound enthusiasm, and pausing to stroll around each level and admire her surroundings. The place was even more charming than it had looked from the street. More spacious, too, with a library and conference room on the ground floor, a living room and kitchen on the second floor, and two bedrooms and a sitting room on the third floor.

The furnishings were both tasteful and expensive, decorated throughout in sweeping shades of bone and brown, with rich parquet floors and gleaming marble bathrooms. The updated kitchen was fully stocked, and complete with every sophisticated appliance known to mankind. The living room bar was also fully stocked, boasting every top brand of liquor, and a floor-to-ceiling Subzero wine rack filled with an impressive selection of reds and white—the latter wines on top, the former on bottom, so as to be kept at precisely the right temperatures. As for the bedrooms, there was a large master bedroom with an adjoining bath, and an ample-sized second bedroom. Both bedrooms had thick cream-colored carpeting and magnificent cherry furniture. A vase filled with fresh flowers sat on the bureau of the master bedroom and, to Sabrina's amazement, the linens on the bed had been freshly changed, and the covers turned back. Quite a feat, given the fact that Carson had just offered her the place an hour ago. Obviously, he'd taken the necessary steps in the hopes that she'd accept. Well, those steps had worked. The entire brownstone felt homey and warm, as if it housed permanent residents, rather than occasional visitors from Ruisseau's European operations.

"Nice, huh?" Dylan asked, leaning against the master bedroom door frame and watching her reaction.

"It's lovely." Sabrina walked over to the flowers and sniffed. "Roses, jasmine, and ylang-ylang," she pronounced. "The floral essences in C'est Moi. I recognize the scents from the lab."

"Impressive sniffing."

"Impressive apartment." Sabrina turned to face Dylan, shaking her head in wonder. "Who took care of getting it ready in such record time?"

"Marie, Carson's secretary. She's as good as they come, a crackerjack assistant in every way. She's the most organized human being on the planet. Carson got word to her that he'd hired a consultant for an indefinite period of time. She took care of the rest. The food, the flowers, everything."

"She's obviously a treasure. I'd appreciate if either you or Stan would introduce me to her first thing tomorrow. I want to thank her. The personal touches are just what I needed."

"No problem."

"Did you know all this was being done behind the scenes?"

"Um-hum. That's why I brought you here first. You were weaving on your feet when we left Carson's room, and you fuzzed out more than once during our meeting with Stan. I was beginning to think we'd have to admit you to Mount Sinai as a patient if we pushed any harder. Then, when I heard you make plans to meet your mother at the hotel . . . let's just say I figured you could use some space before the next round. So, here we are, Madam President—home sweet home."

Sabrina shot him a look, wondering if he was being compassionate or sarcastic. "Thanks—I think. As for the apartment, when Carson said I should move into one of his extras, I wasn't expecting all this. Are you sure you don't need to keep it available for the company's use?"

"You're the company now, too, remember? Besides, we've got two other apartments if someone from Paris blows into town. Carson wanted you to have this one. Unless you'd rather move into his place. He said to make that available to you, too, if you'd prefer. It's on Central Park West, and it's huge."

"Now wouldn't that be cute?" Sabrina returned dryly. "Especially if we were to continue that arrangement after Carson came home—which he will. I'm not sure who'd appreciate it more, the tabloids or Susan. The new, young management consultant shacked up with the great-looking, middle-aged CEO. Nice publicity. We could say it was all thanks to C'est Moi. But of course that would backfire when Carson and I decided to make the announcement that I was his daughter. We'd go from a sex scandal to an incest scandal. Neither one would do much for Ruisseau's reputation, or its sales. So I think I'll pass."

Dylan's lips curved into one of those sexy, crooked smiles. "When you put it that way, it does sound like a bad move."

"Um-hum. Besides, Central Park West isn't really my thing. This place is. It's ideal."

A satisfied nod. "Yeah, I think it suits you. Classy, impressive in an understated way, and naturally beautiful—no enhancements required."

"Thank you." This time her thanks were genuine, although she was somewhat surprised by the compliment. This was more like the Dylan she'd had dinner with last night—charming, putting her at ease. It was a far cry from the mercurial guy she'd crossed paths with today.

The one-eighty was baffling. His moods today had ranged from harsh when they'd left Carson at lunchtime, to distant when they'd converged in ICU late in the day, to crisply businesslike when they'd met with Stan. So why now was he being so warm and accommodating, even flattering? On top of that, she sensed different undercurrents than before—ones that rattled her, where the others hadn't.

She had a pretty good idea why. What she didn't know was where those undercurrents were leading.

Damn, it would be so much easier if she could read this man's mind.

"So it's a go?" he asked.

Sabrina blinked. "Excuse me?"

"The apartment?" he reminded her. "Is it the one you want to live in?"

"Oh. Yes. Consider it signed, sealed, and delivered."

"Almost. We've still got to move you in. I was just

waiting for your nod of approval before I contacted the Plaza Athenée, and arranged to have your things packed up and sent over. I'll make that call now. It'll be taken care of within the hour. You can sleep here tonight." He whipped out his cell phone.

"Wait a minute." Sabrina reacted on gut instinct, feeling more than a twinge of irritation. She wasn't used to having her life controlled. And she didn't plan on becoming used to it, either. "I'll take care of the arrangements. I'll settle my account in person, when I meet my mother for dinner. I'll also pack my own things."

Dylan's gaze was steady, although one brow rose—whether in annoyance or amusement, Sabrina wasn't sure. "Whatever you say."

Tension crackled in the air and, abruptly, Sabrina reached the end of her rope. This whatever-it-was had gone on long enough.

Abandoning diplomacy, she folded her arms across her breasts and stared Dylan down. "Look, I'm too tired to play games. Don't try the take-charge approach to show me who's boss. It's not necessary, and it won't work. I don't intimidate easily. Further, if you've got something on your mind where I'm concerned, just spit it out. If it's resentment, I understand. Three days ago I didn't even know Carson Brooks, except as a name in *Business Week*. You've been an integral part of his life for almost twenty years. My coming on as president of Ruisseau must really piss you off."

This time Dylan reacted, anger flashing in his eyes as he went from lounging in the doorway to jerking upright, his posture rigid. "Is that what you think? That I'm threatened by your place in the company, or in Carson's life for that matter? Quite the opposite, Sabrina. I see how much Carson's investing in you—and I don't mean financially or even professionally. I've spent the past few days praying I could convince you to get tissue-typed, praying you'd be a donor match, praying that, if you were, you wouldn't balk and decide not to go through with the kidney transplant. Now I've got to pray that you won't desert Carson on another level. That you won't decide Ruisseau's not for you, or cave under pressure from your family, or just not give enough of a damn, and go back to head up CCTL full time. *That's* what's on my mind where you're concerned."

Sabrina blinked at the fervor in Dylan's voice. His sincerity wasn't even a question. That he doubted hers—well, wasn't that natural? Given how reluctant she'd been to accompany him to New York, how reserved she'd been about making commitments, how ambivalent she'd been about accepting everything Carson offered—could she blame Dylan? He didn't know her, not really. He had no idea how seriously she took those commitments she did make. And Carson was his family—his *only* family. He wanted to protect him, and he felt helpless to do that under the circumstances. Wouldn't she feel the same way if the tables were turned?

"I'm sorry," she heard herself say. Raking a weary hand through her hair, she walked over to the bedroom doorway, facing Dylan head-on. "I've been so caught up in my own emotional meltdown, I became insensitive to yours. I'll try to make up for that now by being as honest as I can. Yes, I'm in shock. My life's been turned upside down. Yes, I'm worried about the fallout where my family's concerned. And, yes, I'm committed to the continued success of CCTL. That having been said, I won't change my mind. Not about anything. If I'm the best kidney match, I'm going through with that surgery. If I can do the job the way Carson wants it done, I'm stepping up to the plate as president of Ruisseau. And, most of all, I'm getting to know my father. He wants that. And so do I. Does that put your mind at ease?"

A muscle worked in Dylan's jaw. "Very much so. Thanks." He took a step closer, until she could smell the musky scent of his cologne—some Ruisseau brand, no doubt, one that suited Dylan perfectly—mixed with the lingering scent of his soap. "Oh, and for the record," he added, tipping up her chin so their gazes locked. "I wasn't pulling a power trip when I said I'd take care of the hotel. I was trying to take something off your plate. It's getting pretty crowded these days."

"You're right. It is." Sabrina was having trouble breathing. She and Dylan were standing entirely too close, and the mood between them was far too intense. She was stunned by how off-balance it made her feel.

Or maybe not so stunned. There was something about Dylan Newport she found incredibly exciting—a hard-edged sexiness she'd never been attracted to before, but now was. Between that, and the fact that he was so damned challenging, so mentally stimulating . . . okay, so the moment of truth had arrived. Time to put a name to those undercurrents. *And* time to put some serious distance between her and Dylan if she wanted to consider her options before she acted on them.

Averting her gaze, Sabrina took a step backward, then made a move to go around Dylan and leave the intimacy of the bedroom ASAP. "I was relieved to see that Carson was stronger this evening," she declared, her voice bright as she strove to make casual conversation. "He was so wiped out this afternoon that I—"

Dylan's arm snaked out, caught her around the waist, and brought her up against him. "You asked what was on my mind where you're concerned," he said huskily. "There's one thing I didn't mention. This."

There was no time to react, no time to protest—not that Sabrina wanted to. Dylan's mouth took hers in a kiss so consuming she felt it down to the tips of her toes. Like everything else about him, Dylan's kiss was hot and proficient, his lips slanting over hers, moving with hungry precision as he deepened the caress. His tongue plunged inside, rubbing against hers with a sensual thoroughness that awakened every nerve ending in her body.

Sabrina heard herself moan, responding to him on sheer instinct. One minute she was standing there, drowning in sensation, and the next minute she was kissing him back, her motions just as fervent as his, her fingers clutching the lapels of his suit jacket, gripping tightly and holding on for dear life.

The wildness between them swelled, exploded, and Dylan lifted her up and into him, swerving around and pinning her to the wall with his body. Through the confines of their clothes, his erection pulsed against her, made her insides clench in response.

"So good," he muttered, cupping her breast. "So damned good." His thumb found her nipple, rubbing back and forth until it hardened and throbbed through the sheer material of her silk blouse and bra. "God, this is an even bigger mistake than I thought." He kissed her again, his mouth eating at hers as his fingers began unbuttoning her blouse.

Somewhere in the insanity of the next few moments, Sabrina pulled her mouth away long enough to drag air into her lungs. "Dylan . . ." she managed, feeling the air against her skin. Her blouse was open. She *wanted* it to be open.

What in God's name was happening?

"What?" he asked thickly, his breath hot against her mouth.

"We can't. . . ."

"I know." His lips shifted to her neck, her throat, tasting her skin as they burned a path down to her collarbone, then back up to her mouth. "I know—but I don't care." He was kissing her again, one hand tangling in her hair, the other tugging her blouse out of her slacks, pushing the sides apart to give him access to her skin. His fingers shook as they found the front clasp of her bra, working to release it so he could touch her.

He was backing her toward the bed when she jerked her mouth away. "We have to stop."

"Do we?" He paused, raising his head as her legs came up against the mattress.

"Yes. We do." Her palms flattened against his chest, creating a barrier that was as much for her as it was for him. "I'm supposed to meet my mother at nine. It's probably close to that now."

Dylan swallowed, hard. His breath was coming fast, and his eyes burned with tiny flames that made Sabrina's whole body run hot and cold. "Is that the only reason we're stopping—your dinner appointment?"

She stared at him, too torn to think clearly, much less to answer. "I don't know. Is it?"

A muscle worked furiously in his jaw, and he said nothing for a long moment. Then, he released her, turned away. "Shit," he muttered, dragging a hand through his hair. "I knew this would happen if I touched you. But I couldn't keep my hands off you. That's not about to change. So what the hell do I do?"

Sabrina had sunk down on the edge of the bed, her entire body trembling. She was hardly the one to ask advice on this subject. She'd never experienced such blind passion in her entire life. She was reeling from it. And she had no clue how to go from here.

She busied herself by rebuttoning her blouse.

"Sabrina."

She raised her head, met Dylan's gaze.

"You're Carson's daughter. Things are already way too complicated. If we get involved . . ."

"I know," she said quietly.

"Yeah, well, I'm glad *you* do." He rubbed the back of his neck, and Sabrina could see that he, too, was reeling from what had just happened—or almost happened. "I need a drink," he said flatly. "Do you want one? Or would you prefer to wait and have one with your mother?"

"In this case? Both." She gave him a shaky smile. "I'll need one later. And I sure as hell need one now."

Dylan glanced at his watch. "It's eight forty-five."

She nodded. He was letting her know that she had just enough time to get herself together and get over to the hotel. Whether or not she decided to ignore that and share a drink with him, was her call.

She reached for the telephone on the night table. Lifting the receiver, she punched in her mother's cell phone number.

"Hello?" Gloria's voice sounded preoccupied.

"Mother? Are you all right?"

"Yes, dear, I'm fine. I'm just in the middle of a meeting."

Sabrina's brows drew together. Had her mother run into a client? "With whom?"

"I had time to kill before you got here. So I set up an appointment."

"Oh." Sabrina felt a wave of relief. "In that case, would you mind if we pushed dinner back a half hour or so? I'm running late."

A slight hesitation. "Not at all. Finish up what you're doing. If I'm through first, I'll get us a table."

"Perfect. Thanks. I'll see you in a little while." Sabrina hung up, then inhaled sharply. Okay, good. She'd bought herself some time.

"Merlot, right?" Dylan was still standing there, watching her.

She nodded. "I'd better fortify myself, and fast." She stood, glancing down at her disheveled state. "I'd also better make myself look presentable. I'll use the adjoining bathroom over there, and meet you downstairs." A rueful look. "The living room is safer ground than the bedroom. Under the circumstances, I think it's better if we have our wine there."

"You're right about that." Dylan looked grim. "Then again, I'm not sure *any* ground is going to be safe. Not as long as we're together in the same room."

When Sabrina came downstairs five minutes later, Dylan was standing at the living room bar, polishing off a glass of merlot. He glanced up when she walked in, gesturing at the other filled goblet on the counter before reaching for the bottle and refilling his own. "There you go."

"Thanks," Sabrina said. She picked up her glass, frowning as she saw how unsteady her fingers still were. Her hand was trembling enough to make the merlot swish around a bit, and she tried to remedy that—and to calm her nerves—by taking a good hard swallow.

Dylan wasn't even pretending. He downed his second glass of wine as if it were water, then turned toward her, still looking as grim as he had upstairs. Not just grim, but upset and worried, maybe even guilty.

Those were the last things Sabrina wanted.

"We're going to have to deal with this—and soon," he informed her. "Although I have no idea how. But tonight's not the night to get into it. You've still got another chapter of family drama to get through, and a pile of paperwork to read before you go to sleep. Not only that, but tomorrow you're starting an enormous new project—and a whole lot more, as we both know. So let's shelve this for a day or two."

Sabrina inclined her head, studying him intently. "I agree. But in the meantime, I want to clear up a few things, just so we're on the same page. I'm fine. *Really* fine. I realize that last night I told you I had limited experience with men. So my guess is you're afraid I'll read too much into things, or that I'm fragile and I'll fall apart. I won't and I'm not. So stop looking so freaked out."

Dylan shot her a look, then refilled his glass yet again. "I'm glad to hear *you're* fine. *I'm* not."

"Why?" she asked, her lips twitching a bit. "Are you inexperienced, too?"

"Very funny." Dylan took a gulp of merlot. "The problem is, I'm too damned experienced. I grew up on the streets. That means discovering sex when the only part of you that understands it is the part of you that's having it. It means getting what you want, when you want, and as often as you want; knowing just where to go to make that happen."

"Sounds great," Sabrina noted, swirling the wine around in her goblet. "You're lucky you didn't end up with a disease."

"You're right. I am. Then again, I wasn't stupid. Or careless. Not after the way I was conceived. I used condoms. No exceptions. That was one of my three cardinal rules."

"What were the other two?"

"Number two was no virgins."

"Really?" Sabrina's brows rose, and her voice dripped with sarcasm. "How gallant of you."

"Not so gallant. I didn't want the responsibility, or the hassle. Too much potential baggage. Not my thing."

"I see. And rule number three?"

"No emotional attachments. I needed to know I was always in control. Caring strips you of that control." Dylan finished his third glass of merlot, stared into the empty goblet. "Funny thing about cardinal rules. They die hard. Even when you get older and more mature, even when you've left behind the reckless kid you once were, those cardinal rules go with you. They become part of the person you grow into."

"Well, thanks for the lesson. It was fascinating." Sabrina set down her glass. "Now, I'd better be getting over to the hotel. Keep the limo. I'll catch a cab."

"I don't need it. My apartment's three blocks away. I'll walk."

"Stagger, you mean," Sabrina amended pointedly. "You just guzzled three glasses of wine."

"I've got a high tolerance. I'm not drunk, at least not nearly as drunk as I need to be. So, the limo's yours."

A shrug. "Suit yourself." She headed for the stairs.

"Sabrina—wait."

The imperative tone of his voice stopped her in her tracks, and she turned slowly to face him.

"I lost control a few minutes ago," he stated flatly. "I wanted you so much I was blind with it, oblivious to everything except getting you in that bed. I would have chucked aside all the rules. I would have blocked out all the complications. I would have done anything to get inside you. That's never happened to me before. Not in thirty-five years. It blows my mind that it could happen in an instant, with a woman who's so off-limits, it's not even funny—a woman I met two days ago under the worst possible circumstances. It blows my mind more that I can't wait for it to happen again—and it will, unless you've got a hell of a lot more willpower than I do. So, like I said, I'm glad *you're* fine. But *I'm* not."

Sabrina wished Dylan's words didn't make her feel so damned good. But they did. She knew the wine had loosened his tongue. But she also knew the explanation was genuine. The fact that he was not only as caught up in the chemistry between them as she was, but as startled by its intensity—and as unable to ignore or erase it—made the turmoil she was experiencing a whole lot more bearable.

"Aren't you going to say something?" Dylan demanded.

"Something honest, you mean?" She gave him a half-smile. "Fair enough. Here goes. Maybe I'm not *that* fine. I'm not sure what I am. I haven't had a coherent thought in the past half hour. When I do, I'm sure I'll be as freaked out as you are by what all this means, the complications it's going to create or worsen. But right now, all I can manage is to walk out of here, get into that limo, and try to behave like a normal, rational human being—one who didn't just lose all sense of reason and act so out of character it's incomprehensible. I've got to put what just happened between us away while I deal with my mother and then educate myself about Ruisseau."

Her smile faded, and she gave voice to a truth she knew Dylan would understand—one that was rooted in a sentiment the two of them shared. "Tomorrow morning when I walk into that office, I've got to come off like gangbusters. Nothing less. Carson's counting on me. And I refuse to disappoint him."

"You won't. If I'm sure of anything, it's that." Dylan's half-laugh was filled with irony rather than humor. "Bizarre, isn't it? I'd never have believed I'd say that, much less feel confident that it's true. But after watching you when you're with him, seeing the way you two connect, and then listening to what you told me tonight . . ." Pausing, Dylan cleared his throat, then finished his thought with simple, fervent directness. "I said you were lucky to have Carson as a father. I'm beginning to think he's equally lucky to have you as a daughter."

To Sabrina's astonishment, she felt tears burn behind her eyes. She made no move to disguise them, distinctly aware that she was breaking one of her own cardinal rules, one she'd learned early on in her career: Never let your vulnerability show; never reveal a glimpse of your soft underbelly. Adhering to that rule now seemed, somehow, trite and unworthy—both to Carson and to Dylan.

She swallowed, her voice a little choked as she replied. "You have no idea what it means to me to hear you say that." She gave Dylan the candor he deserved. "Especially now, when I'm scared to death about what lies ahead. Thank you."

"Don't thank me. And don't be scared." Dylan watched the play of emotions on her face, and his gaze darkened. Sabrina knew in her gut that he was wrestling with the desire to cross over and pull her into his arms. She also knew that if he did, she'd have to fight like hell not to give in. She'd want to. She *already* wanted to. But if she did, all the complications they'd alluded to would come crashing in on them without ever having been assessed.

In the end, he stayed where he was, although the sparks flying between them were electric. "Take dinner in your stride," he advised quietly. "As for tomorrow . . ."

He raised his empty goblet in a toast. "There's no doubt about the way your Ruisseau debut will play out. You're going to knock 'em dead."

9:30 P.M.
Middle Village, Queens

As he trudged home to his tiny apartment, Russ asked himself for the hundredth time what his best course of action was. Going to the cops was out. Mr. Brooks was very loyal. He'd want to handle this himself first. Besides, Russ didn't have the proof in his hands. Taking it would have been too risky. As it was, he'd stayed two hours later than usual. He'd dug through the accounting files as fast as he could. What he'd really wanted was to access the computer, where he'd probably find a whole lot more, but he didn't know the department's password and he didn't have time to fiddle around guessing.

It didn't matter. He'd seen enough. Too much. He knew that being a good investigative reporter meant having thick skin, but that wouldn't work. Not this time. It just felt too personal.

He turned down a side street, head bent as he wrestled with his choices. Mr. Brooks was still really bad off in the hospital. He wanted to go to him directly, but he couldn't. The next logical choice was Mr. Newport. He could go to him first thing tomorrow, tell him everything. Then, it would up to Mr. Newport to make the decision. That approach sucked, too, because Mr. Newport had enough to deal with. He and Mr. Brooks went way back. And he was really messed up about Mr. Brooks getting shot. Still, he, of all people, would know what to do. And he'd want to know.

But, boy, was this a mess. And once it was out—well, the shit was really going to hit the fan.

Russ never saw the figure huddled in the alley near his apartment.

There was the slightest rustle as it stepped out of the shadows and came up behind him. There was no fore-warning, only a stark sense of realization and a blind, searing pain as the blade plunged into his back.

He crumpled and fell to the pavement.

The assailant rifled his pockets, took the money clip and the Seiko watch, even though neither were worth the trouble. But it had to look like a burglary.

Leaving Russ in a growing pool of blood, the figure vanished into the night.

16

9:35 P.M.
Plaza Athenée

Sabrina hurried through the lobby. Shrugging out of her jacket, she paused to tell the concierge she'd be checking out of the hotel this evening and to make the necessary arrangements. She then went straight to the lounge, mentally rehearsing what she would—and wouldn't—share with her mother tonight.

The "wouldn't" was Dylan. It was too soon, there were too many if's, and she was too confused.

For now, she'd stick to the facts. There was more than enough drama in those.

She reached the bar, and stopped in her tracks.

There, sitting at a small cocktail table, was her mother, Detective Whitman, and Detective Barton.

Both detectives rose when Sabrina walked over.

"Hello, Ms. Radcliffe," Detective Barton greeted her. "It's good to see you."

"You two are my mother's appointment?" Sabrina asked curtly, glancing at her mother for corroboration. Gloria looked composed, her usual elegant self. But that did nothing to put Sabrina's mind at ease. God only knew what these two had accused her of.

"It's all right, Sabrina," Gloria said, responding to the worried look on her daughter's face. "I called the detectives right after I spoke to you. They were kind enough to meet me here. I cleared up a few things for them." Her lips curved. "Like where I was between five and six o'clock Monday evening and with whom."

"We'll check out your alibi right away, Ms. Radcliffe," Detective Whitman assured her. "I don't expect any problems." A polite smile. "A six-person dinner party gives you more than enough witnesses to verify your whereabouts. Thank you for being so forthcoming. It helps to have someone make our investigation easier rather than harder."

Whitman turned to Sabrina. "How's Mr. Brooks tonight?"

"That answer varies from minute to minute," Sabrina replied tightly. "He vacillates from stronger and more lucid to weak, exhausted, and out of it. Some of that is because of the painkillers the hospital's giving him. Let's just say he's hanging on and fighting like hell. My fingers are crossed."

"He's lucky to have so many people pulling for him. I'm sure that will make a difference." Whitman exchanged a quick look with her partner. "We'll leave you ladies alone now. I'm sure you have a lot to catch up on."

"Thank you, Detectives." Gloria extended her hand and, with a lovely smile, shook each of theirs in turn. "Again, I appreciate your coming here."

"How long were they with you?" Sabrina demanded, the minute she and her mother were alone.

"An hour or so." Gloria rose. "Why don't we go into the dining room? Our table's ready. We can talk while we eat."

Inside the dining room, they ordered their meals, waited for their sparkling water to be poured, and then plunged into the multitude of topics they needed to discuss.

"Tell me about Whitman and Barton," Sabrina began.

Gloria shrugged. "Right now, they're either very relieved or very disappointed. I think they really believed I shot the man. The fact that I have an alibi—one they can confirm five times over—makes me a dead end."

"They believe *everyone* shot Carson. They come off like attack dogs. I'm sorry they put you through this."

"It wasn't so bad. At first they were accusatory and suspicious. But after I gave them the facts from my perspective, they relaxed. By the end, we were just fine. I even gave Detective Whitman a few good hints on the best Manhattan night spots."

Sabrina began to laugh. "Mother, you're amazing. You could charm a cobra into giving up its prey. When you put that cunning diplomacy of yours to work, no one's immune. It never ceases to amaze me. I'm so bad at wrapping people around my finger. I'm queen of shoot-from-the-hip. Who I take after is beyond . . ." Her voice trailed off as she realized where her words were leading.

"I think we both know the answer to that," Gloria replied gently.

"I guess we do." Sabrina massaged her temples. "I feel as if a lifetime's passed since Monday. I always thought I could cope with anything. I was wrong."

"You're coping beautifully. These are hardly normal circumstances."

Sabrina searched her face. "Before we go on, I have to know. How did Grandmother and Grandfather react?"

A sigh. "Pretty much the way you'd expect. The only good news is, their worry over your health softened the intensity of their anger and chagrin over the potential scandal. Let's give it some time. Hopefully, they'll mellow. Speaking of time, when will the tissue-typing results be in?"

"In about a week. If it turns out I'm the best donor match, I've got a battery of tests to go through, a nephrologist to see. . . ." Sabrina sucked in her breath. "We don't need to go through all the details now. If and when it becomes necessary, I'll tell you everything. God knows, I'll need your support. But, Mother, I won't change my mind. Like I said on the telephone, if I'm the best match, I'm going through with the transplant."

Gloria's smile was sad, but tinged with pride. "I know you are."

"There's more," Sabrina added bluntly. "No, nothing health related," she hurriedly clarified, seeing the worried look on her mother's face. "Actually, it involves my career. And, from a professional standpoint, it's huge." She fiddled with her napkin. "Carson and I have this kind of mental connection. It's hard to explain. I hardly know the man, yet I do. And I like and respect him. What he's done with his company is incredible and impressive. The problem is he's concerned about how Ruisseau will hold up while he's in the hospital. He wants profits and morale to continue to thrive. He needs someone to help keep things on track."

"So, he's offered you a job," Gloria guessed. "You're taking on a consulting project for him."

Sabrina licked her lips. She hadn't realized quite how hard this would be. "Yes, and no. That's partly true. It's also the story we're telling the staff, at least for now. But it's more than that. Much more." She met her mother's gaze, stated the bottom line without mincing words. "Carson's asked me to be president of Ruisseau."

Gloria's glass struck the table. "What?"

"It's not instead of CCTL," Sabrina hurried on to explain. "I'll be dividing my time." She went on, laying out the scenario she and Carson had discussed. "He's being flexible, which is good, since I'm not sure of the exact division of time and workload until I tackle both companies simultaneously."

"I take it you accepted the position?"

Studying her mother's face to determine her reaction, Sabrina nodded. "Yes. I did. I had to. Not only for Carson. For me." She waited, holding her breath.

She didn't have long to wait.

"Congratulations." Gloria reached across the table, covered Sabrina's hand with her own. "I think it's wonderful. And not only from one vantage point, from two. You'll have the opportunity to get to know your father, and you'll also have the professional chance of a lifetime. I'm so proud of you."

"You're not upset?"

"No." Thoughtfully, Gloria shook her head. "Quite the opposite, in fact. I've had two days to think about the idea of you having a father in your life. As I told you, I figured out years ago that Carson Brooks was the man I selected for the donor insemination. I truly believed I was doing the right thing keeping that information from you. I was wrong. I wish I'd had the benefit of knowing he planned to initiate a search to find you. That would have changed everything, including my decision to keep you in the dark. But it didn't happen that way. So, to answer your question, no, I'm not upset. I wish the poor man had never been shot. But I'm glad fate intervened where you two are concerned."

Relief surged through Sabrina. But there was another, more difficult audience to win over. "What about Grandmother and Grandfather? How do you think they'll react when I tell them about my becoming president of Ruisseau?"

Gloria turned up her palms in a who-knows gesture. "They could explode. Or they could see the prestigious aspect of things, scandal or not. The presidency of a thriving company—very posh, indeed." Her lips twitched.

Sabrina smiled back. "I see your point. And, if anyone can influence the way they view this, you can."

"Would you prefer I broke the news to them?"

"No. That's my responsibility. And if there's hell to pay, I'll pay it. However, I might need you to help do damage control—if it's needed." Sabrina's brow furrowed. "I think I'll wait until I can give them the whole story, after I'm sure about the way the medical situation is going to play out."

"I agree. They're expecting to hear from you when the blood test results come in. You can tell them everything then."

A sigh. "Selfishly, I'm relieved. The one-week reprieve will take some of the strain off me. I've got a few major hurdles to surmount between now and then. Starting with tomorrow. It's my first day on the job—as a management consultant, of course. My position as an officer of the company will stay under wraps until I'm ready to announce I'm Carson's daughter. And that won't happen without my first alerting Grandmother and Grandfather. Carson understands that completely. He's being very patient with me, letting me call the shots. He wants me to feel comfortable with my new role. Most of all, he just wants me to be happy."

"That's not a surprise." Gloria's eyes glittered with emotion. "Carson Brooks just found out what it means to be a father. A *real* father—not just in fact, but in essence."

*   *   *

11:30 P.M.
Greenwich Village

Jeannie had just fallen asleep when her phone rang. She fumbled for the lamp on her night table, then gave up and just groped around until her hand knocked over the telephone receiver.

She grabbed it and stuffed it under her ear. "Yeah?"

"Hey," Frank greeted her. "Wake up. We've got to get over to Queens."

"Are you nuts? I just shut my eyes for the first time since five this morning. Besides, that's not our district."

"I know. But there's been a homicide. A twenty-one-year-old kid. Russ Clark. He was stabbed to death in front of his apartment. In case you didn't memorize our list by now, he was an intern at Ruisseau."

By now, Jeannie was wide awake. She threw off her blanket and got out of bed. "What's the address?"

17

The elevator glided its way up to the twelfth floor.

Inside, Sabrina smoothed the blazer of her red silk suit. It was her mother's design—classic lines but with the distinctive Gloria Radcliffe flair, making it sophisticated enough to be corporate and high-styled enough to be contemporary. And the color—Sabrina smiled. She could almost hear her mother saying: *Wise choice, Sabrina. Red. The ultimate power color.*

She certainly hoped so. That was the look she'd gone for today. Even her hair, which she normally wore down, she'd brushed into a loose chignon, giving her a more vivid, businesslike appearance without being so severe it rendered her unapproachable.

Hey, she might've left the rat race a few years back, but she hadn't forgotten how to run.

A *bing* and an illuminated number 12 heralded Sabrina's arrival at her destination. She sucked in her breath. Here goes, she thought.

The doors slid open.

She stepped out, making her way through the polished hallway to the sweeping oval reception desk. It was too early for the receptionist to be in, but a security guard, no doubt posted as a result of Carson's assault, stood beside the double doors leading to the interior offices.

"May I help you?" he inquired.

"I'm Sabrina Radcliffe. Mr. Hager is expecting me."

He glanced at his clipboard, and gave a terse nod. "Just a moment." Reaching over, he scooped up the phone, pressed an extension. "Ms. Radcliffe is here." A pause. "Very good." He hung up. "Someone will be right out."

Sabrina nodded. Placing her briefcase on the arm of a chair, she took in her surroundings. The broad expanse of wall space was filled with murals featuring perfume ads, touting all the different Ruisseau brands, together with glowing testimonials to C'est Moi from various television personalities and high-profile sports figures. In the center of the room was a stunning, fully-enclosed glass display case, filled with an array of elegant perfume bottles containing various Ruisseau fragrances. The bottles were positioned just so, artistically arranged at different angles, all on a cashmere tapestry that was draped along the full length of the display.

Very classy.

On top of the glass case sat several perfume samples—including, of course, a bottle of C'est Moi—for visitors to experiment with while they waited.

Shrewd marketing approach.

All in all, this room worked perfectly, setting the stage with the elegance and sensory appeal Ruisseau was known for.

Sabrina picked up the bottle of C'est Moi, studied its sensual lines. A bottle as sexy as its scent. Curious, she tugged off the cap, and sprayed some perfume on her wrist. She'd seen its components, witnessed the chemical process, even smelled the floral ingredients. But she'd never tested the final product.

She waved her wrist around, then brought it to her nose. Wow. Quite a sensory experience. Musky and mysterious, but ultra-feminine, lightly floral, alluringly spicy. No wonder it was such a turn-on.

The double doors swung open, but rather than Stan or his secretary, it was Dylan who strode out to greet her.

Sabrina set down the bottle and blinked in surprise, not only at Dylan's presence, but at Dylan period.

No casual attire today. Unlike his usual blazer and slacks, today Dylan was wearing an expensive Italian suit and silk tie—and wearing them well. Funny, how she'd first thought of him as strictly a T-shirt and jeans kind of guy. Dylan Newport was anything and everything he chose to be.

And today what he chose to be—besides more formally dressed—was a stony-faced bulldozer, bearing down on her with ripping intensity.

"Good morning," he said curtly. "I'm glad you're early."

Rather than being offended, Sabrina felt a pang of uneasiness. The combination of Dylan's tone and the tight control he was obviously exerting over himself—he wasn't being rude; he was unnerved. Something was wrong.

"Good morning," she replied, searching his face for answers. "I thought Stan was going to . . ."

"Let's go to my office." He was already on his way, urging her through the double doors, then leading her down a quiet corridor. He reached a large corner office—his obviously, given that it boasted the brass plate engraved, "Dylan Newport, Corporate Counsel" that he'd described to her—and he paused in the open doorway, gesturing for her to precede him.

The office was very Dylan: unpretentious, uncluttered, and unstuffy. The furniture was teak, all simple lines and clean surfaces from the desk to the sideboard.

One entire wall was filled with open bookshelves stacked with official-looking legal volumes. The room's only adornments were a few pieces of modern pottery on the side tables in the conference area. No expensive knick-knacks, no pretentious artwork on the walls, no intimidating LLD diplomas. Yup, this was Dylan Newport, all the way.

Sabrina took a few steps into the office, dropped her briefcase and turned to face him. "Something's wrong," she stated the minute he'd shut the door. "What is it? Is it Carson?"

"No." Dylan rubbed the back of his neck, his features taut with strain. "It's Russ Clark, one of our interns. He was stabbed to death outside his apartment last night."

"Oh my God." Sabrina pressed a palm to her mouth. "What were the circumstances?"

"There weren't any. No fight, no witnesses, nothing. His watch and money clip were missing."

"So it was a robbery?"

Dylan gave a hollow laugh. "Yeah. Right. I'd be surprised if Russ had more than twenty dollars on him. And his watch—if I remember correctly it was about five years old and worth nothing great when it was new. The kid was twenty-one. He lived in a working class area of Queens. He was busting his ass to get through college. Carson was helping him with scholarship money. Russ worked like a beaver and never complained—long hours, weekends, he did whatever was asked of him. He was one of Carson's favorites. He had spunk. And he worshiped the ground Carson walked on. Now suddenly he's killed three days after Carson was shot." Dylan's expression was angry and pained. "Does that sound like a coincidence to you?"

"No, it doesn't." Sabrina's mind was racing. "So let's

say the two incidents are related. Do you think Russ knew something?"

"Yeah, that's exactly what I think." An exasperated wave of his arm. "Of course I have no proof. But in my gut, I believe it. And I have a feeling Whitman and Barton do, too."

"So they know about Russ's murder?"

"They've been on it since late last night. They were notified because of Russ's employment at Ruisseau, and the possible link to Carson's shooting. They contacted Stan right away, since Russ had no family. Stan called me and Susan."

"Susan?" Sabrina asked, puzzled.

"Russ was one of her YouthOp kids. According to Stan, she fell apart when he told her. And she's still a mess today. When Stan called me with an update—which was about ten minutes ago from the car—he said that Susan was at Carson's bedside when he got there to break the news. She held it together, barely. Before Stan left the hospital, he got Dr. Radison to give her a sedative. She's not going to do Carson any good if she falls apart. By the way, that's where Stan's coming from now, which is why he wasn't here to welcome you."

Sabrina didn't give a damn about the missing welcome. But the reason behind it didn't sit well with her. "Dylan, maybe Stan should have waited a while to drop this news on Carson. If he liked this kid as much as you say, he's going to take it hard. And if he's got Susan's emotional meltdown to deal with, too, it might cause a setback. . . ."

"It won't. Carson won't let it. If anything, it'll make him fight harder, because he'll be hell-bent on finding out who did this. I don't have to tell you how protective of his staff he is. Pumping a bullet into *him* is one thing;

killing one of his people is another. Believe me, Stan made the right decision. Carson would be more pissed if we kept this news from him. Besides, if we'd waited, he would have ended up hearing about it from the cops or someone else. It's better that he heard it from Stan."

"So he's okay?"

"He's furious. And he's upset, probably more so than he's letting on, at least in front of Susan. I'll get over to the hospital later and check on him myself." Dylan looked at Sabrina and, for the first time this morning, seemed to actually see her. "You're welcome to come with me."

"Thanks. That would make me feel a lot better."

He gave her a quick once-over, then a longer, more leisurely perusal, and the tension in his jaw eased a bit.

"Well?" Sabrina asked lightly. "What's the verdict?"

"Can I be honest? Or will you bring me up on harassment charges?"

"I think I can restrain myself. Go for it."

"Okay then. You look incredible. Beauty and power combined. A drop-dead gorgeous corporate dynamo. Even I'm intimidated."

Her lips twitched. "Liar. Nothing intimidates you. But I appreciate the vote of confidence."

Dylan released a sharp breath. "Sabrina, I'm sorry if I came at you like a Mack truck when you first walked in. I'm just infuriated and frustrated. Russ was just a kid. I want to find whoever did this to him and choke the bastard to death."

"Don't apologize. It's a horrible tragedy. I feel sick and I never even met Russ." She pursed her lips. "The only thing I'm hoping is that if the two crimes are connected—and I agree with you that they are—that it leaves twice as much room for error. Whoever did this isn't a pro. Somewhere, somehow, the tiniest shred of evidence exists. And Whitman and Barton will find it."

"If they don't, *I* will," Dylan muttered. "I can't take much more of this sit tight and be patient crap. I'm not the passive type."

"No kidding." Sabrina frowned. "Don't do anything stupid, Dylan. We're talking about a murderer, not a street brawler."

"I realize that." He raked a hand through his hair, clearly trying to get himself together. "Let's change the subject." A quick glance at his watch. "We have about a half hour before the meeting. I can answer any preliminary questions you came up with after reading through that mound of material Stan gave you. If any of the questions is out of my league, we can pull Stan aside before going into the conference room."

Sabrina's shoulders lifted in a composed shrug. "That won't be necessary. The material Stan gave me was comprehensive. Any specifics I need I'll get from each department head. And whatever additional questions crop up as we go along, I'll jump right in and ask for clarification."

"Good." Dylan gestured toward the sideboard, where a steaming carafe sat. "Want some coffee? I'm warning you ahead of time, it's leaded. There's decaf in the coffee room for the less intrepid. We can take a walk down there now, if you'd like."

"Nope." An adamant shake of her head. "I'm in desperate need of the leaded kind. I didn't get much sleep last night."

Dylan shot her a quizzical look as he went over, poured two mugs of coffee. "Did you move into your new place?"

"Um-hum. All done. I soaked in my first hot bath

reading Ruisseau's fourth quarter projections. And I snuggled in my new bed analyzing Ruisseau's financial statements and marketing campaign. Quite a first night in my new home. It was as close to heaven as it gets."

Laughter rumbled in Dylan's chest. "It sounds great. No wonder you need this." He handed her a mug, motioning for her to have a seat in his conference area.

"No complaints," she assured him, nodding her thanks as she sank down in a cozy tufted chair. "All-nighters go with the territory. Besides, in all seriousness, the apartment really is beautiful—not to mention much roomier and more comfortable than a hotel room." She sipped at her coffee. "You mentioned that you live three blocks away."

"Sure do. 341 West 76th Street."

"Is your place similar to mine?"

"In a lot of ways, yeah." Dylan dropped into the opposite chair. "It's a brownstone, too, although the layout's a little different. I'm also a little further west than you are, so I'm close to Riverside Drive and Riverside Park, which is great for when I want to clear my head with a morning run."

"That's right. The park. I'll have to remember that." Sabrina sighed. "I've been skipping my early morning yoga routine. Probably because Melissa's not here to play Jiminy Cricket. Although I'm not even sure that having a relentless conscience like Melissa would help. I need to be able to clear my mind to get the benefits of yoga. And these days—I can't."

"No surprise there." Dylan leaned forward, eyeing her speculatively. "Was last night's dinner with your mother very difficult?"

"Actually, no." Sabrina was touched by the genuine concern in Dylan's tone. Was this the same man who'd said he had trouble mustering sympathy for her? "Other than the fact that Detectives Whitman and Barton were with her when I arrived. That was awkward."

"You're kidding. They actually came to her hotel to interrogate her the minute she checked in?"

"No, nothing that tacky. It was my mother who called them. She knew they had questions for her. She had a chunk of time to kill before I met her for dinner. So she used that time to meet with them."

"And?"

"And they got their answers, including an alibi. After that, they left us to enjoy our dinner."

"Good. So how did she react to your latest news?"

"She was very supportive, even more so than I expected. She encouraged me to get to know Carson, and she was excited about my taking on the presidency of Ruisseau." A troubled frown. "Of course, my grandparents are another story. I still have their reaction to contend with."

Dylan's forehead creased, more in puzzlement than in censure. "If status means so much to them, wouldn't your becoming president of a successful, high-profile company like Ruisseau make them happy?"

"If that's all that was involved, yes, they'd be thrilled. The problem is that that part of the equation is the result, not the entirety. First, the media would have to sink their teeth into the guts of the story—the donor insemination, the whole who-found-out-what-and-when, the how-do-you-feel-about-this angle. There'll be mikes shoved in my grandparents' faces, tabloid reporters hanging around their house, embarrassing them in front of their friends." Abruptly, Sabrina realized how inane this explanation must sound to Dylan, and she paused, studying his expression.

He was watching her intently. But whether he was assimilating or appalled, she wasn't sure.

"Before you judge my grandparents, hear me out, and try to keep an open mind," she requested. "Yes, they're snobs. I won't argue that. They're also well into their eighties. If donor insemination sounded extreme to them twenty-eight years ago, you can imagine how they feel about it now. As for the scandal, they're not as strong as they used to be. Being hounded by reporters, having their lives disrupted, it's going to be hard on them. My only prayer is that their health isn't affected. And speaking of health, that's the biggest factor here—me. I'm my grandparents' soft spot. It's been that way since I was born. They love me deeply. The prospect of my facing surgery, giving up one of my organs . . . they'll be frantic, prisoners to their worst fears. All they'll be able to focus on are the possible complications, the what-if's. And, yes, I feel guilty for putting them through that."

Dylan took a swallow of coffee, and Sabrina could see that his wheels were turning.

"I never thought about it from that perspective," he said at last. "I'm not exactly experienced with various levels of family commitment. I understand loyalty and caring. But the rest—sensitivity to fears and weaknesses—that's all new to me."

"Probably because Carson doesn't have any."

"None that he lets anyone see," Dylan corrected. "At least until now. He's changed this past week. Partly because of his close brush with death, and partly because you came into his life."

"That goes both ways. I've changed, too. So, for that matter, have you. Your open-mindedness about my grandparents just now proves it." Sabrina weighed her next words carefully. "You undersell yourself. You're a lot more sensitive than you think."

"Sensitive?" Dylan looked amused. "Somehow that's not a trait I'd ascribe to myself."

"Let's say you're learning. Who knows? There might be hope for you yet."

He flashed her that lopsided smile. "Is that a professional evaluation?"

"Yup."

"You're going to be hard-pressed getting the rest of the world to believe you." His own quip caused a kind of pained resentment to tighten his features, and he finished his thought aloud, more to himself than to her. "Especially our detective friends. They think I'm a prime suspect for cold-blooded murder."

If Dylan expected her to be shocked by his revelation, he was about to find out otherwise.

"Maybe they *used* to think that," Sabrina informed him. "Not anymore. Not if I got through to them. Which I think I did. I didn't mince words. I was pretty damned persuasive. Between that, and the fact that I'd have no reason to lie, I think they'll change their tune. Or at least they'll give credence to my opinion."

"What are you talking about?" Dylan demanded, with a baffled stare. "Got through to them about what?"

Sabrina took another sip of coffee, offhandedly replying, "When they questioned me the other day, they dropped a few pointed comments implying they had their eye on you. I forced the details out of them by reminding them I was Carson Brooks's daughter and had every right to know the status of the investigation. When I got my answer, I blasted them."

Dylan did a double take. "You stood up for me?"

"In no uncertain terms. I told them they were blind if

they didn't see how much you cared about Carson, and that no size inheritance would motivate you to harm him. I told it like it is. Then again, I usually do." She saw the astonishment on Dylan's face and smiled faintly. "You're surprised."

"Not about your telling it like it is. About your defending me? You bet I am. At the time, you didn't even like me. And you sure as hell didn't trust me."

"I didn't trust you not to manipulate me into helping Carson," she corrected. "I *never* doubted your feelings for him. As for liking you . . ." She shot him a teasing look. "You kind of grew on me."

His gaze darkened a bit. "Did I?"

"Um-hum."

"That's nice to hear. So's the fact that you defended me. Thanks."

"No problem."

There it was again. That overwhelming sexual magnetism that kept pulling at them. It was almost impossible to ignore.

Sabrina didn't try to ignore it. But she did have to nip it in the bud. It was *definitely* the wrong time, wrong place.

She accomplished her goal by glancing around the room in a long, exaggerated motion. "It just occurs to me that we're alone. I seem to recall your saying we shouldn't tempt fate that way. Maybe it's time to head down to the conference room." She placed her coffee mug on the table.

"Point taken." Dylan's crooked smile was back again, and he, too, set down his mug. "But before we go to the conference room, why don't I show you your new office. Don't worry," he added, half-teasing, half-serious. "Your office is closer to Carson's than it is to mine. That means there are at least a dozen walls and a long corridor separating us."

He rose, waiting while she followed suit. "As for the walk down there, you're safe on that score, too. It's a quarter to nine. The office will be bustling by now. So there's no fear I'll give in to my libido."

Biting back a grin, Sabrina picked up her briefcase and headed for the door. "I can't tell you how relieved that makes me."

"I thought you'd feel that way." He reached past her to open the door, and they both ignored the sparks their proximity ignited. "Let's get moving," Dylan said without meeting her gaze. "Stan should be here by the time you've given your new office a quick once-over." He paused, then abruptly seized her forearm and brought her wrist to his nose. "By the way," he said huskily. "You don't need it."

18

9:20 A.M.
Mt. Sinai Hospital

Gloria purposely chose this time to arrive.

She entered the hospital through the rear entrance, wearing dark sunglasses and a hat—just in case any fashion reporters were around. Perfume and fashion were frequently linked, so it wouldn't be too much of a reach to think that someone covering Carson Brooks's shooting might also recognize her. And that was the last thing she wanted, at least until any formal announcements were made.

She took the elevator up to ICU, then made her way down the corridor to the nurses' station. She approached the desk tentatively, wondering if she'd be turned away, hoping this idea hadn't been a huge mistake.

"Yes?" a stout, efficient-looking RN inquired.

Gloria removed her sunglasses and hat, and smiled. "Good morning. My name is Gloria Radcliffe. I'm here to see Carson Brooks. I know he's weak, so I'll only stay a few minutes."

The nurse looked at her as if she'd announced the world was square. "I'm sorry, but visitation is highly restrictive. Do you have Mr. Brooks's doctor's permission?"

"No, but I'd be happy to get it. It's Dr. Radison, isn't it?"

"Yes."

"Is he available? I'll only take a moment of his time."

The nurse was still eyeing her as if she were an escaped lunatic. "He's scheduled for surgery at nine-thirty."

"Perfect." Gloria gave her a bright smile. "Then he can poke his head out for just a minute. Please, this is personal—and very important. All I ask is that you tell Dr. Radison I'm here. If he refuses to see me or to let me visit with Mr. Brooks, I'll leave."

The nurse rubbed her forehead. "What did you say your name was?"

For the first time, Gloria found herself wishing she were dealing with someone who'd heard of her. "Gloria Radcliffe."

"The designer?" An attractive, younger nurse turned around, all glowing and excited—and Gloria wondered if she should have been careful what she wished for. "It *is* you. I've seen your picture in *Vogue*. Your new fall line is sensational."

The stout nurse blinked. "Sorry. I'm not really into clothes."

"That's fine." Gloria spoke to nurse #1 and smiled her thanks at nurse #2. "I'd so appreciate seeing Dr. Radison before he goes into surgery. . . ."

"I'll page him." The stout nurse did that, and was rewarded a minute later when her page was answered. "Doctor, it's Mary in ICU. Gloria Radcliffe is here to speak with you. She'd like to see Mr. Brooks." A pause. "Okay. Yes." She hung up. "He's on his way."

"Thank you." Gloria felt a wave of relief—so much so that she spent the next three minutes sharing fashion tips with nurse #2, whose name turned out to be Peggy.

At last, Dr. Radison strode over, wearing his surgical scrubs. "Ms. Radcliffe?" He looked baffled by her presence. She'd expected that.

Determined to get what she came here for, she extended her hand. "Thank you so much for seeing me, doctor. I know you're on your way into surgery. I'll take exactly one minute of your time."

They stepped into a private area, and Gloria didn't waste an instant. "I'm sure I'm the last person you expected to see."

"That's true," he acknowledged. "And, frankly, I'm not clear about why you're asking to speak with . . ."

"I flew to New York to give my daughter the emotional support she needs," Gloria interrupted, giving him the pertinent information as expediently as she could. "I don't need to elaborate on why she needs that emotional support—not to you. As I understand it, you're one of the few people who knows all the facts. It's because of those facts that I'd like to meet Carson Brooks. Given the circumstances, I think he'll feel the same. Do you have any objections?"

"Objections?" Radison studied her carefully. "That depends on whether or not your visit will upset him."

"Quite the opposite. I'm hoping it will give him peace of mind. You're aware of the very real personal connection he and I have. You're also aware of the health crisis he's facing. If you consider all that, together with his definitive nature, I think you'll agree with me."

"I see your point." The doctor still sounded hesitant. Clearly, he was on the fence about this.

She *had* to convince him.

"I'm assuming he's up for company now, or you would have said otherwise." Gloria didn't have to feign how important to her this was. "Please, doctor, just tell him I'm here. Let him make the call."

Radison mulled it over for a minute, then nodded. "All right." He didn't ask any more questions. He just went down the hall, passed a uniformed police officer, and disappeared into a room.

It didn't take a minute for him to reemerge.

"He'll see you now," he told Gloria, beckoning her down.

Another wave of relief.

"Ten minutes max," the doctor instructed. "And if he tires sooner, the nurse will ask you to leave. He's had a rough morning."

Gloria wanted to ask why, but she refrained. She'd already gotten the permission she wanted. No sense pushing her luck. "I understand. Thank you very much, doctor."

Inhaling sharply, she pushed open the door and stepped inside.

Even hooked up to the various tubes and machines, Carson Brooks was easy to recognize. He was a striking man, though he did look pale and weak. But his keen blue eyes, even dulled by pain and medication, were focused and curious.

"Well, well." He gave a weak grin. "This is one visit I didn't expect. Maybe I should have."

She smiled. "I'm glad you agreed to see me."

"Are you kidding? Finally, after all these years we're on an even keel . . ." His grin strengthened a bit. "I know as much about you as you do about me. . . . Well, almost. I'm minus the interview transcript . . . and a paragraph on your aspirations. . . . Then again, I already know what you want to be when you grow up." With a concerted effort, he raised his arm, and stuck out his hand. "Hey, Gloria. Nice to meet you."

She met his handshake, her eyes twinkling with amusement. "Likewise." Her amusement faded as she surveyed the cardiac monitor, dripping IVs, and other medical apparatus that were helping him fight to survive. "How are you?"

"Better than I was . . . Not as good as I will be." He shifted a bit, wincing at the discomfort. "I'll make it. I've got lots of incentive. . . . More than I did before, thanks to you . . ." He pointed to a chair. "Have a seat." He rested while she complied.

"The doctor said you had a rough morning," Gloria continued, settling herself in the chair. "Are you up for a talk?"

"I could use one . . . to divert me." His features hardened. "The rough morning wasn't about me. . . . One of my interns at Ruisseau was killed last night. . . . Stabbed to death right outside his own front door . . . He was just a kid—a great kid. Twenty-one. He never had time to live."

"How horrifying." Gloria's insides clenched. A boy that age, dead. It was every mother's nightmare. "That poor child. And his parents—dear God, what they must be going through. Who did it, and why?"

"Don't know who . . . As for why, I'd be willing to bet it ties in to me . . . and why I was shot. . . . He was so damned loyal. . . ." Carson swallowed hard. "He had no parents. . . . Grew up like me . . . Was finally on track . . . The whole thing sucks."

Sick at heart, Gloria nodded. "Life often does. *Too* often." She sought the right words to console him. "All I can say is that I'm sure Detective Whitman and Detective Barton will solve both crimes. They're about as dedicated and thorough as they come."

"Oh . . ." A knowing glance. "They got you, too, huh?"

"They talked to me, yes. Then again, they had every reason to. I *was* in New York at the time of the shooting.

And, to their way of thinking, I had a plausible motive for wanting to stop you from contacting Sabrina. The only sticking point in their logic was that I had no idea you were initiating a search for her. As it turns out, I also have an alibi, which made their job easier. I spent that entire evening at a dinner party. So I got crossed off their suspect list."

Carson scowled. "Sorry you had to go through that . . ."

"Don't be. That's their job. It's also why I know they'll find your assailant and whoever murdered that poor young man."

"Yeah," Carson replied tersely. "Anyway, that's why the morning was rough. . . ." He drew a sharp breath, and Gloria could see that he wanted to change the subject.

"So," she said in a light, airy tone. "I think this meeting of ours is long overdue, don't you?"

That weak grin returned. "Oh, yeah, I'd say so." He eyed her intently. "Sabrina has no idea you're here."

He sounded so certain that Gloria started. "You're right. She doesn't. How did you know?"

"The medical technician was just in here to take blood. That means it's after nine . . . and that means Sabrina's in a meeting . . . which I'm sure you already knew."

Gloria reminded herself again of what a good choice she'd made. Even fighting for his life, this man was as sharp as a tack. "Right again. I didn't want Sabrina here for this talk. I wanted to speak with you alone. I'll tell her about it later—or you can. It just wasn't necessary for her to know beforehand. She has enough on her mind. As for the meeting she's in, yes, I know about it. I also know what it represents—*really* represents. Sabrina filled me in last night."

Carson absorbed that piece of information without batting a lash. "And your reaction was . . . ?"

"I surprised myself. I was delighted for her. And not only about taking on the presidency of Ruisseau. About forming a relationship with you." Gloria found herself being honest with him. It was odd, really, but they did share the unique bond of a child, however unconventionally she was conceived.

"Since Dylan Newport first dropped the bomb on Sabrina, I've had several days to reflect, to consider circumstances through the eyes of a more seasoned woman than the one who conceived twenty-eight years ago." Gloria propped her chin on her hand, a faraway look in her eyes. "I never thought I'd question my decision to raise Sabrina alone. I had more than enough love to give her, and more than enough resources to provide her with every advantage. Funny, how time and age change your perspective."

A short, humorless laugh escaped Carson's lips. "Truer words were never spoken. . . . Hey, you're talking to the man who was happy to hand over a vial and never know if he made a kid. . . . Then I turned fifty . . . and suddenly I started wondering . . . wishing it could be different. . . . Hard to believe, isn't it? An ambitious punk like me . . . wanting a kid?" Carson paused, regained some strength. "You did an amazing job, you know. . . . She's incredible. . . . Brains, beauty, and balls—figuratively speaking on that last item, of course . . ."

Gloria chuckled. "I can only take credit for the environmental factors and half the biological ones. Some of her brains and beauty were your genetic contribution. As for the balls, those she has you to thank for."

He wiggled his hand back and forth in an iffy gesture. "Balls aren't always an asset. Sometimes subtlety does the job better. . . . But, hey, it doesn't matter. Judging from her track record . . . with some of those pain-in-the-ass Fortune 500 companies . . . my guess is she inherited a chunk of your diplomacy, too. If *I'd* been consulting for them . . . I'd be kicked out by the end of the first brown-nosing session."

"You're right. The combination works well. Which is exactly what I had in mind when I chose you from your profile." Gloria leaned forward, determined to let Carson know exactly where she stood regarding him, Sabrina, and the future. "I *am* usually subtle. But not now. Since I'm short on time and long on words, now I'm going to be direct."

"Go for it."

"My reasons for being here today—they run the gamut. I wanted to meet you, to close the circle so the reality that you're Sabrina's father could truly sink in—for you *and* for me. I wanted to order you to get well, for our daughter's sake, and to give you further incentive to do so by telling you that I support your building a relationship with Sabrina, and that I support your plans for her professional future. That having been said, there's one other reason I'm here. I wanted to give you an idea of what Sabrina's going through. I think it will help you both."

Respect and gratitude flashed in Carson's eyes. "I'd appreciate that. . . ."

"We'll start with my parents." Despite her terse delivery, Gloria spoke straight from the heart. "You'd never understand them. I doubt you'd like them. Sometimes *I* don't like them. But I do love them. What's more, Sabrina loves them. And they adore her. She's their only grandchild. The sun rises and sets on her. They may be elitist and set in their ways, but they're not unkind or unfeeling. They're frightened. Frightened of disrupting a lifestyle that's been their foundation for years. Frightened of being the center of a media circus. But most of all, frightened of losing Sabrina. The thought of her undergoing surgery, giving up an organ—it terrifies them. Sabrina knows all this. Which means she's feeling a great deal of guilt right now—guilt that conflicts with the unexpected emotions she's feeling for the father who's just come into her life. I'm asking that you please bear that in mind. It's a heavy responsibility for her to carry on her shoulders at a time like this."

Carson frowned. "I won't put her through the transplant. . . . I told her no. . . . My kidneys will start working again. . . . But if they don't, I won't let her be the donor . . ."

"You don't have a choice." Gloria stopped him gently, waving away his protest. "What I said wasn't meant to make you feel guilty; it was said to make you aware. Sabrina's a very strong-willed young woman. That shouldn't surprise you. I'm stubborn. You're stubborn. She didn't stand a chance of turning out malleable. She's made up her mind. No one's going to change that. Nor should we try. For the record, I admire her decision. I'm in New York to support it, not to try to undo it. And if it comes down to the wire, my parents will do the same."

Pausing, Gloria gave a wistful sigh. "I guess what I'm trying to explain to you is that having a family is a double-edged sword. Not having one means being independent, answering to no one, and satisfying your own needs first and foremost. It also means being very, very lonely. You know all about the list I just ticked off; it's been your life up until now. Well, welcome to the flip side—*having* a family. You're getting your first taste of that. It's why you're trying to protect Sabrina's health, even at the expense of your own. Having a family means accepting emotional responsibility, showing compassion even when your reserves are dry, and thinking of others before yourself. It's hard work. It's also the most reward-ing gift life has to offer. You'll see that more and more as you and Sabrina grow closer. In the meantime, just re-member she's torn. Caring is sometimes a hard place to be."

Throughout Gloria's speech, Carson had watched her, listened intently. Now, he nodded, wetting his lips to reply. "I'll do that. . . . You know, I always thought of my-self as pretty damned smart . . . but you're smarter. Thanks for the perspective. . . . Sabrina's lucky to have you for a mother. . . ." He inclined his head, his expres-sion pensive. "You're right about my knowing a lot about the not-having. . . ."

A quizzical, shoot-from-the-hip look intensified his gaze, and Gloria sensed that something personal was coming. She just wasn't quite sure what.

She found out.

"While we're on this subject . . . let me ask you some-thing," Carson stated bluntly. "I know how you felt at the time you were looking for a sperm donor. . . . You wanted to live life on your own terms . . . unattached and inde-pendent. . . . Do you feel the same way now? . . . When all is said and done, was the single life all it was cracked up to be?"

An ironic question, one that had been the cause of much introspection for Gloria these past few days. Still, it never occurred to her that Carson Brooks had gone down this mental path. About the idea of having a son or daughter, yes, but not about having a life-partner.

"Are you going to answer?" he pressed. "Or are you

trying to find a tactful way to say it's none of my damned business?"

"Actually, I was thinking it's an odd question coming from you."

"Why? Because I went the unmarried and successful route, too?"

"No, because that route seems to suit you now as well as it did then. It never occurred to me that you contemplated the idea that any other choice existed."

"You're right. I didn't. Not until fifty crept up on me. . . . With it came thoughts that I might have a kid . . . and the rest just followed suit." He paused to catch his breath. "Talk about alone . . . You, at least, had Sabrina. . . . I had my work, my company, women when I had the time or inclination . . . and Dylan, who's like a son to me. But I got him in his teens. I didn't raise him. . . . So, I got to thinking . . ." Another pause, as he regathered his strength. "You know what? I'll answer my own question first. No, the single life's not all it's cracked up to be. . . . You grow older, smarter, and more alone. . . . At least *I* did. I have someone in my life now. Susan Lane. You'll like her. She's great. . . . But it's not the same as building something from the ground up. . . . We've got no history, no memories to pass on to children . . . grandchildren. If you ask me, I was a stupid fool. . . . What about you?"

Gloria sighed, thinking how funny life was. What a shame that you couldn't be born old and grow young.

"Even twenty-eight years ago, my situation was a little different from yours," she responded frankly. "And not only because I had Sabrina soon after, although I thank God that I did. I also had my parents, my roots, and, as a result, some understanding of what it meant to be tied to others. Remember, too, Carson, that going into the donor insemination, I was thirty-three to your twenty-two. I'd been an adult a whole lot longer than you. I knew that being single was a second-rate formula for happiness. I'd tried to find my soul mate—repeatedly. It just didn't happen. Sure, that would have been the better way to go. Unfortunately, it never turned out to be *my* way. So, no, I don't think living life alone is something to aspire to. But it's something I'd made peace with by the time I sought a sperm donor. If the opportunity had presented itself, I would much preferred to have found my other half, made a life with him, and had children together."

"Does that mean you'd want that for Sabrina?"

Why did Gloria have the distinct feeling she was being led somewhere in particular?

"Are you asking me if I want Sabrina to stop being such a damned workaholic and open up that wonderful heart of hers? If so, the answer's yes. Nothing would make me happier than if the perfect man for Sabrina existed out there somewhere, and that she'd find him—that they'd find each other. I may be a realist, but I'm not without dreams."

"Good." Carson settled back on the bed, linking his fingers on his chest and, despite his pain and exhaustion, looking like the proverbial cat who swallowed the canary. "Because I feel . . . the same way."

Gloria eyed him for a minute. "And?"

"And what?"

"And why did you bring this up?"

A shrug. "Just curious." He tilted his head slightly in her direction. "By the way, when Dylan flew to Manchester . . . and dropped that bomb you were referring to, did you get to meet him?"

"No. I didn't."

"Too bad . . . But you will . . . And when you do, keep a close watch . . . He's going to factor into your life in a big way. . . . He already does in mine. . . . But it's going to get bigger. . . . Ironic . . ." Carson's eyelids drooped as if he were fighting sleep.

Swiftly, Gloria glanced at her watch. The nurse would be tossing her out any minute. But she wasn't leaving . . . not yet. Not until they stopped dancing around the obvious.

"Carson, are you playing matchmaker?" she demanded.

One eyelid cracked open. "Nope . . . Just being observant . . . No matchmaker necessary . . . check out the sparks and see for yourself." A smug grin tugged at his lips. "Grandchildren might be in the cards, after all."

9:35 A.M.
Ruisseau Fragrance Corporation

The ten department heads sat rigidly around the conference room table—and around Sabrina.

As she settled herself in her chair, Sabrina assessed the group, looking around the table, one-by-one, and putting names to the faces.

Obviously, she knew Stan and Dylan, who flanked her on either side.

To Stan's left was Nelson Harte, III, chief financial officer—a go-getter, third generation Harvard Business School grad, financial genius. After that came Alfred Rowe, VP of manufacturing—the former president of Distillation Technologies Inc., a company acquired by Carson twelve years ago. Next there was Sandra Cooper, VP of sales—forty years old, the youngest company VP with the exception of Dylan, polished and savvy as they come, which was a sure-fire reason for her meteoric rise.

Directly to Sandra's left was John Baker, VP of information technology—a rare combination of techno-genius, creative dynamo, and attention-to-detail fanatic. Next came Steve Hollings, VP of strategic planning—innovative, enterprising, a real roll-up-your-sleeves-and-get-it-done kind of guy. Beside him was Rita Whiting, VP of marketing—the brains behind the C'est Moi marketing campaign, sharp as a tack and exuding the energy of a thirty-year-old, despite being well into her fifties. After Rita, came Claude Phelps, the VP of research & development—hyper and eccentric, the mad scientist type, one of Carson's original staff members. Then, Roland Ferguson, the VP of human resources—who'd left the successful recruiting firm he'd started up to come work for Carson.

Finally, there was Dylan—officially titled VP & general counsel, although he'd never changed the plaque on his door to include that pomp and circumstance—and Sabrina herself, the legal president of Ruisseau Fragrance Corporation as of twenty minutes ago when she'd signed the papers Dylan had prepared, Carson had signed, and Stan had witnessed—first for Carson, then for her. She had the title, the authority—and the anonymity, until she chose otherwise. For the time being, her input would be conveyed via Stan, who'd voice her recommendations and cast her proxy votes. Her official role, as far as Ruisseau's entire staff was concerned, would be that of Carson's newly hired management consultant.

A daunting balancing act, to say the least.

Sabrina finished her perusal, having made all the individual connections, and sipped at her coffee. The tension in the room was palpable. She couldn't help but feel an immense sense of empathy. All the VPs were clearly unglued, fiddling with pens, crossing and uncrossing their legs, and looking generally freaked-out as they waited for Stan to address whatever he'd called them here for. They were exhausted from overwork, unnerved by Carson's shooting, and drained from the police interrogations they'd been through.

And now, their COO had called an unscheduled, mandatory meeting. So on top of everything else, they were edgy as hell, unsure what was coming next, and casting uneasy, curious glances at her—the unknown intruder—trying to figure out who the hell she was and what she was doing here.

Stan didn't keep them guessing for long.

"Good morning, everyone, and thanks for being here on such short notice," he began. "I apologize for the late start. I came from Mount Sinai. The traffic was miserable." He folded his hands on the table, looking pretty green around the gills himself. The poor man had to open the meeting by breaking the worst kind of news imaginable to a group already reeling from a murder attempt on their CEO.

"Let me start by putting at least one concern to rest," he wisely prefaced things by saying. "There's no upsetting announcement about Carson's health. He's stable. I just spent a half hour with him. He was awake, talking, maybe even a little stronger than yesterday. That having been said, he was terribly upset. So am I. There's no easy way to break this to you. So I'll just say it. Last night, Russ Clark was stabbed to death outside his apartment."

A collective gasp ran through the room.

"I don't have any details, other than the fact that Russ's money and watch were taken, and that Detectives Whitman and Barton are investigating to determine if there's any connection between this and Carson's assault." Stan rubbed an unsteady hand across his forehead, then cleared his throat to regain his composure. "Ruisseau will be holding a small service in Russ's honor on Monday evening. A company-wide memo will go out later today with the time and place. In addition, Carson has arranged for a YouthOp fund to be set up in Russ's honor. Contributions of any size are welcome. Again, specifics will be in the memo."

Stan gazed around the table, his own expression as bleak as those that looked back at him. "I don't have to tell you how devastated Carson is. You know how he feels about his employees. He asked me to remind you how dedicated Russ was, how hard-working, and how thorough. He would have made one hell of an investigative reporter. And he would have been furious if we let his murder bring things at Ruisseau to a grinding halt. I know it's hard to think about perfume when one of our own's been killed, and our CEO's in intensive care. But we have to put our minds and our energies into doing just that—for Russ's sake. And for Carson's. He's counting on us. I'm counting on you."

Again, he cleared his throat. "On that note, I'm going to continue with the main—and positive—objective of this meeting." He turned toward Sabrina, gave her an encouraging smile. "I'd like to introduce Sabrina Radcliffe. She's the president and founder of the Center for Creative Thinking and Leadership in Auburn, New Hampshire. I'm sure many of you have heard of it, since its success stories are numerous, its write-ups are glowing, and, as a result, its revenues have skyrocketed in the short year it's been in existence. Smart, successful companies send their management teams there for training. We're even luckier. The president herself has come to us. She doesn't do that often, since she's inundated with work.

But, in our case, she's making an exception. As you know, Carson can be very persuasive."

A unanimous chuckle went through the room, as much from relief as from anything else. It was hardly a secret that Carson was a steamroller when he wanted something. But sharing an inside joke felt incredibly good, incredibly normal, at a time when everyone's nerves were raw and everything seemed out-of-control.

The tension in the room thawed a bit.

"Bottom line?" Stan concluded. "Carson is the heart and soul of Ruisseau. While he's recuperating, he wants us to stay on track. We've got tremendous momentum going, especially with the upcoming release of C'est Moi for men. We've got to build on our success and keep it going, make it stronger than ever. Sabrina's here to help us do that. She'll be at Ruisseau for an indefinite period of time, and we're very lucky to have her. She'll be reporting directly to me. She'll also be meeting with each of you on an individual basis and working with each of your departments to maximize its potential. I've told Sabrina what great team initiative we have, how we pull together under pressure, and how she can expect full cooperation from each and every one of you. So please join me in welcoming Sabrina to Ruisseau."

Stan came to his feet, initiating the round of applause that ensued. Sabrina followed his lead, smiling as she rose to meet his handshake. "Thank you, Stan."

"The floor's yours," he murmured, his words drowned out by the applause. "Go get 'em."

"I'll do my best," she assured him, her voice equally quiet.

She turned to face the group, noting the variety of expressions on the faces looking back at her—from pleased to relieved to wary.

All perfectly normal reactions.

"My thanks to all of you," Sabrina began as the applause subsided. "I appreciate the warm welcome." Her gaze flitted from person to person, making sure to include everyone at the table. "I'm very excited to be here. Ruisseau's success stories reach far and wide—even to the rural outskirts of New Hampshire." She got a few return smiles.

Time to get past the dark cloud precipitating her arrival. It was the only way to get things started on the right foot. To sidestep the issue would mean erecting a permanent wall between her and the group, and she could forget maximum efficiency.

"I was shocked and upset by what happened to Carson Brooks, and I'm even more sickened by the murder of Russ Clark," she said, grabbing the proverbial bull by the horns. "I'm used to stepping in when companies need help. Sometimes it's because they're in trouble—whether they're experiencing growing pains, adjusting to a recent reorganization, or requiring new strategic direction in order to jump to that next level. Sometimes it's because they're thriving, and their CEO wants to go that extra mile to make sure things stay that way. Your situation's different. The reasons for my being here transcend business. Your CEO was shot. That's personal, emotional, and professional, thanks to the kind of organization Carson Brooks has created. The man's a genius. Yet, he not only cares about his company, he cares about his people. That's why I'm here."

Sabrina's shoulders lifted in an honest but rueful shrug. "Believe me, it's not easy to step in at a time like this. It's even harder to launch a new product and continue expanding Ruisseau's reach in the luxury goods market on the heels of news like the kind Stan just delivered. But I've met with Carson, and that's exactly what he wants us to do. I understand his vision for Ruisseau. I believe I can help you attain it by keeping the momentum going until Carson is back at the helm where he belongs. But I need you to work with me. In fact, to echo Stan's words, I'm counting on you—all of you."

There were a couple of "I'm-on-board" smiles, several open, supportive expressions, an on-the-fence nod or two, and a few still-wary gazes.

Fair enough.

"The job title 'management consultant' is not my favorite," Sabrina continued. "Sometimes I think it's an out-and-out misnomer, since to many people it suggests I'm the one doing the managing. I'm not. I'm doing the consulting. *You're* doing the managing. You know this company. You know your people and your products. Without your skills, your insights, and your ability to execute, my job is pointless. So let's work together to keep Carson's dream surging ahead until he's well enough to take over himself."

She pulled a dozen photocopied pages out of her briefcase and passed them around. "This is today's schedule. You'll see that each of you has half an hour with me. Marie has double-checked with each of your assistants to make sure there are no conflicts. If we've overlooked something, let me know and I'll rearrange your time slot. No preparations are necessary. I'd just like to get to know each of you, and get a feel for the way you see your department, its challenges, and how it fits in with Ruisseau's strategic direction. Once we've talked, we can arrange full-department meetings for next week, focusing on the key initiatives and projects each department is working on."

She waited until the pages had made their way around

the table and everyone was scanning them. "Whatever unaccounted-for time I have today, I plan to use walking around with Stan, being introduced to as many staff members as possible. I'm not going to bombard you with hand-outs or espousals of my corporate philosophy. I'm not a windbag and I'm not a game-player. I'm a straight shooter, and I'd appreciate if you would be, too. If you have a problem, tell me. If you don't like an idea, say so. If you disagree with a point of view, give me your reasons why and support them with facts. And if you want to run something by me, or to say hello, or just to check me out and see if I'm really the nice person I seem to be or if I'm really a control freak who's just a great actress, come on by. My office is two doors down from Carson's. First-hand experience is always the best way to find out."

Gathering up her briefcase and coffee, she made a mental note of where the chuckles came from—and where they didn't. "I'm heading to my office now. My first meeting's set for eleven o'clock. That's with you, Rita." She turned to the head of marketing, ensuring that she made direct eye contact. Good. Rita was nodding, and she looked enthused.

"So," Sabrina concluded, with a quick glance at her watch. "That gives all of you more than enough time to put your heads together and come up with an initial assessment of me." She headed for the door. "Someone will have to let me know how I measure up. See you at eleven, Rita."

19

6:35 P.M.
Mt. Sinai Hospital

Carson was propped up on his elbows, watching the door like a predatory hawk, when Sabrina and Dylan walked in.

"Well?" he demanded.

"Well what?" Sabrina feigned ignorance, slipping off her jacket and slinging it over the back of a chair.

"Well, Radison told me twenty minutes ago that you were here. . . . It took you this long to waltz into my room? . . . What'd you do, stop for a five-course dinner in the lounge?"

"No," Dylan replied, pulling up two seats, one for himself and one for Sabrina. "We stopped to talk to Dr. Radison. We wanted an update. We had to wait. He was with another patient. There are one or two of those around, you know. Anyway, he told us you were doing better. Although I can see that for myself. You're cranky as hell." Dylan turned to Sabrina. "Like I said, he's a miserable patient."

"No shock there," Sabrina quipped back.

She wasn't fooled by Dylan's bantering tone. He was worried about Carson. She could see it written all over his face. And the way he was scrutinizing his friend, giving him a thorough physical inspection—it was far from subtle.

She found herself doing the same thing.

Walking over to Carson's bedside, she acknowledged to herself that, despite all the medical reassurances Dr. Radison had provided, she needed to see for herself that Carson was okay. She'd been uneasy all day, troubled by what his reaction must have been to Stan's news about Russ. Obviously, he'd jump to the immediate—and no doubt accurate—conclusion that there was a tie-in between his own assault and Russ's murder. So, on top of coping with his sense of loss, he'd experience a sense of guilt. He cared about his employees. He'd feel responsible. And—talk about the straw to break the camel's back—he had the additional burden of shield-ing and comforting Susan. He was a strong man, but he was in a weakened state. There was just so much strain he could hold up under, despite his unwavering show of bravado.

It was amazing how well she understood this man, al-most on instinct. Then again, in many ways it was like gazing in the mirror.

Out of the corner of her eye, Sabrina spotted the dialy-sis machine, which had reappeared in Carson's room and was now sitting idly to the side. The sight made her in-sides twist. Not that its being there was a surprise. She knew Carson had undergone another dialysis treatment. Dr. Radison had told them so. She'd responded by asking him to put a rush on her tissue-typing. But, according to him, that was pointless, since it would be weeks before Carson was strong enough to undergo surgery—should it be needed.

Dammit. She was beginning to feel as frustrated and helpless as Dylan.

"Cut it out, both of you," Carson barked out, interrupt-ing her train of thought. "You're about as subtle as bricks. . . . I'm fine. . . . Strong as an ox . . . I'm just losing my mind, lying here in this bed. . . . Can't do anything but think. And thinking sucks."

"I'm sorry about Russ," Sabrina said quietly, laying her hand over his.

Carson gazed down at her fingers covering his, and an odd expression crossed his face. "Yeah, me, too." His voice was rough.

"Everyone's going to the service," Dylan interjected, closely observing the exchange between father and daughter. "And the contributions to the YouthOp fund are spilling over on Marie's desk."

"Yes, the line at her desk looked like passenger check-in at JFK." Sabrina heard the tremor in her voice, and she mentally beat herself up. Losing control wasn't her thing. And now certainly wasn't the time to change that. What the hell was wrong with her? It had to be fatigue and tension combined with the adrenaline drop that followed a long, roller-coaster of a day. Still, there was no excuse.

She forced herself to get a grip.

"My staff's the best," Carson replied. He was watching her, and Sabrina knew it. "Including Russ. I expected nothing less . . . than total unity." He obviously sensed Sabrina's turmoil, because he gave her hand a hard squeeze before releasing it. "Hey," he chided. "I don't fall apart that easily. . . . Just ask Dylan . . . As for that machine you were staring at . . . it did its job. . . . Dialysis is a piece of cake. . . . Stop worrying."

"I'm not worrying," she retorted. This time her voice was steady. "Not only do you look better, you've got some color, you're breathing more evenly, and you're sitting up without support. As for being strong as an ox, maybe not yet, but almost—that is, if your grip's any indication." Her brows arched. "Or is it fear that's prompting your newfound strength? Are you worried that I destroyed your company in nine short hours?"

"The thought did cross my mind."

"Well, sorry to disappoint you, but Ruisseau's better than ever." Sabrina gave him a smug look, filled with mock-challenge. "I even came up with a few ideas you haven't—at least not yet. But when you hear them, you're going to wish you had."

Rather than take the bait, Carson just studied her, his blue eyes probing. Abruptly, a grin curved his lips. "You're hooked. Damn. It took less time than I thought. . . . One day at the helm, and you're hooked." He settled himself on the pillows, his gaze still fixed on her. "So, how did it feel . . . being president of Ruisseau? What's your take on my company?"

Sabrina sat down and crossed her legs. "The overview? Or the blow-by-blow?"

"Both."

Having expected that response, Sabrina was already reaching for her briefcase. "I took notes."

"Good." While she retrieved them, Carson turned to Dylan, who'd settled himself in the other chair. "In the meantime, what'd you think? Was she all I expected?"

"She was amazing," Dylan reported. "Slapped her cards right on the table and turned up aces. She gave the troops a few minutes to catch their breath, then plunged into basic training. She worked everyone's butt off, especially her own. Despite a few war wounds, the feedback was great. Rave reviews across the board." A wry grin. "The consensus is, she's almost as much of a slave-driver as you are, but with a slightly more genteel and persuasive delivery. In a nutshell, she's a tsunami, but no one realizes they've been hit. A brilliant strategy."

"Gee, thanks—I think." Sabrina edged him a sideways

look, although her real reaction was a one-eighty from the one she displayed. Rather than rankled, she felt pleased and reinforced by Dylan's praise. He didn't hand out compliments easily. By the same token, she didn't usually need to hear them.

If that didn't speak volumes about whatever was happening between them, nothing did. And if that was an indicator of the shape of things to come—she didn't even want to go there. Not now.

God, there was so much emotional turmoil converging on her at once—she wondered if she was going to survive.

"You're welcome." Dylan was watching her, and that lopsided grin went from wry to something else—something knowing and intense.

Was it Sabrina's imagination, or was the room suddenly ten degrees warmer?

"A subtle tsunami, huh?" Carson was muttering with great satisfaction. "Couldn't ask for more. A balls-and-diplomacy combo . . . Just like Gloria planned."

That dragged Sabrina's attention away from Dylan. "Nice phraseology," she commented. "A balls-and-diplomacy combo. I sound like something you order at McDonald's." She paused in her paper-shuffling. "And what do you mean, just like Gloria planned? Did your sources turn that up when they checked out my mother?"

"Nope . . . Came straight from the source . . . She's almost as impressive as you are."

"Excuse me?"

"Your mother. She stopped by today."

The briefcase slid to the floor. "My mother?" Sabrina repeated. "She was *here?*"

"Yup. We had a great visit. . . . Long overdue, too."

Carson nodded at some internal thought. "No surprise you turned out great . . . She's quite a person."

"Wait a minute." Sabrina waved her hand in disbelief. "You're saying my mother came to the hospital specifically to visit you?"

"Uh-huh. Helped me get through my first few minutes alone . . . after Susan left . . . Stan had told us about Russ. . . . Gloria's a wise, compassionate woman. . . . And if you're wondering why she didn't clue you in to the fact that she was coming . . . it's because she knew you had your first day at Ruisseau on your mind. . . . She didn't want to add to your stress. . . . She plans on telling you about our talk. . . . I just happened to see you first. . . . She said, if that happened, I was welcome to fill you in."

"I see." Sabrina wasn't sure she did. "What did you two talk about?"

Carson snorted. "That's a stupid question."

"I'll rephrase. What in particular about me did you discuss?"

"Let's just say that Gloria gave me a lesson . . . in fatherhood. She also told me she supported . . . what I had in mind for you. That meant a great deal . . . to me." He shifted impatiently. "Now tell me about Ruisseau. . . . Who did you meet? What were your impressions?"

Sabrina continued to eye him. "You're not going to elaborate, are you?"

"Nope. But you are. Get out those notes . . . and start talking."

With a sigh, she complied, telling herself she'd worm the details out of her mother later, wondering at the same time if she would. She had a sneaky suspicion that much of this heart-to-heart between her mother and Carson would remain private.

Odd, having two parents looking out for your welfare rather than one.

"Did Stan take you around?" Carson pressed.

"He was terrific," Sabrina assured him. "In between my meetings, he took me from office to office, and cubicle to cubicle. He introduced me to everyone from the VPs to the cleaning staff. I started with Marie, whom I thanked profusely for making my new apartment feel like a home. Incidentally, she's the most efficient, insightful assistant I've ever come across. And talk about multitasking—wow. Be good to her; you won't find another like her."

"Gotcha. What else?"

"Rita Whiting. She and I really hit it off. We tossed around some pretty wild marketing ideas. The energy in that office could've blown up a tanker."

Carson chuckled. "I knew you two would be on the same wavelength." He gestured at her notes. "Go through the whole rundown."

Sabrina launched into an extensive elaboration of her back-to-back interactions, giving him every detail, touching on the various unique talents she'd perceived, the outstanding employees she'd zeroed in on—those she referred to as "the best of the best"—and the occasional weaker link she detected.

The latter were few and far between, a smattering of B's and B+'s in a company full of A's.

"Nothing to sit up nights about. Just things to stay on top of," she clarified to Carson. "And remember, these were only first impressions. I have a long way to go before they're etched in stone."

"Damn good start . . . Right on target, in most cases . . ." Carson had listened intently, his forehead creased in concentration. But now Sabrina could see how exhausted he was.

"Enough," she concluded, putting away her notes. "I just crammed a nine-hour day into twenty minutes. You need to rest. Suffice it to say, you're right. I'm hooked. Even the visit to the lab, and watching the perfume being made, was fascinating. I could picture you doing the extractions, mixing and testing, creating all your groundbreaking fragrances." A brief pause, and she regarded Carson soberly as she realized how true her own words were. "I can't thank you enough. This is a once-in-a-lifetime opportunity."

"Um—I'd say it's a draw." Contentment softened the lines of pain and fatigue on his face. "Having you in my life and in my company—those are pretty once-in-a-lifetime, too."

Sabrina rose. "You get some sleep."

"Where're you going?"

"To pump my mother for information."

A faint chuckle. "Don't bother. She won't tell. . . . She's the one you inherited the diplomacy part of the combo from." He turned to Dylan, who'd also gotten up. "You look crappy . . . like you're about to keel over. . . ."

"Thanks," Dylan retorted dryly. "But I'm holding up fine."

"Yeah. Right." A sudden thought seemed to strike Carson. "Did either of you eat today?"

Dylan squinted, trying to remember. "I had a muffin after the meeting. Other than that, nope. Just lots of coffee."

Carson grunted. "What about you?" he asked Sabrina.

"Same," she confessed.

"Then go get dinner," Carson ordered. "Jesus, you're like two damned college kids. . . . You treat your bodies like shit. . . . Now go get some food . . . and I don't mean a sandwich and coffee. . . . Something substantial. Sabrina, you've got a huge corporate expense account now. . . . Use it."

Her lips twitched. "I already had a corporate expense account."

"Sure you did." Another grunt. "How much does food cost . . . up there in the sticks? . . . You're in the Big Apple now. . . . That CCTL expense account won't buy a pretzel and a soda."

"Damn." Sabrina snapped her fingers. "And that's just what I was in the mood for, too—a salty New York pretzel and a Diet Coke."

Carson glared at her, then shot Dylan a look. "She's more stubborn than you are."

"What a surprise," Dylan replied. "I wonder who she could take after?"

"Get the two of you fed . . ." Carson commanded, ignoring Dylan's barb. "Go somewhere good. . . . Your expense account's nothing to sneeze at either. . . . You run the show. . . . Just take her to dinner."

"I intended to. No mandate or expense account necessary." Dylan arched a brow. "Just tell me, are you picking the restaurant again? Or does that fall under the category of my running the show, meaning I'm allowed the privilege?"

"It depends. . . . Where'd you have in mind?"

Dylan turned to Sabrina, addressing her as if Carson wasn't in the room. "Do you like Spanish? I know a great place in the Village. Amazing shrimp in green sauce and the best sangria around."

"That sounds wonderful," she said. It did, too. The thought of relaxing over a glass of sangria was like a balm to her senses. "And seafood's perfect. After not eating all day, I don't think I could handle anything too heavy."

"Done." Dylan inclined his head in Carson's direction. "I'm taking her to El Faro. Does that work for you?"

"Yeah. Good choice. Crowded, but after a few drinks it won't matter." A corner of Carson's mouth lifted, even as his eyelids drooped. "Get the white sangria. . . . goes well with the shrimp green . . . Get two pitchers of sangria. . . . Tomorrow's Saturday . . . Our new president's day off . . . She can sleep in. . . . So can our corporate counsel."

Sabrina blinked, studying Carson, whose eyes had drifted shut. If she didn't know better, she'd swear he was trying to manipulate the evening so it ended up with her and Dylan "sleeping in" together. But that was absurd. It had to be a coincidence—one that just happened to strike too close to home.

She glanced at Dylan, whose startled expression matched hers. Clearly, the same thoughts were running through his head.

He met her gaze and shrugged. "Let's go. He's half-asleep."

"Apparently." She scooped up her jacket and took a step toward the door.

At the same moment, it swung open, and Susan walked in. She looked pale, the area around her eyes—even concealed by extra makeup—swollen from crying. "Hi." She managed a smile. "The nurse told me you two were with Carson. Don't worry, I won't interrupt. I just wanted to check in on him. After that, I promise to wait in the lounge until you've finished your business."

"That's not necessary. We just wrapped up." Sabrina waved away the offer, walking over to Susan and touching her arm. "Susan, I'm so sorry about Russ. I know he was part of your YouthOp family, and that's how he came to Ruisseau. I've heard such wonderful things about him. I feel terrible."

Fresh tears dampened Susan's lashes, and she blinked them away. "Thank you. Yes, Russ was about the most glowing example of YouthOp's potential there could be. He was special. He would have made a real difference in this world. What happened to him was such a waste. Everyone at YouthOp is heartsick. . . ." An unsteady pause. "Anyway, I appreciate your sympathy."

"Carson's hurting, too," Dylan stated flatly, his tone so pointed that Sabrina flinched. Not that she disagreed with Dylan's feelings. He was looking out for Carson, reminding Susan that she wasn't the only one who'd suffered a loss. But how Susan would react to such a direct hit was anyone's guess. More important, how Carson would react when he woke up and Susan told him about Dylan's barbed comment—that was an even bigger question.

Sabrina got her answer sooner than expected.

"Cool it, Dylan. . . ." Carson's voice, tired but adamant, sounded from the bed.

"It's okay," Susan responded, cutting Carson off before he got himself upset. "Dylan's right. You *are* hurting. And I've been a basket case, which is the last thing you need right now."

"Good. Then we're on the same page." Dylan wasn't giving, not an inch, no matter how ticked off Carson got. "Sabrina and I are heading off to dinner. We'll leave you two alone—to comfort each other." He turned toward the bed, totally disregarding Carson's warning scowl. "Get some rest. I'll be by tomorrow."

"Me, too," Sabrina added. Interesting that Carson now looked fully awake. Whether he'd gotten a second wind or was putting on a show for Susan's sake was anyone's guess.

Actually, there was a third choice. Carson could have been more awake a few minutes ago than he wanted her or Dylan to realize. In which case, he was pulling some very interesting strings.

She tucked that thought away for further contemplation.

"By the way, Sabrina—" Susan's tone said she was trying to smooth things over. "I saw your mother here this morning. I would have introduced myself, but she was heading in the other direction. Did the two of you connect?"

Now *that* revelation came at Sabrina out of left field. Carson hadn't said a word about Susan being aware of Gloria's visit. What had he told her?

She tossed an uncertain glance in his direction.

"There's no way they could have connected, Suze," he interceded, not missing a beat. "Sabrina hasn't seen the light of day. . . . Hasn't even breathed since eight A.M. She's been in meetings from then till now. . . . But I'm glad you reminded me. . . . I almost forgot to tell her about this morning's mix-up. . . . Damned medication clouds my thinking."

He angled his head toward Sabrina. "Your mother called Ruisseau this morning looking for you. . . . Someone screwed up . . . told her you were at Mount Sinai, that your meeting with me was first thing in the day rather than last. . . . So she grabbed a cab and came here. . . . By the time we got our signals straight, you were already in the middle of that big powwow with Stan. . . . She said it could wait. . . . Talk about a comedy of errors . . ."

"I see." Quickly, Sabrina assimilated the story Carson had fabricated. She was very touched that he'd gone to such lengths to honor his promise not to divulge who she was, even to Susan. After all, Susan wasn't just anyone— she was a fundamental person in his life.

A person who deserved to know the truth, not along with the rest of the world, but privately and in advance.

Sabrina was the only one who could make that happen.

"Your poor mother." Susan grimaced, mistaking Sabrina's silence for irritation. "She rode all the way uptown for nothing. She must have blown half a business day. Will she be very upset?"

"Not at all." Sabrina recovered, regained her stride. "My mother's used to my insane schedule. She won't be the least bit upset, especially since we just had dinner together last night. I'll give her a call from my cell as soon as I leave the hospital."

Susan's relief was tangible. "How long will she be in New York?" she asked, a hopeful note creeping into her voice. "I'd love to meet her."

"Hey, Suze. . . ." Carson's voice emerged from the bed again. "The poor woman's probably swamped. . . . I know her daughter is. . . . I'm not giving her a chance to breathe . . . much less have time for herself. . . . Not with the rates she charges . . . Now let these two go to dinner. . . . Come over here and sit with me."

"Carson—it's okay," Sabrina broke in, referring to much more than the introduction. "I'm sure my mother would love to meet Susan." She gave Carson a gentle nod.

"Fine . . ." Comprehension flickered in his eyes, but he kept his face carefully expressionless. "The two of them can get together over lunch . . . but you'd better make it the weekend if you want to join them. . . ."

Sabrina understood. Carson was keeping up the pretense, giving her a final chance to change her mind. He wasn't going to say a single word, not until and unless she gave him the go-ahead.

"Goodnight, you two." Firmly, he dismissed her and Dylan, holding her gaze as he let her off the hook. "Eat and drink hearty."

The ball was in her court.

She fielded it, with a lot more ease than she'd anticipated.

"We will—soon," she said, putting an end to the charade. "First I want to talk to Susan." She turned to do so. "Susan, the truth is, my mother's not in New York on business. And she didn't come to Mount Sinai to see me. She came to see Carson."

"To see . . ." Susan blinked, clearly bewildered. "I don't understand." Her fingers fluttered through the air in confusion. "Why would your mother visit Carson? And why wouldn't he tell me if she had?"

"Because he was protecting me."

"From what?"

"It's a long story. But it's time you heard it." A pause. "I *want* you to hear it—for your sake, and for Carson's." Sabrina angled around, assessing Carson's energy level. "Are you up for this? Or should I take Susan out to the lounge and talk to her there?"

"No way." He shook his head, and Sabrina could see he was grappling with a wealth of emotion. "I missed the original announcement. . . . You know, the one where they say, 'It's a girl' . . . There's not a chance I'm missing the second one. . . . If you're telling . . . I'm listening."

"I'm glad," Sabrina said simply. She put her hand on Susan's arm, gestured toward a chair. "Have a seat. Whatever you're expecting, it's not this."

20

The world looked a lot rosier after three glasses of sangria.

Then again, they were a necessary reprieve after the day Sabrina had just charged her way through.

Buffeted by waiters making their way through narrow aisles carrying covered dishes of food, lulled by the din of enthusiastic patrons and the tantalizing smells of Spanish cuisine, Sabrina felt cradled within a lovely sense of cocooned isolation. So this was the eye of the hurricane. Well, it was a great stopping point.

With the edge of her spoon, she toyed with an orange slice at the bottom of her glass. She wasn't drunk. But she wasn't sober either. Between the languid effects of the wine, the filling warmth of the food, and the sharp adrenaline drop that signified the end of a Guinness Book week, she felt exquisitely relaxed.

"A penny for your thoughts," Dylan said, watching her over the rim of his own glass.

She smiled. "I was just thinking that Carson was right. This is exactly what I needed. I think I was about to implode."

He nodded, refilling both their glasses. "Today was a day to write home about. The fact that you survived is a coup."

"I think you said that yesterday. And the day before."

"Probably. But today was in a class by itself." Dylan spooned more rice onto their plates, then added shrimp and drizzled green sauce over the top. "Eat. You need to recharge."

"Okay. But I've already had two portions. I think I'm restored." She stuck her fork into the food, then into her mouth, savoring the garlicky flavor of the green sauce. "I did a pretty good job of anticipating things at Ruisseau. But that chat with Susan was pretty unexpected. Not that I'm sorry. It needed to be had. It's just that I was already reeling with stimuli. . . ." She shook her head.

"Yeah. Just when you thought the day was over, you found yourself recapping the story of your conception yet again."

"The good news is, it wasn't *too* painful. Susan took it well, even though she was shaken up. And she had a right to know before the rest of the world found out. She and Carson are pretty tight."

"That they are."

It was hard to miss the curt note in Dylan's voice.

Sabrina put down her fork. "You're still pissed at her. Why? Do you really think her personal grief over Russ's murder is *that* unfounded?"

"It's not her grief that's pissing me off. It's the self-centered way she's handling it. Not only is she so focused on her own pain that she barely notices Carson's, but she's leaning on him big-time. I know she's used to his being a rock. We all are. But, for God's sake, the man's been shot. He's fighting for his life. He's far from out of the woods. All his strength has to go into recovering. And he's a man, not a god. The least she could do is let him do the leaning for a change."

"I see your point. But, in Susan's defense, I'm sure her reserves are shot. She's been at Carson's bedside practically round-the-clock. Now this horrible thing happened to Russ. It's a lot to deal with. And let's not forget one thing more—Carson's not exactly the lean-on-others type. You, of all people, know that."

"All the more reason that those who care about him have to *make* him lean, especially at a time like this. *You,* of all people, know *that.*" Dylan gave her a pointed look. "Aren't you the woman who blew a gasket because I wanted to facilitate your move from the Plaza Athenée to your new place, even though a little help was precisely what you needed—and you knew it? Hell, Sabrina, you're just like him."

"I guess I am," Sabrina acknowledged thoughtfully. "Sometimes help has to be shoved down my throat. Okay, you're right. Susan's well aware that Carson's stubborn as hell about showing weakness. In this case, she should be forcing him to get over that—and forcing herself to be strong." Sabrina took a sip of sangria. "You know her a lot better than I do. Do you doubt that her feelings for Carson are genuine?"

"Nope." Dylan gave an adamant shake of his head. "That's the one thing I don't doubt. If I did, I'd be in Carson's face, whether or not he wanted me there. Someone's got to look out for the guy. As it is . . ." His voice trailed off. "Let's not talk about this anymore, okay? It only ticks me off. And I want us to unwind."

"Fine with me." Sabrina glanced around the small, crowded restaurant. "I like this place. It's loud, it's jam-packed and, at the same time, it's cozy. Is that possible—or is it an illusion created by imbibing half a pitcher of sangria?"

Dylan chuckled. "Both. Sure it's possible. But it's better when you're mellowed by wine."

"Mellowed. Yes, I'm certainly that. What worries me is

what I'll be after pitcher number two, which is on its way."
She eyeballed the one sitting in front of her, empty except
for a wooden spoon, half-melted ice, and a sliver of apple. "I
can't believe we're actually going for a second batch. I don't
care what Carson said—I think it's only fair to warn you
that I'm a cheap drunk. If I go for more than another glass or
two, I won't just be sleeping in. I'll be slumping over."

"I'll make sure you stop before that happens."

"Promise?"

"Promise."

"Well . . ." Her eyes sparkled. "In that case, a little
more mellowing out can't hurt."

"Glad to hear it." A corner of Dylan's mouth lifted.
"Because reinforcements have arrived."

As he spoke, the waiter appeared with the second
pitcher. He topped off each of their glasses, then placed
the pitcher on the table between them, and left.

"Ummm." Sabrina's eyes slid shut as she savored her
first cold sip. "I think this batch is even better than the
first. My glass has almost twice as many oranges and
lemons as last time."

"Really." Dylan sounded amused. "You multiplied
that out with your eyes closed?"

"I didn't need to multiply," she replied, her lashes lifting. "I inhaled. The stronger citrus aromas told me what I
need to know."

"Ah. That remarkable olfactory sense. I can't wait to
see you apply it to perfume." Dylan watched her take a
second swallow, and his eyes darkened as she licked a
few drops off her lips. "Actually, there are a lot of things I
can't wait for."

The electricity between them crackled to life again—
its impact jarring. Sexual tension sizzled through them,
between them.

This time Sabrina explored, rather than fought, it. "Tell me something, counselor." She propped her elbow on the table and regarded Dylan intently. "Did you take me here so we'd relax, or so we'd be on safe ground because we're among lots and lots of people?"

He set down his glass, folding his hands on the table and leaning forward. "I took you here because the food and the sangria are great, and because it's far away from offices and hospitals. As for safe ground, I told you there is none." His voice lowered, took on a rough, provocative quality that sent shivers up her spine. "The crowd's irrelevant. The setting's irrelevant. I want you no matter where we are and no matter who we're with. I think you know that. What I want to *do* with you can't be done in a restaurant—*any* restaurant, busy or quiet. It requires total privacy, long interrupted hours, and a very big bed." He paused. "Actually, the bed is optional. I could improvise."

Sabrina had never been seduced by words before. But there was a first time for everything.

Waves of heat shot through her, throbbed in all the right places. She swallowed, hard, savoring and fighting the sensations all at once.

"Too blunt?" Dylan asked. "Or too much to handle?"

"Neither. Too close to what I want."

Those orange sparks glinted in his eyes. "The complications that stopped us in our tracks yesterday—I was going to wait to bring them up. But I think we'd better get past them, fast. How does now work for you?"

"Now works fine—if I can think straight." *Or if I want to,* Sabrina added silently to herself. She took a fortifying gulp of sangria.

"Let's start with the biggie." Dylan wasn't mincing words. "You're going through a lot of upheaval right now. An affair with me would be another complication."

"True. But maybe it wouldn't be an affair. Maybe it'd be something simple, like a one-night stand."

"Uh-uh." Dylan pushed aside his glass. "Not a chance. Not with us. One night would merely whet our appetites. Trust me."

She arched a brow. "About this, I guess I should. You're the one who discovered sex the day he reached puberty. That makes you a pro."

"It makes me experienced enough to know that with us—" He sucked in his breath. "Let's just say that once I get inside you, neither of us will be coming up for air for a long, long time. That's a given. Now, is it what you want, even with the complications?"

"Yes." Sabrina had never run away from anything in her life, and she wasn't running away from this. "It's just what I want. I only hope it doesn't push me past overload. But if it does, so be it. I'm a big girl. I can cope—I think. There's only one way to find out."

"Ditto, on all counts." He noted the dubious expression in her eyes, and addressed it. "Don't kid yourself, sweetheart. Experienced or not, I'm way out of my league on this one. I told you so last night. And I meant it." He reached over, took her hand, and brought her palm to his mouth. "But the bottom line is, I no longer give a damn."

Sabrina had to grit her teeth against the pleasure of his touch, his breath against her skin. "O-okay, we covered complication one. What are the others?"

"Mixing work with play. Becoming part of the media hype when your relationship to Carson gets out. Other things I can't come up with right now because all I can think about is getting inside you." Dylan's warm, open mouth moved against her palm in slow, teasing sweeps. "Your turn. Do any of those complications matter enough to change your mind?"

"No. There's only one potential obstacle that matters—and I'm not even sure it's valid."

"You're talking about Carson, and the way he'll react when he finds out."

"Y-yes." Sabrina caught her breath as Dylan bit down lightly on her palm, sending shock waves shimmering through her. "But after the way he just acted . . ."

". . . it could be that that last complication's nonexistent." Dylan was tasting her skin, lingering at all the pleasure points.

"So you did notice."

"Um-hum."

How was she supposed to think straight when every caress was shooting straight to her loins?

Carson. They were talking about Carson, and whether or not he would be bugged by their getting together, or cheering them on.

"It wasn't my imagination then. Carson was pushing us into bed together," she managed weakly.

"Sure seemed that way to me." Dylan's tongue traced the inside of her wrist. "Unless it was a coincidence that he happened to be out of it just long enough to tell us both to get drunk and sleep in—and then, wham-o—he was wide awake when Susan walked in."

"That was my take on it, too." Sabrina tried to recall the conversation, but all she could think about was her libido, which was screaming at the top of its lungs. "I wonder if he has an agenda when it comes to us."

"Maybe. Maybe not." Dylan's breathing had become uneven. She could feel it against her damp skin. "Frankly, I don't care. I want you. You want me. We're consenting adults. Yes, I respect Carson's opinion of me. But that doesn't include needing his approval to take you to bed. The only person whose approval I need is yours." He dragged her fingers slowly across his parted lips, circling each fingertip with his tongue. "Do I have it?"

She would have replied, if she could speak. All she could muster was a nod.

Dylan took in the play of emotions on her face, and his jaw tightened. "Is there anything I'm forgetting on the complications front?" he demanded. "Because I thought I could wait. I can't."

"Neither can I."

The tension peaked, and splintered.

"Forget the second pitcher of sangria," Dylan ground out, releasing her fingers to shove his hand in his pocket and grope for his wallet. "I want you sober. I want your mind totally clear. That way, you'll know when I make you lose it."

That did it for Sabrina.

She was shaking as she tossed her napkin on the table, pushed aside her still-full glass. No arm-twisting was necessary. She wanted her mind as clear as Dylan did. "Get the check."

"Done." Dylan was already signaling the waiter.

Three minutes later, the receipt had been signed, and they were making their way toward the door.

"Whose apartment's closer?" Sabrina asked, her voice so raw she hardly recognized it.

"Yours. But we're going to mine."

"Why?"

The look Dylan gave her could melt stone. "Because I've got two boxes of condoms there."

The tension in the car was so thick you could cut it with a knife.

Sabrina and Dylan climbed out in front of Dylan's

brownstone, and he sent the driver away, saying he'd walk Ms. Radcliffe home. Whether or not the driver sensed how frantic they were to get at each other, neither of them cared.

Dylan unlocked his front door, steering Sabrina inside. He slammed the door shut and flipped the lock. "The grand tour's going to have to wait," he said thickly, backing her against the wall. He tugged her blazer down her arms, lowering his head and covering her mouth in a kiss that burned through them both.

Shaking her arms free of the garment, Sabrina let it drop to the floor, tearing her mouth away from Dylan's long enough to answer breathlessly, "I don't want a tour. I want this." She resumed the kiss, her palms gliding inside Dylan's suit jacket, up his shirt front.

He was unbuttoning her blouse, sending a few buttons scattering to the floor as he yanked it free of her skirt, spread the sides apart to give him access to her skin. His lips burned a path down her throat to her cleavage. "Decision time. It's too dark for you to see your surroundings. So I'll describe. You choose." He pulled the pins out of her hair, tunneling his fingers through it as it tumbled to her shoulders. "The fireplace is across the hall. There's a shag rug in front of it. The living room's to our right. It has a wide, cushy sectional sofa. The den's to our left. It has a leather recliner that tilts way, way back. Upstairs, there are two bedrooms. The guest room's got a queen-size bed and a huge area rug. The master's got a king-size bed and extra pillows. What's your pleasure?"

Sabrina paused in the process of unbuttoning his shirt, tipped up her chin. "Where are the condoms?"

"In the master."

"Sold."

His mouth came down on hers, hard, and he tangled a hand in her hair, anchored her head to deepen the kiss. His tongue plunged inside, rubbed against hers, and Sabrina shoved open his shirt, pressed herself against the hair-roughened surface of his chest. Her nipples hardened through the sheer silk fabric of her bra, burned into his skin, and Dylan's control snapped.

"We're going up there—now." He swung her into his arms, strode through the darkened hall and up the flight of steps.

"If you'd turn on the lights, I could walk," Sabrina murmured, burying her lips against his throat, pressing hot kisses there.

"That would take too long." Dylan's voice was hoarse, and he shuddered with each stroke of her lips. "All that matters is getting your clothes off and getting you under me."

He carried her into his bedroom and lowered her onto the bed, following her down.

They came together without prelude, their kisses hot and frantic, their fingers yanking impatiently at the clothes that separated them. Dylan unhooked her bra, and his mouth was on her nipples, sucking them until Sabrina was moaning and squirming, every tug of his lips shooting straight to her loins. He went with the motion of her body, moving from one breast to the other as he worked her skirt and panty hose off, not pausing until she was completely naked.

Sabrina's hands were equally busy. By the time Dylan tossed the last of her clothes to the floor, she'd unzipped his slacks and dragged them down. She slipped her fingers inside his briefs, finding and exploring his erection from base to tip.

"Shit." Dylan exhaled the word in a hiss. He vaulted

off the bed, kicked free of his clothing, then scooped
Sabrina up long enough to pull back the bedding,
place her on the sheets. He came down over her, covering her, his solid weight pressing her into the mattress.

The contact was electrifying. The entire experience
was electrifying, pushing them both into major sensual
overload. Whatever was happening here was too intense,
too impalpable to assign a name.

They didn't try.

They kissed, again and again, unable to get enough of
each other's taste, each other's touch. Sabrina inhaled
Dylan's scent—that musky cologne and outdoorsy soap,
mixed with Dylan, just Dylan—his own heady masculine
scent more potent now that his skin was damp with
sweat, sensitized with arousal. She wrapped her arms
around his back, her mouth slanting under his repeatedly,
hungrily, her body arching to increase the exquisite friction of skin against skin. Dylan anchored her head in his
hands, devouring her mouth over and over, his thighs
wedging between hers as their kisses deepened, became
hotter, more demanding. His hand slid down, defining
the curves of her body, then reached between her legs to
touch her.

Sabrina stopped breathing at the contact, then whim-
pered as his fingers slid inside her, his thumb rasping
over her clitoris. Her body reacted instantly and of its
own accord. Her inner muscles resonated, loosening and
tightening all at once, and everything inside her went liquid, desire pounding at her brain as her hips lifted, seeking more.

"God, you feel so damned good," Dylan muttered, re-
peating the motion. "Hot. Wet. That's right, sweetheart.
Tighten around me. Like that. Again." His fingers

pressed deeper, higher inside her, and Sabrina heard herself cry out. "Sabrina, I'm losing my mind."

"So am I." Her hand moved between them, her fingers closing around his erection, feeling it pulse in her hand as she caressed it. "Don't go slow. Not this time. We've got all night for slow. But this time . . . it has to be now. . . . *Now* . . ." Her fingertips circled the head of his penis, absorbing droplets of fluid. "Dylan . . . please."

His control shattered.

With a muffled curse, he rolled away from her, jerking open his night table drawer and groping inside until he found the box of condoms. He pulled out one foil packet, tore open the wrapper with his teeth and, in a few quick, urgent motions, guided the condom into place.

"Ah, remembering cardinal rule one," Sabrina murmured as he knelt over her.

"Yeah, by a thread." Dylan hooked his arms beneath her knees, opening her for the deepest possible penetration. "Another second and I'd have been too far gone to remember. That's what you do to me. As it is, I've kissed rule three good-bye. Staying detached's not an option. I'm so involved I can't think straight." He fitted his body to hers, and pushed slowly inside.

Sabrina sucked in her breath. "That feels . . . amazing. But it's not enough." She arched, trying to deepen his penetration.

"Don't . . ." Dylan got out between clenched teeth. "You're tight. I'm trying not to—"

"Stop trying. I need you all the way inside me." Sabrina's fists knotted at the base of his spine, pushing him forward and anchoring herself so she could lift up—hard. "To hell with rule two."

She glided around him—slick and trembling—and Dylan lost it entirely.

The muscles in his back flexed, and he thrust deep, burying himself inside her.

The meaning behind her last comment penetrated his passion-drugged mind a split second after he got first-hand confirmation.

He went deadly still, the muscles in his forearms rippling with the strain of holding back. "Damn." He dragged air into his lungs. "Sabrina, are you okay?"

"No . . . I'm . . ." She could barely speak, the pleasure jarring along her nerve endings was so intense. She shifted under him, her body adjusting to the incredible sense of fullness, the clawing hunger that coiled tighter inside her now that he was there, stretching and filling her. "Don't stop. . . . Dylan, please . . . I'm . . . dying. . . ."

A hard shudder ran through him. "Not yet you're not." He began moving, each thrust slow and deliberate, his penis rubbing on her and in her, the excruciating friction pushing her closer and closer to where she needed to be. "But you will be—soon." He lowered his head and kissed her again, his breathing hard and ragged as he ate at her mouth.

She responded blindly, her mouth as frantic as his, her nails digging into his shoulder blades. "Faster," she gasped, her inner muscles coiling tighter, clamping down on Dylan and stripping him of his last shred of self-restraint. "God, I'm so close. . . . I . . ."

Dylan gave a hoarse shout, and his hips pumped convulsively, driving him all the way into her in quick, powerful motions so forceful they shoved the two of them farther and farther up on the bed, until they were flush against the headboard. The thick piece of cherry wood slammed against the wall with each relentless thrust, and the mattress springs groaned and squeaked beneath the onslaught.

Neither of them cared. Without stopping or slowing, Dylan dragged a pillow up to cushion Sabrina's head, and he planted a palm on the wall to brace them from the impact. Sabrina didn't even notice. She wasn't aware of anything except what was happening inside her—and what was about to happen. Her head tossed back and forth, and she sobbed inarticulate words of need that didn't register any more than the heated phrases Dylan was rasping in her ear.

They went over the edge in rapid succession, Sabrina first—by a heartbeat. She climaxed violently, biting back a scream as the spasms boiled up inside her, slammed through her, spiraling out in rhythmic waves that pulsed around Dylan, tore another muffled shout from his chest. He pushed into her contractions, erupting in his own mind-numbing orgasm, gripping the headboard as he came. He continued thrusting in quick, jabbing motions, letting Sabrina's climax milk him until he collapsed on top of her, half-dead.

For long minutes, their harsh, rasping breaths were the only audible sound in the room. Sabrina sank into the mattress, feeling utterly replete, her mind devoid of thought, her body sated. She would have been perfectly content to lie there like that indefinitely, if it hadn't been for the dull pain in back of her neck that began to gradually make its presence known.

She frowned, shifting ever so slightly, and winced. "Ow."

That got Dylan's attention. He raised up on his elbows, his brows knit in concern. "I hurt you. Dammit, Sabrina, I didn't mean to be so rough." He gathered his strength, lifted himself off of her. "I just wish you'd told me you'd never—"

"Dylan," she interrupted, squirming into a sitting position and massaging the spot where her neck throbbed. "If you want to ream me out for not mentioning my virginity, go ahead. But you didn't hurt me. Your headboard did. I feel like someone took a hammer to my neck."

"Oh. Yeah." A slow grin twisted his lips, and he leaned forward, took over the job of massaging her neck. "I tried to buffer the blows, but solid cherry wood is hard to negotiate with."

"Ummm." She relaxed, her eyes sliding shut as she let Dylan ease her taut muscles. "I don't remember slamming into it."

"Let's say your mind was elsewhere."

One eye cracked open. "Stop sounding so smug. Your mind was right there with mine."

"It sure as hell was." His hot gaze moved slowly down her body, lingering in all the right places, drinking in her nakedness in a way his earlier urgency had precluded. His view was limited, since her body was cast in shadows, illuminated only by the filaments of moonlight trickling through the window. "When we make love again, I'm putting on the light. I want to see—and learn—every inch of you."

"Do I get to do the same to you?"

"I'm all yours, sweetheart."

There was something profound about those words, a double entendre they couldn't ignore.

The enormity of what was happening between them struck home, hard.

"Damn." Sabrina exhaled sharply, averting her gaze and dragging an unsteady hand through her hair. "It wasn't supposed to be this unbelievable."

"But we knew it would be," Dylan stated flatly, in true diehard realist form.

"Physically, yes. But the rest . . ."

". . . it felt like more."

She nodded. "It could just be me. At the risk of sounding corny, this was my first time. Maybe I'm overreacting."

"Nope. That explanation's not going to fly. To begin with, you're not the corny or the overreacting type. Also, it *wasn't* my first time, but I'm as blown away as you are. More so, in fact. This definitely wasn't in my game plan, not after thirty-five years of going solo."

Sabrina felt a little like she was sinking in quicksand, except that she didn't want to be rescued. "The timing's awful."

"True. But the feelings are pretty amazing." He reached over, capturing her chin between his fingers and bringing her around to face him. "Are you sorry?"

"That we made love, that it was so mind-blowing, or that it triggered a whole new set of emotional complications?"

"Take your pick."

She blew out her breath. "No, no, and no." A quizzical look. "You?"

"Not on your life."

"We shouldn't get ahead of ourselves." Sabrina wondered who she was trying to convince—Dylan or herself. "We should take it a day at a time. No expectations, no commitments. There's so much going on right now, neither of us can shoulder more pressures and demands. So let's just take it as it comes, okay?"

"Sounds like a plan."

Sabrina cleared her throat. "What about rule two—are you upset?"

"Only that you didn't tell me." Dylan's fingertip traced her shoulder. "I would have gone slower, been more gentle. . . . Oh, who am I kidding?" He gave a humorless laugh. "No I wouldn't have. I was wild to get at you. Nothing short of death could have stopped me or slowed me down. I was surprised, yeah, but not shocked. I knew you were inexperienced. You told me what your life was like. Somewhere in the back of my mind I'm sure it occurred to me that this was a possibility. It wouldn't have made a damn bit of difference." A grimace. "So, that's two cardinal rules out the window."

"I'll keep you honest about rule one," Sabrina vowed with a faint smile. "It's the least I can do after being the cause of your abandoning the others."

"Fair enough." Dylan was reaching over to his night table, clicking on the lamp.

"Please tell me that doesn't mean what I think it does." Sabrina gave him a wary look. "Please say I'm getting more than five minutes to recover."

He chuckled. "You are. In fact, you're getting help recovering."

"Meaning?"

"See that door?" He pointed to the far corner of the bedroom.

"Yes."

"It leads to my bathroom. In there's the most amazing, relaxing, enormous stall shower you've ever seen—complete with massage sprays and twin shower heads. Great for sore necks and any other parts that need soothing. Interested?"

"Maybe." She shot him a deliciously seductive glance. "Are you joining me?"

He flashed her that irresistible, sexy grin. "It might cut down on your recuperation time."

"I'll take the risk. I'm a fast healer."

"In that case . . ." He rolled to his feet, lifting her off the bed and into his arms. He paused long enough to scoop up the box of condoms, before heading purposefully for the bathroom. "I've got a Jacuzzi, too. After you're recovered, we'll put it to good use."

21

Monday, September 19th, 7:15 A.M.
Ruisseau Fragrance Corporation

Sabrina stared out her office window, watching the city come alive as she sipped a cup of very strong, very leaded coffee. She was exhausted, having flown in from Manchester late last night following a whirlwind weekend at CCTL—a full three-day session with two Fortune 500 companies, including three intensive training workshops a day per company, plus mounds of paperwork to catch up on, and mega-questions to answer from Melissa. She'd worked with the companies, conducted the workshops, tackled the paperwork, and fielded the questions—answering some, deferring others—then hopped on the last plane to LaGuardia, collapsed in the waiting limo and finally, finally toppled into her bed—only to find that she was too wound up to sleep.

It shouldn't surprise her.

Two careers. Two homes. A father she was getting to know and like more every day. Tests about to come back that would hopefully change the course of her life and give Carson back his. And a torrid love affair that had exploded out of control the minute it began.

She sighed, massaging the back of her neck and reminding herself that there were departmental reports sitting on her desk waiting to be read—the main reason she'd come in here at dawn.

She'd wanted to visit Carson first. But Dr. Radison

had said he was asleep after a fitful night. The fitful
night, he'd assured Sabrina, was a positive sign—at least
in Carson's case. He was healing, getting his strength
back, and, as a result, going bonkers lying in that hospital
bed. All his parts were on the mend—all except his kidneys, which still hadn't shown any sign of kicking in.

The tissue-typing results would be in today.

Sabrina's insides clenched just thinking about it. She
felt as if she'd been waiting for this for a month, rather
than a week and a half. Dr. Radison had tried to get the
results on Friday, but they weren't ready. Neither was
Carson, as Radison continually reminded her. It would
still be six weeks before they were ready to concede that
his kidney failure was permanent, and at least that long—
barring any unforeseen complications or infections—before his wounds were sufficiently healed and his strength
restored to the point where he could undergo a transplant.

And that entire scenario was contingent upon Sabrina
being the right donor match, or on that right match
miraculously appearing out of nowhere. Otherwise, the
timetable would drastically alter as they extended the
search beyond Carson's circle of associates, since no one
tested thus far had turned out to be compatible.

Sabrina gulped down the rest of her coffee and walked
to her desk, sitting rigidly at the edge of her chair. She
was so damned wired. She should be in bed, catching up
on a few hours' sleep before another busy, crazy week.
Instead, here she was, in the wood-paneled office that
was now hers, looking over status reports that would help
her shape the tenor for this week's meetings.

Funny that the facet of her life she'd expected to be
the most overwhelming was, in fact, turning out to be her
salvation.

Ruisseau.

She'd loved every minute of her first week here. Donna, her secretary, had to physically pull her out of her office on Friday so she wouldn't miss her flight to Manchester. It wasn't that she didn't look forward to going to CCTL. She did. Walking in there felt like coming home. But Ruisseau was a different kind of home—a home that would soon be permanent in a whole new way, once the announcement she'd drafted on the plane had been made. Then, she'd be the official president of two amazing organizations, each entirely different from the other, each pivotal in her life for its own reasons.

Talk about being torn between two lovers.

Yeah, well, maybe professionally. But not personally.

For the umpteenth time, her thoughts strayed to Dylan and the relationship she was sinking deeper and deeper into every day. Oh, they were playing by her rules, making no demands, asking no questions. No one at Ruisseau had any idea they were involved, and Sabrina meant for it to stay that way, at least until she knew where the relationship was headed and the staff knew who she really was. As for priorities, work always came first, and Carson came before that. On the surface, it was light and airy—no strings, no plans, no big deal.

Behind the scenes, it was fervent, consuming, and downright terrifying.

It wasn't just that they couldn't keep their hands off each other, although the sex was so intense, it left Sabrina shaking. It was how well they worked together, challenging and pushing the boundaries, generating an energy that was palpable. It was how they encouraged, provoked, and sometimes bulldozed each other into considering new perspectives, stretching their individual knowledge to reach new levels of thinking. It was how much they respected and—sappy as it sounded—*liked* each other.

True, they'd met less than two weeks ago. And, yes, that meant there were still lots of unknowns, lots of testing—and learning—unfamiliar territory. But the very personal, life-or-death circumstances that precipitated their meeting and continued to define their day-to-day lives had accelerated everything, snowballed their relationship into supersonic motion. So two weeks felt more like two months.

Plus, they were so much on the same wavelength.

It didn't matter that they were different in countless ways, with backgrounds that were polar opposites. Beneath it all there was an integrity, a loyalty, an ambition and drive, passion and perfectionism that they shared. Not to mention that Dylan was, by far, the most secure human being Sabrina had ever met. Nothing she did, no accomplishment she made, threatened him. He was totally comfortable in his own skin. He was also as opinionated as she—blunt as hell when he disagreed with her, both privately and publicly, straightforward with his praise, and equally straightforward with his criticism. She turned to him as often as she did to Stan, asking questions, getting input, testing theories.

No, actually she turned to him more. And not because of their personal involvement. Because of Stan, and whatever was going on with him.

She'd noticed it all week long, although she'd kept it to herself, at least until today, mostly because she felt guilty saying anything negative about Stan given how tight he and Carson were.

Besides, she liked and respected the man. He was a sharp COO and a dedicated stand-in mentor. He counseled and supported Sabrina, easing her transition as best he could.

What worried her was that he was so jumpy and distracted, that beneath the cutting-edge mind, there was an undercurrent, an edginess that Sabrina couldn't quite put her finger on. But she had to mention it to Carson, to get into the insecurity issue he'd alluded to when he spoke of Stan. She had no choice. It was as if Stan were worried about where his place in the company was, and that that worry was making him increasingly strained as the days progressed. He worked his butt off, but it was more the effort of a freaked-out man than a productive one—like he was dancing as fast as he could, but it just wasn't fast enough to grab hold of whatever brass ring he had in mind. Sabrina couldn't ignore the possibility that it was her arrival, her new position at Ruisseau—and in Carson's life—that had triggered Stan's behavior, or at least exacerbated it.

The issue had to be addressed.

But in the meantime—and as a result of Stan's insecurity—she found herself walking down to Dylan's office more often than not, to run an idea by him or to pick his brain.

No self-esteem problems there. And no baggage to tiptoe around.

With Dylan and her, it was bust-your-butt and leave your ego at the door. It was insane work hours where they ordered in Chinese food to sustain them through forgotten dinners. It was jumping into limos and speeding to Mt. Sinai twice a day to bring Carson up to speed and to get health updates that made them feel more at ease. It was arguing over in-house changes and C'est Moi's continued vulnerability if Carson refused to patent the formula. And once, after a particularly grueling day of meetings, it was a run in Riverside Park at one A.M.

Then there were the nights—equally frenetic, far more devastating.

They'd spent every one of them together last week, sometimes at her place, sometimes at his. Inexperienced or not, Sabrina wasn't a starry-eyed teenager. Her assumption had been that physical attraction—no, more like obsession—would taper off once lovemaking transitioned from fantasy to reality. Well, it hadn't. True, they'd only been sleeping together for a week, but she'd expected at least the frantic edge to have worn off. Wrong. They wanted each other with the same urgency as the first time, even at three A.M, when they'd spent the past four hours making love.

They were on the verge of using up the last of Dylan's two-box supply of condoms. They'd already restocked—putting boxes in both her place and his. And Dylan had started carrying some with him, for those times when the bedroom just seemed too far away. Usually, they barely made it through the front door before they started undressing each other, stumbling as they headed for the nearest piece of furniture.

On Thursday—their last night together before she left for New Hampshire—they hadn't even gotten past the hall. They'd made love on the mahogany table in Dylan's entranceway. He'd stripped her from the waist down, lifted her onto the table, and taken her in hard fast strokes that brought them both to climax in seconds. Just thinking about it made her body throb and . . .

"Good morning."

Sabrina's head snapped up, and she could actually feel hot color flood her cheeks as she saw Dylan leaning in her doorway.

"Hi," she managed.

A corner of his mouth lifted and he walked in, shutting the door behind him. "Well, I don't have to ask what *you* were thinking about."

"No, I guess you don't." She propped her elbows on the desk and interlaced her fingers, resting her chin on them. "Then again, I thought I was alone with my fantasies. What are you doing here at seven something-or-other in the morning?"

He perched on the edge of her desk. "I needed a break from three nights and three mornings of cold showers. I was starting to develop frostbite."

Sabrina's lips twitched. "That sounds dire."

"It was. Care to rub some feeling back into my extremities?"

She couldn't help but dissolve into laughter. "That's quite a pick-up line, Mr. Newport. Very unique. Still, I wouldn't count on it bringing a high ratio of success."

"It worked this time. I got you to laugh, despite those deep circles I see under your eyes." He studied her intently. "You look beat. Rough weekend?"

Sighing, Sabrina pressed her palms to her cheeks. "It wasn't the weekend. I can handle the workload. I can even handle the time-juggling."

"It's the tissue-typing results. They're due in today."

"Yes. I spoke to Dr. Radison a little while ago. He should be calling me any time now." She raised her head, met Dylan's gaze. "I'm afraid," she said quietly, opening up to him in a way that was still very new to her. "Afraid that I won't be a match. And afraid that I will."

"That's called being human." Dylan walked around behind the desk, tugged her to her feet. "Come here." He drew her against him, tipped up her chin and kissed her. "I know this is taboo," he murmured, circling her lips with his. "We're at work. But no one's in the office yet. Give me ten seconds to make you feel better."

She smiled, reaching up to wrap her arms around his neck. "You're good. But not *that* good. If you really want to make me feel better, you'll need more than ten seconds."

"Then consider this a prelude." He covered her mouth with his, nudging her lips apart and taking her in a heated kiss she felt to the tips of her toes. "It'll be okay. Hang in there. And, by the way, I missed you."

"I missed you, too," she admitted. "Even yoga didn't help."

"You must be doing the wrong stretches. Or maybe you're doing them in the wrong positions. I'll work on both with you tonight."

Sabrina smiled against his mouth. "Now you're a yoga instructor?"

"Better. I'm a magician. I can get every one of those beautiful muscles to relax." He winked as he released her. "Promise."

"I'm going to hold you to that." Sabrina's smile faded and she ran her fingers through her hair. "God knows, I'll need it." She met Dylan's gaze. "It's not just what's ahead of me at Mount Sinai. It's what's ahead of me here. I've decided to make the announcement today. It's time."

Dylan folded his arms across his chest. He didn't look surprised. "When?"

"At the end of the day. I left a voice mail for Donna last night, when I got back from CCTL and was still delusional enough to believe I'd get some sleep and she'd beat me in here this morning. Instead I was so revved up that I had insomnia and stared at the ceiling for three hours. Anyway, I asked her to send out an in-house e-mail calling for a full company meeting today at five-thirty. Whoever can't make it will hear the news in a matter of hours by phone chain, I'm sure. I'm not trying to make a big deal out of it, but I don't want the staff to think this only concerns the VPs. It concerns everyone."

Dylan nodded. "Are you waiting until the blood test results come in? Is that why you timed your announcement for the end of the day?"

"No." Sabrina shook her head. "Originally that's what I had in mind. But it suddenly occurred to me that the two things aren't connected. If the blood work turns out the way I'm hoping, Carson will get my kidney. That's a given. But if it doesn't, if I can't be the one to make the transplant possible, I'm still his daughter. I still want to be part of Ruisseau—and of Carson's life. It's time I shared that with the rest of his family—his staff. No, the reason I picked the end of the day is to give everyone a chance to juggle their schedules and to give me a chance to meet with Dr. Radison and talk to Carson."

"To say he'll be thrilled that you're going public with this is the understatement of the year."

"Telling him will be the highlight of my day." Her expression brightened. "Actually, I had an idea. Do you think we could videotape the meeting? Then we could play it for him in his hospital bed. My first choice would be for him to make the announcement himself, but I doubt the medical staff would go for us setting up video-conferencing in ICU. So this is the next best thing. He'll be able to see the event firsthand. You think that's overkill?"

"I think it's terrific. He'll watch the tape a hundred times. He'll probably make all the nurses on night shift watch with him—that is, those who are still speaking to him." Dylan eyed her intently. "What about your mother? Have you prepared her for the media circus?"

A nod. "She knows my plan. I'll be calling my grandparents this afternoon to fill them in, as well. That's going to be a difficult conversation, especially if it turns out I'm a compatible kidney donor. The president of

Ruisseau part they'll handle; the surgery is another thing entirely. But they're bright people. It won't come out of left field. And my mother will drive over there this evening, to help field the media if they start calling—and to ease things with my grandparents' circle of friends."

"What about you? Are you ready? The media's going to hunt you down like a fox."

"I know. I'll manage."

"You'll stay at my place tonight," Dylan stated flatly. "At least that way they can't hound you until the wee hours of the morning."

Sabrina gave him a faint smile. "But you can?"

"Mercilessly. Any complaints?"

"Not a one."

Their welcome moment of banter was interrupted by the ringing of the phone.

With a deer-in-the-headlights look, Sabrina leaned over her desk, picked up the receiver. "Sabrina Radcliffe." A pause. "Can't you just tell me . . . ? Fine. I'm on my way."

She hung up, turned to Dylan. "That was Mary in ICU. She said Dr. Radison wants to see me now. He's on his way up from the lab—with the results."

"Did she give you any information?"

"No." Sabrina spoke slowly and calmly, but inside she was quaking. "She said he needs to speak with me directly." Scribbling a note for Donna, Sabrina snatched up her purse and headed for the door. Abruptly, she stopped and turned around, wetting her lips with the tip of her tongue and fighting her stubborn need to always appear strong. "I'd rather not do this alone. Would you go with me?"

A tender look flashed in Dylan's eyes. He picked up the phone, dialed his secretary's extension and got her

voice mail. "Nina, it's me. It's about seven-thirty. I'll
be out of the office for a chunk of the morning. My
cell will probably be turned off, so I'll check in with
you when I can. If there's an emergency, call Mount
Sinai. I'm joining Ms. Radcliffe there for a meeting."
He replaced the phone in its cradle. "Come on. Let's
go."

8:10 A.M.
Mt. Sinai

Dr. Radison was waiting when they were shown into his
office. His brows lifted when he saw Dylan, but he didn't
comment, just gestured for them to have a seat.

"I asked Mr. Newport to be here with me," Sabrina explained in response to the questioning look. "I want him
to be part of this discussion. In all ways but blood, he's
Carson's son. He's been part of his life a lot longer than I
have. So even though my biological ties are crucial here,
so is Dylan's presence."

"I have no problem with that." Dr. Radison opened a
file on his desk. "I won't waste time. Here's what we've
got. Without getting too technical, there are six criteria in
the crossmatch test. If three or more of those criteria
match, a transplant is feasible. Obviously, the more, the
better. In your case, we've got five out of six."

Sabrina's heart started racing. "Five out of six? That's
very good, isn't it?"

He nodded. "In addition, it doesn't appear that Mr.
Brooks has any antibodies that would attack your kidney.
In short, these results are extremely positive."

"Positive," Sabrina repeated. "But not conclusive. Not
to the point where we know the transplant's a go."

"Assuming it's needed," Radison reminded her. "And,
no, we're not at that point. Not yet."

Dylan leaned forward. "What happens now?"

"Now, Ms. Radcliffe sees Dr. Renee Mendham, one of the finest nephrologists in the country. Dr. Mendham's already got Ms. Radcliffe's medical history. I forwarded that on to her. I'm sure she's reviewed it. Next, she'll do a complete physical and a battery of lab tests. We have to make sure Ms. Radcliffe is in perfect health. Otherwise, there's no way we'd consider letting her undergo transplant surgery."

"And if all that goes smoothly, there's that renal angiogram you mentioned," Dylan remembered aloud.

"Exactly. That will give us a look at Ms. Radcliffe's kidneys, the surrounding arteries and veins that transport the blood supply to and from them, and the ureters that do the draining into the bladder. The idea is to get a technical look at the area to determine which kidney will be taken for the transplant—preferably the left because the vein is longer—and to establish the details of your specific procedure. Obviously, we also want to make sure there are no anatomical complications that would preclude the surgery. Dr. Mendham will describe the test to you in detail. It's an out-patient radiological procedure, using a local anesthetic."

"There are still so many question marks," Sabrina murmured. "I want guarantees."

"There are none. But concentrate on the fact that you've cleared some major hurdles. The results of the tissue-typing and crossmatch put you right up there in the probable category. Let's move forward with that in mind."

"How soon can I see Dr. Mendham? Today? Tomorrow? Say the word, and I'll clear my schedule."

Radison shot her a wry look. "I'm beginning to see the

family resemblance. Father and daughter steamrollers. Lucky for you, I'm getting used to it, after two weeks with Mr. Brooks. So I jumped the gun and called Dr. Mendham. She moved her schedule around, as well. She'll see you Wednesday morning at ten." He passed a business card across the desk. "Here's her office address and phone number. She's a shoot-from-the-hip, top-notch nephrologist. You'll like her."

"I'm sure I will. Thanks for accelerating the process." Sabrina picked up the card and studied the information. Then, she raised her head. "Have you filled Carson in yet?"

"Of course not. These test results are yours, to hear and to share. If you're asking if you can share them with him now, the answer is yes. He woke up about five minutes after you called. Let me warn you, he's ornery as a bear. He's also forbidden me to let you donate your kidney, no matter what the tissue-typing results show. Have fun."

"I might not have fun, but I'll get my way." Sabrina rose, acknowledging Radison's droll warning with a stubborn lift of her chin. "Like you said, father and daughter steamrollers. Well, when I'm on overdrive, there's no stopping me. Be prepared for some choice words from Carson to rock the halls of ICU. Ignore them. I promise to keep him from going overboard and jeopardizing his condition. Besides, it won't take him long to figure out that this is one battle he won't win. He's getting my kidney if I have to transplant it myself."

"How reassuring." Radison came to his feet as well. "I'll go alert the nurses, tell them to man their battle stations. Mr. Newport, I hope you're a good referee."

Dylan's lips curved in amusement. "Actually, I think

I'll let Sabrina and Carson duke this one out. It should be quite a showdown. It'll also be a once-in-a-lifetime chance to see Carson bested." His amusement vanished, and a look of intense emotion crossed his face. "He couldn't have picked a better time to lose. And, as a result, to win."

22

8:35 A.M.

8:35 A.M.

Carson was in heated argument with a nurse when Sabrina and Dylan walked in.

"Don't bother bringing me that liquid crap, because I'm not eating it," he was barking. "No Jell-O. No applesauce. No hospital shit period. Starting tonight, I want steak, medium-rare, and a baked potato. Or some grilled red snapper. Move me to that cushy floor, Eleven West. The one that's more like the Ritz-Carlton than a hospital. Over there, they'll bring me some *real* food."

The trim, middle-aged nurse finished taking his vital signs, glaring at him as she jotted them down. "Believe me, Mr. Brooks, moving you out of here is one of our top priorities. The second Dr. Radison gives the word, you'll be on your way. Eleven West's already been alerted. As a result, half the staff members there have requested transfers."

Sabrina cleared her throat to stifle a chuckle.

The nurse glanced up, spotting Dylan and Sabrina. "Ah, you have visitors. My cue to go. What a shame." She leveled a no-nonsense look at Carson. "Your bland, uninspiring breakfast should be here any minute now. Eat it. It's the only way to build up your strength so you can make that move to Eleven West." She hurried to the door, rolling her eyes at Sabrina and Dylan. "Good luck," she muttered under her breath. "He's in top form today."

"So I see." Sabrina folded her arms across her breasts

and gave a resigned shake of her head as she walked toward the bed. "I go away for a few days and you escalate your campaign to terrorize the staff. Okay, I'm back. Now you can pick on someone your own size."

"You're not my size. You're tiny. Only your mouth is big."

"That's heredity for you," Sabrina retorted. "Like all my obnoxious qualities, I got that one from you." She used her sparring time to scrutinize Carson, noting the changes that had taken place since she saw him on Friday. She was relieved and encouraged by what she saw. He had real color in his face, his breathing was even, and his chest tube was gone, as were several of the contraptions he'd been hooked up to last week.

For the first time, Sabrina knew in her gut that her father was on the mend.

"Sit," Carson ordered, gesturing for her and Dylan to pull up chairs. "You're even crankier than I am," he informed Sabrina. "And you look lousy. Didn't you get any sleep this weekend?"

"Not a wink. I was too excited about rushing over here for a dose of emotional abuse."

Carson's lips quirked. "When did you get back?"

"Late last night." Sabrina pulled her chair directly up to the bed. "And before you ask, yes, I did Ruisseau work on the plane—both ways."

"She was also at her desk before dawn today, reviewing stacks of departmental updates," Dylan added, lowering himself into his seat and crossing one long leg over the other. "She comes in earlier than you do and stays later. Frankly, I don't think you're paying her enough."

"Great. Now I've got two wiseasses to contend with." Carson eyed Dylan, his caustic words belied by his affectionate tone and the warmth in his gaze. "Why are you here this early? Did you just miss me? Or did Nina boot you out?"

"I asked Dylan to come with me," Sabrina provided. "I wanted him here when I got the tissue-typing results— which I just did. I came here straight from Dr. Radison's office."

"How are things going at CCTL?" Carson demanded, pointedly ignoring the subject Sabrina wanted to broach. "Are you satisfied with the way it's being run in your absence? And how did things go with those two megacorporations that dominated your weekend? Did you get them on track, or were they the old-school types whose mind-sets are so rigid there's no getting through?"

"CCTL's running like clockwork," Sabrina replied without missing a beat. "Deborah and Mark are doing a bang-up job. The weekend was a success. Both companies went home with a clearly delineated strategy, and as a far more cohesive team than when they arrived. And the blood test says you and I are a match made in heaven. So, if you need a kidney, you're getting mine. Anything else?"

Carson's jaw set, and he gave a hard shake of his head. "It's not happening, Sabrina. I already told that to Radison."

"I know. And I told him I was coming in here to set you straight. This isn't your choice to make. It's mine. And I've made it."

"Not if I say no, you haven't."

"I beg to differ with you. I'm twenty-seven—way too old for you to order around. You wanted to meet your daughter. Well, you have. You wanted me in your life. You've got that, too. Now I want something from you. I want you to learn how to grit your teeth and accept my help. Because you're getting it whether or not you want it. I'll declare you incompetent if I have to, and sign the papers as your next of kin."

"Really." Carson was clearly enjoying this battle of wits. "And how will you manage that? I'm not incompetent. I'm more lucid than you are."

"I'll lie." A corner of Sabrina's mouth lifted, and she slid a sidelong glance at Dylan. "I know an amazing lawyer who, I'd be willing to bet, would take the case—to protect Ruisseau's interests, of course."

"Don't bet," Carson cautioned. "You'd lose. The lawyer you're looking at doesn't lie. He also doesn't screw me over."

"True." Dylan took his cue, jumping in with both feet. "But, in this case, I'd make an exception."

Carson's head snapped around, his stunned gaze boring into Dylan. "You're kidding."

"Nope. The way I see it, I might be lying, but I wouldn't be screwing you over. I'd be doing you the biggest favor of your life. You're just too goddamned stubborn to see it." Dylan blew out an exasperated breath. "Carson, stop being an obstinate pain in the ass. Give in gracefully. You're not going to win."

"The hell I'm not."

"Fine. Then call Sabrina's bluff. I'll come up with some great language declaring you mentally incompetent. Keep raving that you're not accepting an ideal donor match, and you'll only lend credibility to my argument. And if I need witnesses, the nurses in ICU would line up to support my claim. They already think you're nuts."

"Sorry, Dylan, but your knight-in-shining-armor bullshit's not going to work. You and I both know you're full of it. You might try, but you could never pull this off. I know a dozen people, including Radison, who'd testify that I'm a hundred percent lucid and able to make my own decisions. They're not about to perjure themselves to help you realize your sentimental goal. This might shock you, but not everyone feels the same way about me as you do."

"I don't blame them," Sabrina commented dryly. "But that's not the point. What you're saying is that if I tried declaring you incompetent, you'd fight it—right?"

"I'd fight it and I'd win. Remember, Sabrina, I'm the ultimate street kid. There's no beating me when it comes to getting down in the dirt and slugging it out."

"I agree." Sabrina interlaced her fingers calmly. "And I'm the ultimate corporate shark. It's a role I don't much like playing, but when I do, there's no beating me when it comes to going for the jugular. It just so happens that I was trained on a different, but equally brutal, battlefield than you. So, here we have it. You played your hand. Here's mine. I'm seeing a nephrologist on Wednesday. She's got a battery of tests to run. It's going to be another month before I get the go-ahead. But once I do—which I will—and if your kidneys still haven't kicked in on their own, then you and I have a date in the operating room. If you refuse to let me be your transplant donor, I'll break my agreement with Ruisseau, walk out of your life, and never look back. Your turn."

Carson stared at her for a moment, trying to determine if she was serious or bluffing. Obviously, he didn't like the answer he found, because a flash of naked pain crossed his face. Sabrina knew she'd caused that pain, and it made her insides twist. But she stood her ground, kept her impassive veneer in place.

"I'm not bluffing this time, Carson," she reinforced quietly. "I mean it. Either I'm your daughter or I'm not. If I am, accept my heartfelt need to be there for you. Act

SCENT OF DANGER 307

like a father. If you can't, then I guess we've got nothing to build on. And nothing more to say."

A long minute of silence ticked by.

"Damn, you're good," Carson muttered at last. "I guess the corporate battlefield's even bloodier than the streets." He threw up his hands. "Fine. You win. I'll take your damned kidney."

She smiled sweetly. "Thank you. Now that that's settled, I have some other news to share. I think this news will be a lot easier for you to swallow. In fact, it might even make you stop bellowing like a moose."

He arched a suspicious brow. "I'm listening."

Sabrina didn't make him wait. "I did one other thing on the plane ride back to LaGuardia besides my Ruisseau work. I drafted an announcement telling the entire staff who I am and what my position in the company is. With your approval, I'd like to make that announcement this afternoon."

Carson coughed, reaching over for a glass of water and taking a few swallows. "Tickle in my throat," he muttered, fooling no one, since they all knew how affected he was by Sabrina's decision. Regaining his composure, he placed the glass on the nightstand. "Are you sure you're ready?" He studied Sabrina's face. "There's no timeline here. And no pressure—not from me, or anyone else."

"I realize that. I don't feel pressure. Not from anyone or anything—including today's blood test results. I made this decision separate and apart from what I learned from Dr. Radison today. I want to make this announcement, Carson. I planned on doing so whether or not I was a compatible donor match."

She paused, then blurted out her thoughts without censoring them. "I've had an amazing couple of weeks. Getting to know you has been like being infused with a constant jolt of adrenaline—and we've just touched the tip of the iceberg in terms of our relationship and what it might grow into. As for having a hand in running Ruisseau, I've never felt more alive, more challenged—and more honored. Your company encompasses all the positive team spirit and drive for success that I try to convey in my CCTL workshops. It's awesome to see its effects firsthand. I'm chomping at the bit to see what happens next. Most of all, I'm dying to get you back in that CEO chair, so I can work by your side. There's so much we can accomplish. And with you back where you belong, and me there to add my energy and perspective to the equation, Ruisseau's going to go through the roof."

A corner of Carson's mouth lifted. "So you *were* bluffing about walking away if I refused to take your kidney."

She shook her head. "No, I wasn't. Which—given the superlatives I just spouted, and how excited I am to take part in Ruisseau's future—should tell you exactly how much my decision to be your kidney donor means to me."

A heartbeat of silence.

"Yeah. It does." Carson reached out, squeezed her arm briefly before extending his hand. "Let me see that announcement."

Sabrina gave it to him, watching his expression as he read it through. "Change anything you want," she urged. "If I had my way, it would be you making that announcement."

"It will be." He raised his head. "What time did you call the meeting for?"

"Five-thirty."

"Good. That gives us plenty of time." He turned to

Dylan. "Call Marie. Tell her to get me a good videographer. She's got a list of them. Find someone who's available today. I want him in ICU by this afternoon, equipment in hand. I need the works—tripod, recording deck, lights, microphone—you know the drill. In the meantime, you take care of things at the other end. Set up the necessary VCR equipment in the conference room at Ruisseau. When the company's new president is introduced at five-thirty, the one introducing her is going to be the CEO." He handed the page back to Sabrina, gave her an approving smile. "By the way, what you wrote here is great. Use any part of it you want to. But you'll be delivering it *after* I make the announcement."

Anticipation glinted in Sabrina's eyes. "Nothing would please me more."

"Nothing, huh? I could argue that one." There was an amused, knowing look on Carson's face, and Sabrina could swear he darted a quick glance in Dylan's direction before looking back at her. "But we'll save that for another time. Right now, we have other things to discuss. Like the media. Have you thought about how you're going to handle them? Because they'll be breaking down your door by tonight."

"I'll handle them with as much candor and as few words as possible."

"Not a word about knowing that formula," he reminded her. "Remember."

"I remember."

"Now let's get to Gloria. Have you run all this by her?"

"We discussed it over the weekend. She's steeled and ready, prepped for the media feeding-frenzy that'll take place in Massachusetts—Rockport *and* Boston. She'll run interference for my grandparents, and address whatever personal questions she has to. She's a pro when it comes to the press."

"Not a surprise. She's a class act. Will your grandparents be okay?"

"My fingers are crossed, but, yes, I think they will be. I'll call them as soon as I leave the hospital and tell them everything they need to know, including the tissue-typing results. They need to hear the entire situation, and they need to hear it directly from me. I can handle it. And, in the long run, so can they."

Carson frowned. "I hate that you have to go through this. This whole scandal thing is what I wanted to spare you from."

"I know. But I'm tough. I inherited that from both my parents—and my grandparents, too. Wait till you meet them. They're pretty damned formidable."

"So I hear." Carson was clearly preoccupied, and not with apprehension over meeting her grandparents. "The media's been getting updates on my health," he said pensively. "They know where things stand. Once news that you're my biological daughter leaks out, they're going to jump all over the kidney issue."

"Fine. Again, I'll stick to the facts, giving as few details as possible. I'll say the doctors are still hopeful that your kidneys will resume normal function. I'll add that, in the meantime, I'm being tested, but I don't have any conclusive results. When I do, they will, too. Period."

"Shit. This is going to turn into a tabloid circus." Carson rubbed his forehead.

"If it does, it does. We'll deal with it." Sabrina lay her hand on his arm. "Carson, you can't let this upset you. It'll affect your blood pressure, and your recovery. I've already told you my family will survive this. I'll make sure of it. As for Ruisseau, your staff's a tight, united bunch. Their only concerns are making the company thrive and finding out who shot you. Sure, they'll have some adjustments to my stepping in as president, but they're not about to be thrown by a bunch of reporters grilling them over your being a sperm donor. Is it Susan you're worried about? Will she flip out over the press coverage?"

"What?" Carson looked at Sabrina as if she were crazy. "Of course not. Susan's known this was coming since we told her who you are. Besides, talk about a pro. She's so used to having flashbulbs go off in her face and being asked if I'm as good a lay as I am a businessman, that nothing frazzles her. No, I'm not worried about Susan. Or about Ruisseau. It's you I'm worried about. You're going to be getting it from all sides—your grandparents, antsy staff members from CCTL and Ruisseau, eager news correspondents, and scum-of-the-earth tabloid reporters. You're already carrying the whole goddamned world on your shoulders. The last thing you need is another load. Goddammit, if I were only out of here, I could shield you from some of it. . . ." He slammed his fist to the bed. "This sucks." His head jerked around, and he gazed straight at Dylan. "You're going to have to do it for me. Take care of her. Do what you can."

Dylan nodded, although his expression was wary, as if he were trying to figure out how much Carson knew. "I will. I'd already planned to."

"I figured as much. I don't know what you had in mind, but get her away from Ruisseau and from her apartment tonight. The press will be camped outside both. Take her to your place. Cook dinner. You make a decent linguini in white clam sauce. It wouldn't make Zagat's top fifty, but it's better than average."

"Gee, thanks. Okay, I'll be Julia Child and the diversionary committee all rolled into one. Not to worry."

"Excuse me," Sabrina interrupted. "I'm not some fragile piece of china that needs to be handled gingerly. I won't break."

"I know." Carson dismissed her comment with a wave of his hand. "You're tough as nails. No surprise. You're my daughter. Which is exactly the problem—you're my daughter. And, hell, was Gloria right about the protective instincts this whole parent scene conjures up. I'm just beginning to find out what a wimp you become when your kid's well-being's at stake." He snorted. "This fatherhood thing is something else."

Sabrina smiled, not only at Carson's words, but at his expression. He might be bitching up a storm, but he didn't look upset. What he looked, was self-satisfied and overprotective. Like he was settling into the father role quite comfortably, rather than with the irritation he was feigning.

"That takes care of the media issue," he concluded. "So, we've covered kidney donors, sperm donors, and presidential announcements. Before we kick into high gear with this videotaping thing, is there anything else? Any other bombs you want to drop on me today? Any business issues we need to discuss?"

That brought Sabrina down to earth with a thud.

She hesitated, unsure whether or not now was the time.

Instantly, Carson picked up on her hesitation. "What is it?"

"It's Stan," she forced herself to say. "I feel really uncomfortable broaching this topic, not only because Stan's helped me adjust, but because you two go back so many years. Unfortunately, I think I have to."

"This is business. Not personal. Shoot. What's on your mind about Stan?"

"To be blunt, he's a mess. I have no idea what's wrong, but he's coming apart at the seams. It's possible he's having trouble adjusting to my role at Ruisseau—my *real* role, since he's the only other person who knows the whole truth—or it's possible he's having trouble adjusting to my place in your life. Or maybe it's something entirely different. Whatever it is, I seem to be the only one who's picked up on this in a major way. That could be because he's more on edge around me. I remember your implying he had an issue with self-esteem. I think we should get into that so I'll have a better handle on how to deal with him."

"You're not the only one who's picked up on it," Dylan corrected, catching her completely by surprise. "I have, too."

Sabrina gave him a startled look. "You never mentioned anything."

"You never brought up the subject."

She couldn't argue that point. "Fair enough. Then again, neither did you."

"Yes he did," Carson refuted. "Dylan brought it to my attention this weekend. I was wondering when you'd do the same, and stop letting personal feelings stand in the way of that corporate shark you were describing before. This is my company. Yours, too, for that matter. There's no room for stupid emotions like guilt or discomfort."

"What about a stupid emotion like insecurity? Doesn't that apply?"

"You win on that one," Carson conceded. "I'm a soft touch when it comes to Stan. It's a problem. Don't let me get away with it. When I need a swift kick in the ass, give it to me."

"With pleasure," Sabrina replied sweetly.

"Here's the story with Stan. Yeah, we go way back together. I told you he worked for that fertility specialist your mother went to at the time of the donor insemination. Stan's the one who tipped me off to what this mystery lady was looking for, and how much she was willing to pay the right sperm donor. He encouraged me to go for it. I did. And with the twenty thousand dollars Gloria paid me, I started Ruisseau. For me, that was the beginning of everything."

"So you felt indebted to Stan."

"Big time. He's a great guy, and a great friend. On top of that, he's sharp, with a good business mind. Hiring him was a no-brainer. We didn't use fancy titles like COO back then. There weren't enough of us to bother with titles, anyway. And I was never one for protocol. Hey, I wasn't exactly your typical corporate exec. I spent most of my time playing around in the lab or scribbling ideas in a notebook."

A nostalgic grin touched Carson's lips. "I was determined to make the sexiest-smelling perfumes in the business. Hell, I was twenty-two. At that age, sex is a top priority—the number one recreational activity. Although even sex didn't give me the high that building Ruisseau did. Anyway, I had some pretty tough competition. The powerhouse designers, the European perfumers—everyone was fighting to control the market on whatever scent was the rage that year. The professional woman's scent, the outdoor macho-guy's scent, the romantic evening by candlelight scent and, of course, the supreme accomplishment—to create the ultimate turn-on fragrance that set every man or woman on fire."

"C'est Moi certainly fills that bill," Sabrina murmured. "I've never smelled anything so sensual."

"Yeah, well, it took years to perfect. Then there were all our other scents—formulating them, fine-tuning them, test-marketing them, promoting them, and sometimes trashing them. Stan was right there with me through all the research, all the frustration, all the setbacks. He screwed up two marriages because of the number of hours he spent at work. He busted his ass, and I mean busted his ass. Even when something didn't come easy to him, he never balked. He just kept at it until he could master it; or, if not master it, at least be comfortable working with it. At times that's been rough."

Sabrina pursed her lips thoughtfully. "I get it. I'm reading between the lines. What you're saying is that Stan is bright, but he's not the genius you are. Few people are. But few people have to work right beside you. Stan does. And sometimes he feels the strain."

Carson nodded. "Something like that. So my guess about this past week is that he's seeing me in you all over again. It's probably throwing him for a loop. Not to mention that the cops are all over him. Apparently, they questioned both his ex-wives. Not a fun scene. So try to cut him some slack, okay?"

She frowned. "Why would Whitman and Barton question Stan's ex-wives? Is he up there on the suspect list now?"

"He was asleep in front of the TV the evening I was shot. That doesn't count as an alibi, not in their minds. And he acts like a nervous wreck around them, which makes them more suspicious."

"Yeah, well, everyone's a little testy around those two," Sabrina muttered. "I almost punched them out when they implied my mother was a suspect." An uneasy thought struck her, and she attacked it head-on. "Carson, you said I shouldn't let you be a soft touch when it comes to Stan. So I'll ask you flat out—is there any chance he *is* the one who shot you?"

"Nope." Carson didn't looked pissed off by her suggestion. But he did look certain of his reply. "Sentiment aside, I know Stan's innocent."

"How can you be so sure? If his insecurity runs deeper than you realize, isn't it possible that his feeling of being second-best drove him to do something drastic—even if it's something he regretted as soon as he'd done it?" She paused, rolling her eyes. "God, I sound like something out of a bad movie."

"Yeah, actually you do." A corner of Carson's mouth lifted. "I guess daughters can be as irrational and overprotective as fathers."

"I guess so."

"To answer your question, Stan's insecurities are irrelevant. He didn't do it. How do I know? Easy. Because I'm still sitting here talking to you. The gunshot wasn't fatal. If Stan had pulled the trigger, I'd be six feet under. He's a crackerjack shot."

Sabrina tensed. "Stan owns a gun?"

"Calm down. No, not anymore. But when we were in our twenties, when we lived in that first dump we shared, hell yeah, he owned a gun. It was a cheap nine millimeter by the way, not a twenty-two. Anyway, Stan was convinced we were sitting ducks for muggers and lunatic drug addicts. He drove himself crazy thinking they would break in and kill us for the pathetic wad of cash—maybe twenty or thirty bucks—that we had on us. Finally, he did something about it. He went out and took shooting lessons. He was good—damned good. I watched him at target practice a couple of times, and it was one bull's-eye after another. He bought the gun for protection, then sold it when we moved up and out."

"That was years ago," Sabrina pointed out, feeling compelled to see this notion through, no matter how crazy or farfetched. "If he hasn't held a gun in all this time, he could be rusty. That would explain a less than dead-on shot."

"Uh-uh." Carson shook his head. "He got rid of the gun, not the skill. He still drives up to a shooting range in Yonkers a couple of times a week for target practice. It's good for his ulcer; it helps him let off steam. And, before you ask, yeah, I know for a fact he hasn't lost his touch. A couple of months ago, he rode up with Susan and me to her parents' farm, and did some outdoor target practice. He was dead-on accurate every time. Trust me, Sabrina. If Stan had been the one who shot me, I'd be dead."

"Okay." Sabrina felt a surge of relief. Regardless of her concerns over Stan's behavior, she truly liked the man. And while she had a hard time picturing him as Wyatt Earp, she was pretty sure she understood the gist of who he was. The thought that she could be so wrong about someone, that he would actually shoot Carson in cold blood—well, it was something she didn't want to consider.

"Feel better?" Carson asked.

"Um-hum." Sabrina's wheels were turning, this time in a slightly different direction. "Carson, would you mind if I met with Stan privately and told him what was on my mind? Not about the shooting, obviously, but about my concern that it's me who's making him ill at ease? I think I could help smooth things over without pushing any buttons or rubbing the second-best thing in his face. Plus, I want to give him a heads-up about the announcement we're making this afternoon. He deserves to know ahead of time, not find out along with everyone else."

"That's fine with me. Go for it. The more you bond

with Stan, the more productive your work relationship will be . . ."

". . . and, as a result, the more productive Ruisseau will be," Sabrina finished for him.

"You got it."

"Done." Sabrina rose. "I'm out of here. I've got a million things to do. First up, is calling my mother and grandparents. I'll do that in the limo. I'll also call CCTL, set up a conference call with Deborah and Mark. They know pieces of the puzzle, but they need to be aware of the entire situation, including the fact that the press is going to be camped on their doorstep. Once that's done, I'll turn my attention back to Ruisseau. I've got to get things on track, read those reports, go over the R&D results, see if Stan's free for lunch, have Donna and Marie get the conference room ready . . ."

"Hey, easy," Dylan interrupted. "You'll collapse by noon. I'll get going on the videographer. After that, I can supervise the conference room setup."

"You've got a pile of legal papers so high you can't see your desk."

"They'll wait a day. This comes first."

"Don't forget dinner," Carson reminded him. "At your place. I don't want Sabrina going to her apartment tonight. Not until every reporter's either given up and gone home, or fallen asleep on the sidewalk."

"I haven't forgotten." Dylan looked distinctly amused. "I'll even brew espresso. That'll kill time and keep us both up until the wee hours, when I can sneak Sabrina past the snoozing media-mongers. Okay?"

"Not really." Carson scowled. "Then you'll both be wired till dawn, and crash just in time to screw up a day's work."

"There's no pleasing you, is there?" Sabrina said with

mock irritation. "Why don't I just bring a sleeping bag and camp out on Dylan's living room rug?"

"Now *that's* an idea. Not the living room rug part—I think Dylan can come up with something better than that. But staying at his place? Good solution. See? And you said there's no pleasing me." Carson waved the two of them off before they could probe his underlying meaning, which was becoming increasingly clear with each pointed comment. The question was, how much of his Cupid-playing was based on having actually figured out what was going on, and how much was based on matchmaking for what he *hoped* would go on?

"Well? Get going," he ordered them. "You've got your work cut out for you. Oh, and on your way out, tell someone at the desk to page Radison and let him know about the taping in ICU later today. If he gives his okay without bitching or making trouble, maybe I'll be nice and give him a twenty-second walk-on part."

23

11:20 A.M.
Midtown North Precinct

Frank chewed his piece of gum like a demon, partly because he was starving and partly because he was frustrated as hell.

This damn Brooks shooting kept turning up more questions and fewer answers.

The bullet analysis had been a bust. Ballistics couldn't tell them a thing besides what they already knew—that it was a badly distorted slug fired by a .22 Walther TPH from below and behind the victim. Nice gun. Light. Easy to hide. Not hard to get. Not cheap. But the suspects in this case weren't poor.

Whoever shot Brooks hadn't stabbed Russ Clark to death. Frank was almost positive of that. The stabbing had been a dirty, back-alley deal, and the angle of the wound suggested it had been done by someone who, although not a pro, wasn't new at this either. As a rule, white-collar criminals who took shots at CEOs with expensive pistols didn't hone their stabbing skills or hide out in seedy alleys. They didn't wield butcher knives, either, which was what the weapon that killed Clark had been. It had sliced through his flesh, lacerated his liver, perforated a couple of major blood vessels, and the poor kid had bled to death.

No finesse there, that was for sure.

Still, the two crimes were connected. Frank and Jeannie were convinced of that. Clark didn't have an enemy in the world. He didn't owe anyone money, didn't even have any credit card debt. And there was no steady girlfriend, jealous or otherwise. He was clean as a whistle.

The only plausible reason for his being murdered was because he'd found out something that threatened Carson Brooks's assailant. Either Clark had uncovered some incriminating evidence, or stumbled upon the identity of the shooter. Either way, he'd been disposed of. By a hired hand, judging by the crude manner in which he'd been killed.

There was no point in trying to coordinate the key suspects in the Brooks case with those who were minus an alibi at the time of Clark's murder. Two different people had done the jobs. But Frank would bet his badge that whoever had hired the thug to knock off Clark, was the one who had shot Brooks. That person had had the right access to the building, the smarts to get by the surveillance cameras, and the class to fit into a fashionable midtown office building in case he was spotted. It hadn't been a pro, or Brooks would be dead. But it hadn't been a street punk either.

Idly, Frank wondered if Brooks's assailant had used his hired hand for more than just stabbing Clark. Like for getting hold of a gun, for example. Hell, a well-connected punk could do that no sweat, without ever dirtying his employer's hands. Made sense. Also made sense that he could lead Frank and Jeannie straight to the son of a bitch who'd hired him—*if* they could get their hands on him. So far, they'd turned up nothing. And there was a sense of urgency building inside them both—an innate awareness that the clock was ticking. Whoever had shot Brooks was desperate. And that opened the door to all kinds of grim possibilities and repeat performances.

Frank yanked the list of suspects that was sitting on his desk toward him and pored over it again.

Dylan Newport. The guy had grown up on the streets. He'd know how to unearth the right scum to kill Clark. As for Brooks's shooting, he had both motive and opportunity. So, the fundamentals all checked out. But Frank wasn't buying it—not anymore. Jeannie was right. Newport was too devoted to Brooks to bump him off for money, and too smart to do it under such incriminating circumstances. And as for arranging to kill a twenty-one-year-old kid in cold blood—nope. It just didn't fit the guy's character.

Stan Hager—now there was one that seemed to fit a whole lot better. Hager had grown up on the streets, too, so he'd know how to find the right contact to stab Clark. As for shooting Brooks, Hager had no alibi and a motive that seemed more and more plausible each day. He hadn't just walked in Brooks's shadow for thirty years, he'd raced at warp speed to keep up. And now—well, talk about someone reaching the breaking point. The guy was like a time bomb ready to go off.

Both Hager's ex-wives had confirmed that motive when Frank and Jeannie interviewed them. They'd each described their ex as an obsessive workaholic who was consumed with the need to keep up with and live up to Carson Brooks. Nothing else in his life came close.

Interesting though. When Frank had conducted his heart-to-heart with Lily, Hager's first wife, she'd confessed that for a good chunk of their marriage she'd sensed that Stan was cheating on her. She couldn't put her finger on why she felt that way, since he was fixated on his work, nor did she have a clue who the woman might be. It was just a gut instinct—but one that persisted right up to the time of their divorce.

Frank had passed that tidbit along to Jeannie when she'd gone to chat with Hager's second wife, Diane. Jeannie, in turn, had asked Diane if she'd ever suspected Stan of being involved with another woman. Diane had shrugged it off and said, yeah, sure, the thought had occurred to her, especially since he wanted sex about as often as he wanted any other kind of fun— which was not nearly often enough for her. But, she'd assumed that most of that was due to his obsession with work. On the other hand, yeah, there were times he seemed distracted, times he came home late and looking like he'd just showered. So another woman was a distinct possibility.

Odd. Hager had been single for some time now. So if there was someone else, why would he still be keeping the whole thing hush-hush? Unless he was no longer involved with the same woman, or unless it was she who wanted the secrecy, maybe because she was married.

Or maybe for some other reason.

Hager was a good-looking guy. He was also rich and not much older than Brooks. Doubtful he was living an entirely celibate life. So what was the story there?

"Hey. A penny for your thoughts." Jeannie walked over, perched on the edge of his desk.

"They're not worth that much." Frank scowled, doodling on his pad. "Do you think Hager's gay?"

"Nope." Jeannie didn't look a bit surprised by Frank's train of thought. "I asked Diane that very question, point blank, probably for the same reason you're asking it now—this whole long-term mystery woman thing. Anyway, Diane said no way. Hager's apparently a pretty amazing lover, when his mind is in it. That's why she didn't get out of the marriage sooner. Plus, I watched him interacting with the staff of Ruisseau, when he didn't realize I had my eye on him. There's no doubt about it; he definitely notices women, not men."

"Yeah, I agree. Plus, he'd have no reason for keeping it a big secret if he was gay. Carson Brooks isn't exactly a judgmental guy. He wouldn't give a damn who Hager was sleeping with."

"Not to mention that after a thirty-year friendship, I doubt a shrewd guy like Brooks would be oblivious to the fact that his best friend was gay. No, if there's a mystery bedmate, it's a woman, not a man."

"Do you think it was the same woman throughout both Hager's marriages? And, if so, who the hell is she and why is her identity still being kept so hush-hush?"

"You're wondering if this factors into this case," Jeannie murmured. "I'm right there with you. I can't shake the not-quite-right feeling about Hager, either. He's hiding something. Whether or not it ties in to whoever he's sleeping with or not, I'm not sure. But there's definitely something he doesn't want us to know. The question is, why would a sexual affair prompt Hager to murder Carson Brooks? And what about Russ Clark—why would Hager want him stabbed?"

"Speaking of Clark, there's something else bugging me. The kid wanted to be an investigative reporter. Whatever the hell he was poking into that spooked someone enough to get rid of him, he must have kept notes. So where are they? We've torn his apartment apart and gone through everything at his desk at Ruisseau."

"We're missing a major piece of this puzzle," Jeannie agreed. "It's right at our fingertips, too. I feel it."

"More than one piece. Ferguson's not sitting right with me, either. And not because of his iffy alibi. Believe it or not, I actually buy the guy's story that he was home grilling a steak. But he refuses to make eye contact with either you or me—no matter what we ask him, and he jumps out of his skin before we even say hello. The guy has something eating at him."

"We've got a couple of nervous Nellies over at Ruis-seau, that's for damned sure." Jeannie ripped open a package of Milk Duds and popped one in her mouth. "Still, I don't see Ferguson at the helm. His life's about as boring as it gets. And his street contacts are nil. Where would he find a street punk to stab Clark, and to buy him a gun?"

She didn't wait for a reply, but popped another Milk Dud in her mouth, chewing thoughtfully. "Here's a name that's back in the picture again, along with an interesting twist. Etienne Pruet."

"The French perfumer who's Brooks's chief competitor?" Frank's brows rose. "We crossed him off our list over a week ago. He was in Paris when Brooks was shot."

"We did and he was. Here's the twist. I just got a call from Jason Koppel at Merrill Lynch. He did some more poking around. It seems that Pruet assembled all his top execs behind closed doors in his Paris headquarters. He was determined to come up with something—anything— that would stop C'est Moi's spiraling sales before the men's version hit the consumer market, and the whole phenomenon exploded in Europe."

"Wait a minute. You lost me. Why is Pruet worrying about Ruisseau? His fancy-schmancy French corporation's profits are sky-high. The company's been in the fragrance business for something like three hundred fifty years."

"Longer. Koppel said something about them achieving prominence as the royal perfumer of King Louis the something-or-other—I think it was the fourteenth—in the mid-1600s. Hoity-toity, huh?"

"I'm overwhelmed," Frank returned dryly. "But I still don't get it. Are you telling me our information was wrong, and Pruet's company is hurting?"

"Not hurting. But not happy. Ruisseau is kicking butt with the advent of C'est Moi. And it's now spreading to the European market. Up till now, Pruet's aristocratic roots have kept him on top with elite fragrance-wearers over there. But this is the twenty-first century. It's a new world. Sex outsells pedigree. C'est Moi is threatening to take a chunk of Pruet's sales. And without knowing what's in that formula, they don't know what they're competing with or how to win."

"So Pruet's got an incentive to get rid of Carson Brooks, the only person who knows C'est Moi's formula. Fine, that's motive. But what about opportunity? If the guy was in Paris . . ."

"Then he couldn't have done it," Jeannie finished for him. "But that doesn't mean that one of the other ten people at his New York branch—including a couple of executives on the rise—couldn't have done it. They were here."

"And you're standing at my desk to let me know we're heading over to that New York branch to talk to those ten people."

"In half an hour," Jeannie confirmed, polishing off her Milk Duds. "The office is right down Fifth Avenue—just three blocks from Ruisseau."

"Good. Next question—what about Hager? When do you want to meet with him again?"

"Meet with him or push him to the wall?" Jeannie muttered. It was a rhetorical question, since she knew full well what the answer was. "Yeah, you're right. It's about time we stopped dancing around him. We're getting nowhere fast. How about late today? We'll call and set up an official appointment. That'll give Hager a whole afternoon to sweat over what we want."

"Let's not give the same heads-up to Ferguson," Frank said. "With him, it's better that we just drop in. I have a gut feeling that, if anyone would crack under the pressure of a surprise attack, he's the guy to do it."

"Fine. No preparation time there. We'll just make an appointment with Hager and do a drop-in on Ferguson." Jeannie reached for the phone on Frank's desk.

Simultaneously, her cell phone rang.

She punched the SEND button. "Whitman." Her brows lifted slightly. "Well, hello." A pause. "Really. Yes, I understand. Any more details you want to give me? Okay, fine. We'll be there. You're welcome."

She pressed END and turned to Frank. "You're never going to believe this one."

"Try me."

"That was Carson Brooks. Apparently, there's going to be a company-wide announcement at five-thirty today, informing the entire staff of Ruisseau that Sabrina Radcliffe is his daughter. He's making the announcement himself, via a prerecorded videotape, from his hospital bed. He asked us to be at Ruisseau when the tape is played—for protection purposes."

"Protection." Frank digested that information thoughtfully. "I wonder if Brooks is afraid his daughter will be mauled by the press, or if his fears run deeper than that."

"You know the answer to that, Frank. Brooks is as perceptive as they come. He's well aware that there's a killer out there somewhere, one with a motive we still haven't identified. I'm sure he's also aware that that killer might try again, in any number of ways. One is to go for Brooks directly, which isn't likely as long as he's in Mount Sinai with round-the-clock police protection. The other is to go at him through his daughter."

"Especially if that daughter is about to officially acquire an extremely powerful role at Ruisseau."

"Which you can bet she is. She's smart, she's successful, and she's his flesh and blood. It's a no-brainer."

"Agreed. So if Brooks's shooting was in any way related to his position at Ruisseau, today's announcement might instigate the shooter."

"Maybe. Maybe not. But it's clear that Brooks doesn't want to take any chances."

"I don't blame him."

"Me either." Jeannie crumpled up the empty Milk Duds box and tossed it into the trash. "And to think this morning started off ordinary."

"Whatever ordinary means these days." Frank pushed back his chair and rose. "This also solves our problem about when to meet with Hager and Ferguson. We'll be at Ruisseau at five-thirty anyway."

"We sure will." A gleam of anticipation lit Jeannie's eyes. "Except that we'll get there early and surprise them."

1:45 P.M.
Ruisseau Fragrance Corporation

Sabrina tried Stan's extension to see if he was ready for their lunch.

Lunch. If you wanted to call it that. Donna had ordered in sandwiches, which were being delivered to Sabrina's office sometime within the next half hour. That gave Sabrina forty-five minutes before her meeting with R&D. Forty-five minutes to broach the subject of Stan's discomfort around her and break the news of today's announcement, in between bites of a turkey sandwich she had to wolf down since she hadn't eaten a thing all day.

Talk about a fast-paced agenda.

Then again, why should lunch be different than the rest of the day had been?

Sabrina dropped her head in her hands and massaged her temples.

Her morning had been a soap opera. First, there'd been the conversation with her mother. Gloria had taken the news of Sabrina's donor compatibility with her usual controlled dignity. But Sabrina could hear the tremor in her voice, and she knew her mother was frightened. She'd tried soothing her to the best of her ability, but there were no guarantees she could offer. Nor did Gloria request any. She just told Sabrina she was behind her, and said she'd fly to New York as soon as the press—and her parents—were under control.

Which led Sabrina into Act Two: the drama with her grandparents.

Abigail and Charles Radcliffe had been beside themselves, despite whatever groundwork Gloria had laid. Sabrina's grandmother had wept; her grandfather had lectured. They both had practically pleaded with her to reconsider donating her kidney to a man she barely knew.

It had taken close to an hour to get through to them, to make them understand even on a basic, fundamental level why she had to do this. And, no, telling them about her newly acquired position at Ruisseau hadn't helped. They'd been so worked up, they'd scarcely paid attention to her announcement, much less focused on the prestige it denoted.

Act Two had ended on a taut, emotional note.

Closely followed by Act Three: CCTL. Sabrina's conference call with Deborah and Mark, and the announcement that had ensued, had resulted in mass pandemonium. The two of them had known that Sabrina's assignment at Ruisseau and a back-to-back personal matter she wasn't ready to discuss yet would keep her away from the center for a chunk of time. But a long-term management consulting gig was one thing. Becoming president of the company she was consulting for—not to mention the daughter of its CEO—*that* was a total shock. Their concerns weren't limited to how they should handle the press. They extended to how they should handle the staff, the clients, the future.

Sabrina had reiterated the temporary solution they'd already put in place, assuring them that she had no intention of abandoning CCTL. She promised to fly back on Friday and spend the entire weekend hammering out details.

After that, she'd asked them to put her through to Melissa. That hadn't been a cakewalk either. Melissa had been stunned, then worried—more about Sabrina than about CCTL. She'd asked a million detailed questions, and they'd probably still be on the phone now if Sabrina hadn't promised to have a drink with her the minute she got in Friday night, during which time she'd fill her in on everything.

Dylan had been right, Sabrina thought, wishing the Tylenol she'd taken for her headache would kick in. It was barely past the half-day mark, and she was about to implode.

A knock on her door brought her throbbing head up. "Come in."

Stan strolled in, carrying a brown bag that he waved in front of her. "Lunch and I arrived at the same time," he pronounced, shutting the door behind him. "So I took it off Donna's hands and saved us some time." He gave

Sabrina a tired smile as he walked to the desk, placed the bag down, and emptied out the contents. "Turkey on rye, roast beef on a roll. Fine dining at its best."

"I'm sorry about that." Sabrina helped him arrange the sandwiches and set up the two containers of coffee. "There wasn't time for a restaurant. Not today."

"No apology necessary." Stan sat down and took a sip of coffee, eyeing her over the rim of the cup. "You look like you're about to collapse."

"Great. It shows already? I can hardly wait till the grand finale. I'll probably drop in the middle of the meeting."

"No you won't. You'll gulp another cup of that—" He pointed at her container of coffee. "Then you'll go into the bathroom, glare at your reflection in the mirror, and give yourself a major verbal beating up. After that, you'll march into the meeting and be fine."

Sabrina's brows rose. "That sounds amazingly accurate. Have you been spying on me?"

"No need. That's what Carson does."

She blew out her breath. "It's pretty scary being his daughter. I'm not sure what's harder—what others expect of me, or what I expect of myself."

Stan's sandwich paused midway to his mouth, and he blinked in surprise. It was the first time Sabrina had blatantly displayed any vulnerability in his presence.

"Don't look so stunned," Sabrina said dryly. "Did you think that because I'm smart and self-assured that I was just taking this whole thing in my stride? If so, I'm either a better actress than I thought or you're not looking close enough. Carson's my father, yes. But he's had twenty-eight years to earn the respect he gets. I'm a rookie by comparison. Raw talent's nice. But it's just the beginning. I've got a lot to learn about Ruisseau. That's why

I'm so appreciative of what you and Dylan have done for me. You've helped make this transition easier. I can't thank you enough. That's part of what I wanted to say, one of the reasons I asked you to have lunch with me."

Stan put down his roast beef sandwich. He had an odd expression on his face, like he wasn't quite sure how to handle her personal candor. "You're welcome," he said simply.

"As for the other reason I wanted to have lunch, that one I'm sure you guessed."

"You want to talk about this afternoon's meeting."

"Right. Obviously, you realize it's something pretty important for me to assemble the entire staff. Well, you deserve a heads-up about the agenda, not only because of the support you've shown me *and* because you're the company's COO, but because of the special place you have in Carson's life."

"You're coming clean, so to speak," Stan guessed, taking a bite of his sandwich and chewing it. "You're telling everyone who you are to Carson and what you are to Ruisseau."

"Yes." She nodded, watching Stan's reaction. He looked pensive, yes. But he also looked exhausted. And torn. That part was weird. What kind of internal battle was he fighting? Okay, fine, he was freaked out by having another Carson-type at the helm. That much Sabrina got. But there was something else eating at him. What was it?

"I think it's time we got my identity out in the open," she continued, still scrutinizing Stan's face, his body language. "Obviously, so does Carson. I hope you feel the same way."

"Yeah, I do." His answer was blunt and, seemingly, frank. "It'll make things much easier once you're official—in both a personal and a professional capacity. Secrets never manage to stay that way for long. After today, everyone will know who you are and what your future is at Ruisseau. And they'll hear it from you."

"Actually, they'll hear it from Carson. He's making the announcement himself, by videotape."

"Even better. It'll hold more weight coming from him." A quick glance at Sabrina. "No offense intended."

"None taken. You're right. Like I said, I harbor no illusions about my place in this company. Carson's the heart and soul of Ruisseau. That's never going to change." She leaned forward, trying a tactic she hoped would work. "Stan, you don't need to walk on eggshells around me. I'm tough. I don't fly off the handle when I'm challenged. And I refuse to accept special treatment because I'm Carson's daughter. I'm counting on you to remember that, and to make sure everyone else does, too. The staff will follow your lead. If you kowtow to me, they will, too. In which case, I can't do my job, and Ruisseau can't fulfill its potential. Agreed?"

He took another bite of his sandwich, chewing it slowly as he considered what she'd said. "Yeah," he said finally, with a terse nod. "Agreed. Although I won't lie to you. This is going to take some getting used to."

"I never thought otherwise. That's what change is about. On the other hand, only idiots fix what's not broken, or implement change for change's sake without retaining the strengths of the previous organization. You've been here since the beginning. Tell me what works. Yell at me if I screw up. Believe me, Carson does. Constantly."

A hint of amusement. "I'll remember that."

"You won't have to. You'll hear him. He's not shy about putting me in my place." She propped her elbows on the desk, interlacing her fingers and resting her chin on them. "There's one more thing. It's good news—very good news, although I'm not supplying the press with details. My blood test results came back. My compatibility as a donor match is very high. If it becomes necessary, I'm pretty sure I can give Carson one of my kidneys."

Stan blew out a huge—and very genuine—sigh of relief. "That's the best news I've heard yet. Thanks for telling me." He paused, a flicker of comprehension dawning in his eyes. "I'm not the only one you told. You must have spoken with your family, and with CCTL. No wonder you look so beat."

She nodded. "It was a rough morning, yes."

"Your grandparents must be overwrought."

"They'll handle it. So will I."

"What about Dylan?"

Sabrina blinked. "What about him?"

"I assume he knows."

"He was with me when I told Carson, yes."

"That must have been a pleasant conversation," Stan noted wryly. "Did Carson blow your head off?"

"Pretty much. But we came to terms."

"And Dylan? How did he take the news of your test results?" Stan gave a sympathetic shake of his head. "He must be torn—concern over you, concern over Carson. I don't envy the guy."

Okay, now Sabrina was starting to feel distinctly uncomfortable. "I'm not following you. Dylan is as relieved as I am, and as you are. This was the outcome we were hoping for. It's why Dylan flew up to New Hampshire to find me to begin with—as you well know."

"Sure, but that was before you and he—" Stan broke off, abruptly realizing he was trespassing on a do-not-enter zone. "Sorry. I didn't mean to overstep. Let's change the subject."

Dammit. Stan knew about her and Dylan. How? And who else knew?

"Sabrina, relax," Stan said, responding to the brooding expression on her face. "No one's gossiping at the water-coolers. It's just speculation, although the vibes between the two of you are kind of hard to miss. But so what? Dylan's Ruisseau's corporate counsel. You're Ruisseau's president. There's no big-time conflict of interest that I can see. So live your life and don't worry about what people say or think."

"Like you do?" The question was out before she could censor it.

His eyes narrowed. "What does that mean?"

There was no turning back now. Still, she chose her words carefully. "It means you worry a lot more than I do about the way you're perceived. In my case, I'm choos-ing to keep my private life private. In your case, you're eating yourself alive. Cut it out, Stan. No, you're not Car-son. No one expects you to be. You're good at your job. You'd never do anything to compromise Ruisseau's inter-ests or to hurt its CEO. And that's all that matters—right?"

For a long moment, Stan just stared at her. He looked as if he'd been punched. A flush crept up his neck and a myriad of emotions flashed across his face—surprise and irritation, which Sabrina had expected—mixed with something that looked disturbingly like self-consciousness and guilt. "Right," he said finally. Blowing out his breath, he dropped back in his seat. "You're a piece of work, Sabrina. Talk about a Carson-clone."

She'd upset him. That was a definite. But whether that was because he was disconcerted by her blunt analysis or whether it was something deeper and more serious—the jury was still out on that one.

"Look, Stan, I didn't mean to insult you," she said, deciding that now was not the time to pursue this. "I'm stressed out and tired. Let's concentrate on getting through today. Then, we'll set guidelines for the future, okay?"

"Works for me," Stan replied stiffly.

"Good." She gestured for him to eat. "Let's polish off these sandwiches. I've got so much to do between now and five-thirty, I might have to skip that trip to the ladies' room where I smack myself around for courage."

He nodded.

The rest of the meal lasted less than fifteen minutes, during which time they made perfunctory chitchat. Sabrina knew Stan was still pissed off or freaked out by what she'd said. But that wasn't what was bothering her. She'd find a way to smooth things over, to get their relationship back on the right foot—if that's all that was needed.

What was really bothering her was that she couldn't get past her own uneasiness. Something about Stan wasn't sitting right. His anxiety smacked of more than insecurity. And what had he meant by the statement that secrets didn't manage to stay that way for long? Why did she feel like there was some kind of underlying message there, something he hadn't meant to let slip?

When it came to Stan Hager, Sabrina felt a fine layer of mistrust that she just couldn't get past.

ANDREA KANE

prominent father in the newspapers over the next few weeks—and he might find the discussion when they were joined by the media. The impression and comfort alone before the remaining...

24

6:23 P.M.
Ruisseau Fragrance Corporation

You could have heard a pin drop in the conference room when Carson Brooks finished his taped statement and the screen went dark.

Someone flipped the lights back on, and Sabrina wasn't surprised to see more than a hundred pairs of eyes staring at her. The wall between the two main conference rooms had been removed, opening it into one huge room so that everyone could fit inside. The meeting was closed, a staff-only event, but Marie had faxed a brief statement to the press minutes before the meeting began, which was doubtless being delivered on business networks everywhere as breaking news. Sabrina knew what would be waiting for her outside the building tonight when she left.

That was for later. For now she had the staff—a stunned, curious throng of people watching her and waiting for her comments.

She hadn't expected to be this choked up. Carson's words hadn't been sentimental or emotional. They'd been factual. He'd simply stated that she was his daughter, that he'd only recently learned of her existence, and that he was delighted to announce her joining Ruisseau on a permanent basis as its newly appointed president, reporting directly to him. He said he suspected they'd all be reading colorful details about Sabrina's conception and her prominent family in the newspapers over the next few weeks, and he urged them to use discretion when they were grilled by the media, and compassion and consideration before bombarding their new president with questions. He concluded by saying that they were fortunate to have someone of Sabrina's caliber, quality, and professional experience as Ruisseau's president. He then asked for everyone's cooperation in making her transition a positive one, and urged everyone to join him in welcoming Sabrina to her new place at Ruisseau.

It was a carefully planned, well-executed announcement.

Carson had given Sabrina his ringing endorsement, while keeping the facts scarce to allow her to pick up the ball and run with it in whatever direction she chose. As for spin, he'd left that to the media.

So there was no explanation for why Sabrina felt emotional. Yet she did. She felt as if she were standing at the edge of a pivotal precipice—one that, once she leaped across it, would change her life forever.

The prospect was exhilarating and daunting all at once.

She wet her lips, walked to the head of the table. From the corner of her eye, she saw Dylan, leaning against the wall, arms folded across his chest as he watched her. Stan was beside him, looking sheet-white, which was no surprise, given that Detectives Whitman and Barton were hovering next to him, just inside the door. They'd explained their appearance by saying Carson had asked them to come—which Sabrina didn't doubt—but it hadn't stopped them from closeting themselves in Stan's office for half an hour, grilling him about God-knows-what.

She couldn't think about that now.

Glancing down at the sheet of paper in her hands, Sabrina abruptly folded it in two and put it aside.

"I'd prepared something to say," she told the staff. "But as I look it over, the words seem suddenly very trite. Suffice it to say that as shocked and overwhelmed as you feel, I was twice as shocked and overwhelmed. I've had time for the reality to sink in. Oh, I'm still a little overwhelmed. But I'm also honored. Honored, proud, and excited. You know what I want for this company. I told you my vision the day I came on board—some of you in person, some in a memo I distributed. If anything, a week with all of you has made me want that vision for Ruisseau even more. I intend to make it happen, with your help, and with Carson at the helm. Rather than having me talk endlessly, why don't you ask the questions that are on your minds, and I'll do my best to answer them. And don't be shy. Believe me, the press won't be."

A titter went through the room.

Sabrina spent the next hour discussing professional issues—reassuring people that their jobs would remain intact, that Ruisseau would continue on its present track and with its current objectives—and addressing more human issues—admitting that she'd been shocked and awed to find out Carson Brooks was her father, acknowledging that she still had kinks to work out before she was comfortable with the balancing act of running CCTL and being president of Ruisseau.

The last few questions were the hardest.

"Ms. Radcliffe," Claude Phelps asked, his mouth set in a tight, grim line. "What about the formula for C'est Moi—has Carson shared that with you?"

Sabrina didn't blink or avert her gaze. "I'm not going to answer that question, Claude. Because it's not mine to field. Whatever decisions our CEO chooses to make, or not to make, are his to disclose. I'll only answer questions that pertain to me, to my vision for Ruisseau, or to my philosophies as they might affect you. Any questions you have for Carson, you'll have to take up with him personally."

Claude scowled, but fell silent. Across the room, Dylan gave her a thumbs-up.

"I'll take one more question," Sabrina stipulated. She was starting to feel a little woozy. "Then we'll call it a day." A day. Right. With the media hounds waiting outside. "Yes?" She acknowledged Eve Rogers, one of Ruisseau's up-and-coming product managers, who'd stuck her hand nervously in the air.

"I may be out of line," Eve began, shifting a bit as she spoke. "But I know we're all wondering—and worrying—about Mr. Brooks's health. Could you tell us what's rumor and what's fact? Will he be all right?"

Sabrina nodded, bracing herself for where she knew this was headed. "Carson is the strongest human being I've ever met. He's going to pull through this. I'm sure you saw that much from watching him on tape. He's chomping at the bit to get out of the hospital and back to his desk. Just ask the nurses. They're drawing straws to see who's forced to go in there and deal with him in his current—intolerant, shall we say—state of mind." She smiled, as a universal chuckle echoed through the room. "By the way, no, you're not out of line. Everyone at Ruisseau cares about Carson. He regards all of you as his family. I think you know that."

"We do." The young woman stood up straighter, pushing her glasses higher on the rim of her nose. "What about his kidneys? Have they recovered, or are they still failing?"

"The doctors are being cautious on that prognosis,"

Sabrina replied. "Apparently, in some cases, it can take up to two months for kidney function to return. The bullet caused a lot of trauma. So it's too soon to tell."

"Meaning his kidneys aren't functioning now?"

"Right. He's had several dialysis treatments, and responded very well to them. He's playing the waiting game—not very well, as I said—the same way we are." She rolled her eyes. "Trust me. Mount Sinai will never be the same."

Another chuckle went through the room.

"Ms. Radcliffe—" Eve asked what she, and everyone else, really wanted to know. "We're aware that the hospital was searching for a compatible donor match. Since you're Mr. Brooks's natural child, I was just wondering . . ." Her voice trailed off, and she looked a little panicked that she'd overstepped.

"You were wondering if I'd been tested to see if I fit the bill," Sabrina finished for her. "The answer is yes, I have been tested. We don't have conclusive results yet. The process is complicated, and may take up to a month to complete. But when those results are in and when I have more current information on Carson's kidney prognosis, I'll share the outcome with all of you. In return, I ask that you pass as little as possible on to the press, out of respect for Carson's privacy. Is that fair enough?"

A uniform nod and a murmur of yeses ran through the room.

"Thank you. I'm sure we'd all like to go home and get some rest. This has been quite a day—for all of us. I'll be at my desk bright and early tomorrow morning, ready and eager to assume my new responsibilities. I appreciate all of you taking the time to be here to share in this announcement."

Sabrina was aware of the applause, but she was so

light-headed that she wondered if she'd embarrass herself by fainting on her way down from the head of the table. She walked slowly, methodically, stepping into a swarm of people who had no more desire to let her go home to rest than they had to dance naked in the streets.

She was screwed. She'd be here for hours.

As if on cue, Dylan made his way through the crowd, planted himself in Sabrina's path. "Excuse me, Sabrina, but I need you to sign some legal papers before you head out. I don't mean to keep you, but I've got to get the documents over to Carson tonight."

"All right. Fine." She wanted to weep with gratitude as he pressed a firm palm against the small of her back and practically shoved her out of the room.

In the hall, he took her arm, led her down the corridor and toward his office.

Sabrina blinked in surprise when she saw Detectives Whitman and Barton standing outside Dylan's door. She hadn't seen them leave the conference room.

"Your limo's parked outside, right near Fifth," Whitman informed Sabrina. "The press is gathered around it like a bunch of hornets. Go out of the building, veer toward Sixth, and head over to the park. We have a squad car there that'll get you to Mr. Newport's apartment intact."

"Thank you so much," Sabrina breathed.

"Don't thank us. It was your father's idea." Barton folded his arms across his chest. "A pretty good one, though, judging from what's going on. Congratulations, by the way."

Sabrina didn't have time to answer. Dylan was already dragging her toward the elevator.

The next few minutes were a blur. The elevator down to the second floor. The stairs the rest of the way down, letting them out on the far side of the lobby. Veering outside. Getting swallowed up in rush-hour pedestrian traffic. Central Park. The welcome sight of a NYPD squad car.

Manhattan traffic had never looked so good.

An unknown time later, they turned onto West 76th Street, stopping in front of Dylan's apartment. He tugged her out of the squad car, unlocked his front door, and pulled her inside.

"Come on." He led her into the living room, eased her down on the sofa, and poured her a glass of wine. While she was sipping it, he went into the kitchen, emerging with a tray of crackers and cheese. "Eat," he ordered, putting the tray down in front of her.

Sabrina gave him a wan smile. "My hero." She gobbled up five or six crackers and brie, then drank a little more wine before setting her goblet on the table and sitting back with a sigh. "I'm not sure, but I think you just saved my life."

Dylan sat down beside her. "You scared the shit out of me. You looked like a ghost when you walked away from that conference table." He slid a hand beneath her hair, rubbed her neck gently. "Sabrina, you're not a superhero. You're human. Give yourself a break."

She acted on impulse, on adrenaline, on sheer gut instinct.

"Whatever you say." She scrambled to her knees and scooted closer, tugging at his tie even as she leaned up to kiss him. "You're right. I need a break. I feel like I'm about to shatter. And I need you to help me do that." She traced his lower lip with her tongue. "Make love to me."

No second invitation was necessary.

Dylan made a harsh sound, capturing her head between his hands as her lips brushed his. He took over the kiss without preliminaries, his mouth ravaging hers with three days of pent-up sexual hunger combined with the emotional overload of the past few hours.

They didn't make it upstairs.

They yanked at each other's clothes, unable to get at each other fast enough. Buttons popped, fabric ripped, and still it seemed to take forever for them to be naked, to feel skin against skin.

Dylan couldn't stand it anymore, and he tore himself away from her, kicking free of the last of his clothes and leaning over her, putting one knee on the sofa and tearing her panties in two, tossing the shreds of silk aside.

"I've got to get inside you," he muttered, kissing his way down her body, making her moan and writhe as he did.

The sofa, wide and cushy or not, was too narrow to accommodate their frantic motions. Dylan solved the problem by flinging some cushions on the floor, and tumbling Sabrina onto them. "Okay?" he managed, poised over her.

"Yes . . . yes . . . just hurry." Sabrina was in no mood for slow and seductive. She needed Dylan and she needed him now.

Judging from the smoldering look in his eyes, she wasn't alone.

He moved between her thighs, propping himself on his elbows to take some of his weight. Sabrina wrapped her legs around his, arched to take him, her fingers digging into his biceps, pulling him into her.

He pushed deep, hard, stretching her and filling her. The sensation was beyond description. Every nerve ending in Sabrina's body screamed to life, everything inside her tightened, tightened. . . . God, he'd barely gotten inside her and she was about to come, it was so spectacular.

Too spectacular.

A heartbeat away from orgasm, Sabrina froze. "Dylan."

His lips were buried against her throat, and he didn't answer, his breath a warm, unsteady rasp against her skin. He was pulsing inside her, as close to the edge as she was.

He withdrew slowly, then pushed all the way back in. "God." A hard shudder wracked his body. "I can't wait. You feel too good."

It took Sabrina a few seconds to speak, the pleasure was so acute. And all her energies were focused on fighting the climax that was about to peak inside her. "Dylan!" She shoved at his shoulders.

This time her tone registered. He raised his head, stared down at her with eyes that were almost black with passion. Sweat dotted his forehead, dampened the ends of his hair. "What's wrong?" He forced out the words. "Does it hurt?"

"No. No, but . . ." God, it would be so easy to dismiss the whole thing, to wrap her arms around his neck and pull him down to her, to lose herself in this exquisite, unimaginable madness.

And if it were just the two of them, if there was nothing else at stake, she would.

"Sabrina . . ." Dylan's fingers were shaking as they touched her cheek. "What is it?"

"You're not wearing . . . a condom."

Shock dilated his pupils. "Shit." He gritted his teeth, all the veins in his neck standing out as he called upon his failing reserves. "Don't move. Don't even breathe. It'll be too much."

She understood. She felt the same way. She almost screamed in frustration when he pulled out of her. Fists clenched, she waited while he crawled over to his pants and yanked out a foil packet. He could barely get the thing on, his hands were shaking so badly. But he was back in seconds, his body so taut, Sabrina could feel him vibrating.

"This is going to be barbarically quick," he ground out, already pushing into her. "I'm sorry."

She shook her head. It couldn't be quick enough for her. She was dying.

He plunged deep, and Sabrina cried out, the tension coiling too tight to bear, then unraveling in spasms that shook her to the core, and milked Dylan well past the point of no return.

He shouted her name, thrusting into her climax, meeting it with his own. His entire body convulsed, again and again, his hips pumping wildly as he came.

Recovery took longer than the act itself, both of them struggling to drag air into their lungs. The cushions hadn't survived the chaos, and were shoved haphazardly around on the floor, leaving nothing under Sabrina but the area rug. Dylan's full weight was on her, and the hardwood floor beneath the rug anchored her so he was even deeper inside her than usual.

Moving seemed too exhausting to consider.

Neither of them considered it.

Time passed.

Eventually, Dylan gathered up his strength and lifted himself off of her. He looked dazed and spent, yet there was a fine tension rippling through him that Sabrina sensed right away. She lay quietly, watching him, uncertain whether to address the issue or let him take the lead.

Neither happened.

Dylan stood up, and went into the bathroom to deal with the condom. A minute later, he emerged and walked back over to where she lay. His lids were hooded, but he looked intense, brooding, as he loomed over her.

"We need to talk," he stated flatly.

"Okay." Sabrina's muscles felt like water. She moved them gingerly, wondering if she'd be able to stand.

Dylan eliminated the problem by dropping down to his knees beside her. He cupped her face between his palms and gazed directly into her eyes. "I'm in love with you. I don't want to take it a day at a time. I don't want to do without commitments and expectations. I don't give a damn about the other pressures and demands in our lives. They'll be here tomorrow, and the next day, and the next. We'll deal with them—together. I want permanence. I want marriage. I want children. And I want them with you."

Sabrina just stared at him, his words penetrating her mind slowly, like a fine wine, until they registered.

Then, she did something she rarely did.

She burst into tears.

Covering her face with her hands, she wept, all the emotions of the day spilling out in a rush.

Dylan pressed her head against his chest, kissed her hair. "I hope that's not an answer," he murmured, his fingers trailing gently up and down her back. "Because it's not great for my ego."

Sabrina laughed through her tears. "And I hope that incredible speech wasn't your way of trying to divert me from the fact that you promised to cook me dinner. No matter how eloquent or spectacular you are, I want that linguini in white clam sauce."

"What about the chef? Do you want him, too?"

She raised her head, gazed at him through wet eyes. "You've turned my entire life upside down."

"Ditto," he said softly.

"I knew who I was. I knew where I was going. I knew what I wanted." She dragged a hand through her hair. "God, I'm such a mess. A new life, a new identity, and a man who makes me feel things I never counted on feeling."

"What things, Sabrina? What is it I make you feel?"

She swallowed, hard. "You want the words."

"Damn right I want the words."

Two tears slid down her cheeks. "Dylan, it's only been a few weeks. . . ."

"It only took a few minutes. We both know it. We both feel it. Now say it."

"Okay." She wasn't about to fight this one. It was a losing battle. She could deny it till the cows came home, but she was head-over-heels in love with this man. And he deserved to know. "I love you," she said in a quavery voice. "I don't want to take it a day at a time. I don't want to do without commitments or expectations. The truth is, if you ever look at another woman, I'll choke you."

His lips twisted into that sexy, crooked smile. "Thanks for the warning. But the risk is nil. No one exists for me but you." His expression intensified again. "What about the rest?"

"The rest?"

"Marry me. Have my children. Build a life with me."

"Dylan, I want to say yes." She struggled for a semblance of sanity. "But there's so much going on now. My life is on overdrive. I don't even know which end is up."

"I do," he said in a husky, teasing voice. "Want me to show you?"

"Be serious."

"I am." He sobered, slid his palms over her shoulders. "The way we feel about each other is the only constant in all this insanity. As for the rest—planes fly from

New York to Manchester in a little over an hour. Telephones and e-mails reach everywhere, all over the world, in a matter of minutes. We can live in two places, merge our two lives, do any goddamned thing we want to. We can work it out—if we want to badly enough. Say yes."

She reached up, caressed his jaw. "You have a way of making me believe anything's possible."

"Doesn't that tell you something?"

"Um-hum. It tells me that I already have my answer. And now, so will you. Yes. My answer's yes."

"Finally." He turned his lips into her palm. "I'm crazy about you. I lose my mind when we're together. I guess that means I'll be losing it for good."

Sabrina laughed softly. "Any complaints?"

"Not a one."

He was already starting to get that smoky look in his eyes. And much as Sabrina wanted to make love with him again, there was something important they needed to discuss first. Something she needed to make him understand.

"Dylan?" She rose to her knees, wrapped her arms around his neck, and held his gaze. "Before—when you were inside me—I wouldn't have stopped you. I wanted the same thing you did. It's just that . . ."

"You don't need to explain," he interrupted. "You're not ready. I understand. I was a careless jackass. My only excuse is that I'm so in love with you I lose all touch with reality."

"Me, too. Believe me, pragmatism had nothing to do with why I stopped you. I could barely breathe, much less think. But I had to try—for Carson's sake."

His brows drew together. "Carson?"

She nodded. "The transplant. I've got to be ready for

surgery, just in case he needs it. I can't get pregnant, not now."

Realization—and guilt—flashed across Dylan's face. "I really am a selfish bastard. I claim to be so damned devoted to Carson, and here I am forgetting what he might need more than anything else."

"You didn't forget. We were making love. It's not exactly a natural leap to think of Carson's medical condition while we're tearing each other's clothes off."

"You did."

"Barely. And just in the nick of time. One more second and . . ." She shivered, traced his lips with her fingertips. "You're an amazing lover. The way you make me feel defies words."

He lowered his head, kissed his way down the side of her neck. "I return the compliment. I can't get enough of you."

"M-m-m." Her eyes slid shut. "See? That explains it. You're not selfish. I'm just intoxicating. I bewitched you."

He chuckled, his breath warming her skin. "You sure as hell did. And you're welcome to keep doing so for the rest of our lives." He cupped her face, kissed her slowly, tenderly. "Are you starving?" he murmured between kisses. "Or can the linguini wait?"

"Oh, I'm starving all right." She gave him a look that was pure seduction. "What linguini?"

25

7:55 P.M.
Mt. Sinai Hospital

Carson's eyelids drooped. He didn't want to doze, but he couldn't seem to keep his eyes open.

He was totally wiped out. The excitement, the intensity, the activity level of the day—it had taken a lot out of him. Not that he would have changed any part of it. Not for the world. After today, he could publicly acknowledge his daughter and have her in his life.

It was okay to rest now. He'd be getting an update from Stan any minute now, letting him know how the announcement had gone over, and if Sabrina and Dylan had managed to elude the press. He wanted to know that she was safe and sound, that the cops had gotten her to Dylan's the way they promised.

His forehead creased. That was his only nagging worry. Had revealing Sabrina's identity put her at risk? Would whoever shot him somehow find out that he'd shared the formula for C'est Moi with his daughter, and go after her, too?

He'd talk to Whitman and Barton tomorrow. If they didn't see his logic and agree to a police escort for Sabrina, he'd hire a private bodyguard to watch her.

But not tonight. Tonight she'd be fine. She had the best bodyguard in the world: Dylan. And she and Dylan were well on their way to what he viewed as the ultimate and spectacular inevitable. Hell, with the way he felt about Dylan, and now Sabrina—it was a father's dream . . .

He must have drifted off.

He had the dream again. Relived the Monday night shooting. In slow motion, the same as always. He was standing at the window. Heard the pop. Felt the pain. Smelled the sweet odor. Saw the colors, the carpet. Heard Dylan's voice. Then, the paramedics. The blood—so much of it. Wet and sticky. Dizzy. The tingling in his limbs. Trying to breathe—inhaling that sickeningly sweet smell. Blood and carpet cleaner. And there was something else. Something he should remember, but couldn't. Whatever it was, it was just out of his grasp.

At some point he became aware that he wasn't alone.

Not in his dream. In reality. Here. Now.

He forced open his eyes. Dusk had settled over the hospital room, casting it in shadows. Someone was there. It wasn't a doctor or a nurse.

Stan? Was that Stan standing next to his IV drip, saying something to him?

Maybe not. Maybe it was part of the dream.

Because when he opened his eyes again, Stan was gone. He was alone.

He drifted off again.

And dreamed.

"Carson?" Susan's voice dragged him back to consciousness, and he forced open his eyelids, seeing her worried face. "Are you okay?" she demanded. Her hand was cool as it stroked his face.

He realized he was sweating.

The dream. It did it to him every time.

And he realized something else. It was dark. Pitch

dark. Not in his room, but outside his window. Son of a bitch. How late was it?

"Carson?" Susan repeated, her increasingly alarmed tone telling him she was freaking out because he wasn't answering. "What is it? Are you all right?"

"I'm fine. Just groggy. What time is it?" he asked hoarsely.

"Ten-thirty."

"Ten-thirty?" The cobwebs vanished, and Carson sat bolt upright. "Why did you let me sleep so long?"

"Honey, you were exhausted." Susan still looked worried, although hearing how coherent he was seemed to bring her some measure of relief. "Here." She poured him a glass of water. "Drink this." She waited while he did. "You were having that nightmare again," she told him quietly. "It was bad this time. You were thrashing around and muttering something about smelling blood. And you asked for Stan."

He frowned, remembering. "Stan—was he here?"

Susan nodded. "He came by to tell you about the meeting. But you were pretty out of it. Dr. Radison suggested that he come back in the morning."

"Dammit. The meeting." Carson pushed back the covers, tried to get up. "I have to know. . . ."

"Don't." Susan stopped him, blocking his path so he couldn't get out of bed. "The meeting went fine. I can give you a recap. Stan said the staff received the news about Sabrina with great enthusiasm, and that she answered questions like a pro. No sticky moments, except when Claude wanted to know if you'd told Sabrina the formula for C'est Moi, and when a product manager asked if Sabrina had been tested as a potential kidney donor."

Carson pursed his lips. "And?"

"Stan said she handled things perfectly. She deflected Claude's question, telling him he'd have to direct any inquiries regarding decisions you've made to you personally. As for the tissue-typing, she said she was in the process of being tested and would fill the staff in when the results were conclusive and when she knew if your kidneys were going to recover on their own. And she told them to respect your privacy and stay away from the press."

"Good girl." A proud smile curved Carson's lips. "No bullshit. No embellishing. Just straight facts. Then what?"

"Then, Whitman and Barton did their job. Sabrina and Dylan got out of the building without incident, made it to the squad car. and were driven, safe and sound, to Dylan's apartment."

"How does Stan know they got there okay? Did he check in with Dylan?"

Susan sighed, visibly prepping herself for Carson's outburst. "I didn't hear that part from Stan. Detective Whitman called and told me about it herself."

"And you didn't wake me?" Carson barked. He was already reaching for the phone. "What time did Whitman call?"

"Around eight-thirty. She said to let you sleep."

"Yeah, I'll just bet she did. She didn't want me firing questions at her. Well, tough." He punched in a number. "I'm calling her cell phone. She'd better answer or . . . Yeah, Detective Whitman?"

At the other end of the phone, Jeannie—who was still at her desk, going over the information she and Frank had gleaned from Stan Hager today—munched on another potato chip. "Hi, Mr. Brooks. I was wondering what took you so long."

"I just woke up. Tell me what happened."

"Exactly what you wanted to happen. Your daughter and Mr. Newport were delivered to his apartment, unscathed, uninterrogated, and in one piece."

"Was she all right?"

Jeannie put down the bag of chips. "Physically, she was fine. Other than the fact that she looked white as a sheet. She answered questions for over an hour, following a day that, from what I heard, was a circus."

Carson's lips thinned into a grim line. "You're sure the press didn't get to her?"

"Positive. Although from what I hear, things are hopping at Beacon Hill, and the phones are ringing off the hook at CCTL."

"Shit. How do you know that?"

"We checked with Gloria Radcliffe. She filled us in."

"Is Gloria home or with her parents?"

"She's home. Her parents went to bed. A rough day for them, I gather."

"Shit," Carson repeated. "Okay, I'll take it from here. Except for one thing. What do you think about assigning police protection to Sabrina?"

Jeannie blew out a breath. "Realistically? There's no way. Not the way you mean. We can beef up police presence near your office, even arrange for routine check-ins with Sabrina, and a patrol car monitoring her neighborhood at night. But round-the-clock one-on-one protection? Uh-uh."

"Then I'll hire a bodyguard."

If Carson was expecting a protest, he didn't get one. "I don't blame you. It's your daughter. Your job is to protect her. Ours is to make sure there's nothing to protect her from."

"I hear you." Carson's wheels were turning. "I'll take

care of my end. You take care of yours." A pause. "And detective?"

"Yes?"

"Thanks."

He disconnected the call, then peered over at his nightstand where he'd placed a napkin with a phone number scribbled on it. He grabbed the napkin and punched up the number.

"Who are you calling?" Susan asked, perching at the edge of the bed.

"Gloria Radcliffe. I want to make sure everything there is okay."

Susan looked puzzled. "Why not call Sabrina? I'm sure she's spoken to her mother."

"I'm sure she has." For the first time, Carson's features relaxed, and he shot Susan a hint of a grin. "But I'm not bothering Sabrina. Not tonight."

"You think she's conked out?"

"Nope. I think she's otherwise engaged."

"Ah." Susan got his drift, and fast. "You're hoping that she and Dylan are solidifying things."

"That's a classy way of putting it. But, yeah, that's what I'm hoping." He turned his attention to the phone, as Gloria's answering machine picked up, instructing the caller to leave a message.

"Hey, Gloria, it's Carson," he announced. "I'm sure you're screening your calls, but if you're there, pick up. I want to—"

"Hello, Carson," Gloria interrupted him, sounding bone-weary and worn. "Is everything all right?"

"That's what I called to ask you," he replied. "I'm fine. Status quo. Susan's here, she sneaked me in some decent food, and all's well." His hand tightened on the receiver. "How bad is it?"

"About what I expected. My mother swallowed a tranquilizer, my father swallowed two martinis, and the phones have been ringing off the hook—in Boston and here. The good news is, the photo of me that they're flashing on the business networks is flattering and shows off one of my newer designs. So that's good for business."

Carson chuckled. "You're one strong lady, you know that."

"So I've been told."

He cleared his throat. "I tried bullying Sabrina out of the transplant. It didn't work."

"I knew it wouldn't."

"I'm sorry."

"Don't be. This is what I expected. And concern for my child—*our* child—aside, I'm relieved that she can help you, assuming you still need the help by then."

Carson exhaled sharply. "When are you flying down?"

"When my parents either calm down or agree to join me. Right now, they've got an army of friends who want answers. The head of their damned country club even called. It's like Peyton Place revisited. It brings to mind all the reasons why I left Beacon Hill."

"Is there anything I can do?"

"Just get well," Gloria said quietly. "Soon. Sabrina's going to need you, and not just at work. I didn't meet Dylan Newport yet, but I intend to, the minute I get back to New York. I've been paying attention to that personal situation you hinted about . . ."

"And?"

"And you're definitely onto something. When Sabrina called before . . . let's just say that, killer day or not, she was very relieved that Dylan was with her. It was nothing she said, just her tone. The same tone I've been hearing all week. Sabrina's not the mushy type, or at least she never was till now. Something's brewing. And that something is Dylan. In which case—let's just say I'd be as thrilled as you if our daughter's heart led her to follow a traditional path."

"Like down an aisle?"

"Um-hum. And if that happens, guess who's got to be strong enough to be her escort?" Gloria sounded as if the one bright spot in her life right now was the fact that Sabrina might have found her key to happiness. "Like I said, she's going to need you. So get well soon."

"Count on it," Carson assured her. "In the meantime, when things get tough over the next few days, soothe yourself with the fact that you and I are going to have some amazing grandchildren in the not-too-distant-future."

A slight chuckle. "I'll do that."

"Stay in touch."

"I will."

Carson placed the phone back in its cradle. He stared broodingly at it, wishing like hell he could get out of this goddamned hospital bed and move life's events along— on the investigation front, on Sabrina and Dylan's courtship front. He needed to be in control, to make things happen. This whole victim routine—lying here, doing nothing—it was killing him. His fists clenched at his sides, as he fought the incredible sense of pent-up frustration and impotence.

"Hey." Susan unclenched one of his fists, and interlaced her fingers with his. "Everything will work out. You'll see."

"Yeah, I know," he replied with a scowl. "But it would

work out a helluva lot faster if I were the one running the show."

"You will be. Before you know it, this whole ordeal will be over and you'll be in control again."

"That's not good enough." His scowl deepened. "Time's not on our side. I've got this bad feeling. It keeps nagging at my gut. I don't know what it means. But I don't like it."

11:35 P.M.
Yonkers, New York

The garden apartments were on the Yonkers-Tuckahoe border, a nice area in Westchester County to call home. The buildings were brick, modern, but with a homey touch. Set back from the main road, they were hidden by a line of pine trees, planted to ensure the privacy of the tenants. The apartments weren't inordinately expensive, not by today's standards, but they were tasteful, with manicured grounds, an outdoor swimming pool, and a small tennis court reserved for residents only. As for the tenants themselves, they were, by-and-large, in their thirties and forties, upwardly mobile and financially comfortable. Many of them commuted daily to Manhattan, hopping on the train and riding the short distance on Metro North to Grand Central Station.

For a single woman like Karen Shepard, who spent most of her life at the office, building a solid foundation in a solid corporation, and the rest of her time with friends or at the gym, it was a great place to live. Especially since she wanted to keep a low profile, to live somewhere where the tenants came home tired and late, and were, on the whole, too wrapped up in their own

lives to pry into hers. That way, Stan could drop by and
spend two or three nights a week in her bed—during both
his married and his unmarried years—without anyone
noticing or, quite frankly, caring.

It was a great arrangement for them both.

Except that when Stan veered into the parking lot that
night, he felt anything but great.

He jumped out of his car and made his way to the double glass doors outside Karen's building. Impatiently, he
pressed the button marked 3F, and paced around, waiting.

The answering buzzer sounded.

He grabbed the door, yanked it open, and tore through
the lobby and up the stairs like gangbusters.

She was expecting him. He'd called her earlier this
evening to say he was coming, then again from the car to
let her know he was on his way. They hadn't originally
made plans to see each other tonight. But after his late-
day interrogation—which had thrown him so badly he'd
puked up his lunch—their getting together was a necessity. And not just for sexual pleasure or mutual gain. For
survival.

Karen opened the door the minute she heard Stan's
footsteps, stepped aside to let him in. He blew by her,
wired to the hilt. Even so, he felt that sharp jolt of sexual
awareness he always felt in her presence, the same pull
that had drawn them together the first time they'd met,
and still made him hard the minute he saw her. Even at a
time like this, when his life was in chaos and his ulcer
was about to eat him alive, she got to him.

She looked sensational, as always, her honey-brown
hair loose and silky, curling around her shoulders as if to
embrace them. Her robe was a delicate Chinese print,
belted around her slender waist, concealing every inch of
that incredible skin he couldn't get enough of. Her dark

eyes were filled with questions as she shut the door behind him.

Jesus, he thought, turning to face her. Between her
pristine attire and that wide-eyed expression, she
looked more like a young virgin on her wedding night
than a forty-one-year-old woman who'd been his lover
for nearly two decades and was practically insatiable in
bed.

"What is it?" she asked, tucking a strand of hair behind her ear. "You sounded terrible on the phone. And
you look worse." She sized him up for another instant,
then headed over to her sideboard. "I'll make you a
drink. Sit down and tell me what's going on."

"Sit down? Forget it. I can barely stand still. But I'll
take the drink—a couple of them, in fact."

She poured him a shot of bourbon, and handed it to
him. "One's enough. Unless you're spending the night. I
don't want you driving home drunk. Can you stay?"

His brows rose as he tossed down the shot. "When
have I ever been able to say no to that invitation?"

"Never," she replied frankly. "At least not till now. But
tonight . . . something's very wrong."

"Yeah. Very wrong." He put down the glass, rubbed
his forehead.

Karen watched him, more worried about his state of
mind than whatever had caused it. "Stan." She walked
over, loosened his tie and unbuttoned his shirt. "Whatever crisis has you so frantic, let it wait a few minutes.
You need to unwind."

He made a pained sound, pulled her against him like a
drowning man. "I'm not sure that's possible. I feel like a
cornered rat."

"Oh, it's possible." She kissed his neck, molded herself to him until his body responded, his erection puls-

ing against her. "As for how you feel, I'd say you feel pretty damned good. Tense, but good. Whatever's gnawing at you, let me make it go away for a little while."

She knew what his answer would be. It always was. When it came to each other, neither of them was capable of saying no.

Stan was already unbelting her robe, pulling her toward the bedroom as he did. He pushed the garment off her shoulders, stripping off his own clothes as she lay back on the bed, waiting for him.

He took her with an intensity that bordered on violence. Afterward, he rolled away, flung an arm across his eyes, and lay there, his breathing ragged.

"I'm sorry," he muttered. "I didn't mean to be so rough."

"Don't apologize." Still breathless herself, Karen propped herself up on one elbow. "That's one thing that you, of all men, never need to do—at least not in bed. You're an incredible lover. I don't need to tell you that. And you weren't rough; you were desperate."

"Desperate. Yeah, that's a good word for it."

"Is it Carson's announcement? I saw the clips on TV. I can't imagine the news came as a surprise to you. From the hints you've been dropping, I realized something big was in the works. You must have known Sabrina Radcliffe was Carson's daughter."

"Yup, I knew," he confirmed grimly.

"So why are you so freaked out? Is it the media? Are they jumping all over you?"

"No, Karen, they don't give a rat's ass about me. It's Sabrina they're interested in."

Her shoulders lifted in a shrug. "What's the problem then?"

He moved his arm away from his eyes, angling his head to face her. "The problem is, the press might not find me fascinating. But the cops do."

Karen frowned. "More so than before?"

"Oh, yeah. Barton and Whitman were in my face today, and, boy, did the gloves come off."

"They came to Ruisseau just to see you?"

"No. Evidently, Carson asked them to show up for the meeting, to make sure the press didn't bug Sabrina. And to make sure no one took a shot at her, would be my guess." He blew out his breath. "Anyway, they arrived at Ruisseau a good hour before the meeting. First, they paid a surprise visit to Ferguson, who's already sweating bullets. He fell all over himself saying he knew nothing about my personal life. In his frenzy to avoid mentioning what he knew about you and me, he told them everything else."

"What's everything else?"

"Oh, the fact that I'm a workaholic, the fact that Carson's tweaking the customary chain of command by having the company president report to the CEO rather than the COO. Oh, and the fact that I'm so dedicated to my career that the only recreational activity I have is my twice-a-week target practice."

Karen digested that thoughtfully. "Okay, fine. So what? None of that's a secret. Everyone who knows you knows you're a workaholic. Carson's decision to have Sabrina report to him isn't really such a reach. She is his daughter. As for the fact that you enjoy target practice, that's common knowledge, too. Carson's certainly aware of your trips to the shooting range in Yonkers. So Roland didn't really do much harm. I know you're worried he'll cave under pressure. So why don't you just give him a bottle of Valium and send him on vacation? The police won't care if he leaves New York. He has an alibi for last Monday night."

"He might. But I don't," Stan reminded her. "None I can share without incriminating myself. As for what was and wasn't a secret, all but the workaholic part was news to Barton and Whitman. They didn't know Carson was bypassing me on the corporate ladder. And they sure as hell didn't know I'm a crackerjack shot. To them, it looks like Carson doesn't trust me, and that I kept my shooting skills a secret for some sinister reason. They came marching over to my office and closeted themselves in there for forty-five excruciating minutes." A muscle in his jaw flexed. "They brought up Russ Clark, wondered if I had any idea what dirty business dealings he might have uncovered at Ruisseau that would make someone kill him."

"Oh God."

"My sentiments exactly. And there's more. You'll never guess whose name came up during my little police interrogation."

"Whose?"

Stan's gaze was as bleak as it was direct. "Etienne Pruet."

Every muscle in Karen's body tensed. "Etienne's? Why?"

"Because they got wind of the fact that he was worried about the buying frenzy that would result when C'est Moi was released in Europe. He was concerned that it would take a bite out of his sales. And rightfully so. Sex sells. We all know that."

"Okay." Karen sat up, pulled the sheet around herself, and leaned back against the headboard. She had to stay calm, to think this through. "So they know Etienne was uneasy that C'est Moi would put a dent in his profits.

They're looking toward motive and, in their minds, Etienne has one. But he was in Paris when Carson was shot. He couldn't have done it."

"True. But, as luck would have it, he's in New York now, ready and eager to offer the police whatever assistance he can. So Whitman and Barton are heading over to his New York office tomorrow to question him—and all his employees."

"*All* his employees?" Karen repeated weakly. "Why?"

"Because even though Pruet was in Paris, his New York staff was right here in the Big Apple. The detectives are trying to figure out if any of those people might be guilty. And I do mean *any* of them."

"I hear you." Karen wet her lips with the tip of her tongue. "I understand what you're warning me about. What I don't understand is why the detectives were discussing any of this with you."

"Because Pruet's company and Ruisseau are both key players in the fragrance business. No one knows better than you that we're major competitors, or that it's natural for the big guns at Ruisseau to keep tabs on the big guns at its rival—including who's who, who's up-and-coming, and who's hungry to get ahead."

"Right. So you're saying the detectives questioned you about Etienne's staff. Which employees in particular?"

"All of them. They ran down the list of the entire New York staff, asked me about each and every one."

Karen paled. "Including me."

"Oh, yeah, including you."

"What did you say?"

"What do you think I said? 'Hey, Detectives, now that you ask, I've got a hot and heavy twenty-year affair going with the executive assistant to the head of Pruet's New York division?' " Stan snorted. "I lied through my teeth. I told them I'd met you a couple of times, at meetings and at professional functions. I said that all I'd heard about you through the grapevine was that you were bright and ambitious, and that you traveled frequently to Paris for Pruet because you spoke fluent French. Period."

A fine sheen of perspiration dotted Karen's forehead. "Maybe that was a mistake. Maybe you should have told them we were involved. After all, who you sleep with is no one's business."

"Oh, come on, Karen." Stan threw off the covers and rose, pacing naked around the room. "We both know that's a crock. It's everyone's business, even though we've managed to keep it a secret all these years. Because this isn't just a chance affair. It's a business arrangement, just as it has been from the beginning—one that benefits us both. Okay, there are perks. In my case, I'm crazy about you. In your case, you're crazy about my money and about the way I make you feel in bed."

She leaned forward, crossing her arms over her breasts, and staring him down. "That's unfair. To begin with, I'm in love with you and I have been since I was twenty-one. Yes, I like wearing beautiful clothes and getting expensive jewelry. And, yes, I'm wild about the way you make me feel in bed. But money and sex aren't the only reasons I'm with you. Any more than the only reasons you're with me are for the marketing updates and sales strategies I pass along."

"True. I'm in love with you. I blew two marriages to hell because of that fact. As for the last part, I think the term for what you described is corporate espionage."

"That's an ugly term. Especially in this case, where it's not even accurate. You've never used any of the information I shared with you against Etienne."

"Big deal. That's not because I'm a great guy; it's because it never suited my purposes. You know why I needed those briefings, and what I used them for. I had to stay on top. I had to be the best COO in the business." A bitter pause. "I had to live up to Carson's expectations." Stan paused, rubbed the back of his neck. "I feel lousy that Russ is dead. But if he really did have something on me, it's a damned good thing he didn't get to Carson with it. Because if Carson had the slightest idea what I've been doing, he'd kick my ass out of Ruisseau so fast I'd have whiplash."

"He's never going to find out."

"I'm glad you're so sure of that. Because I'm not. The detectives are sniffing around me like bloodhounds, Ferguson's seen us together and is about to crack like an egg—bonus payoff or not—Russ Clark's murder smacks of a company tie-in, and now Sabrina Radcliffe is starting to get suspicious."

Karen went still. "Sabrina Radcliffe? You're saying she knows about us?"

"No, but she knows something. I'm just not sure what. And she's sleeping with Dylan Newport, so God knows what she's shared with him, and vice versa. This whole thing is spinning out of control. I've got to nip it in the bud."

"How are you going to do that?"

"By handling the situation myself. I've already set things in motion. If everything goes according to plan, we might luck out. You just deal with those detectives tomorrow. Stick to the same story I gave them, about how we barely know each other."

"What about my alibi for the night Carson was shot?"

"Say you were at the movies—alone. Find out what was playing that night, in case they ask. Just stay cool. They have no reason to suspect you. Not unless you give them one."

"Don't worry," Karen assured him. "I won't."

"Good." Stan walked over to the window, stared out into the night sky. "If we can get past this one, maybe we can still save our asses."

26

11:55 P.M.
341 West 76th Street

The flames in the fireplace burned steadily, casting a warm, orange glow through the downstairs sitting room. The intimate light and occasional crackle set a romantic atmosphere for the room's two occupants, who were draped across the shag rug, enjoying their dinner as they stretched out, naked, beneath two oversize blankets.

"M-m-m." With an appreciative sigh, Sabrina swallowed another bite of linguini in white clam sauce. "Carson was wrong. This is definitely Zagat's material."

Dylan chuckled, lifting the glass of sauvignon blanc to Sabrina's lips and holding it while she took a sip. "It's the wine. It heightens the taste buds."

"Uh-uh." She gave an emphatic shake of her head. "If anything heightened my senses tonight, it was you. An amazing lawyer, lover, *and* cook. I'm beyond impressed." Her eyes twinkled. "Do you plan to cook all our meals naked?"

"That depends. Do you plan to eat them all naked? If so, count me in."

Sabrina's lips curved. "And here Carson said you could do better than having me camp out on the rug. I'll have to tell him he was wrong."

"We used the sofa, too," Dylan reminded her. "And later, I have plans for the bed, and the Jacuzzi, and that great recliner I was telling you about. What can I say? I'm a creative guy."

"You're an energetic guy," Sabrina said, with a half-groan. "I'm not sure I have your strength."

"I'll renew you." His fingers traced her spine, caressing lightly.

Sabrina's eyes slid shut. "Dylan, we have to get *some* sleep. Tomorrow's a workday—my first as president of Ruisseau. How do you think the troops will react to my napping at my desk? I doubt it'll win them over."

"They're already won over." His lips brushed her shoulder. "You knocked their socks off today."

That reminded Sabrina of something she'd better share with Dylan, although she wasn't sure how he was going to take it. "Speaking of the troops, I think you ought to know that, super-discreet or not, you and I are a known item. Apparently, everyone in the office knows we're involved. Stan as much as told me so."

"Of course they do." Dylan gave an offhanded shrug. "I'm sure they figured it out the first time they noticed me undressing you with my eyes. They're a shrewd bunch. They're also a caring bunch. My guess is, they're cheering us on." He tipped up her chin, rubbed his lips lightly against hers. "So am I."

"Me, too." Sabrina gave another contented sigh. "I must say, this was a wonderful end to a turbulent day."

"The day's not over," Dylan corrected.

"U-m-m, I forgot. The Jacuzzi, the recliner, the bed . . ."

"Well, yeah, there's that." Dylan gave her that bone-melting grin of his. "But we also have plans to make. Like, when am I meeting your mother? When are we breaking our news to Carson? And, most important of all, when am I slipping a wedding band on that beautiful ring finger?"

"Wedding band?" Sabrina arched a brow. "Now wait just a minute, buster. You're not getting out of an engagement ring. Now that I've shocked myself by falling in love and wanting to get married, I'm not skipping any of the steps along the way."

"There's not a chance I'd let that happen. I've been a renegade all my life. Not this time. This time I want to enjoy every traditional, sentimental ritual there is." Dylan's fingers threaded through her hair. "Need I remind you that Ruisseau is practically across the street from Tiffany's? I planned—with your permission, of course— to take you there tomorrow at lunchtime. We'll pick out an engagement ring and a set of matching wedding bands together. Then, I'll get down on one knee right in the middle of Fifth Avenue, and ask for your hand. How's that?"

Sabrina's lips twitched. "The part about the rings is perfect. As for the proposal, I suggest we move it to Central Park, or at least to the sidewalk on Fifth Avenue. New York motorists aren't the romantic types. They'll mow you down like a blade of grass."

"Good point. Okay then, either the sidewalk or the park, depending on how patient I'm feeling."

"You're never patient."

"Untrue. It's been—" He glanced at the wall clock. "—fifty-two minutes since I made love to you. I think that shows commendable restraint on my part."

"I stand corrected." Smiling, Sabrina nuzzled closer to Dylan, as eager as he to resume where they'd left off before their growling stomachs had compelled them to eat. "I tell you what. We'll just finish making plans. The dishes can wait."

"Good. Because I can't. So talk fast." He was already exploring the contours of her body, his palm cupping her breast, his thumb teasing the hardening nipple.

"You're the one who insisted we make plans," Sabrina reminded him breathlessly, wriggling closer and reveling in his touch.

"That was when I could still think. Now I can't. My libido eclipsed my brain. So, like I said, talk fast." He was already tearing open a foil packet, dealing effectively with the condom.

A soft laugh. "Yes, sir. You asked about meeting my mother. She's dying to meet you. I can hear it in her voice every time she *doesn't* mention your name but wants to. So we can arrange that ASAP. Carson we can tell tomorrow. He'll probably host an engagement party on Eleven West the minute they move him there. Did I talk fast enough for you?"

"Sounds good. And no. Now, come here." Dylan gripped her waist and pulled her over him. Nudging her thighs apart, he set her astride him, lowering her slowly onto his erection.

"Dylan?" Sabrina splayed her hands across his chest, needing one more serious, sane moment before she lost herself in their lovemaking.

He heard the solemn note in her voice and paused, watching her from beneath hooded lids.

"You asked about the timing of the wedding. I wish it could be right away. But it can't. We have to be realistic. If Carson needs a transplant, it'll be a while before he's himself again. A few months at least. And until he is, I want to wait. I know you do, too."

"Absolutely." Dylan's response was emphatic, his gaze intense as it held hers. "You're also forgetting something else. Carson's not the only one who'd be involved in this transplant. You'd be the donor. Both of you would need recuperation time."

"I guess you're right. I didn't think of that."

"Well, I did. I want you to be a hundred percent when we walk down that aisle." Dylan's hands slid to her hips, his thumbs making lazy circles on her skin. "So you see? I'm way ahead of you in the planning department. We're getting married. Soon. We'll know in a month if the transplant's happening. If it is, we'll wait—for however long it's necessary. And after that, we'll have the rest of our lives together. That's enough planning for tonight. Okay?"

Sabrina nodded. "Very okay."

"You're sure now?" he teased. "There's nothing else you want to discuss?" He eased her down a fraction, gliding the tiniest bit farther inside her. "The flowers?" Another fraction downward, teasing her body and his own. "The food?" A little more. "The invitations?" He arched upward, stopping when he was halfway there, making Sabrina twist and cry out in frustration. "The guest list?" he rasped, driving himself as crazy as he was driving her. "The—"

"No," Sabrina gasped. She grabbed his hands, yanking them away so he could no longer hold her immobile. Then, she sank down on him—hard—forcing him all the way inside her. "I don't want to discuss anything." She raised herself upward, then sank down on him again. "I just want this."

A harsh groan escaped Dylan and he dragged her mouth down to his, his hips lifting to keep him as deep inside her as possible. "God, so do I."

"Good," Sabrina managed, as their bodies took over. "Because if I don't get it, you're fired."

Tuesday, September 20th, 3:05 A.M.

It was in the deepest part of night that he made his way to Dylan's apartment building. He stood outside, scouted the area.

He was alone.

They were in there. He knew that much.

He assessed the vertical bars that protected the ground floor windows. Protected. That was a joke. There was more than enough space between bars for what he had in mind. He selected the window closest to the door. That way, their means of escape would be blocked off.

By now they were probably upstairs, fast asleep in the bedroom. Well, guess what, guys, he thought. It's wake-up time. Wake up and die.

He was just about to reach into his knapsack, when he heard the crunch of tires on the street. He whipped around. Shit. Some cops patrolling the area.

He sauntered off, keeping his steps slow and even, just a kid with a knapsack trotting along West 76th. Then, he ducked down an alley and held his breath.

The patrol car passed by, neither cop even glancing in his direction.

Gotcha suckers, he thought smugly.

Then, he turned back to go do his job.

3:08 A.M.

Dylan jerked awake.

He wasn't sure exactly what had roused him, but his street instincts were kicking in, warning him that something wasn't right.

He peered around the darkened sitting room where he and Sabrina had fallen asleep. She was curled on her side on the rug, her breathing deep and even. The apartment was silent. Everything seemed fine.

So why did it feel like it wasn't?

He got up, moved restlessly around the apartment, checking doors and windows, then verified that the burglar alarm was on.

It was. Everything was in order.

He went back to the sitting room, lay down beside Sabrina and wrapped an arm around her, drawing her close. She murmured something unintelligible and snuggled against him, obviously not sharing his sense of unease.

Fine, so it was his imagination working overtime.

He shut his eyes, finally drifting into a light doze.

3:50 A.M.

This time no one was around.

No cops cruising the area, no late-night pedestrians. Nothing. He stood there for ten fucking minutes to make sure. But the street was deserted. And with the cops having just driven by, it'd be a while before they did a repeat performance.

He had enough time to do his thing.

But he sure as hell wasn't wasting any of it.

He pulled the two whiskey bottles out of his knapsack, unscrewed the caps, and retrieved the two rags he'd brought. He doused the rags in the gasoline he'd filled the bottles with, then stuffed them into the mouth of the bottles.

Okay, he thought. Here goes.

One more quick scrutiny of the area. All cool. Action time.

Reaching into his knapsack, he groped around, pulling out a lighter and a piece of steel pipe. He had only one chance to get this right. And he wasn't going to blow it. The stakes were too high.

In one unbroken motion, he lit the rags, then smashed the pipe against the window pane, shattering the glass. He flung the bottles into the apartment, one after the other, aiming for the short wall by the door to get the greatest possible impact.

He heard the glass splinter, saw the fire engulf the wall.

By the time the blaze spread, flames licking at the carpet and climbing up the drapes, he was gone.

Dylan jolted upright the instant the window shattered and the burglar alarm screamed to life. He vaulted to his feet in time to hear the crashes—one, two—and the *boom* of an explosion.

He grabbed his pants as the smoke detector began a shrill screech.

He smelled the gasoline, saw the eerie glow flickering from the hallway. And he knew damned well what it was.

"Sabrina!" He shouted her name, even though she was already struggling to a sitting position, looking tousled and disoriented.

"Dylan?" She blinked, shoving her hair out of her eyes. "What's going on?"

"The apartment's on fire." He grabbed his shirt and tossed it at her, as he zipped up his pants. "Put that on. Hurry. We're getting out of here."

"Oh my God." She was instantly wide awake. Even without looking, she knew Dylan was right. She could smell the flames. Flames and gasoline. And the heat was getting stronger, closer.

She yanked on the shirt.

"Wrap this blanket around you," Dylan instructed, already helping her do that, then flinging the second blanket around himself. "The backyard's fenced in and the key to the back door's hidden in a drawer. We've got to get out of here—*now*. Our chances are better heading straight for the front door. I'll go first. Follow right behind me. And stay low to the ground. If the smoke gets bad, we'll crawl."

Sabrina's eyes were already stinging, and her nose was burning terribly. But she nodded, doing as Dylan said, staying low and following him into the hallway.

The full length of the hall was in flames, and the front door frame was a rectangular inferno.

Dylan knew they were in trouble.

He also knew it would only get worse. They had to get out of here—now.

He turned to Sabrina, beckoned her forward. "Come here." He unwrapped the blanket from around him and pulled her inside, blanket and all, anchoring her against him. Then, he wrapped his blanket around them both, enveloping her in as tight a cocoon as he could, and muttered, "Hang on. We're making a break for the door."

Gritting his teeth, Dylan urged them forward, and they bolted through the hallway like a pair of sprinters. He could feel the heat of the flames, and the smoke that was choking him, making his eyes water, but he refused to give in. Next to him, Sabrina was seized by a horrible coughing fit, but he ignored that, too. Gripping the blanket so it enveloped his arm and hand, he reached through the flames, and flipped open the front door lock. Even through the protective layer of acrylic, the metal was unbearably hot, but he didn't give a damn. He braced himself, then grabbed hold of the doorknob, twisted, and pulled.

The cool night air slapped at his face, but it didn't compare to the burning heat all around him. He heard Sabrina's whimper, knew the blanket was in flames, but he also knew it was the only protection they had for what needed to be done. He anchored Sabrina against him and made a dive for the pavement, cushioning Sabrina's fall with his body. He landed hard, a sharp pain shooting through his skull as it struck the concrete. He fought the pain, holding Sabrina tightly, and rolled the two of them back and forth across the pavement until the flames subsided and his strength ran out.

He collapsed, waves of dizziness blending with throbbing pain.

From far away, a fire truck siren blared.

The last thing Dylan remembered before blacking out was hearing Sabrina dissolve into a violent spasm of coughing.

It was the most beautiful sound he'd ever heard.

27

Mt. Sinai Hospital

"I'm fine," Dylan insisted hoarsely as he followed the pinpoint of light the emergency room doctor was moving back and forth in a horizontal line in front of his eyes. "I just have a lousy headache."

"That lousy headache is a mild concussion," the doctor corrected. "You hit your head pretty hard."

Dylan forced a smile. "Yeah, but I stopped the blanket from burning, didn't I?"

"That you did." The doctor put away his medical instruments and checked the bandage that covered an ample section of Dylan's chest. "Good. The bleeding's stopped." He stepped away, planting his feet in that doctor-about-to-issue-a-lecture stance. "Look. You're a lucky guy. Besides the concussion, you've got that whopping gash on your chest, cuts and scrapes on your arms, a few impressive lacerations on your face and neck, and minor burns, plus a scratchy voice from those few minutes of smoke inhalation. Considering what could have happened . . ."

"Yeah, I know." Dylan moved his head and winced a bit.

"The painkiller should start working soon."

"Good. Fine. Thanks. Can I see Sabrina now?" Dylan demanded. "You said she was all right. So let me go to her."

"She *is* all right," the doctor returned sternly. "She was treated and released. And you don't need to go to her. Last I saw her, she was pacing outside your door, where I asked her to wait until I finished examining you. She takes orders about as well as you do." Seeing the profound concern on Dylan's face, the doctor's demeanor softened. "She really is fine—thanks to you. You took the brunt of the fall. Her cuts and scrapes are minor, and she's got minimal burns. The toughest part for her was the smoke inhalation. It affected her more than it did you. Not so much her lungs, which are pretty clear, but her nose and throat. They were badly irritated. But she'll be herself in a couple of days."

"Thank God."

"I'll send her in now. Oh, by the way, there are a couple of detectives here who want to speak with you, too."

Dylan's mouth thinned into a grim line. "Let me guess. Detectives Whitman and Barton."

"Yup. That's them."

"They'll have to wait a minute. I want to see Sabrina first."

The doctor nodded. "Remember, I want you to sit still for a while longer, just to be on the safe side. No sudden movements."

"I won't dance, I promise."

"Good. Let me know if you experience any lightheadedness or nausea." With a tight smile, the doctor opened the door and stepped outside. "Ms. Radcliffe? You can come in now." He blocked her path as she reached the door. "He's got to take it easy. Understood?"

"Yes. Understood." Sabrina's voice was scratchy, but audible. She strode in, relief flooding her face as she saw Dylan. She went right to him, touching his jaw with gentle fingertips and leaning up to kiss him. "Hey."

"Hey, yourself." He scrutinized her from head to toe, at least as much of her as he could see. She was wearing a hospital gown, which covered a lot more of her than his shirt had. Her cheeks had a few cuts and smudges on them, and a section of her hair was singed. A couple of scrapes and bruises marred the skin of her forearms, and her breathing was definitely raspy. Most of all, her eyes were teary and red, and she kept blinking, trying to make the burning go away.

Despite it all, she was fine. Alive and fine.

And worried about him.

"Does your head hurt a lot?" she grated out, coughing once or twice between words. "The doctor said you had a concussion. And your chest . . ." Her features tightened as she studied the bandage. "Oh, Dylan. Is it a deep gash?"

"Just a cut. But you can dote on me anyway." He glanced down at himself. "Hmm. Naked from the waist up, injured, with an impressive-sized bandage on my chest. Pretty damned sexy, huh? Makes me look like James Bond."

Sabrina snickered, and promptly began to cough. "Don't make me laugh. It hurts."

"It's that sensitive nose of yours." He traced it with his forefinger. "Is it badly irritated?"

"It burns a little. It'll get better. And you didn't answer my question. How's your head?"

"My head is fine. All of me is fine, now that you're here."

"I can't believe this happened." Sabrina dragged both hands through her hair. "Someone actually tried to kill us."

"*You,*" Dylan corrected. "Someone tried to kill you. I just got in the way of his plan."

Sabrina met Dylan's gaze. "I'm sorry."

"For what?"

"Putting you in danger. I had no idea . . ."

"Sabrina, I love you. If anything had happened to you and I hadn't been there to stop it . . ." He drew a sharp breath. "Don't apologize, okay?"

"Okay." She licked her lips. "But I will say thank you, inadequate as that sounds. I'd be dead if it weren't for you. I've never seen anyone move so fast in my life."

"Hey, if you've dealt with one Molotov cocktail, you've dealt with them all."

"Obviously." With a pensive expression, Sabrina contemplated the situation. "Whoever did this knew I was at your apartment."

Dylan shrugged. "According to what you told me about our involvement being public knowledge, that could have been anyone."

"Not really. Knowing we're involved doesn't mean knowing I spent tonight at your place."

"True. On the other hand, whoever did this might have trashed your apartment first, then headed over to mine when he realized you weren't home."

Sabrina's eyes widened. "I never thought of that."

"I'm sure Whitman and Barton did. They must know a lot more than we do by now. We should talk to them, find out where things stand."

"I agree." Sabrina went to the door and croaked out a few words to the nurse outside. "She'll send them in," she told Dylan, before dissolving into another spasm of coughing.

"Sit down," Dylan ordered her. "And stop doing so much talking. I'll take the lead for a change." He watched her strained, shaky motions as she pulled over a chair, and he realized how much this ordeal had thrown her, bravado or not. "Hey," he said, determined to lighten the gravity of the moment. "Speaking of taking the lead, I have a bone to pick with you."

"What?" Sabrina gave him a quizzical look as she sat down.

"Earlier tonight, you threatened to fire me if I didn't make love to you right away. That's sexual harassment. On the other hand, it's also a major turn-on. So I've decided not to file charges. Instead, I've decided to do whatever I have to, as often as I have to, and as fast as I have to, to keep my job."

Sabrina's lips twitched. "I told you not to make me laugh."

"Can I make you do other things instead?"

"Dylan . . ."

"Okay, I'll be good." He grinned, caught her fingers and brought them to his lips. Kissing them gently, he sobered, watching her pale, anxious expression. "It'll be okay, sweetheart," he promised hoarsely. "Whoever did this is scared. That means they're vulnerable. Whitman and Barton will find them."

"I hope so," she managed.

As if on cue, Jeannie and Frank strolled through the door.

"Never a dull moment with you two," Jeannie commented, shaking her Q-tip head. "I haven't had a full night's sleep in two weeks." She handed a shopping bag to Sabrina. "I picked these up when we checked out your apartment. I thought you might want them. Your place is untouched, by the way. No sign of anything, not even a jimmied door. Whoever did this went straight to Mr. Newport's. They obviously knew you were there."

Sabrina glanced in the bag, recognized her clothes and underwear, and gave Jeannie a grateful look. "Thank you so much," she grated out. "I wasn't looking forward to going home . . . in a hospital gown." Another bout of coughing.

"You sound lousy," Frank noted. He glanced at Dylan. "What about you? Is the concussion too bad for you to fill in a few pieces for us?"

"Nope," Dylan assured him. "This is one time I'm looking forward to talking to you." Quietly, he filled the detectives in on exactly what had happened. "My guess is that the same hired punk who stabbed Russ, did this," he concluded. "Every street kid knows how to make a Molotov cocktail. It doesn't take a rocket scientist. And by deciding to handle it this way, whoever hired him could keep his own hands clean."

"I agree with you," Jeannie said. "So let's see your theory through. Whoever hired the punk shot Carson Brooks, then paid someone to stab Russ Clark when the poor kid uncovered some incriminating information. Now, that head honcho is threatened by Ms. Radcliffe coming on as company president, so he goes this route. It can't be coincidence that this happened the night of Carson Brooks's big announcement."

"No, it can't," Dylan concurred. "But what's not clicking for me is, what's the common denominator? What's going on at Ruisseau that's significant enough to make someone go to these lengths?" His expression darkened. "And please don't start on the inheritance bit again. I'm the only one that scenario would fit. Even if you still believe I'd kill Carson, you've got to realize that what happened tonight would kind of preclude my chances of getting rich. Dead guys can't inherit."

Jeannie opened her mouth to reply, but Sabrina cut her off. "Look," she croaked out. "You'd better not still be stuck on the sick idea that Dylan's guilty. . . ."

"Ms. Radcliffe, save your breath," Jeannie interrupted. "We're not. Mr. Newport's not on our short list anymore."

"Gee, I'm flattered," Dylan said dryly. "And all I had to do was almost die to get crossed off."

"No, we chucked your name a while ago." A corner of Jeannie's mouth lifted. "Like lawyers, detectives have instincts. Ours are usually right."

"Great. So where do your instincts go from here?"

Jeannie cleared her throat. "To a few different places. What are your thoughts on Etienne Pruet?"

An odd expression crossed Dylan's face. "Why? He was in Paris when Carson was shot."

"Yeah, because he was worried about C'est Moi's impact on his business," Frank put in. "Which left his worried New York staff here, angsting over whether or not their futures were on the line."

"That sounds kind of far-fetched," Sabrina rasped. "To kill a competitor to slow the market penetration of his product?"

"No. To *stop* penetration of his product," Frank corrected. "Remember, if your father was dead, no one else could duplicate C'est Moi."

Dylan and Sabrina exchanged glances.

"Until now," Dylan informed the detectives. "Carson shared the formula with Sabrina last week."

Jeannie's jaw tightened. "Who knows about that?"

"Just us." Sabrina's pause was uneasy. "Unless Stan found out somehow."

"What makes you bring up Stan Hager's name?" Jeannie jumped all over that one.

"I don't know." Sabrina shrugged. "He's just been acting odd. Nervous, upset. Maybe he found out that Carson told me the formula and that threw him for a loop."

"Or maybe it's more." Frank rubbed his chin.

Dylan's eyes narrowed. "Meaning?"

"Meaning we've got some things to work through. Stan Hager's one of them. As soon as we've got our ducks in a row, we'll discuss them with you. As for Pruet, we're meeting with him and his New York staff in a few hours. We'll let you know how that goes."

Dylan had opened his mouth to pursue the subject, when the door opened and the ER doctor stepped in. "How do you feel?" he asked Dylan.

"Better."

"Good. Because there's a wheelchair on its way. When it arrives, get in it. No arguments. Even though you're feeling stronger, I don't want you walking yet."

"Walking where?" Dylan asked, his brows drawing together in puzzlement.

"You and Ms. Radcliffe are taking an elevator ride."

"Why?"

The doctor sighed. "Apparently, the incident that took place at your apartment tonight was reported on TV a few minutes ago. The early edition business news broke it. They gave a brief overview of what happened. And they described it as a close call for both of you."

"So?"

"So, Carson Brooks saw the TV clip. He's making a huge scene in ICU. He won't stop bellowing until he sees for himself that you're both all right. I told Dr. Radison I'd send you up there as soon as you felt up to it, to calm him down."

Sabrina was already on her feet. "Poor Carson. He must be frantic."

"The poor nurses," Dylan amended dryly. "They must be rioting."

Jeannie looked like she was biting back laughter.

"Yeah, well, you'd better get your friend to simmer down. I've heard him when he's ticked off, and it's not pleasant." She stepped aside as the wheelchair was brought in.

"Oh, for God's sake, I don't need that," Dylan protested.

"I say you do," the doctor contradicted him. "So either you use it, or you don't go. In which case you'll help us hire new nurses after the ICU staff quits."

"When you put it that way . . ." Dylan levered himself off the examining table and maneuvered himself into the wheelchair. Actually, he didn't mind being forced to comply. His head was still throbbing pretty badly. And his chest stung like hell.

"The nurse is bringing in a hospital gown for you to put on. She should be here any minute." The doctor turned to Sabrina. "Would you like something to wear over your gown? I realize that parading around like that doesn't do much for your modesty."

"I'd rather get dressed," Sabrina replied. "Detective Whitman was kind enough to bring me some of my clothes. Not only would I feel more comfortable, but Carson will be less upset if only one of us looks like a patient."

"No arguments there." The poor doctor sounded as if he'd try anything that might succeed in mollifying Carson. "And no problem. You've been discharged, so there's no reason you can't get dressed. Go ahead and change. You can use the room next door."

"Thank you."

After Sabrina had excused herself and stepped out, and the doctor had vanished to attend to other patients, Dylan spoke up, maximizing the time he had alone with the detectives.

"Two things before you go. First, any idea what the damage was to my apartment? The fire department was there on a dime, but the fire was burning like hell when the ambulance took us away."

"Your downstairs is a mess," Frank supplied. "The hall's destroyed, and your living room furniture was charred to the point where you might have to chuck it all. The rest of the ground floor isn't much better. The good news is, your two upstairs levels are pretty much intact. They're smoky, but that'll clear up with some fresh air and a cleaning service. The downstairs you'll have to renovate."

Dylan nodded. "That's a small price to pay for being alive. It's also better than I expected."

"Your insurance will cover it," Jeannie pointed out. Again, that hint of a smile. "In the meantime, I'm sure Ms. Radcliffe will let you bunk with her. She seems fond of you."

"Yeah, thanks." Dylan kept his face carefully expressionless. "Good observation. I'll mention your suggestion to her."

"What was the other thing you wanted to discuss?"

"Stan." Dylan cleared his throat. "Listen, Detectives, I'm bound by attorney-client privilege. That having been said, I want this case solved yesterday. So I'll go out on a limb and say this much—I think you might be barking up the wrong tree if you think Stan shot Carson. Look elsewhere. If you still come up empty, if you're pushed to the wall and need some concrete facts, I'll see what I can do to give you some."

Jeannie's eyes narrowed. "What you're telling us is that there's something going on with Stan Hager."

"What I'm telling you is that whatever it is that's going on with him, it isn't attempted murder, or conspiracy to murder. Trust me on that one. When you're getting your ducks in a row, don't spend too much time on this particular duck."

"Even though the duck in question knew Ms. Radcliffe was at your place tonight?"

"Yeah, even so. Lots of people saw Sabrina leave with me. They all could have made the assumption that we spent the night together. From what I hear, our relationship is far from under wraps." Dylan spoke tersely, emphatically. "I repeat, Stan's not your duck."

"What about Roland Ferguson?"

"What about him?"

"Should we discount him as a duck, too?" Frank asked sarcastically. "Does whatever the hell he's freaked out about tie into Hager, or into this case?"

Dylan blew out his breath. "The former. Forget Roland. He's harmless."

"Why didn't you mention any of this before?"

"Because, like I said, I'm bound by attorney-client privilege. Plus, this is the first time I've picked up on the fact that Stan is a key suspect. Till recently, it was me you had your eye on. Besides, to be frank, you grilled the hell out of everyone. It was hard to tell who was a bona fide suspect and who you just felt like provoking."

"Yeah, we are a nasty duo," Jeannie responded in a wry tone. "Everyone says so. But, hey, it keeps us employed."

"Could be because they're afraid to let us go," Frank surmised.

"Nah." A corner of Dylan's mouth lifted. "The NYPD isn't an easily intimidated bunch. My guess is they keep you around because you're good at what you do, browbeating included. You might not have a lot of civilian friends, but I'd say your jobs are secure."

"Thanks for the vote of confidence." Jeannie met Dylan's gaze. "Ms. Radcliffe isn't on the inside about this Stan Hager situation, is she?"

"Not at this point, no."

Jeannie studied Dylan for a long, thoughtful moment. Then, she nodded. "All right, Mr. Newport, we'll play this your way—for now. But if another day goes by and we have nothing, I'm coming to you for answers." A meaningful stare. "So when you get up to ICU, I'd suggest you talk to your *client* and get his permission to spill the beans. Got it?"

Dylan didn't let any reaction show on his face, or come through in his voice. "I hear you."

At that moment, the nurse came in and handed Dylan a hospital gown.

He'd just finished putting it on when Sabrina reentered the room.

Silence greeted her.

She glanced from Dylan to the detectives and back again. "What did I miss?"

"Nothing," Dylan assured her. "Our allies here were just leaving. Keep us posted, Detectives."

"We will." With that, Jeannie and Frank headed out.

"Okay, what was really going on?" Sabrina demanded in a hoarse rasp.

Dylan didn't insult her by lying or feigning ignorance. "We'll talk about it later. I want to get upstairs before Carson kills someone."

"Fair enough. *If* we talk about it later."

"We will. I promise. All I ask is that you give me five minutes alone with Carson first."

Sabrina scrutinized Dylan's expression. "It's privileged," she correctly deduced. "No problem. Talk to Carson. But, after that, you're talking to me."

"Or I'm fired?" Dylan teased.

"Nope. You're too good an attorney. I'd only fire you if you refused me in bed. Which I don't think you ever will. So your job's secure."

"Glad to hear it." He grinned, settling himself in the wheelchair. "And you're right. 'No' isn't in my vocabulary when it comes to you. Now, would you help me steer this stupid thing?"

"My pleasure."

28

Three nurses were restraining Carson, who was demanding to be allowed out of bed, when Sabrina wheeled Dylan into the room.

"Carson," Sabrina called out in a scratchy voice. "Stop tormenting those poor nurses. Dylan and I are fine. We're here. Abuse us instead." Her insides twisted when she saw the white-faced apprehension on Carson's face—apprehension that transformed to relief when he saw that she and Dylan were all right, then to anxiety when he saw that Dylan was in the wheelchair.

"Just a precaution," Dylan assured him immediately. "The doctor was afraid you'd take a swing at me and make my concussion worse."

"You have a concussion? How bad is it?" Carson barked.

"It's mild. Please, calm down." Sabrina glanced at the three nurses, who were mopping their brows, totally spent and at their wits' end. "Thanks so much," she croaked with a grateful smile. "Please. Go take a break. Put your feet up and have a cup of coffee."

"Spike the coffee," Dylan advised. "You won't be the first to do that after going a few rounds with this guy."

"Sounds good," one of them muttered. "Our shift's over in ten minutes. A seven A.M. cocktail might be a first, but till Eleven West gets him, I doubt it'll be a last."

She assessed Sabrina and Dylan, her demeanor softening. "We heard the news. Are you both all right?"

"Good as new," Sabrina assured her. "Now go home and get some rest. We'll take it from here."

The RNs didn't need a second invitation. They blew out the door like three fleeing bandits.

Carson didn't even seem to notice. He was eyeballing, first Sabrina, then Dylan, and back again. "You scared the shit out of me," he accused, clearly shaken. "What happened? Who did this? What did the cops find out?"

Sabrina pushed the wheelchair over to his bedside, then walked over and took his hand. "Carson, listen to me. We'll answer all your questions and stay as long as you like. Just please, settle down. Dr. Radison stopped us on the way in, and warned us that this kind of excitement could raise your blood pressure and cause a setback. So take a few deep breaths and lie back. Dylan and I are both fine, thanks to his quick thinking and amazing reflexes. He saved our lives."

Carson squeezed her fingers, then gave Dylan a look filled with profound emotion and pride. "Doesn't surprise me. He's one in a million—always has been." Swallowing hard, Carson brought himself under control. "On the news they said something about an explosion and a fire. They're speculating it was a Molotov cocktail. Was it?"

"Two Molotov cocktails, actually," Dylan amended. "I heard both bottles break. Whoever threw them must have assumed we were upstairs and wouldn't have a chance of getting to the front door in time. Fortunately, we were down in the sitting room. We made a break for it before the fire got out of hand."

"How'd you get the concussion? How much smoke did Sabrina inhale that she can barely talk? And what other injuries don't I know about?"

"My throat's scratchy," Sabrina replied. "My eyes are still burning. Mostly, my nose is irritated. Not a surprise, given how sensitive it is. Other than that, I've got a couple of burns and some cuts and bruises—nothing worse than you'd get from falling off a bike. Dylan, on the other hand, had to outdo me—as usual. He came away with a big gash across his chest, more impressive burns than mine, and a concussion." Her light tone vanished. "Of course, that could also be because he used his body to protect me when we ran through the fire and when we hit the concrete." She dissolved into a coughing spasm.

"Sabrina," Dylan interjected. "Rest your voice."

She waved away his protest. "He wrapped blankets around us and made a mad dash for the front door. By the time we got outside, the blankets were on fire. He shoved us to the pavement—slamming his head in the process—and rolled us around until the flames were out. Then he passed out. Talk about being scared to death. I crawled over to make sure he was breathing. I could barely find a pulse. By the time the ambulance arrived, I was beyond frantic."

Dylan angled his head toward her, a surprised expression on his face. "I didn't know that."

"How could you? You were unconscious."

"Beyond frantic, huh? Did you call me your hero and beg me to live?"

Sabrina shot him a look. "Very funny. No, as I remember it, I threatened to kill you if you died."

"Wow. That's even worse than firing me." He turned to Carson. "She threatened to do that, too, earlier tonight. It was a different set of circumstances, of course. But she was frantic then, too. I tell you, Carson, she's one demanding president. I'm lucky I'm still employed."

Hot color flooded Sabrina's cheeks. "Can we stick to the subject?"

Carson's lips had begun to twitch. "I'm beginning to think there's more than one of those."

"There are," Dylan assured him.

"Dylan . . ." Sabrina's voice might have been raspy, but there was no mistaking the warning note there. "Cut it out."

"You're the one who asked him to settle down," Dylan reminded her. "I think we can do one better. I think we can get him to grin like a Cheshire cat." He gave Sabrina a quick, conspiratorial wink. "Don't worry. What I'm planning won't make you blush. I just say we go with the good news first. After that, we can get into the messy details of tonight's break-in, and the conversation we had with Whitman and Barton. What do you say?"

Sabrina got his drift, and she had to agree that it made sense. "I say there's no time like the present."

"What good news?" Carson demanded.

Dylan arched a quizzical brow at Sabrina. "Who gets the honor—you or me?"

"You've known him longer." She smiled, then coughed again. "I'll save my voice and watch like a fascinated spectator."

"*What good news?*" Carson blasted.

"Okay, okay." Dylan gave him that lopsided grin. "I'll make it short and sweet. I'm wildly in love with your daughter. Fortunately, she feels the same way about me. I asked her to marry me. She said yes. Now how's that for an incentive to get well? We need you to walk her down the aisle."

Disregarding the quiet demanded in ICU, as well as the twinges of pain he caused his injuries, Carson let out a whoop and punched the air triumphantly. "Yes! I knew it! Gloria knew it, too. We were both right. Damn, I can't wait to start spoiling my grandchildren."

The grandchildren bit didn't even register. Sabrina

was too fixed on the part before that. "What do you mean, 'Gloria knew it, too'?"

An offhanded shrug. "I think that's pretty self-explanatory."

"No, it's not. Dylan and I knew *you* were playing matchmaker. You weren't exactly subtle. But where does my mother fit into this equation? She's never even met Dylan."

Carson rolled his eyes. "You forget how smart Gloria is, and how well she reads you. She guessed where this was headed right after I told her you couldn't keep your hands off each other. She's probably starting a line of designer booties as we speak."

Twin spots of red stained Sabrina's cheeks. "You told her we couldn't keep our hands off each other?"

"Not in so many words. I was a little less crude. I think I said something about sparks flying between you. But she got my drift. Hey, don't sell your mother short. According to my nurses, two surgeons tried to hit on her the day she visited me. Believe me, she's no stranger to sex. And you and Dylan are about as transparent as the couples in the C'est Moi ads. You undress each other with your eyes whenever you're in the same room. To tell you the truth, I was a little worried that you'd never make it out of El Faro, at least not fully clothed."

"Oh, God," Sabrina groaned, covering her hot face with her hands.

"What'd I say?" Carson asked Dylan, totally baffled.

"Go easy," Dylan suggested, amused by Carson's utter lack of comprehension when it came to this particular difference between himself and his daughter. This was one time when upbringing and experience—or lack thereof—superseded heredity. And while Dylan understood both perspectives, and was personally unbothered by Carson's pointed innuendos, Sabrina most definitely was not. "You're embarrassing Sabrina," he explained to his friend. "She's not used to your, uh, uninhibited approach."

"What do you mean uninhibited? I'm just stating facts. Why would Sabrina be embarrassed? She's as forthright as I am."

"Not about this, I'm not." Sabrina's head came up. "We're talking about something personal, something intimate. Besides," she added with an incredulous stare. "Aren't fathers supposed to freak out when they discover their daughters are sleeping with someone?"

"I don't know. I never read the father handbook." He shot her an impish grin. "Besides, even if I had, I'd toss it. Dylan is the finest human being I know. You two are so well suited, it's staggering. If he was using you, I'd break him in half. But I've seen the expression on his face when he looks at you, and on yours when you look at him. This is a hell of a lot more than lust. So, why would I freak out? I'm thrilled."

A tiny smile played at Sabrina's lips. "To tell you the truth, so am I."

"Good. Now that we've got that straight, tell me what date you've set and I'll be out of here in time to buy my tux."

Sabrina sobered. "We haven't set a date yet. Nor are we going to, not for a month. After we know where things stand with the transplant, then we'll make plans."

Carson scowled, opening his mouth to give her a hard time.

"Don't even bother." Sabrina cut him off. "Dylan and I are in total agreement on this one. We both want the bride and her father whole, healed, and ready to dance the night away before we finalize the where and when. Period. End of subject." She softened the statement with a more welcome add-on. "But we're officially engaged as of last night. Dylan's taking me to Tiffany's . . ." She broke off, wrinkling her nose in disappointment. "We were going to go today, but it'll have to wait until Dylan's concussion's better."

"Bullshit," Dylan refuted. "Our plans stand. I'm getting myself released the minute we leave Carson's room. I'll go home, take a hot shower, then get dressed and head into work. You, on the other hand, will spend the morning resting. After that, we'll go to Tiffany's. . . ."

"No way." Sabrina overruled that decision. "It's my first day as president of Ruisseau. I'm going into the office, even if I sound like a croaking frog. I don't want to rest. Oh, and one more thing. You won't be going home for that shower. From what I heard in the ambulance, your first floor is a disaster, and your entire apartment is smoke-filled. You'll have to make other living arrangements for a while."

"Gee," Carson piped up. "You can stay at my place on Central Park West. Or . . ." He snapped his fingers. "I know. You can stay at Sabrina's apartment. It's so convenient. It's only a few blocks away from yours. You can pick up your clothes on the way from the hospital and move right in."

"Now *there's* a spontaneous idea. Thanks, Carson." Sabrina shook her head in disbelief, marveling at his sheer audacity. "You took the words right out of my mouth. Dylan is more than welcome at my place."

"I accept." That didn't take Dylan more than three seconds. "Now, back to the issue of Tiffany's. We're going as planned. I promised you a proposal today, either on the sidewalk of Fifth Avenue or in Central Park. You're getting it. I'm not dumb enough to wait for you to change your mind."

"No chance of that," Sabrina assured him. "Once my mind's made up, it doesn't get changed." Abruptly, a thought pertaining to another aspect of their plans struck her, and she frowned. "It just occurred to me, we were going to call my mother later and tell her about our engagement. We'd better not wait. She's probably waking up about now. If she sees the news, she'll lose it."

"Go ahead and use my phone," Carson urged, pointing to his night table. "Call her right away. Oh, and you can tell her I said 'I told you so.'"

"I will."

Dylan waited until Sabrina had gotten through to her mother and was happily, if hoarsely, chatting.

"Carson," he said, lowering his voice. "We have a problem. It can't wait anymore. We've got to talk about it now."

Carson didn't flinch. "Is this about Stan?"

A nod.

"Does Sabrina know?"

"Not yet."

"Then let's wait for her to hang up. She's got to be told the whole situation, especially if it's coming to a head. She's got a right to know. She's president of the company. She's also family."

"I agree. But I needed to get your permission first."

"You have it. When she's finished assuring Gloria that she's okay and telling her your incredible news, we'll talk." Carson inspected Dylan closely. "You're sure you're all right?"

"Yeah. But it's pretty obvious that whoever did this was gunning for Sabrina. Whatever's prompting his actions, he wants her out of the way, too."

"I know. That possibility was eating at me all day. I

talked to Whitman and Barton about it, and they're thinking along the same lines. They can't give me round-the-
clock protection for Sabrina, so I'm hiring a bodyguard.
He'll be glued to her side every minute, until we've
caught the wacko who's behind this." Carson's mouth
thinned into a tight, grim line. "Tell me what Barton and
Whitman said, other than their suspicions about Stan."

Dylan blew out his breath. "They're still centering
their investigation on the gang at Ruisseau. Not that I
blame them. It certainly seems to be a company-related
motive based on the attacks—first you, then Russ, now
Sabrina. Even *I'm* starting to eye staff members up and
down, wondering if maybe, maybe . . . Anyway, you get
my drift."

"I don't like it, but I get it."

"I don't like it either, but we've got to be practical
here, and leave our emotions at the door. Someone's a
murderer. That someone has to be found, whoever and
wherever he is. By the way, I told Whitman and Barton
that Sabrina knows the C'est Moi formula. That sparked
their interest, especially in light of last night's attack. It
also reminded them that there are motives outside Ruisseau. They're rechecking those avenues."

"Competitor time again," Carson muttered. "I'm beginning to wish I'd never shared that damned formula
with Sabrina. If it turns out that whoever's responsible
for these sick attacks found out that I told her, and if all
this is about stopping production of C'est Moi, then I'm
the one who put Sabrina in danger. Hell, maybe I underestimated the risk of making her company president."

"Cut it out," Dylan returned flatly. "That's pure speculation. It's also garbage, given your feelings for Sabrina.
And let's not forget that Sabrina has some say in this. She
can't wait to get to her desk. She's bursting with energy

and enthusiasm over her new position at Ruisseau. This presidency's tailor-made for her. You know it. She knows it. She wouldn't change her mind under *any* circumstances, danger included. Look. Between me and your bodyguard, we'll keep Sabrina safe. Put that worry out of your head. And remember something else. Sabrina's not the only victim here. You're a victim, too. So was poor Russ, who paid with his life."

"Don't remind me." Carson's jaw tightened. "Which competitors are Whitman and Barton talking to?"

"They're going for the obvious. They're heading over to Pruet's this morning to question his New York staff."

"Shit." Carson's fist made an imprint on the bed. "Talk about a best-case, worst-case scenario. Determining that this scumbag shooter works anywhere but Ruisseau—that would take the weight of the world off my shoulders. But Pruet's, of all places . . . that opens up a whole new can of worms. Does Stan know that's where Whitman and Barton are going?"

"My guess is, yes. Whitman and Barton showed up at Ruisseau about an hour ahead of time yesterday, and spent a chunk of that time with Stan. I'm sure they talked to him about his take on Pruet's staff, hoping to gain some insight into different personalities and their professional agendas. And if that's the way their chat went down, Stan's smart enough to cover his bases."

"Christ, what a mess."

At that moment, Sabrina hung up, and turned to face them.

"How's Gloria?" Carson asked.

"Relieved that we're okay. Worried about who did this and whether he'll try again. Elated that Dylan and I are getting married. Heartened that she has something positive to share with my grandparents. And hoping to fly down later this week to meet her prospective son-in-law. Oh, she sent a return message to you. She said to stop gloating. She said to remind you that she's the one who pointed out where the relationship was headed, and how fast it was headed there." Sabrina folded her arms across her breasts, rolling her eyes to the ceiling. "Honestly, the two of you are like obnoxious teenagers, fighting over who did a better job of playing Cupid."

Carson's lips curved. "I'd say it was a dead heat."

"Okay, now let's get to what you two were talking about," Sabrina continued hoarsely, but without missing a beat. "I heard the recap Dylan gave you. I also heard him bring up Stan. Evidently, you've decided to clue me in on whatever's going on with him. That would be helpful, since I can't get a handle on it without having all the facts. It obviously ties into Whitman and Barton's visit to Pruet's. I'm all ears. And, for the record, I don't need a bodyguard. I can take care of myself. Lastly, if I ever again hear you blame yourself for getting me on board at Ruisseau, I'll put a dead skunk in your desk drawer. That'll mess your nose up for weeks."

A chuckle rumbled in Carson's chest. "I thought it was just your olfactory sense that was heightened. Obviously, your hearing's right up there, too. You managed to catch every detail of two separate, simultaneous conversations. Not bad."

"That doesn't take acute hearing. It takes the training of a management consultant combined with the brains and multitasking abilities of a woman."

"Right." With a look of pure sympathy, Carson gazed at Dylan. "Want some advice? Expect to stay on your toes for life. And when the two of you fight? Don't bother trying to win. Just concede up front, and skip to the making up part."

"Gotcha." Dylan seemed more pleased than intimidated. "That sounds like a damned fine strategy."

"Yoo-hoo," Sabrina interrupted. "We were talking about Stan."

"Right. Stan." All humor vanished, and a worried pucker formed between Carson's brows. "The demands of his job have been a major source of stress for him from the beginning. He wanted to be the best COO imaginable. We've already gone over the reasons why."

"His need to keep up with you, and to please you. Yes, that much I get."

"What you don't get is how far he'd go to make that happen." Carson glanced back at Dylan. "I know it's his own damned fault, but I can't help thinking I pushed him into it."

"How? By being brilliant?" Dylan returned dryly. "Carson, in life we make choices. We also accept our own strengths and our own limitations, along with the fact that others might be smarter or better than we are. Stan can't accept any of that. As for his choices, they suck."

"He's never crossed the line."

"That depends on where you draw it."

"I'm lost again," Sabrina interjected.

Dylan propped his elbow on the arm of the wheelchair and turned to face her. "In a nutshell, Stan stays on top of his game by keeping tabs on the competition's marketing, sales, and research strategies. And I don't mean by reading their press releases. I mean *before* those strategies are released or implemented."

Sabrina's jaw dropped. "You're saying he's getting inside information? From whom? Which of our competitors are selling out?"

"Just one. Pruet. And it's not as cut-and-dry as selling

out. But, yeah, Stan's got an inside contact. He has for twenty years."

"I don't believe this." Sabrina sank down into a chair. "Carson, how can you say that's not crossing a line? That's industrial espionage, for God's sake."

"It would be, if money were being exchanged, and if Stan had actually done anything with the information he got hold of," Carson defended immediately. "But it isn't and he hasn't. All he's done is assuage his insecurities by feeling like he's one step ahead in the fragrance industry."

Dylan grunted. "Let's not make his actions sound so noble. First of all, we limited his opportunities to use anything he learned. And second, even if he'd managed to use his inside information, you're always two steps ahead of the competition. So there was no worthwhile material that would benefit Ruisseau. I shudder to think what would have happened if Etienne Pruet had been half the genius you are."

A muscle worked in Carson's jaw. "I like to think Stan would stop short of using what he knew. He's been a jerk, Dylan, but he cares about me, and he cares about this company. I don't think he'd put it at risk. Besides, the situation's more complicated than that. There are emotions involved."

"Yeah." Dylan rubbed the back of his neck. "Stan's contact is Karen Shepard," he explained to Sabrina. "She's executive assistant to Louis Malleville. And Louis Malleville is . . ."

". . . the head of Pruet's New York division," Sabrina finished for him. "And since there's no money involved, I'm guessing the payoff is sex. Boy, this just keeps getting better and better."

"Stan's crazy about Karen," Carson stated flatly. "On

the mornings after he's spent the night at her place, he still acts like a teenager who just had his first lay. Both his marriages broke up because of Karen, whether or not his ex-wives figured it out."

"He told you all this?"

"No." Carson shook his head. "A couple of years after the affair began, I started getting some bad vibes about Stan's frenzy to stay on top of things, his erratic behavior, and his periodic disappearances. I kept an eye on him, and put together a few pieces. Then, I hired a PI. He got me the information I needed about Stan's ties to Karen."

"Yeah," Dylan added dryly. "For obvious reasons, Stan's kept the relationship a secret."

"For twenty years?" Sabrina asked in amazement.

"Yup."

"Great secret. Who else knows about it?"

"The three of us, my PI, and, most recently, Roland Ferguson," Carson replied.

"Wait." Sabrina held up her palm. "How did Roland get into this equation?"

"I'm not sure exactly how he found out." Carson shrugged. "I sure as hell wasn't about to march into his office and ask. But he's head of human resources. For all I know accounting gave him copies of phone records and Karen's number showed up repeatedly. It doesn't matter. However it happened, he knows. Stan's been keeping him in check since then, which has been about the last year or so."

"Keeping him in check—does that mean paying him off?"

Carson averted his gaze. It was obvious he was loath to answer.

"I'll take that to be a yes," Sabrina presumed aloud. "Carson, this is serious."

"It's not serious. But, yeah, it's snowballing," he admitted.

"Did Stan use company funds to bribe Ferguson?"

"No." Carson wasn't happy with her using the word bribe. But he didn't call her on it. "Like I said, Stan never crossed the line. That includes stealing. He paid Ferguson with money from his personal account."

Grimly, Sabrina turned to Dylan. "When did you get included in this juicy secret?"

"About ten years ago. Not long after I passed the bar exam."

"I needed Dylan's legal guidance as to how I should handle things." Carson scowled. "It was a lousy dilemma. I didn't want to hurt Stan, but I sure as hell wasn't going to ignore behavior that could end up screwing over Ruisseau. Dylan and I made sure to isolate Stan from making decisions for Ruisseau that utilized information he had on Pruet, whether properly attained or not. That way, we minimized our risk. Ruisseau was protected, and Stan was protected."

"Wow." Sabrina felt a wave of compassion for Dylan. "What a great quandary to step into as a new lawyer. Talk about walking a legal tightrope. You must have felt like you were caught between a rock and a hard place."

"I did." Dylan shifted in the wheelchair—and winced a bit.

"Is it your head?" Sabrina asked at once.

"No, my head's better, thanks to the painkiller. It's just the bandage on my chest. It's pulling. I'll be happy to get rid of it." He shifted again, easing the discomfort. "I'm fine. Anyway, to answer your question, yeah, I wasn't happy with our iffy legal footing. Carson and Ruisseau were my primary concern, even though I knew how protective Carson was of Stan. Frankly, if the information exchange between Stan and Karen had been a little more formal, or if Stan had used what he found out to benefit Ruisseau in any way, I would have been on him like a hawk. But the fact is, nothing concrete took place. Nothing in this entire mess is black and white. It's all gray. Stan was, and still is, nuts about Karen. They spend two or three nights a week together. How do you differentiate pillow talk from industrial espionage when nothing's been used to benefit Ruisseau?"

"I see your point." Sabrina's nose and throat were beginning to burn badly, and she could see that Carson was starting to fade. This conversation was taking its toll on everyone. "I also see why this is coming to a head now. Whitman and Barton view Stan as a key suspect. You can clear that up by explaining what's really going on with him."

"We can also give him an alibi," Dylan told her. "Dollars to doughnuts he was at Karen's apartment when Carson was shot. It was a holiday weekend. Since Stan's last divorce, he's spent every one of those at Karen's place—day and night. And one small correction—it's not that we *can* explain. We *have* to explain. I told Whitman and Barton they were barking up the wrong tree. Not just to protect Stan, either. I don't want them wasting time drilling someone who's innocent. Not when the real murderer's still out there somewhere. Whitman got my drift. She gave me a day to get Carson's okay to forgo attorney-client privilege."

Carson frowned again, clearly fighting to keep his eyes open. "If you tell them the truth, will they have anything on Stan?"

"Not unless there's more going on here than we know.

Remember, Stan has no idea you're aware of his twenty-year fling with Karen. Once you tell him, we can spin the explanation we give Whitman and Barton to his advantage. We'll describe it as a hot-and-heavy love affair that Stan kept under wraps because he was afraid of how it would look. You'll assure the detectives that Stan's just being his insecure self. Tell them you knew about the affair, and that no aspect of it has compromised the business ethics of either fragrance company. Since nothing illegal was done, that interpretation will work just fine." Dylan gave a humorless laugh. "Occasionally, spin works to our advantage."

He eyed Carson, wrapping up quickly as he saw how exhausted his friend was. "If you're asking if Whitman and Barton could go after Stan for small stuff, like giving Roland shut-up money—sure, if they want to, although there's no proof that was a payoff. By the same token, they could also go after Stan, and me, for getting hold of Gloria Radcliffe's confidential medical records. But I doubt they will, not when they have bigger fish to fry. They're not interested in bringing Stan up on charges. They have more important crimes to deal with. Crimes like murder and attempted murder." A shrug. "Even if I'm wrong, it's a chance we'll have to take. There's no choice. We have to give them the facts."

"And *you* have to rest," Sabrina informed Carson, placing her hand on his shoulder.

"I'm not tired."

"Then let's say we are. Dylan and I need to get him released and moved into my apartment. And you need to regain your strength for a conversation with Stan."

"Yeah." Carson nodded, stretching out his arm. "Before you go, hand me the phone. Punch up Stan's number."

Dylan glanced at his watch. Seven forty-five. Stan would be at the office.

He pressed the appropriate buttons and handed Carson the receiver.

Carson held it to his ear and waited until he heard the click that signified a connection, followed by Stan's preoccupied voice.

"Stan Hager." There was a whirring sound in the background.

"It's me," Carson replied.

"Carson. I just got in and heard the news. Are . . . ?"

"Yeah, Sabrina and Dylan are fine. They're about to leave the hospital. Listen, I need to see you. But first I need to get some sleep. It's been a rough morning. So wait a couple of hours. Then get yourself over here. That'll give me time to rest and you time to finish whatever the hell it is you're shredding."

A taut pause.

"Okay," Stan said finally. "I'll be there. What do you need me to bring?"

"Yourself." Carson hung up. "Damn fool," he muttered, already drifting off. "He must have kept notes or something . . . and now he's shredding them. . . ." One heavy eyelid lifted. "By the way . . . you're getting that bodyguard, like it or not. . . ."

"Okay," Sabrina conceded quietly.

The eyelid slid shut. Carson was asleep.

Sabrina and Dylan exchanged glances.

"Shredding papers?" Sabrina murmured. "This is getting dicey."

"Yeah," Dylan agreed. "But let's keep two things in mind. One, this is Stan. He's paranoid enough to be shredding love notes. And, two, this is Stan. He's Carson's oldest friend. So let's do what we can—for Carson's sake."

Nodding, Sabrina stood, walking around to grab hold

of the back of the wheelchair. "Let's get going. I'll stop at the nurses' station and tell them to hold Carson's calls. He needs to sleep."

No sooner had she spoken than the phone rang. Sabrina made a dive for it, so it wouldn't disturb Carson.

"Hello?" she said hoarsely.

A tiny hesitation. "Sabrina? Is that you?"

"Yes. Who's this?"

"Susan." She sounded totally freaked-out. "I heard the news. Thank God you're all right. What about Dylan—is he okay, too?"

"We're both fine. Very lucky, very grateful, and very much alive," Sabrina assured her.

"Why didn't someone call me? I'm beside myself." Susan's voice quavered, and she gave a hard swallow. "I saw the news. I didn't know what to do. I wanted to call Carson right away, but I was terrified that I'd upset him if for some reason he was still asleep and didn't know about the break-in. Finally, I couldn't stand it anymore. I had to know if you were all right."

Sabrina felt a pang of guilt. "Susan, I'm so sorry. We should have called you. Things were just so hectic. We were in the emergency room until a little while ago and then we came up here to calm Carson down because he'd just seen the clip on TV. I'm sure he would have called you afterward, but he just drifted off. I think the emotional upheaval really wore him out."

"The poor man." Susan sniffled, and Sabrina realized she was weeping. "He must have been berserk."

"He was. But he's calm now." Sabrina glanced at the bed, saw that Carson's breathing was deep and even. "He's sleeping peacefully."

Another pause, followed by the sound of running water and a gulp. "I'm here. I just had to take something to help me calm down. I'm not big on tranquilizers, but in this case—" Susan broke off, taking another gulp of water. "This whole nightmare is really beginning to get to me. One thing after another. My nerves are shot. I don't know how much more I can take before I crack." Abruptly, she stopped herself, as if realizing how unglued she sounded. "Forgive me, Sabrina. You sound terrible. You must feel worse. You just went through hell, and I'm going on and on about how upset I am. I'll hang up now and give you a chance to go home and rest. I was going to visit Carson this morning, but under the circumstances, I think I'll wait. He's exhausted and I'm a wreck. I won't be any good for him. I'll head into YouthOp, get some work done. Maybe that'll help me get myself together. I'll drop by the hospital later this afternoon."

"Good idea." Sabrina's wheels were spinning. It *was* a good idea, and not only because of Susan's frame of mind. But because when Carson woke up, he had an unpleasant confrontation to face. His meeting with Stan would, no doubt, drain the hell out of him. The last thing he needed was a social visit, even from Susan, and especially if she was as overwrought as she sounded now. By later today, he'd be restored and, hopefully, so would she.

"Susan, we really are fine," Sabrina reiterated, trying to soothe her in the interim. "Again, I apologize for not calling you."

"I understand. And I'm sorry for overreacting. We'll talk later today. In the meantime, you take care."

A click signified she'd hung up.

Sabrina frowned as she replaced the receiver.

"What was that all about?" Dylan asked.

"Susan was checking up on us. She was practically hysterical. It's like she's coming apart at the seams."

"Yeah, she does that. Without much regard for the people it affects."

"Dylan." Sabrina shot him a quick look. "That's the second time you've reacted that way about Susan. She really bugs you, doesn't she?"

He glanced over at the bed. "Let's take this conversation elsewhere, okay?"

"Good idea."

They left Carson's room, headed for the elevator to go back to ER and get Dylan discharged.

The elevator doors slid open, and Sabrina pushed the wheelchair inside, maneuvered herself in behind Dylan.

The doors shut behind them.

There was no one inside but the two of them.

Dylan angled his head, gazed up at Sabrina. "You asked if Susan bugs me. The answer is yes."

29

Dylan got a clean bill of health, along with a warning not to overdo from the staff in ER. With that, he and Sabrina were on their way.

They left the hospital, and were surprised to see Sabrina's limo waiting outside the emergency room exit. Surprised or not, they were thrilled to take advantage of climbing in, once they saw the line of news correspondents waiting to interrogate them about their close call.

As their driver pulled away, he informed them that, at the request of Detective Whitman, he'd stopped at the Midtown North Police Precinct, and picked up the clothing and personal items that the police had rescued from Dylan's smoky brownstone and brought to their precinct. As a result, he could take them straight to Ms. Radcliffe's.

Sabrina was grateful. She was also relieved. She was eager to continue the conversation she and Dylan had begun in the elevator at Mt. Sinai.

While the driver helped Dylan carry in his bags, Sabrina went into the kitchen and brewed a huge pot of coffee. She carried it into the living room, placed it on the coffee table, and waited until she and Dylan were alone.

He joined her, dropping onto the sofa and running both hands through his hair. "Damn, that coffee looks good. Thanks for making it." A quizzical glance. "It's not decaf, is it?"

"No way," Sabrina assured him, sitting down on the adjoining love seat so they could maintain eye contact.

"Not after the night we had. It's ultra-leaded. This way, we can hydrate ourselves, warm up, and get our caffeine fix all at once."

"Don't forget to add 'and talk,'" Dylan reminded her, taking a huge, grateful swallow. "I know you're chomping at the bit—even though you're supposed to be resting your voice."

"I'll rest my voice later. Or, better yet, I'll listen. You talk. Unless your head hurts too much."

"Nope. My head's much better. I'm in fine shape for talking."

"Good. Because I want to hear what you meant when you said Susan bugs you."

"Was it really such a surprise revelation?"

"Of course not." Sabrina sipped at her steaming coffee. "But I can't help feeling like the reasons behind it are more than just the fact that she's emotionally selfish."

"They are."

"Let's start with my most fundamental concern. Last time we touched on this subject, you said you believed Susan genuinely loved Carson. I've got to assume you meant that."

"Definitely." Dylan set down his cup. "I'd never lie about that, or look the other way if it weren't true. Like I said, if I thought Susan's feelings for Carson were anything but real, I'd go straight to Carson with it. Hey, I was planning on going to him with a lot less. I was just trying to find a way to say what I had to without pissing him off."

"About what? What is it about Susan you feel honor-bound to tell Carson?"

"That's the problem. I can't give you a specific answer. My entire argument is based on instinct. My feelings about Susan are ambiguous, at best. Sometimes I think she's full of it, and sometimes I think she's everything she seems to be and I'm imagining things. She sends out mixed signals. But my gut instinct just won't shut up. And it tells me that most of what she does, she does for personal gain. No matter how altruistic her actions appear."

A major piece fell into place. "You're not talking about her commitment to Carson. You're talking about her commitment to YouthOp." Sabrina leaned forward. "Is it that you don't think her heart's really in it?"

"I think her heart's in the perks she gets from running it. Carson's her principal supporter and her biggest fan. That certainly solidifies her place in his life. On top of that, the columnists eat it up in their personal interest stories. The participating schools praise her up and down. To read about her contributions, you'd think she was a regular Mother Teresa."

"But you think she disingenuous, that she doesn't really care about the kids."

"I wouldn't go that far. She cares. The question is, who comes first—her or the kids? My guess is, she does. All the time, personally and professionally. Her reaction since Carson was shot is just one example of that. Her needs first, his second. Sure, she helps the kids. Like I said when we talked about Stan, we're not talking black and white. We're talking gray. There's just something about her priorities—it comes through in the way she runs her charity functions, the angle she takes when she's interviewed. She puts herself in the limelight—subtly, but every time the opportunity presents itself. Then there's the way she disburses the funds. . . ."

"You think she's misappropriating them?"

"Let's just say I've never seen such a posh office occupied by the head of a charitable organization. An office which, I may add, I'm one of the few outsiders who's seen. And that's only because I do the legal paperwork that allows a YouthOp kid to intern at Ruisseau. She never conducts interviews there. It might make her look materialistic, rather than benevolent." Dylan rubbed a palm over his jaw. "I could be way off base. She could have paid for the damned interior decorating with her own money, for all I know."

"She told me she grew up on a farm in upstate New York. I doubt she has a huge trust fund to dip into. What did she do before she started YouthOp?"

"Various corporate positions, mostly in the public relations departments. Could she have saved a bundle that she's now spending on herself? Of course. She sure as hell spends it on her clothes and makeup. I've never seen that woman in the same outfit twice, or with a hair or eyelash out of place. As for the place she calls home, she lives on the Upper West side—not far from here. Nice area, not cheap. And hey, I'm sure the apartment's furnished to the nines, also."

Sabrina had to stifle a smile. "You really don't think much of her, do you?"

"That's not the issue. It's just that my warning bells go off when I'm around her. She's done nothing overt. She makes all the right moves at all the right times. Maybe that's part of the problem. She's *too* smooth, *too* impeccable. I don't know. I only know that I can't turn those warning bells off. Remember, Sabrina, when it comes right down to it, I'm a street kid. I grew up relying on my instincts to survive. They rarely failed me. That hasn't changed. And when it comes to Susan—they just can't get comfortable."

Sabrina was feeling more uneasy by the minute. Dylan was a clever, astute man. If his feelings on this

matter were so strong, she wasn't about to pooh-pooh
them. "You said you planned to bring this up with Carson. Why didn't you?"

"Because we were always busy. Because we never got
a quiet minute alone. Because I wanted to be wrong."
Dylan blew out his breath. "And because I knew he'd dismiss it as crap. I guess I was hoping to have something
concrete to show him or tell him, anything to prove my
concerns had merit. But nothing presented itself. Finally,
I thought, screw it, I'll go to him anyway, if for no other
reason than to keep him on his toes by putting the bug in
his ear. That never happened. He got shot, so I obviously
put the whole discussion on hold. I'm sure as hell not
going to add to his burden with this petty garbage. He's
going through enough. Whether Susan is Florence
Nightingale or a social-climbing schemer whose main
goal is to enrich herself and score Brownie points, it can
wait until Carson's stronger."

"Maybe it doesn't have to."

Dylan arched a brow. "What does that mean?"

Sabrina put down her cup. "It means that I've learned
to trust your instincts. There's only one person whose instincts I trust more: mine. Susan and I haven't spent a lot
of time together. When we did, it was in the ICU lounge.
We talked about YouthOp, and she got very emotional.
On the other hand, maybe she's just a drama queen about
everything. She certainly was a basket case on the phone
before. She wasn't even ready to see Carson, that's how
upset she was. She wanted time to compose herself. She
was going in to YouthOp to do some work."

"So?"

"So—" Sabrina's chin came up and a purposeful glint
lit her eyes. "You're right that this Susan-issue pales in
comparison to everything Carson's been through in the

past weeks. But it still affects his well-being. And that's something you and I need to look out for. He loves this woman. If she's not everything he thinks she is, it's up to us to find out."

"I see." Dylan's lips twitched. "So now we're on a crusade?"

"Let's just say that I'm interested in seeing this incredible organization where Carson finds great interns like Russ Clark. By the same token, I'm sure Susan could use some company. She was so distraught when we spoke. I say we kill two birds with one stone. It's still early. We can shower, change, and pay a quick visit to YouthOp before we head into the office."

9:45 A.M.
Mt. Sinai Hospital

Stan popped another Zantac into his mouth and gulped it down with water.

Dr. Radison was in with Carson now, checking out his vital signs and whatever else surgeons did after their patients went through a traumatic morning like the one Carson had just endured.

When Radison was done, it was his turn up.

He refilled his cup, drank some more water, then tossed away the paper cup and headed back to the lounge. He began to pace. There was no point in standing still, much less sitting down. He was a wreck, and his stomach was killing him. He'd spent the whole morning trying to figure out what Carson wanted to see him about. He'd sounded deadly serious. Had Whitman and Barton paid him a morning visit? Had they actually accused Stan of trying to kill Sabrina, on top of shooting Carson? Had they managed to convince Carson he was guilty?

If so, what could he say in his own defense? Just his

luck, he'd been with Karen again. How many times could he spout that crap about being home alone and falling asleep in front of the TV? Why was it that whenever some dire crime occurred, his alibi was one he didn't dare provide?

Talk about being in deep shit.

The thought of Karen made him glance at his watch. Whitman and Barton were still with Pruet's staff, probably grilling the hell out of them. Normally, Karen was cool as a cucumber. But under the kind of pressure being exerted, he prayed she'd hold up. Because if those detectives found out about the two of them, he'd be in jail with the key thrown away.

He could hear the charges now. Collusion. Industrial espionage. Expensive gifts provided in exchange for sexual favors and corporate secrets. And motive for attempted murder? How about fear of his CEO-slash-oldest-friend finding out what he'd been up to for the past twenty years and pulling the plug? Couldn't get a better motive than that. Oh, and what about motive for attempted murder number two, tonight at Dylan's place? Let's see. The CEO's daughter had just been made company president. She was smart as a whip, and already suspicious of Stan. Hell, he even had the perk of being one of the few people who knew she'd spent the night at her boyfriend's.

It was a tidy little package. He'd be handcuffed and led away before he could catch his breath, if he didn't do something to save himself.

But how?

He'd told Karen he was taking matters into his own hands, nipping things in the bud. Well, he'd planned to. He'd already taken steps to achieve that end, although he'd veered in a different direction than he'd

originally intended. But he had to live with himself—
and, hopefully, with Karen. If those damned detectives
had only solved the crimes, he could have slithered off
into the sunset, leaving minimal upheaval in his wake.
Instead, they'd come up empty and now there'd been
another murder attempt, which meant a stepped-up investigation and an accusation waiting right around the
bend. An accusation against the most likely suspect—
him.

He was damned if he told the truth and damned if he
lied. And he'd just run out of time.

"Mr. Hager?"

Stan nearly jumped out of his skin as Dr. Radison approached him from behind. He whipped around. "Yes?"

The doctor gave him a curious look. "Mr. Brooks is
asking for you. He's doing well, by the way. No lasting
effects from this morning's shock, if that's what's got
you so on edge."

"Great." Stan's relief was as tangible as it was real.
Carson had to get well. He had to. Because no matter
how things played out, Stan had a painful and long-
overdue confession to make.

"You can go down to his room now," Radison
prodded.

"Oh. Thanks." Stan sucked in his breath, straightened
his shoulders, and marched down the hall. This whole
meeting could be a no-biggie. Maybe he was blowing the
whole thing out of proportion. But he didn't think so.

He pushed open the door and walked in.

Carson was sitting up in bed. He did look stronger,
and there were only a few tubes and contraptions still
hooked up to him, plus his IVs and that shunt-thing in his
arm used for the dialysis. But his expression was intense,
brooding, like he had something heavy on his mind.

Stan knew that look. And it wasn't a good sign.

"Hey," he greeted his friend, pulling up a chair and forcing himself to sit down and appear relatively calm. "Radison says you're doing great."

Angling his head slightly, Carson gave Stan a penetrating stare. "I'm not going to beat around the bush. And I'm sure as hell not going to sugarcoat what I have to say. Not to you. Not after what you've done. Whitman and Barton are another story. They'll get the modified version. That way we can minimize the trouble you get into. I'm not sure you deserve the protection. But you're my friend, so you're getting it. As for now, when we're one-on-one, you're going to hear exactly what I think of you. Then, we'll get into the song and dance we're going to lay on the cops to save your ass."

The knot in Stan's gut tightened, and he paled as his worst fears were confirmed. "You honestly believe I tried to kill Sabrina tonight?" he blurted out. "Worse, you think I tried to kill *you?*" He groped for his pills, popped another into his mouth. He didn't give a damn how many he'd taken. His insides were on fire.

He reached over to Carson's tray. Taking a glass, he poured some water from the pitcher with a hand that shook so badly the water sloshed everywhere. Then, he swallowed the pill and put down the glass. He was sweating, and he yanked out a handkerchief, mopping at his forehead. "Christ, you really think I'm a killer. The scary part is, I can't blame you. But I'd never . . . I'd never . . ." He broke off, dropping his head in his hands as he realized how lame anything he said would sound.

"Hey." Carson's voice brought his head up. There was an odd expression on his friend's face—a combination of sorrow, pity, and nostalgia. "You've suffered a hell of a lot, haven't you?" Carson muttered. "I guess in many ways that's punishment enough. No, Stan, I don't think you tried to kill anyone. In fact, I know you didn't. It's time the cops knew, too. So later today, we're going to tell them."

Taken aback by Carson's response, Stan turned his palms up in a baffled gesture. "I've already told them. Repeatedly."

"They need proof. You've got it. Give them your alibi."

"What alibi? I was home watching TV and—"

"You weren't home watching TV," Carson interrupted. "You were in Tuckahoe, screwing Karen. Just like you were last night when Sabrina and Dylan were attacked. Once the cops know that, they'll go away."

Silence.

"And before you ask, I know everything. About Karen, about the updates on Pruet, about the twenty years it's been going on. The works."

Stan sank weakly back in his seat. "I don't believe this. Why didn't you call me on it? Why didn't you do something, like throw my ass out the door?"

"Because you're a better COO than you give yourself credit for. Also, because you're my oldest friend. And don't make me sound quite so soft and squishy. I *did* do something. I kept tabs on you like you wouldn't believe. My PI practically lives up your ass. I also made sure you were isolated from any projects that might entice you to use what you'd learned from Karen. You have Dylan to thank for that. He's a hell of a lawyer. He kept you clean, and now he's laid out a plan to help keep your ass out of jail. But before I get into that, tell me two things. Where do things stand with Ferguson, and what the hell were you shredding when I called today?"

"Dylan's in on this, too?" Stan managed in a faint voice.

"Damn straight. I'm not a lawyer. I needed to protect Ruisseau. That's what I pay Dylan for. Now answer my questions—Ferguson and the shredding."

Ferguson. The shredding. Jesus, Carson really did know everything. And apparently, so did Dylan.

"I'll answer your questions. Just tell me who else knows."

"Sabrina. I told her a few hours ago. Whitman and Barton will come later. I wanted to talk to you first."

Nodding, Stan rose, drawing in a breath and running a shaky hand through his hair. "Ferguson's off the hook. I told him so this morning. What I was shredding were any personal notes from Karen, copies of Pruet's internal memos, and details I'd jotted down based on what Karen passed along. I never used any of it, by the way. I'm not sure I could have brought myself to, even if they'd been needed. I felt like a shit. I just needed to feel in control." A hard swallow. "No point in telling you what you already know. Just tell me what you don't know, and I'll fill you in."

"How did Ferguson find out what was going on?"

"He saw Karen and me come out of a hotel together—twice. We were rarely that stupid or careless. Just our luck, the two times we met in the city instead of at her place, Roland spotted us. He recognized Karen from some industry event they'd both attended. The second time he saw us together, he also overheard us saying some guilty good-byes and making plans to meet at her place where no one from Pruet's or Ruisseau could see us. Our conversation sounded pretty incriminating. The next morning, Roland confronted me. I freaked out. I gave him two personal bonus payments of ten thousand dollars each. He's been a twitching wreck ever since. Like I said, I let him off the hook today. I told him my plans. Needless to say, he was relieved."

Carson's eyes narrowed. "Your plans? What plans?"

Stan planted his feet firmly apart, and crossed his arms over his chest. "I won't lie to you. There's been too much of that already. Originally, I was just going to shred anything that could incriminate me or hurt Ruisseau, then bribe Roland with as much money as it took to get him to resign his position and to move far, far away. I told myself I'd make it up to you. I'd comb the globe until I found the best VP of human resources known to mankind to replace Roland. I'd never discuss business with Karen again. I'd bust my ass to help Sabrina, and to make her transition as easy as possible. I'd do it all, and I'd do it with the morals of a boy scout. But guess what? That bogus attempt at altruism didn't work. I discovered that my conscience has a lower threshold than I thought. It wouldn't shut up. Also, my insides feel like shredded wheat. My peptic ulcer has graduated to a bleeding ulcer. I'm killing myself, and I'm not ready to die. The only way to stop that from happening is by taking a major stand—now."

His shrug with filled with weariness and defeat. "Look, Carson, I can't keep fighting to be what I'm not. So I changed my original strategy, decided to go about things differently. Instead of bribing Roland, I gave him back his integrity this morning. I told him I was going to resign as soon as the cops caught whoever shot you, at which point I could tell you everything and walk off into the sunset. Actually, the conversation we're having now changes that timing. Since you already know everything, we can give the cops my alibi, tell them whatever you and Dylan decided on, and I can resign now rather than later."

"The hell you can." Carson's eyes blazed and his jaw set. "Let me get this straight. You're saying you figured that if you spilled your guts to me now, I'd assume that anyone who'd screw around with my company, might also put a bullet in my back."

"Something like that, yeah."

"Well, you were wrong. Your logic sucks. Just like it sucks that you never came to me, not in twenty years, and told me what was really going on with you and Karen. It sucks that you thought I'd just throw you to the wolves. It sucks that you didn't think I'd get it that you were in love with this woman. It sucks that you don't realize how well I know you, that I know how nuts you are about proving yourself. It sucks that you never caught on to the fact that I feel guilty as hell for making you feel so desperate that you had to go to these lengths to stay on top. And you know what sucks most of all? That after all we've been through together, all the years we've been friends, I had more faith in you than you had in me. Or in yourself, for that matter. You really are an asshole."

"That's a fair assessment. As for the last part, thanks for the compliment." Stan smiled faintly, his tone as wry as his expression. "It's good to know that, even with my life coming apart at the seams, some things never change."

"Yeah. Things like our friendship. And your job. You're not leaving Ruisseau. You're not going anywhere. Try handing me your resignation. I'll tear it up and throw it in your face. Now sit the hell down," Carson ordered, pointing at the chair. "We'll go over the explanation Dylan laid out for us to share with the detectives. It's pretty close to the truth. Once we're in sync, we'll contact Whitman and Barton, and arrange for you to give them your statement. Oh, and call Karen. Let her know what's going on. Tell her she's keeping her job and you're keeping yours. I'll give Pruet a call. If he feels better, Karen can sign a confidentiality agreement. But I doubt he'll insist on that. He'll be satisfied with her verbal assurance that whatever happens in her professional day isn't discussed outside the office. As for you, the employment agreement you signed as COO already binds you to maintain confidentiality about Ruisseau.

"And one more thing." Carson shot Stan a no-bullshit look. "On a personal note, would you get off your butt and ask this woman to marry you? It's the only way you're ever going to get this marriage thing right."

"I will." Stan's throat was working convulsively as he lowered himself into the chair. He stared at the floor, and there was no sarcasm in his tone when he spoke, only gratitude and humility. "Thanks, Carson. I said it when we lived in that cockroach-ridden dump, and I'll say it now. You're one hell of a friend."

"Yeah, well, that goes both ways. Without your passing along that sperm donor information twenty-eight years ago, Sabrina would never have been conceived. And without your digging it up again now, she'd never have come into my life. So we're even. Now let's stop slobbering and get busy."

10:25 A.M.
YouthOp, East 23rd Street

Whatever tranquilizer Susan had taken hadn't done much good.

She was shaky and uptight as she ushered Sabrina and Dylan into her office.

"I hope our dropping in isn't an inconvenience," Sabrina said.

"Not at all. I'm touched that you're here." Susan took

out a tissue and dabbed at her eyes. Then, she sat down behind her desk, folding her manicured hands in front of her. "It's good to see for myself that you're both all right. I just wish I'd known you were coming. I'd have had a fresh pot of coffee ready, maybe brought in some muffins from that little bakery down the street."

"Thanks. But we just downed an entire pot of coffee. Any more caffeine and I think we'll twitch." Sabrina smiled politely, settling herself in a chair and glancing at her surroundings.

Okay, Dylan was right about the office. It looked like a Maurice Villency showroom, all cream leather and exquisite lacquered wood. Even the paintings on the wall screamed Upper East Side gallery.

Interesting. Especially since the rest of YouthOp's modest-sized office space was a complete one-eighty— inexpensive, spartanly furnished rooms with basic berber carpeting, and metal desks and file cabinets.

"Your office is lovely," Sabrina commented, pausing as the scratchiness in her voice swallowed her words. Simultaneously, she became aware of a disturbing odor aggravating her nose—an odor that sidetracked her big-time.

"Pardon me?" Susan inquired, brows drawn in question.

Sabrina forced herself to keep it together. She couldn't let her reaction show. She had to shelve it, to think about the implications later.

"Your office," she repeated, operating on autopilot. "It's lovely. Did you decorate it yourself?"

"Actually, no. I worked with a professional decorator." Susan didn't look the least bit put off by the question. On the other hand, her fingers were still trembling from the upset of the day. "He's on the expensive side, but he's phenomenally talented. For months I was on the fence about whether or not I should spend thousands on my office. But, the truth is, I'm in this room over fifty hours a week. So, in the end, I decided to splurge. I sold one of my stocks and went for the works. I've never been sorry. I'm far more motivated when I feel good in my surroundings." She gestured at her stylish taupe suit, striving for a lighter note. "It's like putting on one of your mother's designs when you're going through a bad time. It lifts your spirits—most of the time," she added ruefully, clearly self-conscious about the emotional state she was in.

She drew a calming breath, then glanced at Dylan. "I should give you my decorator's name and number. From that news report I heard, it sounds like the explosion and fire at your apartment were bad. The place must be in shambles."

"The ground floor's a disaster," Dylan confirmed with a nod. "Aside from that, I got lucky. The firefighters put out the flames before they could spread upstairs. But, yeah, I'm going to have to do some major renovating. The hallway as I knew it is gonzo."

"Wow." Susan shook her head in dismay. "I'm hardly an expert on Molotov cocktails, but it's hard to believe a couple of bottles could do that amount of damage." A concerned frown. "Where will you live in the meantime—at Carson's place?"

A heartbeat of silence.

"No. Dylan's staying with me," Sabrina supplied, seizing the awkward moment by transforming it into an opportunity to deliver their big news. "Which brings me to the one happy development we were able to share with Carson today. Dylan and I are getting married."

"Oh, my." Susan blinked, then leaned across the desk to squeeze both their hands. Her own palms were icy.

"That's wonderful. It's just the outcome Carson was hoping . . ." Her voice trailed off.

"You don't need to protect him," Dylan assured her dryly. "We're already onto the fact that he was doing a little not-so-subtle matchmaking. Fortunately, he didn't have much work to do."

"Obviously not." Susan's smile didn't quite reach her eyes. "So when's the big day?"

"We're not sure yet. We're waiting until we know Carson's prognosis, and have a better idea when he'll be on his feet and ready to walk me down the aisle. Then, we'll set a date." Sabrina's voice was getting raspier again. And the tingling in her nose was intensifying.

But it was the reason for it that was freaking her out.

She began to cough.

"Can I get you some water?" Susan asked at once.

"Please," Sabrina grated out.

Susan hurried out to the bottled water dispenser in the outer office and began filling up a paper cup.

"Are you okay?" Dylan's lids were hooded, his expression pensive.

"No." Sabrina squeezed her eyes shut as tears filled them.

"Sabrina?" Dylan grabbed her arm. "What is it?"

"It's my nose. . . ." She dissolved into another spasm of coughing. "After the water . . . let's get out of here."

"Yeah. Good idea."

When Susan walked in, Sabrina was taking slow, deep breaths through her mouth.

"Goodness." Susan looked alarmed. "Are you all right?"

"Smoke inhalation," Dylan explained, taking the cup and handing it to Sabrina. "After she drinks this, I think I'll take her outside for some air."

"Of course." Susan twisted at the tissue in her hands, watching nervously as Sabrina sipped at the water.

Slowly, the fit of coughing subsided, but Sabrina's eyes continued to water.

"Susan, I hope you understand . . . if we leave," she managed, her voice breaking and scratchy. "We just wanted to . . . make sure you were doing better . . . and to tell you our news."

"I'm very glad you did. I'm so happy for you both." Susan led them through her doorway, quickly showing them out. "As for understanding, of course I do. You've been through a terrible ordeal. Go home and rest."

Five minutes later, Sabrina sank back in the limo, leaning her head against the cushioned neck rest, as the car made its way uptown.

"Better?" Dylan asked, smoothing her hair off her cheek.

"Actually, no. I feel sick to my stomach."

Dylan tensed. "The aftermath of last night?"

"No, the meeting with Susan."

A harsh glitter came into Dylan's eyes. "So you heard it, too. Yeah, I'd say you have reason to feel sick. I just keep wracking my brain, trying to come up with a logical explanation."

"Oh, there's a logical explanation, all right," Sabrina bit out. "And it makes me ill."

The vehemence in Sabrina's tone gave Dylan pause. "Are we talking about the same thing?" he demanded.

"We sure as hell are. You're talking about the fact that when we were discussing the damage to your apartment, Susan said it was hard to believe that a couple of bottles could do so much damage. How did she know it was 'a couple' of bottles? The news didn't mention it. No one mentioned it. No one knew but you. And the only people you told were the detectives and Carson, none of whom have spoken with Susan since then. The detectives are with Pruet, and Carson's sleeping."

"So who told Susan?"

"She already knew," Sabrina stated flatly.

"It sure as hell seems that way. But let's not jump the gun. We can't be sure."

"We damned well can be." Sabrina glanced at her watch, then flipped open her cell phone and dialed. "Detective Whitman? It's Sabrina Radcliffe. Are you finished at Pruet's? Okay, good. Don't go back to your precinct yet. I need to see you right away. It's urgent. Dylan and I are on our way to Ruisseau. Could you meet us in my office ASAP? Thank you."

She punched END.

"Sabrina, what is it?" Dylan pressed. "I know what Susan said sounds incriminating, but we can't assume she's involved without having more evidence than that."

"We've got more evidence. It's right here." Sabrina tapped her nose.

"Your reaction in Susan's office, you mean?"

"Yes, my reaction. The tingling in my nose just wouldn't go away because of the odor."

"What odor?" Dylan's voice had gone deadly quiet.

Sabrina angled her head, met his gaze head-on. "The smell of gasoline."

30

The tension in Sabrina's office was so thick you could cut it with a knife.

Dylan was perched at the edge of the desk, Sabrina was sitting behind it, and Frank and Jeannie were seated across from them, digesting all they'd just been told.

Jeannie tapped her pen against the side of her leg, her eyes narrowed in concentration. "Let's start with the smell of gasoline. If you're right, then one theory is that whoever made those Molotov cocktails was in Ms. Lane's office."

Sabrina slapped a palm on her desk. "First of all, I *am* right. Don't insult me. I know the smell of gasoline, and that was it. Second of all, if Susan's only involvement is that her office was used as a laboratory—without her knowledge or consent—how do you explain her little slip about the 'couple of bottles' that were used? She had to know what was going on."

A frown. "That bugs me, too. My first instinct would be to say that whoever threw those bottles last night and stabbed Russ Clark to death is affiliated with YouthOp. Which makes sense. Not every street kid is reformable. And those who aren't make the people in charge look bad. In the case of YouthOp, that would be Ms. Lane. Maybe she's protecting the kid—and herself, in the process."

"Bullshit." Dylan rose, pacing restlessly around the room. "Susan would go to great lengths to keep her nose clean. But she wouldn't protect a murderer, certainly not one who could lead us to the person who shot Carson."

"You're *sure* she used the phrase 'a couple of bottles'?" Frank asked for the third time.

"Yes." Sabrina glared at them. "My olfactory sense is hypersensitive. My hearing's just plain old keen. Dylan's hearing is just as good. And we both heard the same thing. Loud and clear. So can we move off that sticking point?"

"I think we should," Jeannie agreed. She still looked bugged. "Something's not connecting. Obviously these two murder attempts are related. It doesn't make sense for them not to be. And yet, if Susan Lane is the mastermind, I just can't think of an explanation for Carson Brooks's shooting."

"As an aside, Susan knew Dylan and I were together last night," Sabrina added to the mix. "Carson's been filling her in on the progress of our relationship. Oh, and Russ Clark came to Ruisseau from YouthOp. There's another tie-in between the two organizations."

"I hear you. And I'm not arguing with your logic. When it comes to last night's attack, the YouthOp connection can't be ignored. So let's work with your theory. Let's say the worst is true—that Ms. Lane hired one of her kids, some lowlife scum, to kill you off. Maybe she wanted you out of the way so no one would stand between her and her ambition to become Mrs. Carson Brooks, at which time she could stake her claim on your father's fortune. That's a solid motive. But it doesn't provide a single link to Mr. Brooks's shooting. The weapon's easy. She could have gotten it from her scummy little sidekick. But what about motive and opportunity? She had neither—no motive, not as long as she was still Mr. Brooks's girlfriend and not his wife. And no opportunity, not when she was en route to the U.S. Open."

Sabrina dragged a hand through her hair. "You're right, especially about motive. There's not a damned thing she'd gain by killing Carson. Plus, I'm convinced she loves him. She doesn't want him dead."

"Maybe killing him wasn't her intention," Dylan suggested. "Maybe she just meant to hurt him. That way she could get loads of publicity from hovering by his side, nursing him back to health. I can see the headlines now: 'YouthOp's beautiful and benevolent leader lavishes her beloved Carson Brooks, millionaire CEO of Ruisseau Fragrance Corporation, with love and tender ministrations as he recovers from his wounds.'"

Frank shook his head. "If that were her plan, she'd have gone about it differently. A bullet in the back? That runs a high risk of being fatal. An inch in the wrong direction, and he'd be dead. It's too chancy. If she wanted him hurt and needy, she'd have had her punk attack him in the alley, steal his wallet, and break a few ribs. No, Mr. Newport. What happened in Mr. Brooks's office was attempted murder."

Jeannie was studying her notes. "Let's get back to opportunity, and see that through, before we even try to figure out motive. Ms. Lane was at the U.S. Open. The game began at five after seven. She caught a cab there, since Mr. Brooks had the limo. She'd have to leave her apartment by sixish."

"It was a holiday," Frank reminded her. "That means no rush hour."

"Still, there'd be holiday traffic heading in and out of the city. Tuesday was going to be a workday. The world was coming back to life after the summer. Anything less than an hour would be pushing it." Jeannie chewed the end of her pen. "She'd need time to get dressed and ready. . . ."

"That would take an hour by itself," Dylan muttered. "Between her wardrobe, her hair gunk, and her layers of makeup, it's a full-time job."

A corner of Jeannie's mouth lifted. "Yeah, she is the put-together type, isn't she? Okay, let's say an hour, including showering, makeup, the works. That means she'd have to be in her apartment around five o'clock in order to get to the Open on time. Mr. Brooks was shot at approximately five-forty."

"It doesn't fit," Sabrina murmured.

"Unless . . ." Jeannie's head came up. "We're all assuming Ms. Lane was on time for the match. Maybe she wasn't. Maybe she was late. If she shot Mr. Brooks, for whatever reason, she could have been dressed and ready when she headed over to Ruisseau. A light trench coat would have been enough to hide whatever she was wearing so she couldn't be identified. It would also provide her with deep enough pockets to conceal her weapon. She could have fired the shot, left the building, and headed home. She'd be there by six-fifteen, even in heels and walking leisurely, so she wouldn't look suspicious. She'd have enough time to lose the overcoat, throw the gun in the Hudson, and hail a cab by six-thirty. She'd be late, but not by a lot."

Frank considered that scenario, and nodded. "Makes sense. It's certainly possible. The question is, how do we find out? We can interview every damned cab driver in the city to find the one who drove her to Queens. But that's going to take more time than we've got."

"We don't need to do that." Jeannie turned to Dylan. "Mr. Brooks was a big tennis fan, right?"

"Right."

"Then my guess is, he was a regular at the U.S. Open. After all, it's the premier tennis match in the world, and it's played right here in Queens."

"He was. He went to every game he could. Why?"

Rather than answering his question, Jeannie asked another of her own. "And when he attended these games, where did he sit?"

Realization dawned in Dylan's eyes. "He has a courtside box. He reserves all six seats for the entire two weeks of the U.S. Open, for important customers and Ruisseau employees."

"Bingo." Jeannie gave a triumphant nod. "So we have a couple of options here. Let's get some footage of the televised network coverage of that Monday night match and see if we can spot Mr. Brooks's courtside box, which should be empty except for Ms. Lane. That should make it easier to spot her arrival. Also, let's find out who reserved tickets in the nearby courtside boxes. Ms. Lane's a very attractive woman. I'd bet money that someone noticed when she got there, and if she was in her seat when the game began."

"That's brilliant." Sabrina felt her adrenaline begin to pump.

"Don't get too excited," Jeannie warned. "At least not yet. Besides, even if we do find proof that she was late, there's still the problem of motive. We have none. We've got to take this one step at a time. Let's not get ahead of ourselves."

"Okay. You're right."

Inclining her head, Jeannie shot Sabrina a probing look. "Tell me something, what made you become suspicious of Ms. Lane to begin with? I have a gut feeling you didn't go down to YouthOp for a friendly visit. I think you went to check out Ms. Lane. Am I right?"

"Yes." Sabrina met directness with directness. "In my case, I can't say the word suspicious applied, at least not yet. I was bothered, especially after talking to Dylan. And I was protective, since Carson is my father, and Susan's a big part of his life."

"What about you, Mr. Newport? I take it your feelings in the matter were stronger."

"Stronger and more definitive—yes." Dylan was equally frank. "I've known Susan longer than Sabrina. I've spent a fair amount of time in her company, both with and without Carson. And she makes me feel uneasy, irked, and worst of all, mistrustful. I could elaborate with a few more adjectives, but you get my drift."

"We get it," Frank said. "What's it based on? Elaborate on that instead."

Bluntly, Dylan filled them in on his ambivalent take on Susan, from her me-first attitude, to her desire to be in the limelight, to his misgivings about her priorities at YouthOp.

"Wait." Jeannie help up her palm. "Stop at the YouthOp issue. Are we talking about a woman who's promoting her own agenda, or about something more serious—something criminal?"

Dylan blew out his breath. "I just don't know. I can't give you facts. I was hoping to get those today, but our visit took a different turn. All I can say is her office looks like something out of *Lifestyles of the Rich and Famous,* her charity events cost as much as an inaugural ball, and her publicity campaigns are huge."

"None of that's illegal," Jeannie pointed out. "Not if it's properly funded."

"We asked her point-blank if she designed her own office," Sabrina said. "She said she hired a decorator, and claimed she cashed in one of her stock holdings to pay for the whole shebang. She probably did. Like Dylan said, the office is a real eye-catcher; far too conspicuous for Susan to assume there'd be no questions asked about how a charitable organization could financially swing such a costly decor. Plus, the sale of stock is too easy to verify. I doubt she was lying. But as for subsidizing everything else out of her own pocket? That's highly unlikely. I agree with Dylan—she's just not the philanthropic type. She's also not a Rockefeller. And we're talking about big bucks here. YouthOp's got only local funding, not state or federal. Susan told me so herself."

"Don't they also have corporate sponsors?"

"Yeah," Dylan replied. "Carson gives a bundle. I know that for a fact. YouthOp has other sponsors, too—some personal, some corporate—although I doubt any of them gives close to what Carson does. Either way, the thing that gets to me is that I don't see enough of that money going to the kids. Listen, I was once in their shoes. I know what they need. Especially the older ones. They're beyond the point where baseball games and pep talks are going to help. They need hard-core support."

"They get internships and scholarship money," Jeannie reminded him.

"True. And I wholeheartedly support that. It made all the difference in my life. But it's step two. Step one is for someone to get them on track, moving in the right direction so they'll take advantage of those opportunities. As I've told Susan before, YouthOp needs to hire some professionals, counselors who go out to the high schools and zero in on kids who could benefit from this program, counselors who can help them along the way. Charity events are great. But once the money's in YouthOp's coffers, then what? Where's it going? To flashy events that are covered by the press? That's what eats at me. The donations should be used to create an environment where these kids feel like there's a place to go, a person to talk to. Russ Clark's a perfect example. If he'd been able to confide in someone about whatever the hell he'd uncovered, maybe warning bells would have gone off in that someone's head. Maybe Russ would be alive today."

"Unless what he uncovered was at YouthOp itself. Then, he wouldn't know where to turn. And, if he did, maybe he couldn't get to that person in time." Jeannie leaned forward, and it was obvious her mind was going a mile a minute. "As Ms. Radcliffe pointed out, Clark came to Ruisseau from YouthOp. We've been assuming that whatever incriminating information he dug up, he found at Ruisseau. Maybe he didn't. Maybe he found it at YouthOp. And maybe he was spotted by Mr. Molotov cocktail, who happened to be at YouthOp at the same time. That would certainly be an incentive to shut Clark up."

Frank twisted around to face Jeannie. "That might explain why we didn't find any notes, scribbled memos—anything that could help us—in Clark's office at Ruisseau. He wasn't checking out this place. He was checking out YouthOp. And if he was keeping some kind of running report, he might have stashed it right where he was poking around. It was convenient and he probably had no idea anyone was onto him."

"Which means that report could still be there—unless the Molotov kid found it. He sure as hell would have looked, to save his own ass. Whatever Russ Clark dug up, we can assume it was incriminating."

"And if it also implicated Susan . . ." Sabrina swallowed the bile that rose in her throat. "That would give her motive to have Russ killed."

"Enough theorizing. We need answers." Jeannie shut her notebook with a thwack. "We've got to get our hands on a list of all the teenagers and young twenties who've been affiliated with YouthOp since its inception. My guess is that would lead us to Mr. Molotov. And the list wouldn't take long to compile, since the organization's relatively new."

"The problem is, who's going to compile it?" Frank muttered. "It has to be Susan Lane. She runs the place. Trying to go around her would be stupid. She'd inevitably find out what we were doing, which would piss her off and make her suspicious."

"Um-hum," Jeannie agreed. "We've got to spin this so we get her cooperation." A thoughtful pause. "Mr. Newport, did Russ Clark spend any scheduled time at YouthOp? I realize he visited the place now and then—the YouthOp staff confirmed that for us when we interviewed them after his murder—but we need more than an occasional drop-in. Did he have any formal reason to go to the organization with any regularity?"

"As a matter of fact, yes." Dylan nodded. "He taught a writing class there every Saturday afternoon to a bunch of twelve- to fourteen-year-olds. There's a subway station a couple of blocks away from YouthOp, so getting there was easy for everyone. The staff might not be aware that that class was going on, since most of them don't work Saturdays." Awareness flashed across Dylan's face. "Which would make it the perfect time for Russ to do some snooping."

"That's enough for probable cause, Jeannie," Frank declared. "We've got an ongoing murder investigation, a connection between the victim, YouthOp, and—after the gasoline Ms. Radcliffe just smelled in Susan Lane's office—the assailant. Plus, we've got statements from

Ms. Radcliffe and Mr. Newport affirming that they heard Ms. Lane use the phrase 'a couple' of Molotov cocktails in referring to last night's attack. It's search warrant time."

"I agree," Jeannie said. "And we'll lay it all out for the judge. But as far as Susan Lane's concerned, let's soft-pedal it. The lower key and less personal we make this visit, the better. Let her believe she's out of the mix for now."

"Right. No point in tipping our hand. Let her think we're just checking out the possibility that some slime-bag kid slipped through the cracks and got into her program."

"She'll understand that in order to find him, we'll need to access the computer, go through the personnel files, and get into the financial records." Jeannie gave an innocent shrug. "After all, you never know if the punk stole money from YouthOp, or if somebody paid him off. You and I both know it's highly unlikely we'll find infor-mation like that neatly listed in the financial records. But it is possible. And it'll give us the grounds we need to re-view the charity's financial transactions. Which, in turn, will give us a chance to see how the YouthOp funds have been allocated—or manipulated—as the case may be. Ms. Lane won't have an inkling that's part of our agenda. Unless we stumble upon something incriminating—*then* she'll know, and fast."

"Just having you walk in with a search warrant will make Susan freak out," Dylan noted.

"Not the way we'll handle it, she won't. We'll ask for her help, make her our ally. Believe me, Mr. Newport, she won't freak out—not if she's innocent," Frank clari-fied. "If she's innocent, she'll thank us. Her organization will be cleansed of a bad seed, and she'll have helped nail him. Hell, she'll look like a heroine in the press. Isn't that what she thrives on?"

"You've got a point," Dylan conceded. "Well, good luck. I'm half-hoping you'll find something to fry her ass, and half-hoping she's innocent as a lamb—for Carson's sake."

"You're emotionally involved. We're not. That's why things go much smoother when Detective Barton and I handle the situation ourselves," Jeannie told him.

"In other words, butt out." A corner of Dylan's mouth lifted. "Don't worry, Detective. Sabrina and I have had more than our share of excitement. This one's all yours. Just keep us posted."

"Will do."

"Speaking of which, what happened at Pruet's this morning?"

"A dead end," Frank stated flatly. "Ten people, nine alibis. Everyone could account for their whereabouts except Karen Shepard, who's the executive assistant to Louis Malleville. She was at the movies alone. We'll check out her story as best we can. Not that I expect to find anything."

Sabrina and Dylan exchanged glances.

"What?" Frank demanded. "What do you two know?"

Dylan reached for the phone. "Let me just make a quick call to Carson, see what he's up to. Then, I'll answer your question."

He'd pressed three buttons when there was a knock on the door.

Sabrina frowned. "I asked Donna not to interrupt under any circumstances. Yes?" she called out.

The door opened, and Stan walked in. He looked exhausted, and like he'd been through hell. But there was a peace in his eyes that Sabrina had never before seen.

"Don't blame Donna," he said quietly. "I pulled rank on her. I knew Detectives Whitman and Barton were here. And I need to speak with them right away. This can't wait."

Silently, Dylan hung up the phone.

"Go ahead, Mr. Hager," Jeannie replied. "We're listening."

31

5:35 P.M.
Mt. Sinai Hospital

If looks could kill, Sabrina and Dylan would both be dead.

Carson glared at them, pushing himself higher up in the bed. "What do you mean you didn't pick out your rings? You both look fine. Much better, in fact. And Marie said you were both at work the whole day. So what gives? What happened to the Fifth Avenue marriage proposal?"

Dylan provided the answer they'd rehearsed, which was the truth, sans the part relating to Susan. With events unraveling so quickly—and so unpleasantly—the last thing they wanted to do was sandwich a joyous and memorable occasion like getting engaged between Stan's confession and Frank and Jeannie's YouthOp investigation.

Especially with Susan smack in the middle of it.

"It was a rough day, Carson," Dylan explained, smooth as silk. "Whitman and Barton were with us at noon which, if you recall, was when we'd planned to go to Tiffany's. That's when Stan walked in. He had a tough hurdle to leap, and we wanted to be there to support him. Plus, Sabrina's nose and throat were still burning her, and my head was aching. A marriage proposal isn't something you bulldoze your way through, like a rough business meeting. It's a once-in-a-lifetime event. So we decided to wait. Tiffany's is opened until seven P.M. every weeknight. For us to go tonight would be pushing it. It's already close to six o'clock. We want time to browse, to pick out just the right rings. So we have a date for tomorrow night. We'll leave work early, which will give us plenty of time for shopping. Then, I'm taking Sabrina to Central Park for a sunset proposal."

"What's wrong with tomorrow morning? You can propose in the sunlight, too."

Sabrina rolled her eyes. "Gee. Aren't you the romantic?"

"No. I'm a get-it-done guy. So's Dylan. You and I both know he can't wait to slip that ring on your finger. So what's really going on? Why can't you be at the doors of Tiffany's at ten A.M. to open the store?"

Another sore subject that seemed impossible to avoid.

Fine. If avoidance was out, then shoot-from-the-hip was the next best alternative.

"Because I've got an appointment with the nephrologist tomorrow morning at ten, remember?"

"Yeah, I remember," Carson grumbled. "I was hoping *you'd* forget."

"Not a chance. Anyway, Dylan's going with me. And so, I'm sure, is Bernard," Sabrina added dryly, referring to the linebacker of a bodyguard who'd been appended to her since mid-afternoon. "By the way, is it okay if he hangs out in the waiting room during my physical exam? He's a great guy and all, other than the fact that he never cracks a smile, but I'm not quite ready to do a strip show for him."

"Very funny. He's not paid to smile. He's paid to keep you safe. And, yeah, he'll wait outside while you get checked out."

"Good. So much for that. And don't worry about the

proposal. By tomorrow night, Dylan's knee will be sore and grass-stained, and there'll be a glistening diamond on my left hand, which we promise to come by and show you. Okay?"

Carson's glare softened, and he appeared slightly mollified. "Yeah, I guess I see your point. Getting engaged is a big deal. Fine, okay, it can wait a day. But come by here afterward, no matter how late it is. I can't wait to see you gushing over your ring."

"If *that's* what this is all about, then you've got a much longer wait than you think," Sabrina retorted. "I don't gush."

Carson's lips twitched. "I guess not. Okay, I'll settle for a rosy glow." He settled himself against the pillows. "Did you at least get Dylan moved into your place?"

"No. Dylan got himself moved into my place."

A snort. "Damn, you're difficult. Semantics are bullshit. But, fine, Dylan moved himself. The important thing is, he's living with you, right?"

It was Sabrina's turn to stifle a grin. "Yes, Carson. He's living with me. But if you don't stop meddling, I'm going to relegate him to the guest room."

"Shut up, Carson," Dylan ordered.

"Gotcha." A chuckle. "All I care about is that you two are on your way. I'll stop sticking my nose where it doesn't belong."

"That'll be a first. Sabrina and I are lucky you haven't ordered Bernard to post himself in the master bedroom and keep a running count of how many times we . . ."

"Time to change the subject," Sabrina announced.

". . . snore," Dylan finished with a straight face. "I was going to say snore."

"Oh." Sabrina shot him a yeah-right look.

"Don't worry," Carson assured them. "Bernard knows

his limits. He'll keep his distance at the appropriate times. That includes when you're at Tiffany's and Central Park, by the way. Believe me, he'll be the soul of discretion. And he'll be staying outside the apartment, not in it. Intimate moments are yours and yours alone."

"See? You are a romantic," Sabrina teased. Sobering, she asked something that had been nagging at her all afternoon. "Did you have a chance to talk to Stan after the meeting with Whitman and Barton?"

"Yup. He called here around three."

"Did he sound okay?"

"Actually, he sounded better than I expected. I guess that's because he and Karen will be paying their own visit to Tiffany's pretty soon. Hell, those diamond rings are flying." Carson's amusement vaporized. "Seriously, Stan said the talk with the detectives went well. Did it?"

"Very well," Dylan supplied. "Stan stuck to our story. He said he'd just come from the hospital where he'd informed you that he was going to tell the authorities the truth about him and Karen, even if they chose not to believe he was innocent of committing a crime. He was frank and to the point—very effective. He even cleared up the issue of Roland's jitters by explaining that Roland didn't realize that the relationship between Stan and Karen was an open book, especially to you. Whitman and Barton were fine with the alibis and the explanation. So that chapter's closed."

"Really." Carson eyed his friend. "It sounds a little too easy. They didn't pump Stan? Didn't try to trip him up? Nothing?"

"Nope."

"Odd, isn't it? Considering how convinced they were that he was involved. Unless, of course, things have

changed and they have their sights set somewhere else—
on someone else. Do they?"

This was the discussion Sabrina and Dylan were most
hoping to dodge—at least until it was necessary for it to
be had.

"What are you two hiding?" Carson barked.

It appeared that the necessary time had arrived.

Still, maybe it could arrive in stages.

"If we tell you, it has to remain among us—*just* the
three of us," Sabrina began, delivering the most impersonal aspect of the facts, that part that would be least
likely to hit Carson like a blow to the gut.

"Fine." Carson waited expectantly.

"It's possible that whoever threw those Molotov cocktails last night and, presumably, who also killed Russ is
affiliated with YouthOp."

Carson's jaw set. "Why do you think that?"

Sabrina didn't flinch. "Because Dylan and I were
there today, visiting Susan. She called your room this
morning after you'd fallen asleep, and she sounded really
rattled. We wanted to calm her down. So we went to
YouthOp, chatted with Susan in her office. There was a
persistent, lingering odor of gasoline. I smelled it the entire time we were there. Which suggests that whoever
threw those Molotov cocktails was, at some point, in
Susan's office."

Carson didn't so much as blink. "Go on."

"The YouthOp connection makes sense," Dylan continued, following through with Sabrina's approach.
"Russ worked there. He could have found out that some
son of a bitch was making extra bucks hiring out as a
paid killer. You know the type. He was probably selling
drugs, maybe even weapons, which means he's already
responsible for God knows how many deaths. It's not a

reach that he'd go one step further, knock off a few people for the right price."

"Not a reach at all. As for weapons, you're figuring he got hold of the twenty-two that shot me, right?"

"Right. And when the little shit realized Russ knew who he was, he stabbed him."

"Not of his own accord, he didn't." Carson's expression and tone were flat. "They don't call them *paid* killers for nothing. So who's paying him?"

"We don't know."

"Ah." Carson fell silent, his lips pursed as he thought. "Tell me, how much of this theory has Susan been told?"

"None of it. The detectives asked us to sit on this. They want to handle things their way. We gave them our word we'd say nothing to Susan."

"Because she might be involved," Carson concluded in that same monotone.

Sabrina blew out her breath. They were up against a wall, and she knew it. "It's possible," she said at last.

"In what way?"

Silence.

"I asked you a question." Carson's wooden tone was gone, and irritation glinted in his eyes. "Stop dancing around the issue. And stop protecting me like a goddamned child. What's Susan's alleged involvement in this? I have a right to know."

"Yes, you do." Sabrina should have realized there was no putting one over on him. "But you're not going to like it."

"I'm sure I won't. But I *am* going to hear it."

"Fair enough." Sabrina turned to Dylan. "You've been wrestling with this for a while. For once, I'm less personally involved. I'll provide the details. You fill in whatever you need to."

Dylan nodded, looking as troubled as she felt.

Sabrina proceeded to tell Carson everything—about the verbal slip Susan had made in her office, about Dylan's intrinsic concerns about her skewed priorities, and about the various scenarios they'd bandied around with Whitman and Barton.

"No wonder you had no time for ring shopping," Carson said tersely when she was through. He adjusted his pillow, propped one arm behind his head in a deceptively casual gesture. But there was a vein pulsing at his temple, and a hard glitter in his eyes. "You've certainly been busy."

"You're ripping mad at us," Sabrina stated.

"I haven't gotten that far. I'm still trying to visualize Susan as being capable of hiring someone to stab Russ to death and to burn you two to a crisp." Carson inclined his head toward Dylan. "Is Susan the personal matter you wanted to talk to me about the night I got shot?"

"Yeah, but purely from an ethical standpoint; nothing of this magnitude," Dylan qualified. "I was bugged, really bugged, by the vibes I was picking up from Susan—her priorities, her agenda with regard to YouthOp, even the allocation of the charity's funds. I knew that by coming to you I was taking the risk of pissing you off. I didn't have anything solid to go on. And, yeah, I realized you'd probably dismiss my misgivings as garbage. But I couldn't live with myself if I didn't say something. If Susan was taking you for a ride, or at least taking your money for a ride, you deserved to know."

Carson stared into space for a long, silent moment. When he spoke, his tone was, once again, emotionless. "Look, Dylan, I've got the same keen instincts you do. I might not be objective on the subject of Susan, but I do know her. Sure, she loves the limelight. She also loves living the high life. Would she compromise her integrity, even screw around with the YouthOp books, if it meant cashing out? Maybe. Would she kill anyone who stood in her way? I can't even fathom it. How did she know there were two Molotov cocktails tossed through your window? Only she can answer that."

With a hard swallow, he continued. "In any case, let's play this out in brutal extreme. Say Susan was ripping off money from YouthOp and, when Russ discovered what was going on, she hired someone to get rid of him. Then, she found out I have a daughter, which translated into an obstacle in Susan's path to me and my money. So she got her punk to knock off Sabrina. Sounds preposterous to me, but you could make a case for it, saying she had motive. But now comes the major stumbling block in this theory. Me. Why the hell would Susan shoot me? She'd get nothing if I were dead. Plus, the woman loves me. Hell yeah, I know she also loves the wealth and notoriety I give her. But there's no way you're convincing me she'd put a bullet in my back."

"No arguments on that one," Dylan replied. "It's the sticking point for us, too—*all* of us, Whitman and Barton included." He cleared his throat. "I don't want to hang the woman, Carson. I'm as confused as you are. I'm not happy with the Molotov cocktail coincidence, or any of the theories that have spun off from it. But let's put those aside. I don't believe she'd shoot you. She's crazy about you. The whole scenario falls flat right there. On top of which, I can't even picture the woman holding a gun, much less using it—on anyone, least of all you. Hiring someone is one thing. But killing someone herself? Uh-uh. Not even a stranger, much less the man she loves. Susan's emotional, she's squeamish, and she's not exactly the rustic type."

"If you're trying to find solid reasoning that'll convince you Susan's not guilty, you can chuck that description. It won't fly," Carson stated flatly, even as an odd expression flickered across his face. "Susan's a survivor. Believe me, she's not squeamish. Emotional, yes, but gutsy. As for the rustic part, you've never seen her camping. You wouldn't recognize her."

"Um-hum. Susan and I discussed that camping trip when we were in the ICU lounge," Sabrina recalled aloud. "It sounds like she holds her own. Then again, that's not a surprise, given the way she grew up. She described that rural town in upstate New York where she lived before moving to Manhattan. She milked cows, planted tomatoes, and did all kinds of outdoorsy things. Sounded pretty rustic to me. I guess that life on a farm teaches you all kind of skills—"

Abruptly, Sabrina broke off, as she remembered another conversation. And, suddenly, the reason for Carson's odd expression made all the sense in the world.

"Carson," she said quietly, "when we were discussing Stan's marksmanship, you told me he drove up to Susan's parents' farm with you to do some target practice. Did Susan shoot, too? *Can* Susan shoot?"

"Yeah, Susan can shoot." Carson's lips tightened. "Damned well. Not as well as Stan, but close. But she doesn't want me dead, and she doesn't own a twenty-two."

"Not a surprise," came Detective Whitman's voice from the doorway. "Mr. Molotov probably got it for her. She'd be an idiot to use her own gun. And one thing Susan Lane is *not,* is an idiot."

Neither Sabrina, Dylan, or Carson had seen Jeannie and Frank arrive. But arrive they had. They'd eased open the doorway, and were standing just inside the room.

"We weren't eavesdropping," Frank supplied. "The nurse said to go right in."

"Looks like you've already done that," Carson observed dryly.

"You're right." They completed the process, shutting the door behind them, and pulling over two chairs to sit down.

"Where is Ms. Lane, by the way?" Jeannie asked.

"Not in the hospital, or we wouldn't be having this talk," Dylan supplied. "She left about an hour ago, went home to take a hot bath and a three-hour nap. She's a wreck from the day—for a change." Dropping the sarcasm, he shot Jeannie a questioning look. "Did you get the warrant?"

"No sweat. We'll be paying YouthOp a visit tomorrow. We also did lots of other homework." She hesitated, glancing uncertainly at Carson.

"They told me everything," he confirmed. "So talk."

"All right. First of all, the TV station was very cooperative. We watched an hour's worth of video clips from Monday night's U.S. Open match. There were three occasions when we got a dead-on view of your courtside box—one at seven-ten, one at seven thirty-one, and one at seven fifty-six. The box was empty during the first two video shots. During the third—the one taken just before eight o'clock—Ms. Lane was in her seat. She was all settled in, so my guess is, she'd arrived a good few minutes before. But she wasn't there for the first half hour of the match."

Sabrina edged a quick glance at Carson. He was sitting very still, listening.

"We also contacted the USTA National Tennis Center, got the names and phone numbers of a dozen and a half spectators in the immediate vicinity of Ms. Lane's seat. We called them all. Guess what? Two of the women and—surprise, surprise—seven of the men, remember an attractive, well-dressed woman with frosted blond hair arrive late. Five of those nine people remembered what the logistics of the match were when that woman arrived—what the score was and where each player was standing, since they were in the process of changing sides. All five reports matched. So we fast-forwarded our videotape to that particular moment. Based on that information, Ms. Lane's arrival time was seven forty-three."

A weighted silence, which Sabrina broke.

"When you first interviewed Susan, she never mentioned to you that she was over a half hour late to the match?" she asked Whitman, knowing full well it was a rhetorical question, needing to ask it anyway.

"Nope." Jeannie glanced at Carson. "How about you, Mr. Brooks? Did she tell you she missed the first chunk of the match?"

Carson shook his head. "Shit. I don't believe this." He raked a hand through his hair. "All right, Detective. I buy it. Susan had all the time she needed to blow my guts out. But why? Believe me, I'm no sentimental jerk. I don't believe love conquers all. But Susan's not insane. She'd need a reason to kill me. So what's that reason? And when you come up with it, you can also tell me why she picked that particular place and time to do it. She, of all people, knew Dylan and I were wrapping up by late afternoon. I was supposed to be out the door at five to get ready for the match."

Abruptly, something seemed to click in Jeannie's mind, because her back went rigid and an intent expression came over her face. "Right. You told us that you weren't supposed to be at the office at the time you were shot, that you were supposed to have left around five. Ms. Lane knew that?"

"Yup. We discussed it that morning, and I confirmed it with her at around three-ish, on the phone."

"What exactly did you say?"

"That Dylan and I were finishing up. That I'd be out the door right on schedule."

"But you weren't. Was that unusual?"

"When it comes to tennis matches, damned straight it's unusual. The Open's one of the few things that gets my juices flowing like my work does. I'm never late for a match."

"What held you up?" Frank asked. "Legal papers to review?"

"Not really. Yeah, Dylan had one more file to go over with me, but it wasn't crucial. It could have waited until morning. I stayed because Dylan said he had a personal issue to discuss with me. I could tell that whatever that issue was, it was weighing on his mind. So I hung around."

"And that personal issue was Susan Lane, and your uneasiness about her." Frank addressed Dylan, picking up on Jeannie's thought process and running with it.

"Yes." Dylan nodded.

Frank leaned forward. "Mr. Newport, when we spoke this morning, you said you made suggestions to Ms. Lane about allocating YouthOp funds differently, providing counselors instead of splashy fund-raising parties. Did you give her any other advice?"

Dylan shrugged. "Here and there. She knew the way I felt. I never accused her of anything illegal, if that's what you mean. . . ."

"But she had a good idea where your head was when it came to her. You're a pretty outspoken guy. And she's a pretty bright woman. She must have picked up on your disgust whenever you walked into her office and looked around. She must have blanched at your suggestions. And she must have known you had Mr. Brooks's ear."

"Not only his ear, but his inheritance," Jeannie reminded him. "Mr. Newport is Mr. Brooks's prime beneficiary."

"*Was,*" Frank corrected. "My guess is that Ms. Radcliffe's going to claim that spot—or at least share it." A humorless laugh. "Share it with, of all people, the man she's romantically involved with. Quite a double-obstacle, huh?"

"Um-hum. A very inconvenient double-obstacle. Especially for a woman who's got her sights set on becoming Mrs. Carson Brooks—after which, it would all be hers; hers and her charity's. Wealth, notoriety, status— hey, she'd be a regular Jackie O. *If* she cleared the path to Carson Brooks."

Frank rose, walked behind the chair and gripped the back. "She's a good shot. I'm sure she's handled a twenty-two. She could master it like that." He snapped his fingers. "One shot, and there'd be no more threat to her future—personal, professional, or financial. The opportunity was perfect. Based upon Mr. Brooks's three o'clock call, he and Mr. Newport were the only people at Ruisseau—and Mr. Brooks would be leaving by five. So at five-forty, there'd be only one person left in the office—Dylan Newport. And that's just the person she wanted to kill. So off she went to do the dirty deed. She found Newport in her boyfriend's office, standing by the window with his back conveniently to her. She stooped down low, took aim, and fired from the doorway. Just one problem. There's not a lot of light by that office window, and it's an eastern exposure, so there'd be little sun at that time of day. Newport and Brooks are about the same height, and with similar builds. All that adds up to a perfect, if unfortunate, case of mistaken identity."

"Wow." Jeannie let out a low whistle. "After she pulled the trigger, she realized it wasn't Dylan Newport she'd shot. It was Carson Brooks." A mocking shake of that Q-tip head. "Imagine how she felt. Especially since she's the high-strung type, a woman who comes unglued easily. Talk about seeing your world go up in smoke. So much for the right corpse. So much for the windfall. So much for your future, if the guy it depends on bites the dust. Man, she must have been a mess. No wonder she was bawling her head off in the ICU lounge. Talk about enormous guilt mixed with colossal failure and sheer panic."

"Yeah, but she recovered enough to try again, through her good buddy, Mr. Molotov. We thought he was just after Ms. Radcliffe. Nope. He had two targets in mind last night. His job was supposed to make bye-bye Sabrina *and* bye-bye Dylan. Hello freedom and hello cash. And what happened? She was foiled again. No wonder the woman's been such a wreck. She's got a lot to be freaked out about."

"Okay, that's enough." Sabrina cut them off and rose. The sick expression on Carson's face had been intensifying by the second. And it was really starting to worry her. "Carson?"

He angled his head in her direction, and there was a kind of empty, shocked awareness in his eyes, mixed with disbelief and guilt. "I'm okay," he managed. "I feel like puking, but I think that's to be expected. If this is true . . ." He broke off, turned to Jeannie. "How do we find out? How do we see this through?"

"We'll call Ms. Lane at home tomorrow morning,

under the guise of our original plan. We'll tell her about our search warrant, and arrange to meet her at YouthOp," Jeannie replied. "Once we're in the door, we'll see what we can find. That will determine how we confront her, and with which crime first. Ideally, we'll get her on misappropriation of funds, then catch her off-guard on the big stuff. To a certain extent, we'll have to wing it. Leave it to us."

"We will." Dylan came to his feet, looking a little green around the gills himself. "Detectives, that's enough for tonight. I think we've all had it. Let's call it a day—for everyone's sake."

"I agree." Jeannie nodded, getting up and waiting while Frank followed suit. "We'll call you as soon as it's over."

"Wait." Sabrina stopped them. "What time tomorrow morning are you two planning on going over to YouthOp?"

"That depends on Ms. Lane. Why?"

"A couple of reasons. First of all, I don't want Susan paying Carson any visits before this whole thing goes down."

"Oh, cut it out, Sabrina," Carson barked. "I'm not a shriveled basket case."

"True, but you're not a diplomat either. You've got all the subtlety of a firing squad. Susan will know something's wrong the minute she sees your face." Sabrina was exaggerating and she knew it. Under circumstances like these, Carson would lie through his teeth if he had to. The truth was, she didn't want him having to face this woman—not alone.

Which brought her to the other potential schedule overlap she was trying to avoid.

"Second, I want to hear the outcome of this little tête-à-tête firsthand. Which means, I want to be here when you call Carson. The problem is, I've got an appointment with the nephrologist at ten. Time is of the essence, so rescheduling with Dr. Mendham is out. Can we work around that?"

Jeannie's gaze met hers, and a current of communication ran between them. Sabrina's message was getting through, loud and clear. She wanted to be with Carson, to help him through this emotional crisis. But she couldn't, wouldn't, do that if it meant neglecting his physical crisis. It was a juggling act. And she needed Whitman and Barton's help to manage it.

"That should be doable." Jeannie nodded, scratching her cheek thoughtfully. "Tell you what. Detective Barton and I will ask Dr. Radison to issue a no-visitors policy for tomorrow morning. He'll leave word at the nurses' desk that Mr. Brooks had a difficult night, that he was badly thrown by his daughter's brush with death, and that he'd been given something strong to help him sleep. As a result, he'll be out for the count until afternoon. That'll put a halt to any early morning drop-ins Ms. Lane might have planned. After that, she'll be kept plenty busy by us. She'll be compiling that list of potential Mr. Molotovs, while we're systematically compiling evidence. It'll take quite some time to do our thing at YouthOp. You'd be surprised how long it takes to review accounting data. Plus, we've got lots of questions to ask. And, of course, we've got to check out the place thoroughly for anything Russ Clark left behind. Trust me. We'll buy you more than enough time to get your physical exam."

"Thank you, Detective," Sabrina said. A wave of gratitude swept through her, and a grudging smile tugged at her lips. "Looks like I was wrong about you. You're a pretty decent human being after all. You both are."

"Yeah, well, don't spread it around," Jeannie warned. "It'll ruin our reputation."

"No chance of that," Frank muttered. "No one would believe her." He headed for the door, Jeannie right behind him. "Good night, all."

"Good night. And good luck." Sabrina waited until the two of them had left the room and shut the door.

Then, she turned, went back over to the bed where Carson was lying, stony-faced, staring at the ceiling. "Hey." She lay her hand over his. "Don't be pissed at me. I know I interfered. But I wasn't babying you. I was caring. Cut me the same slack you wanted from me. I can't help worrying. You're my father."

Carson's gaze shifted, dropping to where her fingers covered his. "I'm not pissed. And, yeah, I *am* your father. *I'm* the one who's supposed to be protecting *you*, not the other way around. Which is why I'm having a hell of a time coming to grips with the fact that it looks like the person who paid to have you killed is the woman who's been my partner for over a year. A woman I cared about." His use of the past tense was deliberate and emphatic. "And who claimed to love me."

"She does love you, for whatever that's worth."

"It's worth shit," he snapped. "So's the fact that it wasn't me she meant to shoot. It was Dylan, and that's worse than if she'd killed me three times over. Then, as if that wasn't despicable enough, she tried again. She hired some piece of shit to kill both of you, *and* stab poor Russ to death to keep his mouth shut. . . ." Carson's fists clenched, his fury a tangible entity. "God help her if Whitman and Barton are right."

"Carson, stop it." Dylan strode over, loomed at the foot of the bed. "Look at that cardiac monitor," he said, pointing. "It doesn't take a surgeon to see that your heart rate's up. So's your blood pressure, I'm willing to bet. So calm the hell down. You can't change what's happened. If—and I repeat *if*—Susan's guilty of everything the detectives speculated, she'll be punished for her crimes. We can't bring Russ back. That's a tragedy that can't be undone any more than your being shot. But we've got to focus on the positive. You're going to make a full recovery. Sabrina and I survived last night's attack. We're alive and well. So cut it out."

With a tight nod, Carson blew out his breath, visibly trying to force himself to relax. "I hear you. But it's easier said than done. I'll calm down. I just need some time alone—to think, to sort things out."

"The hell you do. What you need is a sleeping pill," Sabrina corrected. "I'm asking the nurse to bring one in now. I don't care if you call her every name in the book. You're taking that pill. You need some rest." Seeing him open his mouth to protest, she shot him one of her I-gotcha-on-this-one looks. "Let's put it this way—no sleeping pill and no rest means no rings and no proposal. And who knows when Dylan and I might feel compelled to do something so mushy and traditional again? Actually, our lives are so hectic these days—why, it could be months before we find the time to formalize things. And *that* would push the wedding back indefinitely."

"You're full of it." Carson eyed her knowingly. "You two are chomping at the bit to make this official."

A challenging stare. "Think so? Fine. Then call my bluff. But if you're wrong . . ." She shrugged. "A sleeping pill seems a small price to pay to ensure a romantic, one-day-away engagement. But it's your call, Mr. Matchmaker. So tell me, do Dylan and I go to Tiffany's tomorrow night, or not?"

Carson's mouth snapped shut, and he gave her a dark

look. "Talk about going for the jugular. That's not a bargain; it's blackmail."

"Nope. Just a business deal where, for once, you're not in the power seat." Sabrina arched a brow. "So what's it going to be?"

"Fine. I'll take the damned sleeping pill. You can stay here and watch me swallow it, if it makes you happy."

"That won't be necessary. I trust your nurses." She smiled faintly. "And just to show you that I'm not such a piranha and that I do understand that in any good negotiation both sides should walk away feeling like they got something in return, I'm willing to make a concession, too. When Dylan and I come by tomorrow night, I'll gush my little heart out over my ring—first to you, then to every nurse, intern, and medical technician who walks through that door. Okay?"

Carson's features softened, and Sabrina noted that his cardiac monitor had returned to a more regular rhythm. "Sounds fair."

She leaned closer, meeting his gaze with solemn understanding. "Carson, I know you feel responsible for my safety. But cut the guilt. None of this is your fault. And look at the bright side. Out of this horrible series of events came a few wonderful things, too. Hey, I got a father, a fiancé, and the career opportunity of a lifetime. Those were worth walking through flames for." On impulse, Sabrina bent down, kissed his cheek. "I'll get the nurse to bring in that pill. You sleep. Dream about those grandchildren you're waiting to spoil."

32

Wednesday, September 21st, 1:25 P.M.
Mt. Sinai Hospital

The appointment with the nephrologist had gone off like clockwork.

Dr. Mendham was sharp, to-the-point, and thorough, just as Dr. Radison had described. She'd examined Sabrina from head to toe, asked her a ton of questions, and conducted a whole battery of tests, including a chest X ray and EKG. She'd also explained the renal angiogram in detail, addressed some of Sabrina's concerns, and provided some promising information about the prospect of Sabrina undergoing laparoscopic, rather than conventional, surgery, which would be much less invasive and translate into a quicker, easier recovery.

All in all, the appointment was enlightening and positive. With a modicum of luck, all systems would be go. When Carson was ready, Sabrina would be, too.

In the meantime, however, she was practically jumping out of her skin.

She and Dylan had darted out of Dr. Mendham's office, Bernard looming close behind, and the three of them had jumped into the limo and headed straight for Mt. Sinai. Dylan called the hospital from the car and was told that Carson was dozing fitfully, awakening every few minutes to ask if the detectives had called yet.

They hadn't.

It was twelve-forty by the time the limo got there, and

Sabrina and Dylan went straight to Carson's room, where a brawny police officer was posted outside the door.

"Is everything all right?" Sabrina demanded, recognizing Officer Garner.

"Fine," he assured her. "Everything's been quiet. Mr. Brooks had two visitors—Stan Hager and Susan Lane. Mr. Hager arrived at eight-fifteen; Ms. Lane arrived at eight-forty. They each left promptly and without protest as soon as they were told how exhausted Mr. Brooks was and that Dr. Radison had ordered no visitors until later today. I checked in with Stick and Stone around nine and filled them in. Nothing since then."

"Thanks." Dylan guided Sabrina through the door.

They'd tiptoed into the room in case Carson was asleep, but his eyes popped open the minute they entered. He'd looked tired and drawn, and Sabrina had the distinct impression that Dr. Radison's story about the sleepless night hadn't needed to be fabricated.

Carson pumped them for details on Sabrina's appointment with Dr. Mendham, absorbing all the information with a terse nod. He waved away their concerns about his exhaustion, assuring them that he was fine, other than the fact that he was losing his mind waiting.

It was one-thirty when the waiting ended.

The telephone rang, and all three of them jumped. It couldn't be anyone but the detectives; no one else's calls were being put through.

Carson picked up the receiver. "Hello?" He paused. "Yes, they're both with me. What happened?" Another pause. "Here? Yes, fine, all right. Just hurry up." He hung up. "That was Whitman. She and Barton are driving into the hospital parking lot. She wants to come up and see us." His expression was grim. "She didn't elaborate. But it's obviously not good."

"We didn't think it would be," Sabrina put in quietly.

"No. We didn't." Carson interlaced his fingers and fell silent, waiting and steeling himself simultaneously.

Dylan paced over to the door, standing there and staring at it as if willing it to open.

Eventually, it did.

"Hey." Detective Whitman walked in alone. She didn't mince words, or waste time. "Everything went down as planned. The search warrant was just a formality. Ms. Lane cooperated fully. She was definitely antsy about the fact that we'd tracked Mr. Molotov to YouthOp, but she had no idea that she was also under suspicion. So she kept herself in check. Until we started digging up financial records that were majorly out of whack. Then, she caught on, and freaked out. We told her she wasn't going anywhere, so she cried and wrung her hands and paced around while we searched the place."

Jeannie drew a sharp breath. "We got everything we need. Gross misappropriation of funds, the name and lowdown on Mr. Molotov—thanks to Russ Clark, who'd hidden some pretty comprehensive notes inside the textbook he used to teach his Saturday writing workshops. And we got Mr. Molotov himself who, according to the call I just got from my precinct, was picked up at his apartment, along with a closetful of illegal narcotics and stolen weapons. His name's Joseph Kenman, and he's got a juvenile record as long as my arm. Now, he's in the big leagues—twenty years old and very much an adult. With charges like murder, attempted murder, and conspiracy to commit murder facing him, he's not worried about the drug and weapons crimes Ms. Lane was holding over his head to keep him in line. He's singing like a bird. Not that we need it. Ms. Lane broke down and gave us a full confession."

"All of it?" Carson fired out. "She confessed to hiring that Kenman kid to kill Russ, and to murder Sabrina and Dylan?" His jaw was so tight, it looked like it might snap. "And she admitted to shooting me—or rather, going to Ruisseau to shoot Dylan and mistaking me for him?"

"Yes, Mr. Brooks." Jeannie didn't look happy. She looked resigned. "I'm sorry. But she did. She used your extra key to get into the building through the freight entrance. She avoided the surveillance cameras by scooting up the stairs. The rest happened pretty much like we figured—the shot, the mistaken identity, the works. The twenty-two's at the bottom of the Hudson. She tossed it there from the Seventy-ninth Street boat basin. We'll keep dredging. With any luck, we'll find it. The gun's hot. Kenman got it for her. We certainly don't need to get our hands on it to convict either of them, but it'll be one more nail in their coffins if we do."

A pause, as Jeannie cleared her throat. "I could have told you all this on the phone. The reason I didn't is because Ms. Lane is insisting on seeing you. She's downstairs in the car with Frank. Normally, I'd tell her to stuff it, but I wanted to make sure you had no interest in speaking with her before we take her in and book her. Her attorney's already on his way to the precinct. What do you want me to tell her?"

Dylan's expression was murderous. "How many words would you like it in? You can start by telling her that she's a—"

"Bring her up," Carson interrupted in a hard, implacable voice.

Both Sabrina and Dylan turned to gaze anxiously at him.

"Carson, it's a bad idea," Dylan said flatly. "Let it go.

There's no closure to be had. Not in a situation like this. There's only an opportunity to send your blood pressure soaring, and screw up your recovery."

"I don't want closure." Carson stared Dylan down. "I want confirmation. As for my recovery, it's a nonissue. She couldn't kill me when I was vulnerable, with my back to her. She's sure as hell not going to hurt me now, when I'm the one in control, looking her straight in the eye."

"You're sure this is what you want?" Sabrina asked.

"Yeah. I'm sure."

"Okay, but Dylan and I are staying."

Her bullying tone actually caused a wry grin to twist his lips. "No need to sound so menacing. By all means, stay. There's nothing intimate about what I have in mind." Carson nodded at Jeannie. "Tell your partner to bring her up."

Ten minutes later, Frank shoved open the door and led Susan in. She looked worse than she had when Carson was first shot—her makeup blotchy, her hair mussed, and her eyes filled with haunted realization. Then again, this time it was *her* life, *her* future that was on the line, not someone else's.

Officer Garner continued to stand guard outside the door, along with Bernard, although no one really perceived Susan as a threat. Not now. Standing there, her hands cuffed behind her and her head bowed, she looked more like a broken bird than a criminal.

Her gaze flickered over Sabrina and Dylan, and she winced, averting her head—whether because she couldn't bear the sight of them or because she couldn't deal with the reminders they represented, it wasn't clear. Either way, she didn't speak to them, but looked straight at Carson.

"Carson . . ." She wet her lips, searching his face for some sign of compassion, and finding none. "Can I come closer? I don't want to talk to you from across the room."

"Good idea." Carson stunned everyone by waving away Detective Barton's oncoming refusal, and beckoning her forward. "Don't worry, Detective. I doubt she's packing heat with her hands in cuffs. Let her come over to the bed."

Relief flooded Susan's face, and a flicker of hope lit her eyes as she approached his bedside—Barton close behind.

"I . . ." She struggled for the right words. "You don't know what I went through when I realized it was you. I thought you'd left the building. You said you'd be gone by five. The person in your office was alone. Of course I assumed it was Dylan. He was the only other person at Ruisseau that day, and he spends more time in your office than he does in his own. It never dawned on me . . ." A sob shuddered through her, and she bent over, laying her head on the bed near Carson's pillow. "I'd never hurt you. You have to believe that. I love you. I was just so afraid that Dylan would get to you, tell you things that would turn you against me."

"You mean, like the truth?"

"No . . . yes . . . Carson, please let me explain." She pressed her face against his shoulder, her tears drenching his hospital gown. "I fought my way out of that damned hick town I grew up in. I've been fighting my way up ever since. And I've been fighting alone. I don't have your inner strength. I can't make it by myself. I need security, someone by my side. I need *you*—your love, your name."

"My money," Carson added.

She blew out a shaky breath. "Fine. Yes, that, too. I

need financial security, for me and for YouthOp. I do care about those kids, no matter what Dylan told you. Everything could have been so perfect. But he wouldn't stop poking around. Neither would Russ. And then Sabrina showed up, a daughter you'd never met, but felt obligated to take care of. As if that weren't bad enough, she got involved with Dylan. It was only a matter of time before he shared his suspicions with her. Then, she'd be in my face, too. I couldn't take that. You and I had built a future together. I couldn't let some unknown sperm donation come between us. She'd ruin everything. I couldn't survive that. I love you too much."

Carson hadn't so much as blinked through her long burst of hysteria. But there was a harsh glitter in his eyes, and a hard set to his jaw, both of which said he wasn't even a tad bit moved. Still, he turned his head slightly toward her, drawing a sharp breath as he did.

An odd expression flickered across his face, a sort of self-censuring awareness, as if he'd found whatever confirmation he'd been seeking.

"Get up," he commanded, in a tone so scathing it made even Sabrina cringe.

Susan's head snapped up and, when she saw the icy condemnation in Carson's eyes, she complied instantly, stumbling to her feet. "Carson, please . . ."

"Shut up. If you think I agreed to see you so you could profess your undying love and I'd forgive you, forget it. You'll rot in prison, if I have anything to say about it. Okay, Detective Barton, you can get her out of here."

Stark disbelief flashed across Susan's face. "I don't understand. . . . I thought . . ."

"That I was an asshole?" Carson supplied helpfully. "That I'd melt the minute you told me how much you love me, and forget that you're a murderer? Honey, if that's what you thought, then *you're* the asshole." He settled himself back on his pillows. "So long. See you on the six o'clock news."

Barton took Susan's arm and urged her toward the door. He paused to exchange glances with his partner and shrug, before leading Susan off.

The door slid shut behind them.

Detective Whitman folded her arms across her breasts. "Okay, Mr. Brooks. What was that all about? And don't tell me you wanted to hear her beg. That's not your style. You had an agenda. That agenda involved getting her over to your bed. So what's the scoop?"

A corner of his mouth lifted. "You're good, Stick. Have I mentioned that? Damned good. Remind me to call the police chief and tell him what an asset you and your partner Stone are."

"Thanks. Now, how about an answer? You were looking for something. Apparently, you found it. Care to share?"

"Not *looking* for it, *smelling* for it," Carson corrected. "Since the night I was shot, I've been reliving the experience, in slow motion, from soup to nuts. It just wouldn't go away, not when I was awake, not when I was asleep. And it wasn't because I was traumatized. It was because something was bugging me. Something I couldn't put my finger on. A smell. First, I thought it was just the carpet cleaner and my blood. But there was something else, something that kept nagging at me but I just couldn't place it. Each time I dozed off, I'd wake up in a drenched sweat, with the answer just out of reach. And each time I woke up, who was always by my bedside, cooing her little heart out to make the bad dream go away? Susan. Now I understand why the memory was so strong. It was in my face every day since the shooting. Literally."

He shook his head in disgust. "So much for my genius IQ and my fantastic olfactory sense. Like everyone else, I can be as dumb as a stump. I missed what was right in front of me simply because I wasn't really seeing it—or, in this case, smelling it. But last night, after you all left and I was trying to imagine Susan as the shooter, it hit me. The smell. That sickeningly sweet smell I kept remembering. It was that foamy gunk Susan uses to puff up her hair."

"Mousse?" Jeannie suggested with a hint of a grin.

"Yeah, right, mousse." He snorted. "I still don't understand why companies make that stuff with fragrance. It clashes with every perfume on the market—even C'est Moi. Lousy R&D, if you ask me. Anyway, it's no wonder I've been bugged by that memory. Susan's practically lived in my room since the shooting. I guess she saw my bedside as a kind of confessional—a place to cleanse herself of her sins. It didn't work. And the hair connection finally clicked."

"So you figured it out last night—the tie-in between the odor you remember when you were shot and Ms. Lane's foamy hair gunk." Jeannie's lips twitched as she echoed Carson's phraseology. "And just now, you were looking for proof?"

"Not proof. Just corroboration. My sense of smell is all the proof I need. But these damned tubes in my nose ruin my olfactory sense. So I wanted to get her over here, take a deep breath, and make sure. Well, I did and I am."

Jeannie gave an intrigued shake of her head. "You know something, Mr. Brooks? You're good, too. Damned good. Remind me to call your company and tell them what an asset you are."

He grinned—a worn-out, tight grin, but a grin nonetheless. "Thanks. Just for that I'll let you in on a secret. You see these two here?" He pointed at Dylan and Sabrina. "They're about to get the hell out of this hospital room and head down to Tiffany's to pick out some rings. There's going to be a wedding in the near future."

"That's great." Jeannie shook both their hands. "Congratulations."

"Keep it under wraps for now," Carson added. "I want to make a big, splashy announcement. Who knows? Maybe it'll send the sales of C'est Moi soaring even higher."

"Hey," Sabrina said in mock protest. "Did we just become a marketing tool?"

He shrugged. "You're already prime time media buzz. Let's give the TV networks, the newspapers, and the tabloids something cheerful to yap about. Now, get going. I'll be waiting to see that sparkling baby on your finger."

"Yes, sir." Sabrina snapped off a salute. She paused, studying his face. "You're sure you're okay?"

"Positive. I'll be better when you're engaged." He arched a brow at Dylan. "Now go make an honest woman out of my daughter."

"With pleasure." Dylan chuckled, wrapped an arm around Sabrina's waist. Carson really was okay. He could tell. And that made him feel like a great weight had been lifted off his shoulders. "We're out of here. See you soon."

"Yup." Carson watched them go, then settled back, feeling a surprising sense of peace, despite the pain and trauma of the past day, and the difficult recuperation that lay ahead. Somehow, everything was going to be all right. "See ya, Detective," he dismissed Whitman, letting her know he was ready to drift off.

"See ya, Mr. Brooks. You take care."

One eye opened. "Hey, Stick, are you married?"

Jeannie paused at the door. "No, why? Are you proposing?"

"Nah. You'd turn me down. I'm harder to live with than you are. What about Stone—is he single, too?"

"Nope. A great marriage, and two great kids. Why?"

"I just wanted to know how to address the invitations."

"Invitations?"

"To the wedding." A hint of a smile. "Hey, you're the reason those two incredible kids of mine are safe and able to get on with their lives. Same goes for me. The least we can do is invite you to the wedding. I promise you great food and a great time."

"Sold." Jeannie perked up at the part about the great food. As for the great time—anything was possible. Carson Brooks hung with a very eclectic crowd—corporate execs, regular Joe's, and grown-up street kids. Mix that with Beacon Hill snobs and high-fashion designers, and, hey, whether or not it was a great time, it sure as hell wouldn't be boring. "I'm sure I can speak for Frank and Linda, too. We'll all be checking our mailboxes. When's the date so we can save it?"

"That part's still up for grabs. If you want an answer, ask my kidneys."

EPILOGUE

～

April 2nd, 2:30 P.M.
West 73rd Street

Muttering a few choice curses under his breath, Carson tossed the pile of contracts, specifications, and Internet printouts across the coffee table in Sabrina's living room, and leaned back on the sofa.

"I don't believe this," he muttered, linking his fingers behind his head. "And I thought running a corporation was hard? This isn't a wedding; it's a fucking conspiracy planned by pompous, cutthroat lunatics. Worse, they're all delusional enough to believe they're visionaries. Wedding planners who want to color-coordinate flowers and bathroom accoutrements? What the hell's a bathroom accoutrement, anyway—toilet paper? How about white? That goes with everything, including your gown. And that's just the flowers and the other artsy touches she's proposed. We've also got an orchestra that can change gears so fast—from Sinatra to hip-hop—that I'm convinced they're on drugs, an egocentric photographer and videographer who are like two male turkeys—I know in my gut that in the middle of the reception they're gonna start beating the crap out of each other fighting for center stage—a centerpiece designer who thinks she's Michelangelo, and volatile bridesmaids who have perpetual PMS and can't even agree on the same pair of Donna Karan panty hose. Jesus Christ."

He reached for his bottled water, took a long, cold

swig. "Here's an idea. Let's chuck the whole wedding coordinator thing. I'll walk you down the aisle and give you to that incredibly tolerant guy over there who's held up through this insanity a helluva lot better than I have." Carson pointed at Dylan, who was standing at the sideboard, enjoying his friend's outburst. "After that, you can say a few mushy words, exchange vows and rings, hang around long enough for one dance with your husband and one with me, and then go upstairs for the good part. I hear the toilet paper in the honeymoon suite is fabulous."

Sitting cross-legged on the carpet, paperwork sprawled out all around her, Sabrina burst out laughing. "You know you wouldn't have to twist my arm to get me to go along with you. That woman's driving me nuts, too. But we agreed to make this one concession for my grandparents. According to them, everybody who's anybody has Lilah Wellington do their wedding. She's the most sought-after wedding planner in the business."

"She might be sought-after. But she's certifiable."

"Eccentric," Sabrina corrected, wiping tears of laughter from her eyes. "Just eccentric. And remember, at least she thinks the grand ballroom at the Waldorf Astoria has the right *feel*. Otherwise, we couldn't have the reception there."

"We *need* to have the reception there. It's got to be somewhere big enough to hold the four hundred guests your grandparents are probably going to come up with, plus the two hundred fifty we've put together. I can't wait to hear the grand total."

"Seven hundred seventy-two," Gloria announced, hanging up the phone. "That would be the grand total. My parents just finished cutting down their list to five hundred twenty-two, thanks to the seventeen couples who will be abroad during the last week of June. Otherwise, we'd be topping eight hundred." Her forehead creased in concentration as she scanned the list. Walking over to the sofa, she sank down next to Carson. "Anyway, we can call in our final count, so the invitations will be printed and ready for the calligrapher to address them. They'll be mailed out in four weeks."

Carson hadn't heard a word after the first sentence. He'd whipped around to face Gloria, his jaw dropping. *"Did you say five hundred twenty-two people?"*

"Um-hum." Gloria's lips twitched. "I'll kick in some extra cash, if you're running low."

"Cash isn't my problem. Space is. I don't need money. I need Shea Stadium."

"The Waldorf's equipped to handle well over a thousand guests."

"So's the Javits Center. But this is a wedding, not a convention."

"There, there." Gloria patted his arm in mock comfort. "Look at the bright side of having this huge affair."

"What bright side? All I want is to see these two happily married and figuring out how many grandchildren they're going to give us."

Gloria swallowed her grin. "To begin with—sales. Profits. Ruisseau's, the Gloria Radcliffe fashion line's, and CCTL's. They've skyrocketed, thanks to all the publicity surrounding this wedding. Ever since Dylan's Central Park proposal, both our families and companies have dominated the social and business headlines. As a result, C'est Moi for men burst on the scene and squashed the competition, my spring and summer lines have sold like there's no tomorrow, and CCTL has had to double its staff to accommodate all its new corporate clients. As for you and me, why, we're being credited with creating and inspiring the love match of the century—Sabrina and

Dylan. The media spotlight is bright, their spin is positive—why, even my parents are starting to like you."

Carson shot her a skeptical look. "Don't get carried away. Your parents don't *like* me. We tolerate each other."

"Fine. You tolerate each other. That's still an improvement."

"Yeah. When we first met, they looked at me like I was an ax murderer. Not that I blame them. It was right after the transplant surgery. I was the reason Sabrina went through that ordeal."

He fell silent for a moment, remembering the tension-filled Christmas season of a few short months ago. Between Susan's conviction, his own struggle back to health, and his harsh realization that his kidneys weren't going to rally on their own, it had been one dark, hellish time. The thought of relying on hemodialysis three times a week for the rest of his life—it sucked. He wanted his life back. He *needed* his life back. Christmas and all the joyous spirit it conveyed had been the farthest thing from his mind.

Except that Santa Claus had arrived in the form of an extraordinary young woman who happened to be his daughter.

There was no talking Sabrina out of the transplant. She was hell-bent on seeing it through. And she had.

Luckily, she'd been able to undergo the laparoscopic procedure, which had kept her risks minimal, her recovery time shorter, and her incisions minor. She'd also been able to keep the rib that the surgeon would have had to remove had the conventional surgery been necessary. Still, she'd given up one of her organs. She'd been in the operating room for four hours, not counting prep time and recovery time. That was twice as long as his transplant recipient surgery had been. As far as he was concerned, that was damned unfair. As far as Abigail and Charles Radcliffe were concerned, it was abominable.

He understood where they were coming from. He felt for them. He felt *with* them.

Maybe, in the long run, that's what had finally turned things around. Maybe it was seeing how much he cared about their granddaughter that had made them thaw a tiny bit. Maybe they'd finally realized he wasn't just an anonymous sperm donor. Not anymore. Now he was a father.

"Hey." Sabrina scooted over on the area rug and nudged Carson's leg. "Stop brooding. The transplant's ancient history now. You've had my kidney for over three months. A damned fine kidney, too, if I must say so myself. And a match made in heaven. You and I might kill each other in the boardroom, but our kidneys are as compatible as bread and butter. Not the slightest sign of rejection. You're doing great. I'm doing great. Sales are doing great. My grandparents stopped worrying a long time ago. And they're so into this wedding thing—not to mention the oohs and ahs they're getting from their socially prominent friends—that they've forgotten all about the negative publicity from last fall. They're really strutting their stuff. Which is why we're going along with Lilah Wellington, and the *aura* she wants to create for our special day." Sabrina rolled her eyes, then scooped up the pages Carson had tossed on the coffee table. "So let's get on with our next decision—the cake. Lilah wasn't wild about the milk chocolate mousse filling we selected. She thinks it conflicts with our aura. She wants us to go with dark chocolate."

Carson groaned, flinging an arm over his eyes. "I give up."

"But there's good news," Dylan consoled him, strolling over to stand behind Sabrina. "She's crazy about the tuxes we picked out." A corner of his mouth lifted. "They're in sync with the feel of the Waldorf."

Shifting his forearm away from his eyes, Carson gazed suspiciously at Dylan. "How come you're dealing with this so well? When we first started with this Wellington kook, you were bitching up a storm. Now suddenly, you're all sweetness and light. Why?"

Dylan tugged Sabrina to her feet, wrapped an arm around her waist. "Because then it was January. Now it's April. I'm marrying your daughter on June 30th, which is just a few months away. After that, I'm taking her to a beautiful, private villa in Tuscany where we'll be totally alone for two weeks, and where the aura will be better than anything Lilah Wellington can create at the Waldorf or anywhere else. So I can afford to be tolerant." He paused, winking at Sabrina before he added, "You know, Carson, you can afford to be tolerant, too."

Carson arched a brow. "Yeah? How do you figure that?"

"Because Tuscany's a beautiful and romantic place. And because Sabrina and I will be there at just the right time."

"You lost me." Carson glanced at Gloria, who had started to smile—a smile that broadened as she exchanged a look with Sabrina. "You obviously know what Dylan's talking about," he observed.

"I guessed. And I'm thrilled. You will be, too. Thrilled enough to jump through hoops for Lilah Wellington."

He snorted. "Don't hold your breath. Nothing could get me to do that."

A dubious shrug. "If you say so."

"Okay, I'll bite." Carson eyed Dylan. "What do you mean you'll be in Tuscany at just the right time?"

"We're arriving in Italy on July 2nd," Dylan explained. "That's six and a half months after your transplant surgery. Which is two weeks after the go-ahead date we got from Sabrina's nephrologist, her surgeon, and her OB/GYN."

"Dylan's right, Carson," Sabrina concurred with a teasing grin. "So if this wedding goes off smoothly, and my new husband and I are feeling very relaxed and very adventurous on our honeymoon—well, who knows? My mother might be able to start on that line of designer baby booties right away, with us as her first customers."

Carson sucked in his breath, jerking to an upright position. "Whose idea was the milk chocolate, anyway?" he barked, snatching the paperwork from Sabrina's hand and poring over it. "Dark chocolate's richer, more elegant. It's definitely got an aura. This Wellington woman knows what she's talking about." His head snapped up, and he gazed from Sabrina to Dylan to Gloria, scowling at their three smiling faces. "What's wrong with all of you? Stop grinning like fools. We've got a wedding to plan."